"One of the most provocative, intelligent, and original novelists working in Britain today."
—Irvine Welsh, author of *Trainspotting*

"A terrific thriller . . . puts a very contemporary dysfunctional family at the heart of a very contemporary dystopian reality."
—Lynda Obst, producer of *Interstellar*

"Stylishly crisp, thematically germane—and great fun."
—Lionel Shriver, journalist and author of *We Need to Talk About Kevin* and *Should We Stay or Should We Go*

"I wasn't sure there could be a great pandemic novel. Here it is."
—Ian Rankin, author of the Inspector Rebus novels

"This is an absolutely brilliant read."
—Lucy Mangan, journalist and author of *Are We Having Fun Yet?*

"*How to Survive Everything* is a gritty and (tragically) cool novel. The collision of a broken family and a global pandemic, it reads as a survival guide and feels like (is) a warning."
—David Shields, international bestselling author

"I loved everything about [this book] . . . the voice, the world, the humor, the darkness. . . . Read now, thank me later."
—Antonia Senior, journalist and author of *The Tyrant's Shadow*

"A brilliant, intriguing, harrowing, illuminating story."
—Tim Minchin, comedian, actor, composer, and songwriter

How to survive
everything

Also by Ewan Morrison

Nina X
Close Your Eyes
Tales from the Mall
Swung
The Last Book You Read
Menage
Distance

How to survive
everything

EWAN MORRISON

HARPER PERENNIAL

NEW YORK • LONDON • TORONTO • SYDNEY • NEW DELHI • AUCKLAND

HARPER ● PERENNIAL

Originally published as *How to Survive Everything* in Great Britain in
2021 by Saraband.

HOW TO SURVIVE EVERYTHING. Copyright © 2021 by Ewan
Morrison. All rights reserved. Printed in the United States of America.
No part of this book may be used or reproduced in any manner
whatsoever without written permission except in the case of brief
quotations embodied in critical articles and reviews. For information,
address HarperCollins Publishers, 195 Broadway, New York, NY
10007.

HarperCollins books may be purchased for educational, business,
or sales promotional use. For information, please email the Special
Markets Department at SPsales@harpercollins.com.

FIRST U.S. EDITION PUBLISHED 2022.

Library of Congress Cataloging-in-Publication Data has been
applied for.

ISBN 978-0-06-324732-1

22 23 24 25 26   LSC   10 9 8 7 6 5 4 3 2 1

For Theo and Frances

Man can live about forty days without food,
about three days without water,
about eight minutes without air,
but only for one second without hope.

Hal Lindsey

My Survival Guide

I'm still alive, and if you're reading this then that means you're still alive, too.

That's something.

My name is Haley Cooper Crowe and I'm in lockdown in a remote location I can't tell you about because, if I do, then you and any people you come in contact with could endanger me and the ones I love, plus some of the ones I less than love.

When this shit began I was fifteen years, seven months, two weeks and one day old, but in the first year of lockdown we lost touch with the outside. Then we lost a day, then a week, then all sense of time, so I don't actually know exactly how old I am now.

Hold on … If you're reading this, it's also possible I'm dead, because there's no internet anymore, or so my dad said, and the only way you could get to read this is if you've broken into our safe house and found my cubbyhole in the bunker and discovered this notepad.

If you found me lying there dead, I hope I wasn't too gross.

I told myself if I ever got through this crap alive, I'd spend my remaining days trying to set down how the hell we got here and to make my own non-boring survival guide, with actual practical tips for non-boring people and other teenagers abducted by crazy prepper parents. Actually, Dad's survival manual is pretty much a how-to guide for the crap he put us through, so I'll be using bits of that, too. I thought my own guide could be useful just in case we manage to somehow live through this and then have the next wave of the pandemic to get through, and because, like my dad said, we have to leave something behind for future survivors, so they can rebuild civilisation.

That's kind of awesome, thinking about my little life story being that important, but maybe I should actually focus on actually living long enough to get this written and not being such an egotistical dick.

Actually, truth be told, when you're in phase five of lockdown, things get pretty scary, and these little jokes are just the tears of a very nervous clown. I'm writing this every day because it takes my mind off waiting for death to find us. Anyway, I'm really sorry for the billion or so folk who're probably starving and wheezing to death or being burned alive in the riots and all my old school chums (apart from Sharon Mackay) who're getting generally brutally murdered for the sake of literally a can of peas or something, but I really should start my survival guide properly now.

How Not To React When Faced With A Wheezer

'Wheezer' is our name for a contaminated person and this is a very dangerous problem. First of all, if there's a wall or a fence between you and the wheezer, try not to get in a panic and don't forget to breathe. Holding your breath can make you pass out or hallucinate, and these are not useful things to do when you are carrying a loaded crossbow, which may even be pointing upwards towards your own actual face.

Move your weapon into a safe position and get your fingers the hell away from the trigger, then count your breaths and focus. This was how I tried to control the terror as I hid, crouching in the dirt behind the burned-out pick-up truck we use for target practice. I was on perimeter patrol and the wheezer was right there, just like we'd been warned about in our lockdown training, literally on the other side of the fence.

I counted to thirty-six, then I thought, shit, what am I going to do – stay here shivering and literally piss myself, or take another look? I edged up and tried to frame the contaminated asshole, but the telescopic sights were steamed with my stupid breath. He was maybe sixty feet away, and he wasn't wearing a face mask, for sure.

Jesus, I thought, the day has come: when they plunder our food stash and slaughter the men and contaminate Mother and me and maybe even mad Meg, and then rape us and kill us. Because that's what infected, starving mobs who are internally bleeding to death tend to do. According to Dad, anyway.

Hyperventilating can also make your hand tremble, and if you are using telescopic sights you won't be able to see or aim at jack shit.

My crosshairs were jumping from the wheezer's chest to his feet to the sky and the stupid turf. I was panting and furious and whispering, 'Don't you dare contaminate that fence with your poxy breath!' It might have been wire-cutters in his hand or a gun, but totally not gloves – he was literally spreading the virus everywhere. I was whispering, 'Please, for Christ sake, just turn round and go, don't make me shoot my first human.'

Oh, another **Survival Tip**: In times when you have to remain totally hidden, your walkie-talkie may be your worst enemy.

My walkie-talkie made a crackling noise, and the wheezer turned sharply. I kept totally still, but my chest felt like I'd been hit and I was whispering, 'Get a grip, Haley Cooper Crowe, use your fucking crossbow!' I was lying low, but I could feel the guy's eyes scanning No Man's Land for me.

My eyes blurred and for some random reason I was thinking of me and Danny huddled together, hiding from the dying world, and how bad it was to feel good about that. Like, how totally romantic and stupid.

Survival Tip: When confronting an infected individual, it's a very good idea to stop fantasising about snogging and to decide on whether you are actually going to shoot to maim or shoot to kill, and to assess the consequences if you shoot and miss.

My chest was pounding panicky and if I fired and missed the wheezer, he could run off and return with his starving mob. Also, if I got up to run for help then he'd know our safe house was there and he could shoot me in the back. But if I stayed still and did

3

nothing, he'd just cut his way through the fence and find me shivering like a total asshole. What would I do when he pointed his weapon at me? Say, 'Hey, wheezer, how's this pandemic working out for you? Let's be friends.'

Shoot or not? I am shit at choices and only slightly better at hitting targets. Choose, Haley, for the first time in your stupid life.

Dad's voice was in my head, saying, 'Contamination and starvation drive good people to do evil things. You've got to get stronger, Haley. If I die first, you'll have to protect the others.'

The wheezer was fastening something to the fence, not cutting through it, and wearing some kind of outfit that wasn't a hazmat.

I couldn't decide, so I let the voices in my head decide for me.

Danny's voice said, 'They wouldn't think twice about shooting us, they're no more than animals now.'

OK, I had to shoot the contaminated idiot to protect my family. The guy was a long-goner anyway. God forgive me, and I don't even believe in any kind of God that could have set this plague upon mankind.

I tried to do what Danny taught me. 'Hold your breath and take aim, Haley. You've only got one shot and if you miss, you won't have time to reload before they shoot back.' I thought of Danny's arms around mine, steadying the weapon, his mouth against my ear. 'Hold steady, concentrate on your heartbeat, hear it, it's a countdown to shoot. Count breaths with me now.'

I put my finger slowly round the hair trigger. I counted my breaths, down from ten, nine, eight, just like Danny showed me. Seven, six. I lined up the crosshairs with the wheezer's chest. Five, four. I closed my eyes. 'It's them or us,' Danny's voice whispered. Three, two. I thought of Danny's mouth on mine, our tongues circling. Wait, stop, don't shoot the guy! I thought. But the air slashed and the crossbow kicked and I realised I must have pulled the trigger. I scrunched my eyes tight and waited in cringing silence for the thud of my arrow puncturing a human chest.

Wait. Rewind.

This happened about three or four months into lockdown and you have zero clue what any of this is about or how we even got here. Right?

Start again, Haley.

Like, on the day it began.

The day Dad started Plan A. The day he called Day One.

Plan A

How To Abduct Your Own Children

To abduct your own children from under the nose of your ex-wife on day one of a supposed pandemic, you will need the following:

1. A sturdy off-road vehicle full of gas, with extra fuel tanks prepared.
2. A well-planned and pre-rehearsed 'get out of dodge' road route.
3. A layered script of falsehoods to hide what's actually going on.
4. It's also super-handy if the abduction is on a 'sleepover' night.

This is what my dad, the author of his own pandemic survival guide, rather turgidly entitled *SURVIVE*, had worked out.

It all began at 05:03, on the morning of October 12th. I'm crap with numbers but Dad is obsessed with them. Like: you can survive for three days without water and three weeks without food. Like: two hundred and twenty-three trillion was the size of the debt bubble in dollars and I don't even want to get into that whole argument about the real number of humans who died during the last pandemic. And, like: the spread of virus is exponential and when you put it and the globalised economy together, you get a 'mutually reinforcing positive feedback loop', which means basically a 'species-threatening event'.

Dad used to be a journalist, and he taught me all this stuff. 'Stats can't be trusted,' he said, 'like the people who use them.' And that was the problem. No one believed him, or listened to his warnings – especially not Mother – and so that's what made him do the things he did at 05:03 on that first morning.

You could say he lured us or placed us under extreme psychological pressure, but he didn't hold us at gunpoint – that sort of came later, under Plan C. He definitely lied with the offer of a surprise, so we'd get up, dressed, out the door and into his crummy old SUV.

'Hey, Haley-Boo,' he whispered as he shook me awake, because being sentimental and waking us up at crazy hours is his thang. 'Hurry, I've got a really cool surprise for you,' he said. You know, the kind of cutesy Santa Claus crap you'd say to a little kid, like Ben – who's my little brother, by the way.

So, me and Ben got up off Dad's 'blow-up camping mattresses' – which Mother had of course condemned as unsanitary living conditions. Ben was already jumping around Dad's crappy one-bedroom rental like a lardy space hopper, and I was doing my sleepy-best to cover my lady-bits with the duvet. I reached for my phoney-o, as it wasn't even light yet, but Dad was giving it, 'Don't text your mother! No Snapchat either, get dressed. Quick!'

Six a.m. would have been normal-ish for Dad, but five was weird. Ben was already half-dressed and giving it, 'Haley's on her phoney, Haley's on her phoney!' The beloved blimp was fond of getting me into trouble, especially on the subject of my 'anti-social phone habit' – which was the only one thing my deeply divorced parents ever agreed on, though, ironically, never face-to-face and only over their own phones.

Don't get me started. Seriously, eighty per cent or sixty per cent of all the kids at my school had divorced parents. I'd given up trying to mend it when I was ten. I'd put a total ban on ALL emotions by the time I was eleven. I was so over saying 'I'm so over it.' I'm pretty convinced their divorce made me the indecisive, choice-averse, two-faced, sarcastic, passive-aggressive, asthmatic, whining, overthinking, ADHD, Hamlet-ish brat everyone here in lockdown knows and loves.

Dad was dragging something out of the closet that looked like a cross between a small engine and a computer, and yelled, 'Right this minute, kids! We're leaving NOW!'

Ben gave me that look that said, c'mon Haley, we have to pretend to be excited for Dad's sake! Because we have this secret agreement, me and the Benster, to always pretend everything we did in the twenty-three hours we saw Dad every week was fun, so he wouldn't feel rejected.

It's Better To Be One Year Too Early Than One Day Too Late

When you abduct your children, you will need a 'grab bag' with essential survival items. It should contain the following:

Multi-packs of climbing socks, mountain bars, pepper spray, antibiotics, a rope, a first aid kit, water sterilisation tablets, a compass, flint or some other flame-making device, and a hunting knife which may or may not be for hunting.

Dad had three such 'grab bags' – one each for Ben, me and himself – but we didn't know that either. Neither did we know his old SUV and roof-rack was pre-stuffed with five plastic boxes containing eighty packets of dried peas, a Sundström pandemic respirator kit, twelve HEPA filters, three N95 gasmasks, three Mylar emergency blankets, three fake IDs, a bottle of chloroform, three four-litre gasoline tanks and an illegal weapon.

Just to show you how completely oblivious I was on that fateful 05:00am, while Dad was trying to rush us out the door, the most important thing in my world at that juncture was my choice of footwear.

You see, Dad had got me these tomboy-ish mountain boots, and Mother had got me these girlie, sparkled hi-tops. The problem was how to choose one pair without making one parent feel I preferred the other. Dad was supposed to be dropping us back off at Mother's later that day, as per always, and if I turned up wearing the shoes he'd bought me, it would hurt her feelings. Mother and Dad had both been having this unsaid competition to try to out-do each other with commodities in the battle for my affections, since I was a little divorceling.

Dad was yelling, 'What's keeping you, Halester?'

So, on the day Dad abducted us, I was fussing over the epic choice between mountain boots or femme fashion. Mother or Dad? Choose (a) or (b). Who will I reject today? Can't I just make both sides happy? This is my basic problem – I just can't make any choice, ever. I hate it. Screw it. It's so unfair.

But Dad had that all figured out in advance and wasn't going to let me or Ben have any choices at all. Nada.

Dad grabbed Ben by the hand and literally pulled him out the door, yelling back, 'Haley, if you don't come now, I'm going to leave you here to starve.'

Starve? Wow! I grabbed the first sneakers to hand and ran after Dad and Ben, into his filthy, ten-years-out-of-date, family-sized off-road vehicle. It was still dark outside and as I hopped into my shoes I bemoaned the utter randomness of my non-primary custodial caregiver.

Do Not Tell Your Abductees About The Evidence Or The Plan

It's essential to map human pandemic behaviour data so you can time your escape perfectly. You don't want to get the early-warning signs wrong, after all. Or to be caught too late when a city is put in lockdown with police roadblocks. Don't waste any time explaining to your kids what you're doing. Stick to Plan A.

It was like, five-twenty or something and the streetlights were casting eerie shadows of Dad's speeding 4x4 on the empty roads. The streets started thinning out and trees popped up like adverts between the suburby bungalows. All the traffic lights were on green, like they were sneaking us through on some secret mission. We passed a play park and the kiddie swings and plastic hippos were empty, everything spookily still. A fox dashed across the road before us and hid in a hedge. It was that surreal hour before people get up, when all the secret animals scour the streets and everything looks like an abandoned film set.

Dad was more wired and tired than usual that morning. We

didn't know it then, but he'd been up all night on his computers mapping the spread of CHF-4, or what, he said, would later
become known as Virus X.

If Mister Deadbeat-Dad Ed Crowe is to be believed, he'd
watched the sunrise over China, as the first cases of an unexplained viral disease that caused your lungs to basically turn into
purée, were reported in Hong Kong. Here's what he later said he'd
discovered:

1. Five hundred and four people had already died and the incubation period could be as long as a month.
2. Over the past four weeks, two hundred and eighty thousand people from all over the world had been in the infec-
   tion-centre-city, and these happy tourists had all flown back
   to their home nations.
3. The info had been leaked late because the govt had hoped
   to contain it to stop precisely the viral and economic meltdown that we'd come so close to with the Covid pandemic
   five years ago.
4. The politicians were just so, so sorry, because they'd done it
   again, only worse, cos this virus killed little kids as well, and
   this time around they were deeply, deeply sorry that, yes,
   this virus had come from a laboratory.

Had I known Dad had been up all night gathering his scary
data, I was under strict instructions to report his behaviour back
to Mother. 'Now, Haley, if you hear your father going on about
anything weird from any fake news channels,' she said, years back,
'you must tell me immediately.' But Ben and me had been bliss-
fully asleep.

Dad, as he later claimed, watched the hysteria spread online
through Asia and Australia, then Russia and India, as they each
woke up to discover they too had people wheezing with unexplained symptoms. And so they struggled to shut down their

borders to contain the contagion, before each economy went into panic and then into the aforementioned mutually reinforcing positive feedback loop that, according to Dad, would lead to global war, what with it already being too late to stop the virus. That would end the lives of one billion people for starters, and basically return us to the medieval plague era.

But if he'd told us any of this, it's very doubtful that we'd have got into his 4x4, let alone stayed in it.

Anyhow, as we learned from the last pandemic, divorce and shared custody don't go at all well with lockdown, cos the parents have to decide who gets to keep the kids, and kids don't get to see their other parent anymore till the virus all-clear is given. Like ninety per cent of the time divorced mums win this argument. And Mother did and that's why we didn't see Dad for a whole six months last time this pandemic shit hit the fan.

Actually, when you think about it, Dad was pretty lucky that the end of civilisation coincided with the October school-break, because it meant we had a double sleepover with him, for two nights in a row. If it'd been just one night, like usual, then the end of civilisation would have started on the wrong day and he'd have had to come and snatch us from Mother's house. She'd have resisted and accused him of having a paranoid delusion so he'd have had to use a gun or something, and that would've been pretty embarrassing.

Secretly Prepare Your Children For Years In Advance

To avoid arousing suspicion, and so that you don't terrify your kids when you abduct them, prepare your kids with weird and secret adventures over many years.

OK, you'd think that being sped out of the city at 05:30am, by a father who looks like what Kurt Cobain would have looked like if he'd joined the Marines, would set off alarm bells. Not with us. Dad had been prepping me and Ben for years, only we hadn't realised it.

Dad always took us on little outings called 'vaventures'. The word came from a cute mispronunciation Ben made when he was three, based on va-va-voom or something. Vaventures usually meant something 'exciting' Dad was sneaking into the schedule before he had to drive us back to Mother's.

Vaventures from the past included:

1. Dad turning off all the power in his flat and us having eat 'blackout breakfast' at 04:00am with candles.
2. A trip to the shingle beach to catch so-called 'edible molluscs'.
3. A trip to the nearest snow-covered hill forest to hack down branches to make a bivouac – and all before breakfast.
4. One time he even dragged us out to hunt for copper wires from the rubble remains of a freshly demolished tower block, and we had to sneak past the DANGER – DO NOT ENTER signs.

Ben, of course, thought all this was awesome, and I whined and moaned but gave up asking Dad why, why, why because he always said the same thing: 'I know you're kicking and screaming now, but in the end you'll thank me!'

Dad asked us to keep these vaventures secret from Mother. 'Most people get scared by the truth,' he said, 'and your mother has a particular aversion to it.' And I, of course, told him that asking kids to keep secrets from their primary custodial caregiver is a form of psychological abuse. He patted my head for being 'older than my years', which meant, don't be such a smart-ass, Haley. The upshot was that Mother never knew about Dad's secret vaventures and if she had, she would've most likely legally ended the 'unsupervised visits from your father' malarkey.

They had one of those really nasty divorces. I mean, I used to get these flashbacks to them screaming at each other. He'd done a pretty amazing job actually of getting Mother to trust him again, through doing years of therapy, or at least that's what we'd thought.

We were on this totally empty road winding out of the city. We didn't know it but Dad had rehearsed and timed his 'city escape route' at least twenty times – as he instructs all preppers to do in his manual – so that on the day of our abduction he could drive at speed, pre-aware of any possible blockages, without encountering excessive panic-traffic or police.

Dad sped past the big mall near the edge of the burbs. Usually when we drove past such things, he would deliver one of his borderline rants. Classics like: 'The masses just assume there'll be food on the shelves, fuel in the pumps, money in the banks. The masses have been taught to love their servitude, and they have no idea how this house of cards could fall.' One time he even yelled out his window at these random passing shoppers: 'Wake up, Sheeple!' Yeah, he was always telling Ben and me to 'wake up' and be aware of the world.

'Sheeple' means people who are like sheep, FYI.

But that morning he was spookily silent, and he said, 'Shh, the radio!' The news said, '...reports of deaths have yet to be confirmed ... have broken off diplomatic relations over rumours of a cover-up, meanwhile the World Health Organization...' and Dad turned it down low, smiled to himself and hummed along to a tune in only his head.

In retrospect, this was a massive telltale sign, but I was, as always, giving less than zero fucks, having what Dad's survivalist manual calls 'no contextual awareness'.

Wait, you still don't really know about my dad.

OK, Dad must've been at least kind of normal when he was married to Mother, but when he started living alone he became like the mad inventor dad in *Chitty Chitty Bang Bang*. He ran his SUV on this homemade diesel fuel that was one-part ammonia and nine parts recycled frying fat and urine, or something. He had these huge industrial coffee filters in his kitchen, to drain out all the bits of batter and onion rings. This was essential because the 'fuel' came from all the cafes we used to drive round late at night

– after they closed. It wasn't stealing, Dad told us, but 'creative recycling'. 'One man's crap is another man's gold!' he said.

One time Mother smelled fish and chips on me and Ben and accused Dad of feeding us junk food, and I had to make Ben promise never to tell her the truth because Mother could use Dad's illegal manufacturing of potentially explosive materials as leverage to put a restraining order on him. I told Ben it wasn't really lying because sometimes you had to protect people you love from the truth. Which is basically what we all do to Ben, 24/7.

I guess Dad had normalised his weirdness to us, so, for example, when my foot hit the disassembled crossbow under Ben's car seat that morning as we sped out of civilisation, I just went, 'Yup, that's just Dad being Dad again!'

I checked the speedo and we were doing five miles over the speed limit, just like normal. We passed the sixties housing estates with boarded-up windows and all the other ruined places on the outskirts Dad had taken us to teach us his philosophy of life. We sailed right past, accelerating obliviously into Dad's Abduction Plan A. He was later forced to use Plan B, Plan C and even Plan G, but we had no idea such things even existed at that particular junction or juncture, or whatever.

Confiscate The Phones Of Your Abductees Through Some Simple Ruse

Taking the phones from your abductees is essential, as one simple text message can be enough to scupper your entire plan. Teenagers and tweenagers very rarely part from their phones for more than a few minutes so you will need well-planned strategies to nab those telecommunication devices.

Ben asked Dad where the fabulous vaventure was going to be, and I reminded Dad that we had to be back at Mother's at twelve, due to me meeting up with Shanna, who was my new bestie.

You see, I'd fallen out with Beth, Stace, Lana, Scoobs and Eva, on account of them private group-chatting without me because they thought I'm weird cos of my asthma and ADHD, or some shit. So I was supposed to go to the mall with Shanna for the sale in Blitz. But that was just an alibi, cos really we wanted to spy on Jason in Vodafone – he'd recently dumped me, telling me he was gay, but he still gave me the major moists.

These were my plans for that day.

I waited for the right moment to sneak out my phone, half listening as the radio said that someone who was head of something had become suddenly ill. My phone screen had a seven per cent power warning.

'Damn it, Dad, you total doofus!' I shouted. 'You promised you'd charge it for me last night!'

'Sorry, Hale-Bopp. But hey, who needs a phone when you can speak to real humanoids, huh? Try it sometime.' Dad called me Hale-Bopp sometimes after some goofy comet that comes round every seventy years. Kind of ironic, given that we only saw him one night a week.

Anyway, so Dad had actually drained our phone batteries deliberately in the night, then topped them up by one or two per cent to hide his subterfuge.

I mumbled that he was as bad as Mother and rummaged in the glove box for his charger. Weirdly enough, there was a brand new pack of my asthma inhalers in there, but I gave zero fucks and thought only about getting back online. 'Where's your cable for the cigarette lighter charger thingy, Dad?' I moaned at him. 'It's not here! Why can't you have a proper phone charging socket like every other human being!'

He put his hand out. 'Give it to me.'

I refused.

'OK, if you hand it over, I promise I'll charge it for you,' he said. 'Why don't we see how long you can live without it, anyway? See it as a character-building exercise, Haley. I'll bet you can't go half an hour without it. Prove me wrong.'

So, I handed my phoney over with a sigh. 'You'll really charge it?'

'Sure, when we get to our destination,' he added, with a grin, and he switched off my phone and set it on the dash, where I couldn't reach it.

'Heinous,' I muttered, 'abhorrent, grievous, monstrous!'

Dad accelerated and ignored my moaning for a whole five minutes, so I said: 'Er, are we just going to drive around for miles and miles and then turn round and go back to Mother's? Because, sorry, that's not much of a vaventure. Plus, we should be watching the time because I seriously have to be back at twelve to meet Shanna.'

I thought I'd better text Mother, just to warn her that things had gone awry. I asked Dad for the phone again, but he said, 'Haley, you're not calling your mother, it's way too early, and your phone's dead anyway. I told you, I'll charge it when we get there. Trust me for once, would you?'

We passed a petrol station. It was empty and I recalled that time, during the last pandemic, when Dad had seen ten cars in a line waiting for gas and he'd said, 'You see that, in three hours' time they'll be paying a hundred for a gallon. They'll be queuing for miles. When that ring road gets blocked it'll turn into a stranglehold – no one'll get in or out. The biggest nose-to-tail in history, the last one.'

Of course he was wrong, and things like this were why Mother called Dad 'paranoid obsessive'. There was something else about a personality disorder, but he'd done a shit ton of therapy and had convinced Mother he was now more-or-less fine.

After the petrol station we'd officially 'left the county'. But I still didn't suspect anything was up – Dad, with his many vaventures over the years, had trained us to not be alarmed when he deviated from the map.

He'd also managed to keep it secret that he'd been preparing for this day for the last five years since the last pandemic. His motto, we later found out, was: 'It's better to be one year too early than one day too late.' Or maybe it was 'hour'. In the years when we hardly saw Dad at all, he had been a very busy chap indeed, and all that money he'd not given Mother in child support payments… well, it had gone to something much bigger.

Have A Fake Narrative Prepared For Your Abductees To Buy More Time

Vague promises of rewards buy time, and give greedy teenagers and kids motivation while also creating disorientation.

We passed the sign that said *NORTH* and Dad accelerated way past legal speed and I decided it was game over. 'Very amusing, Dad, but actually, I'm getting too old for this. To be perfectly honest I'd rather you just took us back to Mother. Like, now, OK, thank you very much, *danke, merci beaucoup*.'

He raised an eyebrow and squinted into the rear-view mirror, checking out Ben, who was dozing in the back, cute sibling-style, his little spherical face smooshed against the glass. I say Ben is my *little* brother – he'd just turned six a month before this began – but he weighs about the same as a nine-year-old on account of his eating disorder. Mother blamed Ben's egregious eating on the divorce and Dad blamed it on Mother's 'unsustainable consumer-ist lifestyle'. Classic divorce shit.

Anyway, as we headed into the deeply sheep-filled countryside, I asked the question that had started growing on me over the last few miles.

'Dad,' I said, 'you wouldn't happen to be, you know, abducting us, would ya?' I said it as a kind of joke so as not to offend him. 'Just checking, cos if you are, I might have to make a few calls.'

He laughed. But not like an evil cackle. More like he'd been elsewhere and just tuned back in. He checked out the snoozing Benster again, and with lowered voice he said, 'Haley, can you keep a secret?'

And I thought, oh crap, he really is abducting us, for real!

But this was him cueing up his fake narrative. Note: an effective fake narrative should contain an element of truth in it, so as to not be out-of-the-blue.

'What if I told you,' he said, 'that I just made a lot of money, Haley?'

This was pretty improbable. Dad never had any cash and I knew that he'd recently stopped paying his child support payments, and Mother was officially 'concerned', alluding to his 'mental health issues' and his 'need to just buckle down and get a proper job'.

'Well, how much money we talking?' I asked, thinking it's most likely a measly hundred or something.

Then he says, 'Well, I finally sold an invention.'

And I'm like, 'What? You mean like your bike-powered TV?' Poor old doofus Dad had actually made one such object, though he told us not to tell Mother.

He shook his head. 'Guess again, Hale Storm!'

So, then I'm staring at the random cows speeding by and saying, 'What? The wind-up hairdryer?' and he's laughing but quietly so as not to wake Ben and he says, 'Nope, this one actually works,' and so, I said, 'OK, just frickin tell me!' and he says, 'Nope, guess again,' so I say, 'The water-powered fan?'

'Nope.'

And I'm getting giggly because it's like a kiddie's guessing game. 'OK! The metal glove thingy with the screwdriver fingers? The newspaper sandals? The solar-powered fridge?'

'Nope, nope, nope.'

Now when I say Dad 'invented' these freaky things, I mean they were mostly just held together with duct tape and not likely to become an all-in-one solution to the problems of modern living anytime soon. And I stared at the road thinking of his vast sad legacy of failure, and he's doing a steady seventy and the car is rattling and there's a few cars all heading in the opposite direction but no one else going north.

And this gave me the melancholies, thinking of what a forever hopeful fool my dad truly was and how maybe Mother was right about him being a loser-ish dead-beat. Such insights can make a girl feel a bit lonely in life.

So, I just said, 'OK, Dad, I give up, you win!'

After a short silence his voice went serious and he said, 'OK, we're going north to visit the folk who bought my new invention. That's my surprise. They live a hundred miles away and I'm going to do some final adjustments and, all being well, they're going to pay me today.'

For real? I thought.

But then he said, 'Then I'll pay your mum all the child support I owe her plus some extra. Then who knows, maybe she'll let me see more of you.'

That kind of killed me. Because Dad'll never get it that he could give her the nine months of over-dues plus a million bucks but Mother would always find a way to limit our exposure to him. So I said, 'Sure, Dad, that'd be cool. I mean, to see more of you.'

But then curiosity got the better of me, because I'm shallow and materialistic, like Mother says, and so I asked, 'So, how much are these simple country-folk paying you for your va-va-vention, anyhow?'

'Well, this one is worth twenty grand,' he said, 'and there's ten more friends of theirs interested in buying the same thing. So that's...'

At this point I must have choked because I'd done the mental math and I coughed out, 'A quarter of a million! For real?'

Make A Fake Promise of Expensive Consumer Goods As A Reward

There is an egregious trick that psychologists call 'leading with the carrot'. It is all about animals but it works very well on teenagers too.

All I could think was, Dad could be rich, Dad could be rich! And this was dumfounding and legit hopeful. Then he was on about how he could put a little cash my way, and me being pathetically addicted to my phone (as he says everyone in my generation is), he said he could even buy me a new one.

And me, being pre-wired for the merest possibility of such an offer from either competing parent, spat out, 'Awesome, Dad. Could you buy me a Samsung G80 X-Phone Extra-Lite with two terabytes and three times optical zoom and four gigs of RAM?'

Dad laughed and shook his head as he took a turn-off onto a smaller road.

So I said, 'Pretty please,' doing the cutesies, 'please, please, Dad, cos if I had an X-Phone I could send you proper long vids, and have decent video streaming for our wonderful chats and I could buy that app so Mother could track my phone and then she'd stop getting on my case about where I am all the frickin time, and I could even take the subway or the bus over to yours and have a bit more freedom and not have to beg her for Ubers home to which she always says no, anyway. Please, the X-Phone's on special offer and it only costs 350 and I don't just want one because my friends have one, and it's the newest and coolest and if I have it I promise I'll spend less time on Snapchat.'

And he was still laughing and shaking his head. Then he put his hand out and said, 'Deal.' And we shook.

'You'll get me an X-Phone G80? For real?'

He nodded and said, 'You drive a hard bargain, Hale-Bopp.'

Dad didn't actually have to buy me it, because just the threat of him saying he was going to would trigger the competitive 'buy first' reflex in Mother. It's not like money can buy you love, but in the absence of love, new technology is a pretty good substitute. Actually, it would be a good time right now to ponder how most of the horrific things that were about to happen to Ben and me and Mother might never have been triggered if I hadn't betrayed her for the illusory promise of a new smartphone.

Then Dad said, 'But let's just get to our destination first and make sure this invention of mine actually works before getting our hopes up too high. OK?'

'Deal, Dad!'

And then, for some reason, staring out at the romantic clouds and hills, I said something corny like, 'Really proud of you.' And he took my hand and squeezed it and then I got some emotions because of his strong, wrinkly, old-man hand on mine and he said, 'Proud of you too, Haley-boo.' Which is so corny, but fuck you, he's my dad and I was legit lumping it in the throat.

We chewed up the country miles, and by his stroke of evil genius my deceptive dad then had me actually enjoying the trip, looking forward to arriving at this wherever hillbilly place. I even said to him that it would be cool if we were a bit late for Mother, and I thought, that'll teach her for restricting my phone usage last month after the me-sending-a-pic-of-my-boobs-to-Jason-to-test-if-he-was-really-gay incident. And to be honest, Dad never stood up to Mother, so him defying her schedules for once meant he had some guts. And maybe he'd even end up in a custody battle and renegotiate better terms and that would mean he really cared.

It didn't cross my mind for a second that every single thing Dad had said that morning might be lies, and that the new phone he was promising me would not even operate in the future world he believed would soon be upon us. Because, the way he saw it, within three or four weeks smartphones would lie scattered in the streets beside tear gas canisters, spent plastic bullets, credit cards, oxygen masks and dead bodies. But he didn't tell me that. Not until we'd put another two hours, a wall and some razor wire between us and Mother.

Make Your Kids Question The Safety Of The Home They Want To Return To

Just in case Dad's abduction Plan A didn't work, he had back-up plans from Plan B all the way up to Plan G. Dad had actually considered these options for Ben and me:

1. Drug your abductees so they are asleep for the duration of the abduction.

2. Tie them up. Don't forget to gag them so the screams and pleas won't disturb you when you are driving.
3. Threaten your abductees into compliance with a gun or other lethal weapon that can be used at close range i.e. within a speeding vehicle.
4. Any combination of 1, 2 & 3. Plus Strategy X.

Dad drove us on through ever more rugged, windy roads. We'd been in the car for more than two hours and boredom was killing Ben and me. Dad once said the problem with young people was they mistakenly thought that boredom was a thing other people gave them. Like a virus.

We sped through picture-perfect landscape moments that would have got hundreds of likes. We saw a hovering hawk and like a million sheep. Ben seemed to be incanting a Buddhist-type mantra: 'Will we get there soon?' 'Can we go back to Mum's?' 'What time is it?' 'Are we there?'

Dad turned to me. 'Sorry, kids. Not much longer now.'

Then it was single-track roads, off-the-map roads, and going fast like he knew these tracks super well, which was weird because we were two hundred miles from home. I started doing that very-Mother-thing of compiling lists of complaints against him:

1. Dad's 4x4 hit a pothole and I bashed my nose against the window – and this was his fault.
2. Ben was snoring in the back because this is what obese kids with attention deficit hyperactivity disorder do, apparently – and this was Dad's fault.
3. The vehicle was super cold and the heating didn't work – Dad's fault.
4. It also stank of cooking fat and now so did we – Dad's fault.
5. He was driving dangerously fast down a dirt track and if we crashed – Dad's fault.
6. At first there were cottages and farms, then only the

abandoned ones from millions of years ago. The mountains loomed dark and heavy over us. I've never trusted mountains – they're like screensavers that actually kill people. And this was Dad's fault, too.

We were going to be so late for Mother, and I was about to raise this again when Dad suddenly said, 'It's good that your mum gets some personal time, too.'

And I was like, 'Woah, random! What in the actual hell do you mean?'

'Well, maybe your mum needs a bit of grown-up time once in a while. I'm glad she's moving on.'

Now this was really freaky. Because moving on could only mean, like, shagging some other adult, and the absolute thought of micro-managing middle-managerial Mother actually even looking at another male, let alone the horrific vision of her with make-up on, and like flirting, like out in a pub, like on an actual date, or even touching another man, let alone bouncing about on his love pole ... Anyway, my bile rose and I said, 'What do you frickin mean, Dad? Call a spade a spade, spill the beans, are you saying Mother is like' – and I leaned in and whispered in case Ben woke up – 'do you mean she's, like, dating?'

'Oh,' he said, 'didn't you know? Oh, sorry.'

Oh my actual God. 'What?!' I shouted. 'You're saying Mother is bonking, like, a man? Not that I'm saying she's bisexual, but... for God sake, Dad!'

'Well,' he said, reminding me not to wake Ben, 'I don't know if it's someone specific, or if she's seeing...' Then he paused. 'What did you think she was doing all these Saturday nights when you stay at mine? Come on, Haley, you're an adult now.'

'I just puked in my actual mouth,' I said, because I had. A bit.

'But keep it hush from your brother,' he said. 'Anyway, I'm glad for her, don't you think it's good your mum's having some fun?'

Jesus. Mountains were passing by my furious eye and I was

getting flashes of Mother dearest sipping wine and smiling at this man who was stroking her thigh, and I was saying, Jesus, Jesus. And maybe I even said, 'What, in your actual bed?' This meaning the very large marital bed which Mother never got rid of after the divorce. And maybe I was secretly holding onto the childish fantasy that Mother and Dad's grand pash would one day be re-kindled. But the thought of some male stranger in this bed she used to share with Dad – when she wouldn't even let Dad get past the front door – and maybe this male stranger was even naked and totally tumescent and he's gazing at a picture of me and Ben in the bedroom and saying, 'Your kids look so cute,' as Mother prepares his pink love pole. And I literally mouth-barfed cos this was not just a betrayal of Dad, but a violation of me and Ben and our safe space and everything.

Of course, this was a very clever part of Dad's PLAN A, and the evidence is in his book under 'Delay and Disorientation Strategies'.

There was no boyfriend, no date. It was most likely Mother had actually spent all night before updating her yearly planner and her calorie counter app for Ben's diet, and trawling the net for ever newer gluten-free solutions to the problems of midlife loneliness.

But I was livid and caught up in his lie and so I said to Dad, 'Well, fuck Mother then. Like, not literally, but fuck it, I don't want to go back home today!'

And with that, Dad bought another hundred miles and my total commitment to getting as far away from my traitorous principal caregiver as possible.

But like I say, what was actually happening back home, I found out later, was Mother was panicking as the time for our drop-off came and went. She sent me and Ben dozens of messages, and after calling us and Dad and getting no reply ten times, she was frantic and heading off to a fake destination that Dad had sent her to.

You see, evil clever Dad, under PLAN A section five, had actually sent Mother a cunningly timed auto-send text message that said something like, *Sorry, traffic bad, running late. Meet you at Nando's in the shopping mall at 01:00pm*

And Mother was flipping because Dad was never ever allowed to lay down the schedule. And she was actually getting in her car, right then, two hundred miles away, and on her phone, most likely to Tami, her best-bitchin-bud, and telling her, 'How dare he change my schedules like this?' and asking, 'Has Debra received any messages from Haley this morning?' Or other such freaked-out questions to the rest of the midlife, single-mum, friend-group, panic-phone-call circuit.

But, like I say, I was oblivious and even hating her at this juncture. I gazed out at the forests and mountainous miles speeding past and back at Dad, and I got a lump in my throat as I thought, what a brilliant human he is, how could Mother ever have thrown him out?

And Dad told me another lie then. He said, 'I sent your mum a message already saying I'd have you back at hers for 05:00pm. She's totally OK with it. Chill.'

Then the wheels were skidding and spraying millions of bits of dirt up the side windows and his knuckles were white from gripping the steering wheel. He yelled, 'Hold on, kids!' and steered us headlong into an actual river. My head hit the roof and Ben woke up and was laughing. 'Wow, Dad, total moon landing! Do it again!' Steam roared from the bonnet as we practically turned into a boat.

'You fat phoney freak, do you really think this is fun?' I yelled at Ben. 'Do you have any remote idea what's actually going on in the world?' I recoiled, as water sprayed up on either side of us, fearing we might actually drown.

Ben sniffed and said, 'Dad, Haley called me fat.'

'Apologise to your brother!'

I mumbled an apology, actually feeling pretty out of line because Ben has, according to my online diagnosis, bulimia nervosa, but without the vomiting.

My head bashed the ceiling as the 4x4 hit the other side of the river.

'Ow, that hurt!'

'Wooh!' yelled Ben. 'Do it again, Dad. Again!'

The radio was mere fuzz as we headed deeper into the mountains, literally driving through a field and fifty sheep scattering before us in bird-like patterns. And I probably deserved the headache I was getting. Then some radio news report crackled, saying '...demanding an explanation, while government officials claim this is fake news deliberately created to upset the markets.' And some boring politician was saying something about scaremongering and bio warfare and not to panic, this is all under control, like this is going to be nothing. Dad just turned it off. His eyes were miles away and a smile grew on his lips, so I asked, 'You OK, Pops?'

And his silence became ominous, interrupted only by machine-gunfire from Ben's vexatious computer game.

'Dad, why are you grinning like that?

'We were right.' He beamed.

'We' – who the hell was 'we'?

Trick Your Abductees Into Completing The Final Steps Of Their Own Abduction

Rather than using force to get your abductees over the threshold into captivity, it is best to trick them into entering of their own accord.

The SUV stopped with a jolt in the middle of this marshland. Before us was a high fence of shiny metal, like the ones for keeping deer out or in, but the curly spiky wires round its top made it look military. Dad got out with a big bunch of keys, leaving the motor running. The fence ran as far as I could see before vanishing into a mist of landscapey nothingness. For a second I might have thought, wait, why does my dad have a set of keys to a top-secret military-looking enclosure?

Dad opened the big-locked gate and I was staring at him

through the muddy windscreen, in a kind of daze with a big 'what-the-fuck?' forming.

This was the moment when Dad played his absolute masterstroke.

You see, another secret that Dad asked me not to reveal to my principal caregiver, aka Mother, was the super-covert driving lessons he'd been giving me since I was ten, usually in the back roads of some industrial estate.

So Dad came back to the car, smiled and said, 'Jump in the hot seat and bring her through, Hales.' And all my questions suddenly became a big yeah-yeah-yeah and I jumped straight into mirror-signal-manoeuvre mode as I shunted my aforementioned scrawny ass over and literally got into the driver's seat.

There came a sound like a small nuclear explosion from Ben's accursed computer game and he said, 'Bum! Why am I always dead?' I revved up the engine and yelled, 'Hurry up, Dad, get back in, so I can put my foot down!' Dad jumped in and shouted, 'She's all yours, I souped her up last week. Slow now on the clutch, and wait for the bite.'

We lurched forward and the first thing we passed, as I took her through the huge gates, looked like a burned-out-car from some Middle East war, but I gave zero fucks. Alarm bells be-damned. Nope, I was giving it, first into second, don't over-rev, listen to the engine and hear what it wants.

So yeah, the dirt track and potholes had me plenty occupied, and so I didn't notice a stack of morbidly abandoned refrigerators sitting in ditches, oddly different from the usual junk lazy farmers have strewn around their property.

Nope, I was only thinking, rev it up, hold her steady, then up into third.

I didn't even see the sewage pipes sticking out of stony holes that could only imply some kind of bunker beneath. Or the big, burned hole in the marshland that could only have been the blast crater from a DIY explosive device.

Nope, I was doing forty, and the dirt track was long and the SUV shuddered and felt good and Dad was winking at me. 'That's my girl!'

And here's the irony: I remember thinking, wow, it feels really frickin great to BE IN CONTROL! Which kills me, given that I was riding me and my bro, at speed, into our own prison.

To be honest, I should have clicked what was going on a whole day and a half before, cos when we'd first got to Dad's flat, he made us wash our hands with bleach and soap and then gargle and he scrubbed the soles of our shoes with bleach too cos, he said, a cat had pissed outside his door or something. Plus, he did sort of quiz Ben and me about whether any of our school pals had been abroad recently and he got Ben and me to spit in a jar, one each - but this hadn't set off any alarm bells. Nope. I didn't think 'is Dad testing for us some kind of contamination?' cos it just seemed like Dad's usual eccentric paranoia.

And so, blissfully-unaware-me drove past abandoned rubbish sacks, with crows picking at the innards, and past vertical poles carrying a single swooping electrical cable that I didn't realise was our only connection to the outside world. We passed five old TVs lying in the mud, their screens smashed with little holes and then there was a row of three target-practice soldiers, with their heads and hearts punctured so many times they could only have been shot by automatic weapons. But I saw none of these things that I would, very soon, come to know and loathe as the only markers in the one kilometre square of my imprisonment. Hell no, little old me was oblivious and elated, as I accelerated down the dirt track, kicking up movie-style dust behind us with Ben yelling, 'Weeeehoooo!' and Dad grinning over at me. Like one of those classic Facebook family montage moments that gets auto-set to music by the app, even when you didn't ask it to.

How To Trap Kids In A Safe House

Keep Up The Pretence Of Civility As Your Abductees Acclimatise

The use of façades is very important. Conceal what is really inside with a calculated exterior. N.B. this works for buildings and humans.

It looked like an ancient, abandoned farmhouse surrounded by an old ivy-covered stone wall. It was grey-black, mildewed and decayed-looking against the grey sky, all desolate and *Wuthering Heights*-like. Weird, in other words.

Dad must have sensed my disappointment, as he told me, 'Just wait,' and he jumped out the passenger door. As if on cue, the ancient iron entrance-to-the-farm gate creaked open and, even weirder, there was this woman with long red hair grinning at us, holding this big plastic bucket. Now, I'm the last person to want to reduce a woman to her physical attributes, but let's call her homely, big-boned, perhaps hefty, food-loving or huge-knockered. And hippie-ish too, with that kind of red-cheeked, no make-uped, muddy-handed, nature-loving, probably-smelly energy that always freaks me out. Weirder still was this major déjà-vu feeling – like I totally knew Dad was about to say, 'Hey, kids, this is Meg,' as I steered inside and Dad locked the huge black iron gate behind us.

The farmhouse had a bit of the roof caved in and some broken windows, like it had been utterly deserted for fifty years. I was pretty disappointed that this was our surprise vaventure actually, plus it had started pissing with rain.

I slowed down, just right, put the handbrake on, and I saw Dad go over to this Meg person and I couldn't hear them properly through the windscreen but she asked him something weird like 'all clear?' and he nodded. Then out of the blue she hugged him and handed him her bucket and she ran over and was literally yanking my door open. She had this big, over-eager smile, like in a horror film where the baddie grins and says, 'We've been expecting you.' And her totally bra-less boobs were bouncing under her outstretched arms and she said, 'Here they are at last! The little rascals! Hi Ben, Hi Haley.' And she's wearing this weird mixture of, like, a tie-dye Eighties T-shirt and camouflage pants along with this weird apron with bunnies on it. She had the kind of gnarly hair vegans call 'self-washing'.

Freaky. And there were hugs. Ben always laps that shit up, probably because Mother dearest had to do online classes in expressing intimacy. I stood there dreading contact with this woman's pendulous possessions and her stained apron, and I guess I must have muttered, 'Is that blood?' to her. Which, given that she was supposed to be Dad's client and was supposed to buy his invention, was kind of rude of me.

'Oh that – just a bit of jam,' she said, with gusto. 'I bet you're both starving, I made a chocolate sponge cake, special.'

Ben erupted with excessive 'Yippees!' and I clocked that full-on calorific Ben-bribery was now occurring. Total strangers offering chocolate cake with a smile was way up there with the Child Catcher from *Chitty Chitty Bang Bang*. And it was strange: how did she know about coercing-Ben-with-foodstuffs and know our names? So, I had to cut things off.

'Ben can't eat chocolate anymore because of his condition,' I said to the Meg woman and to Dad, who was already unloading the car.

You see, Mother had asked me to secretly police Dad to see if he was force-feeding Ben treats behind her back. Her endless refrain was, 'I don't think he realises how much damage he's doing to his son's liver.' Seriously, me and the spheroid sibling had this super strict health diet that Mother enforced. Sometimes, I thought she put her bans on random foodstuffs, just so she could blame Dad for making a mistake. 'He fed you flour?!' It was like we were test experiments that Mother sent out into the world to gather incriminating evidence against Dad. Like guinea pig double-agents.

'Well, your mother's not here, and chocolate is actually a really good relaxant and anti-oxidant,' Dad announced, as he set down the big bucket thing that stank majorly of bleach and opened the boot and started unpacking. 'And she's not right about everything. Live a little, it might be the last chocolate cake we'll ever see.'

That was pretty psychotic but not entirely out of his given repertoire.

'Think about it, kids, the cocoa beans are from Brazil,' Dad said, as he unloaded four boxes, going off on one of his classic rants. 'seventy-eight per cent of everything we eat comes in on foreign container ships. This nation can't feed itself. Everyone's forgotten how. We ship strawberries in from Chile, anchovies from Japan. We waste ten calories of hydrocarbon energy just shipping one calorie of food round the globe! It's insanity. Every supermarket has only enough food for two days. How many meals are we away from anarchy, kids?'

'Three!' Ben yelled. Then added, 'Can I have some cake now?'

Dad laughed and winked over at the Meg woman, 'How much would you trade me for a bit of Meg's cake, Ben? Your Xbox? How about a can of diesel? How about I trade you this world-class four-wheel-drive for a slice of that chocolate cake?'

'No way!' Ben laughed. He always made a big show of guffawing at Dad's jokes even when they weren't funny. And the Meg woman was laughing too and weirdly touching Ben's shoulders, like she wanted to pick him up or something.

Dad carried the boxes towards the grubby old farmhouse and he called back, 'Why don't we let your sister decide if you can have some cake?'

Oh, great, put it all on me!

Ben was yanking at my hand then, as if to say, please, please, please? I won't tell Mother, if you don't.

Then, as if Meg's boobs were gravitationally coupled with all small children in the universe, she bent forward to Ben's height and said, 'How would you like to meet the rabbits first?'

And Ben shouted, 'Rabbits! Yay! Rabbits!'

And how did she know that Ben's ADHD means if you get him excited about the next thing he totally forgets what was basically his reason to live like thirty seconds ago? And Meg was giving it, 'Aren't you the clever one!' and literally taking Ben's hand and leading him away. This triggered my sibling-safety instinct, so I said, 'Ben's not supposed to hold hands with strangers, either.'

Then the weirdest alarm bell of all was Meg saying, 'Auntie Meg's not a stranger, is she, son?'

Auntie? Woah, hold it, horsey! So, I flashed detective-style through my mental holiday-snaps, and there had been some grown-ups one time in a forest, back when I was like nine or ten. And if I'd met Meg in the past, did that mean...? I shuddered: seriously, is this woman Dad's mistress? Then a totally vile flash came to me of Dad mounting those mountainous mammories, because every single kid in my generation has been exposed to way too much online porn, but that's a-whole-nother story.

Meg tickled Ben and he let her lead him through the rain and mud towards this ancient doorway with no door, literally hand in hand.

'Why don't you join in for once, Haley?' Dad said. 'Go check out the bunnies with your little brother while I unpack, then we can eat.'

And in his face I saw no sign of deception, because I'm clearly shit at reading faces. I just sort of stared him down. 'Auntie?'

'Figure of speech,' was all he replied. He undid the ropes on the tarp on top of the 4x4 and took down a sort of bit of an engine and a plastic box full of cans from the roof, but all I'm thinking is, shit, maybe Mother and Dad are literally both having GFs and BFs and FBs.

Word of advice: never, ever, ever put the words 'Fuck Buddy' and one of your parents into the same headspace.

'Can I have my phone now, please?' I asked, cos when things get distressing, that's always the best solution.

And Dad took it from his pocket and tossed it to me, with a smile. 'Catch.'

I checked it and it was now totally dead.

Dad said, 'Calm down, all mod cons here, I'm sure we can find a charger. Why don't you ask Meg?'

I stared at him, and he said, 'Or you can have an hour without the net, Haley-Boo, open your eyes to the beauty of nature, stretch your legs.' And to totally wind me up, he added, 'Let Auntie Meg show you around.'

A barn. That was what it was called, this thing Meg had taken Ben by the hand into – or that's what I thought, in my naïveté. I looked round and saw that all the disappointing tumbledown crap on the outside had been a cleverly constructed smokescreen. To my shame, I confess, and it was only then that I began to develop some kind of, what Dad calls, 'contextual awareness'.

Behind the ruined wall was a high gleaming silver fence of what I would agonizingly learn shortly was razor wire. On the interior wall was a big old satellite dish and three gleaming solar panels and there were two mud-spattered quad bikes. There were three mini-windmills lying on the ground, and the propellers of a huge one were half concealed beneath some camouflage material.

I glimpsed the heel of a dirty army boot vanish round an old wall corner and it gave me the shudders. Who? What? How many others? Random weirdnesses were overwhelming me, so I spat out my big question, 'Dad what IS this place?'

He clocked that I wasn't going to let him off without a proper explanation. . He set down his part of an engine - that I would later learn was designed to suck oxygen into an otherwise airtight bunker - and said, 'Come on, let me show you.' Then he threw the big bucket of bleachy water all over his car, which was weirder still, and led me onwards.

Do Not Tie Up, Drug Or Lock Up Your Abductees ... Yet

If you show your abductees parts of the self-sustaining living environment, they will be less traumatised than if you bundle them without explanation into the bunker, with the threat of lethal force.

Dad led me into what I thought was a barn, but it was really a kind of quad, that contained some kind of futuristic eco-garden packed full of Dad's almost-genius inventions. Ben was running around wowing, and Dad was like, 'Haley, let me show you the hydroponic solar tent.'

I couldn't believe it. Cos Dad had been messing around with bits of this thing for years and there it was, like a plastic green-house, with these tubes of pulsing blue light and pipes of moving water with bubbles. Dad grinned and gestured for me to follow him inside and there was classical music playing, probably Baby Mozart or something, and all this lush veg dangling in rows of bags. Like hundreds. And four kinds of lettuce and watercress, and this little pump whirring.

And Dad was like, 'So this is the rainwater transfusion system and the plants hang in water bags, with absolutely no need for soil.'

And my geek-factor kicked in and I was like, 'Because the roots feed directly from the nutrients in the water...'

'Yup, and the water is oxygenated by—'

'—by the solar-powered oxygen pump,' I said triumphantly, and Dad's grinning at me, like we're both part of the same super-geek universal-mind, and maybe he said, 'That's my girl,' and there was a wink of pride.

And I'm seeing this fabulous invention like it's mine too and I'm so proud of Dad for actually, finally, pulling this off. And then he's answering my next question before I even say it, with, 'In summer it captures solar energy into the rechargeable battery rack, so we can grow fruit and veg all year round with our sun lamps.' And sure enough, I'm seeing like half of a tanning booth that Dad must have salvaged and hot-wired with the solar panels. It was awesome in the original sense of 'awe' and 'then some'.

And this totally cancelled out all my questions about what the fuck was actually going on. Then Hippie Meg came in and picked a strawberry/raspberry-looking thing and handed it to me, laughing, 'They're stras-berries!' she said. 'Delicious. Here, love, try one.' And, of course, Ben ran over and snaffled it and everyone was laughing, even though the 'love' thing was super-weird.

Then Dad was pulling back a tarp and saying, 'Haley, Ben, bunny-time!' And there was, no kidding, what looked like a luxury, bunny-super-apartment with a slowly rising bunny escalator, ingeniously made out of some metal bed bases, and a bunny elevator powered by the hamster wheels in the next hutches. Total geek-heaven.

Meg brought a Palomino out of the hutch and taught Ben how to hold it, and the little fluffy thing was so damn cute, and Ben was grinning over at me, like a massive family Facebook moment. But I just had to ask Meg, 'So, like, how long have you known Dad?'

And she said, 'Oh, I don't know, a couple of years.'

So I asked her, 'Did he help you build this place, then?'

Then she kind of looked around and was proud-sounding and she said, 'Help us? He's the one who brought us here.'

Uber freaky. And if Dad had really studied his own Survival Manual, he would've realised that you have to rehearse your survivalist team so they don't go off script. So I said, 'Wait, "us"? Us? Like, how many people is that? What do you mean, he brought you here?'

But then there was a commotion over at the hutches and Meg moved away, totally not answering me. I shot a look at Dad, but he was over with Ben, giving it, 'No, Ben, don't hold it like that! Here, I'll show you.' And the rabbit was struggling in Ben's grip and he nearly dropped it, so grabbed it by the ears. Then Dad shouted in a weird tone. 'Give me it back! They're not cuddly toys, Ben. They're our food.'

Ben stared at Dad in horror then wailed, 'Euwww!' and ran back out the doorway.

Evidence was mounting and it looked to me like Meg was too poor to pay Dad twenty grand for his invention. In fact, this place was so packed full of Dad's inventions that only he could have been living here – like, maybe since he even got divorced.

Just as I was about to interrogate Dad, a lion-sounding engine roared.

'That's my boy, Danny,' Meg yelled at me over the racket. 'He's been dying to meet you!'

I turned and there in the doorway was this guy on a quad bike. He had the body of a grown man but must have only been fifteen or sixteen. He didn't smile or blink or even speak and I was sort of trapped in his gaze, like a human on safari being sized up by a wild animal. He turned the engine off and I could hear barking, like from a huge guard dog locked up somewhere. Then this man-boy Danny-person turned away and I was released from his eyes. I shuddered. Did I mention he was bare-chested? 'Ripped' is even the word, probably from just lifting hay bales or some crap, and he looked a bit like that famous dead actor guy. He had mud on his face and chest, and something darker, like maybe grease from an engine or worse. He was precisely the kind of redneck that a girl like myself considers Neanderthal.

But Ben was jumping up and down beside the quad bike, practi-cally wetting his little blimp bod with excitement and yelling, 'Can I have a go? Can I have a go?' And I couldn't believe it, but Dad shouted over, 'OK, let Ben climb on for a spin, Danny, but slowly!'

And me shouting at Dad then, 'Are you nuts, Dad? Ben can't go on that thing! Mother'll be absolutely furious and whip your ass!'

And Dad just smiled.

Use Delay Tactics To Coerce Without Confrontation

I later discovered that Dad had actually planned to play his fake story out for days, with delay tactics and small deceptions. His next delay tactic was a classic: feigned engine failure. He had his head inside the 4x4 engine and was going at it with a ratchet.

I said, 'I get it, Dad, this is some revenge thing with Mother – you're testing her and that's OK. She's been sort of bugging me, too. It's even kind of cool that you've stood up to her for once, even if this is a bit over-the-top. But just so you know, we really have to be back in time for school tomorrow, so I really have to call Mother now...'

He was actually listening.

'...because Mother'll be getting distressed,' I said. 'You know what she's like ... my God, she's probably got helicopters out looking for us already!'

'I'm sorry, Haley,' he replied, pulling out some wires. 'I'd take you back if I could, but when we hit that bump in the river, I must have damaged the converter. It's going to take a few hours to fix.'

'A few hours!' I yelled.

'Maybe more.' And he yanked another part of the engine out and laid it in the mud.

I had so many questions buzzing round my head but they were drowned out by the redneck's quad bike and Ben's yells of 'Whey-hey' and 'Wooo!' I was absolutely furious, knowing the chances of Dad getting the engine put back together again and driving us back to the city were getting dimmer.

Cunning, the way that Dad made it seem like 'an unfortunate accident'.

'OK, Haley,' he said to me finally, wiping his oily hands. And maybe he'd even practised his lines with Meg and Danny. 'I messed up. Meg's called a friend in the local village and he can get us a converter, but it won't be till tomorrow morning.'

I was shouting then at Dad, for turning me into the kind of uncool emotional teenager that shouts at their Dad.

'I'll email your mum now and explain,' he lied. 'I'm sure she'll understand.'

'Yeah,' I yelled, 'she'll understand alright, she'll understand how totally fucked up you are and she'll make sure you never get to see us again!'

And there was that secret smile of Dad's again.

It was only later that I clicked. It would be Mother who'd be the one who'd never see us again, as long as she lived, because that was exactly Dad's plan.

Use Sentimental Strategies To Win Over Your Abductees

Objects from your past, music, tunes or books, an old expression or an image can all make your abductees 'feel at home'.

So, it was official, we were going nowhere, and staying 'the night'. When I say going nowhere, Ben was still spinning around on Neanderthal Danny's quad bike, and Dad had led me inside the hobbity farmhouse to 'freshen up and have a rest'.

When I get with the spiralling questions, I get this hot flushing feeling, and usually just go round in circles saying 'I'm so confused, I'm just so confused,' and 'I'm hot, why am I so hot? I'm so hot, I can't breathe,' until either Mother or Dad sits me down and gives me my asthma inhaler and a glass of water.

So that's what Dad did, taking me up the rickety, smelly, woody stairs, into this room that Dad said was 'you and your brother's room'. But my inhaler wasn't stopping the freak-out, because inside 'our room' were two military-looking bunk-beds and those kind of huge local maps you see in war-rooms instead of wallpaper. There was a bare light bulb hanging, like an actual prison.

'Just breathe slowly, Haley,' Dad was saying, his hand on my back.

And I'm staring at Baloo as I suck my inhaler.

Baloo was the bear from my early childhood. My first love. My divorce dolly. I'd cried into Baloo, I'd chewed off one of his eyes, and I'd punched, burned and buried him when Mother and Dad had been fighting downstairs.

And there he was, Baloo the guilty secrets bear, restored to full sight with a new eye and his stuffing re-done and sitting on this weird camp bed. And I still couldn't get my breath, and I was asking Dad what the hell Baloo was doing there, because Mother, literally, threw him out years ago.

And Dad said, 'I rescued him.' He smiled and took my inhaler from me because you can over-nebulise and it's not good for your heart.

'You went through the actual trash cans at Mother's house? What, like, at night?'

He told me to lie down and slow down, but outside the vile quad bike roared once again. I told Dad he was really freaking me out and said, 'I really need to email Mother now. Please. You said you emailed her and that she answered saying it was OK to stay, so you must have Wi-Fi and a landline.'

More and more questions un-answered and, like I say, spiral-ling. 'Dad, who is this Meg woman? How does she know me? Does Mother know about her?... Is your engine really busted?... I know Meg's not bought your invention, she's poor, so why did you lie about that? Is she your mistress? Is Danny...?'

Then I stopped. Jesus Christ, is Danny my secret half brother?

Dad smiled and stroked my back and shook his head. 'No, no, of course not.' And I repeated, 'I'm so confused! What's your Wi-Fi password?'

He said there was no internet here. And I told him, 'But that's bullshit, you just said you emailed.'

Dad was standing there, silent, as the quad bike seemed to get faster and louder. So I told him that even if he was abducting us – and it was weirdly kind of sweet because it showed he really cared – could the abduction thing just be for one night because I really had to get back to do masses of homework and then there was school and...

He was silent, just staring out. And I knew it might hurt his feel-ings but I had to ask him the one big thing that Mother would have asked.

'Dad, have you stopped taking your tablets?'

He didn't react.

Mother had told me about the anti-depressants before and

another pill, which was about psycho something, and Dad had done tons of tests and the doctor had said that for three years he had been perfectly normal. But still.

'Dad, please tell me the truth,' I said, and I know he just breaks apart inside when I'm sad and confused and it's his fault. 'I really don't want all the things Mother says about you to be true. Are you OK?'

'Truth,' he said, 'your mother wouldn't accept the truth.' He came and sat beside me, and stroked my head. 'I was hoping, Haley, that we wouldn't have to have this conversation for a few days yet, but you're so smart, I just can't keep anything from you. Can I?'

'Just frickin tell me, Dad!' I shouted.

And so he began going on about 'mutually reinforcing positive feedback loops'. He said, 'Do you remember, when you were a bit younger, during the last pandemic…?' It was all in that slow philosophical way of his and I just wanted to shake him. Then, suddenly, as if my anger had sparked out into the real world, we heard a loud crash from outside. The quad bike roaring then cutting out. A wail from Ben. A heavy thud against a wall. A sound of something snapping. then a horrific silence. Then Danny screaming.

Plan B

How To Do CPR On Minors

To try to save a child's life when they are not breathing and utterly unconscious, you must:

1. Close the soft part of the child's nose using index finger and thumb.
2. Open their mouth a little but keep the chin pointing upwards.
3. Blow steadily into their mouth for about one second, watching for the chest to rise.
4. Repeat four times. If the child does not respond, begin chest compressions.
5. Adults – Do not press too hard on a child's chest as you can easily break their ribs. And even puncture the heart. Many well-meaning adults have killed children this way.
6. Try not to think of the child as Ben and stop screaming!

I tore down the stairs after Dad. He was totally out and sprinting across the mud. My mind was wailing – Poor baby Ben, Dad killed Ben! Mother will kill Dad! – and then I'm staring at the quad bike, upside down and smashed against the wall, one wheel spinning and Ben's legs sticking out from underneath it, not moving. And Danny is panicking, and Meg runs out screaming, and Dad is trying to lift the quad bike off Ben, but it's too heavy, and Danny's backing off and saying, 'He tried to grab the throttle and fuck… fuck… I'm sorry, sorry!'

Dad's yelling, 'Help me get this thing off him!' and he got his back under the quad bike while Danny pulled the bike upwards, and Dad dragged Ben out.

I was like, 'Ben, Ben!' and saying, 'Dad, why isn't he moving?' and Dad's yelling, 'Back off, give me space!' And Dad's lifting Ben to kiss him but Ben is all floppy.

Dad's checking Ben's breath and pulse and wiping mud from his eyes and mouth, then Dad did everything exactly like in the manual with the 'kiss of life'.

Ben suddenly coughed and, random as anything, looks round, all sleepy, and says, 'Did we have the cake yet?'

I'm in total shock, then I burst out laughing, like hand to mouth cos it's not a laughing matter. And Dad's moving Ben's arms, legs, neck – checking nothing's broken – and asking loads of questions, like, 'Ben, can you make a fist?' 'Ben, can you turn your head?' 'Is that sore? Try standing.' And Ben's giving it, 'Why's everyone staring at me, Dad?' and 'Why's the quad bike upside down?' And it's awful but I was weirdly grinning, mostly because my mad lil' bro was not actually kicking the bucket.

Meg ran off to get some water and bandages or something and I'm staring at the Neanderthal fuck-up, Danny, giving him the 'this-is-all-your-fault' look. And Dad's lifting Ben and cradling his neck, like he was a baby again, saying, 'It's alright son, you had a horrible fright, you're OK now.' And I'm shouting, 'No this is not frickin OK, Dad! We need to get him to a hospital right now! He needs Mother.'

But Dad is all calm and cold and he says, 'There will be no hospital and no Mother, either.' Then I'm shouting, 'What the actual fuck? Are you totally out of your mind?'

The next bit was a case study in why people who make decisions with high adrenaline in reaction to stimulus generally mess up, and why people who have a plan of action, and have practised for all eventualities will always beat the aforementioned un-prepped persons.

Ben was on his feet and Dad was brushing him down. I saw my opportunity and I yanked Ben away, shouting, 'C'mon, Ben, we're getting out of here!' And I was literally thinking, even though I've never used fourth gear before, I'm going to drive Ben away, right now, in the 4x4! And I'm dragging Ben out of Dad's hands and towards the open gate, trying to avoid the piles of animal poo. But then Ben yanks me back, saying, 'No, Haley, we haven't had the cake yet!'

And I slide in the mud and poo and I'm falling backwards so I grab for the first thing to hand, and this is literally how I discover what military-grade razor wire is, cos there's a bundle sitting by the wall. So, I'm like some entangled convict trying to escape a maximum security prison, giving it, 'Aw! Aw! Aaawww!'

The really clever thing about razor wire is, the more you try to pull your hand out of it, the deeper it goes into the flesh, so I'm screaming and skidding in shit, and Dad's over me then, giving it, 'Let me do it. Slow down, you can't get it out by yourself.' My hand is now pumping blood all over the mud, and the razor barb is in so deep it's hitting this nerve, and Ben is going, 'Oooh, blood!! Euuuw, euww!' and starting to blubber and I can hear this noise, like a big engine, and the gates are being opened by Danny.

I get a glimpse then, through the gates, of the white-topped mountains beyond, and a shiver runs through me, and I'm telling Dad, 'This is all so fucked up, just call Mother to come and get us! Please!' as he's literally unhooking me like I was a fish.

And then I hear a walkie-talkie and Meg's standing there giving it, 'Sierra Oscar Tango, confirm move to Plan B. Over.' And I'm like, 'What the actual fuck?'

Dad picks up Ben, and Ben's struggling against him, and Meg's bending over me then, helping me unsnag my jeans and leg skin, and I'm yelping the same expletives, and then this huge Range Rover speeds through the gate and this short, muscly, shaven-headed man with tattoos all over jumps out.

There's this big fuck-off rifle on his back and Danny slams the big iron gates shut behind him. Then this man, who I'd later find out was called Ray, stands before Dad and they man-hug super-fast and he says, 'Pickups on storage A and B complete. Plan B ready.' And this Ray creature, he has the kind of working man's accent that comes from wherever the middle of nowhere is and he practically salutes Dad, and asks, 'Lock down the perimeter?' And Dad says, 'Affirmative.' Like Dad's actually a military general. And this Ray takes the huge gun off his back and swings it in front of my and Ben's faces as he turns, like a total asshole.

Real guns are really, really heavy, and when someone points it into your face you can actually feel death in your bones, as I would discover later.

Meg gets her arm under me and lifts me, and Ben, seeing my blood-dripping hand, starts wailing, 'When is Mummy coming? I want Mummy,' in that uniquely repetitive way of his that makes very deep razor wire wounds throb even more. It also made me realise that Ben and me were not going back to see Mother. Not tomorrow. Not the next day or week, or even year.

Ben's yells faded into the distance as Dad dragged him towards the farmhouse. The wind picked up and I felt the freezing air from the mountains on my bloody skin. I got this sense for the first time of how, even if Mother scoured the entire country searching for Ben and me, she'd never find us. Not here. Just never.

The razor wire beyond Dad's head was like some kind of Jesus-crown-of-thorns as he called back, 'Meg, take Haley inside and dress the wound.'

'Affirmative,' Meg called back. Then she grabbed my hand and dragged me, screaming, towards the big dark farmhouse.

To Suture Or Not To Suture

If you get a deep cut from a piece of questionable metal and you don't utterly clean the wound, you can get septicaemia and seriously die from toxic shock.

So, I was in the bathroom inside the farmhouse and Hippie Meg was being all maternal and holding my wrist and saying, 'Oh, that must be bloody sore,' and, 'Let Auntie Meg take care of that for you.'

I'm staring at the blood flowing out of the two perfect holes in my hand and she's saying, 'You're being very brave,' as she thrusts my hand under freezing water and I scream, and she won't let me pull it back and she was like, 'Can you bend your thumb?' And she's yanking my arm around like a real pro and sticking my cut really close to her eyes and asking, 'Have you had a tetanus shot recently?'

I dunno, something happens to me when I'm in shock. Like, I totally just stopped wriggling and I surrendered to Meg's process, and it goes like this:

1. Rinse the wound in cold, clear water for five to ten minutes.
2. Clean the tweezers with isopropyl alcohol and use them to remove any dirt or debris still lodged in the wound.
3. Sterilise the wound with Dettol or another deeply stingy antiseptic liquid.
4. Gently pat the area dry using a gauze pad. Don't use cotton wool, as strands get stuck to the wound.
5. If the wound is more than 0.6 cm deep, or more than 4cm long, you will need stitches and this means sewing your actual skin (see Suture Kits).
6. If the wound is smaller than that, you can use paper stiches or superglue to close the wound.

And it was like Meg had been a nurse or something before, as she fished out some poo and bits of rust from my cut. So, with some predictable whimpers, I let her paper stitch and bandage me. Then I'm staring at the side of her face, thinking, who in the living crap are you people?

Like she read my mind, she said, 'I know you're confused and in shock now, Haley,' and she wound the bandage round my hand and secured it in place with two safety pins. 'But your father will protect you, like he protects all of us. He predicted this was coming and now it has.'

Right, the gun thing was bad enough but a prophecy was nuts, so I trod carefully. 'Look, I'm not judging, really I'm not, but if you don't mind, could you just call my mother or email or whatever? That would be fab, cos Ben really needs her.'

Meg just kept on pinning the bandages, focusing on my hand, and she said, 'Your mother never believed him, she thought our Guardian was mad.'

And I'm like, 'Our what?'

'In an insane society, the last sane man appears insane,' she said.

OK, quoting shit is a major timeout for me, like chanting mantras. Then Meg went uber weird.

'Your father saved so many of us,' she said, throwing back her smelly red hair. 'Danny would be an orphan as I'd have been dead long ago if it wasn't for your dad. Ray would have been in jail. Ed's a great man, he loves you very much and we made a vow to protect his kin.'

Wow! So Dad was some kind of cult leader.

Permit Your Abductees To Explore

Abductees adapt poorly when you threaten them, so allow them to explore the inside of their containment area and ask their own questions.

1. This performs the double function of allowing them to let off steam.
2. They will learn quickly that there is no escape and so can familiarise themselves with the layout of their containment area.
3. This preps them for accepting the procedures that they now have to follow.

With my bandaged hand I marched down the stairs and saw the psychos all sat round their hobbity little fireplace with their pile of rustic food. They stank of wet beast and sweaty feet. Dad was sitting there sharing some tea and plans of some kind with the short-assed soldier-guy, Ray. And Ben was pigging out on chocolate cake with glee, all chummy with the Danny kid who'd nearly killed him twenty minutes before.

I just sort of stood there fuming at them and they hardly even noticed me.

Meg was hugging Danny tight, like forgiving him for 'the accident', and Danny leaned his head onto Meg's shoulder and was massively embarrassed that I saw him. It was only then I clocked that he was her actual full-on son. Then I felt weirdly jealous, cos me and Mother never hugged like that. Which raised the big issue.

'Dad … I … need … to … speak … to … you … privately … outside … now!' I said, trying to muster that scary clarity-voice that Mother used with him.

Meg smiled. 'Come on, love, sit down and get warm. We'll all have a nice chat, shall we?'

I stared at my choccy-smeared brother so happily adapted to his new prison and I stormed out. I don't know where the hell I thought I was going, but no one stopped me.

Doing a recce was something Dad had trained us to do on some of our vaventures. There was the farmhouse and a barn facing each other with the walled quad in the middle. I walked round the outer walls, checking it all out. The whole thing was a big square of old stone, and about eight inches before each wall was a shiny metal fence, about twelve feet high, topped with barbs of razor wire and strung with another wire that had a yellow sign on it saying, *DANGER 7000 VOLTS*. Think history lessons and Checkpoint Charlie, or worse. It faintly buzzed and my arm hairs stood on end when I got near it.

In front of that, lying on the ground, were huge bales of razor wire that still had to be unwound. I stood staring at all of this lethal crap and tried to picture what it was all for. Up to this point I'd thought only about how it was a stinking prison for keeping me in, not a security measure to keep people out. I mean who would want to get in here?

But then I put myself mentally on the other side of the wall, like someone trying to climb in. They'd get to the top then they'd look down and see the razor wire for the first time on the inside. They couldn't climb down inside because then they'd be stuck between the electrified fence and the wall. They couldn't jump, because they'd get tangled in the bales of razor wire.

I made it right round the enclosure, cursing and kicking the dirt, my hand stinging, and my jeans smelling of animal crap. There was a terrifying barking dog sound near a vast solid steel refrigerator hidden in an old stone alcove. I went to the main gate and saw that it had a kind of electronic bolting mechanism, huge. All in all, just frickin great.

The only place to go was Dad's SUV. Half its engine was still lying in the dirt, mocking me. So I was sitting inside it, staring at my stupid bandaged hand, trying not to gag from the stinking animal poop on my knees. I was just so trapped and so angry and on and on it went, in a loop.

There's no escape, no escape, there's no escape.

That was when I discovered the life-saving strategy of the horn.

Let Your Abductees Burn Out Their Useless Tantrums

Don't try to explain the greater reality to your abductees before they expel their anger, because they will not listen. Although it's difficult, you may have to endure a temper tantrum of several hours before the abductee is tenderised through exhaustion, gives up and is forced to listen with an open mind.

Honk, honk. Even I was getting really sick of the stupid car horn, but I figured that if I kept on banging it long enough and being as obnoxious as possible, Dad might just realise his abduction plan was shot and drive us back home.

I must have bashed that horn for a good half-hour, till the stalky moron Ray marched out. It was raining and his shaved head was dripping and his wet T-shirt was tight on his huge tattooed muscles. He thrust a stumpy, scarred finger in my face and yelled at me to 'Fucking stop it!'

I hit the horn again. Quick as a horror film, he opened the car door and grabbed my arms.

'Dad! Dad!' I yelled and Dad ran out, tripping through the mud.

The Neanderthal released his hold and I yelled, 'Dad, this man touched me.'

The Ray-man backed away, mumbling, 'I never laid a finger…' and 'Bloody racket.' Dad tried to calm him and me, by using the word 'calm' a lot, and Ray hobbled back inside like a scolded mutt.

Dad yanked the SUV door wider open and said, 'OK, Haley, you've had your little tantrum. But don't waste my battery hitting that horn. No one out there can hear you anyway. It's thirty miles to the nearest farm.'

I crossed my arms and stared at him, actually hating him and the pathetic camouflage jacket he'd put on, like he was playing at soldiers.

'So this is your protest plan, is it?' he said. 'You're just going to sit in here, not come inside, be rude to these generous people, not eat, not sleep…'

I shrugged lamely.

'Fine, how long do you plan to keep this up?' he said, making it not like a question. 'All night, till tomorrow. Hmm? We have a lot of work to be getting on with, what do you think you will achieve?'

It's really crap the way adults make you do all these clichéd classic teenage reactions like mumbling, and you can't meet their eye, the same way that dogs can't endure the gaze of a human. So I honked the horn again.

He grabbed my hand. 'OK, OK,' he said, 'have it your way.' Then he thought for a minute and said, 'You know, Haley, even if I was to go back for your mother now – for your sake, because your life without her is so unendurable – even if I was to make it the several hundred miles, and I could locate her, she'd contact the police, and they'd lock me up.' He paused like a teacher with one of those questions that answers itself. 'So then I'd be in custody and your mother would still be stuck in the city when the virus lockdown starts, and you'd still be stuck here.'

'What frickin lockdown?' I said. 'Can we check? Like, call someone?' Couldn't he like prove this crap to me?

When you give Dad the silent treatment, it always makes him blurt stuff out, because of his divorce-guilt, most likely. So I tried that.

'Would your mother even come with me anyway?' he said. 'Even if she saw people dying of the virus on TV, would she believe me? How would I convince her?'

I kept on with the silent treatment.

'OK,' he said, and I could see that he'd been through, like, a million variations of this in his head, 'let's just say I was to drive you and Ben to your mother and I tried to convince her to join us, then most probably we'll all get stranded in the city and infected, so no … there's no going back.' His eyes were miles away. 'So that only leaves the kidnap option,' he said, calmly. 'I'd have to use force on your mother to make her come with us, and that would mean she'd be kicking and screaming for two hundred miles, unless I gave her a sedative, or threatened her life in some way.'

I had zero understanding of how he'd jumped into this random scary shit.

'Dad,' I said, 'I hate to tell you but you're sounding like a very mad person right now.'

He shook his head. 'I am simply sharing with you the very difficult choices I've had to make,' he said.

'But, Dad, can't we please, please, please just contact her somehow? Like, send a pigeon or drive to get a phone signal. I mean, if she's in danger like you say, shouldn't we warn her or something?'

I had drained his patience. He muttered about how he'd already told me many times about Mother's inability to see reality. Like, if Dad said something was blue, she'd say it was red, just to spite him.

'Look, Haley,' he said, 'this isn't like when you were a kid, you know, and your mother would want to take you to the swimming pool, and I'd want to take you to the park and we'd ask you, which one do you want to do, and you'd say *both*, so then we'd end up doing *neither*. No, that's not going to work here. You can't have everything both ways, Haley. Your mother made her choice years ago. You've made your choice, too, so you have to stick to it. There will be negative consequences and you'll have to live with them.'

'What "choice" did I make? What? That's not fair! You lied to me, you didn't give me any choice at all. Why do you always pick on me?' I yelled, then added, 'Leave me alone!'

I slammed the door on him and honked the horn, for a really long time.

There's this horrible thing about being a divorced daughter, like how you can make your Dad feel really guilty for hurting your feelings, and use it to get what you want. But the classic strategy wasn't working any more.

'Stay in there as long as you like,' he shouted over the racket. 'It won't make any difference. But it gets pretty cold, Haley. You should get a thermal sleeping bag from Meg if you're planning on doing your little protest all night. Alternatively, you could stop being a spoiled brat and come inside.'

Another choice. Either/or. I hate it. Because it always means believe Dad or believe Mother. So I just kept honking the horn.

'Fine!' he shouted from the other side of the car door. Then he went to the front of the 4x4, lifted up the bonnet and rummaged about inside. There was a snapping sound and then my horrible horn died. He came back and took something out of his pocket, a wire and white box. I thought it was the horn thingy but it was one of those old music things from the last century that didn't connect to the net but somehow had tunes in it.

Out past my windscreen in the rain he was saying, 'The Truth will do you good.' And he waved the headphones and the thingy at me, and he was getting soaked so I told myself, OK, whatever, and I opened the door and he just threw the thingy onto the passenger seat along with my asthma inhaler and said, 'Track Four.' Then he slammed the door shut, turned and headed back inside, sliding in the mud as he went.

I raised my fist to hit the horn again and this time it wasn't against Dad but against myself, because I still didn't know whether the world was ending or my dad was mad. I had zero evidence. I didn't hit the horn, but I had to hit something, so I hit my knees, my arms, my chest. I shouted, 'I hate you, I hate you!' meaning basically myself, then I stopped due to thinking someone might have seen me. Then I realised that maybe no one ever would.

The Three Recommendations

I always found ancient technology spooky, like it reminds you that everything always ends up on the scrap heap – things like marriage. And I was well pissed at Dad but I pushed the stupid Play button anyway.

Dad's voice burst out in the crummy headphones, and he said: '*My name is Edward Crowe and I was an investigative journalist. In 2019, I was employed as a government consultant on the Global Health Futures Survey. The findings of this document were classified at National Security Level 3.*'

All this was news to me. I'd known Dad used to do some stuff for the newspapers but this made him sound important. But maybe it was all just made-up fantasy bullshit. His voice droned on.

'*After the catastrophic Covid-19 pandemic of 2019–21, and the terrible death toll across two hundred and fifteen countries, the GHFS set out to investigate the likelihood of further pandemics, and to make recommendations to the W.H.O. and the G20. My role and that of my working partners – among whom was NYT correspondent J. Samuels – was as neutral media observers on the public information sub-committee during the international risk assessment.*'

It was breathtakingly boring and Dad wasn't skilled at reading aloud. His voice droned on about 'viruses', 'pathogens' and 'crashes' again and again.

'A dozen scientists, Samuels and I, made our recommendations to the GHFS, and these were as follows:

1. We expressed concerns that in the global rush to find vaccines for all known and potentially hazardous viruses, over two hundred naturally occurring and biologically engineered pathogens, were now being cloned and stored in labs around the world. Including government sanctioned chimerical recombinants of Ebola, Sars, Sars-CoV, Mers and Mers-CoV.
2. Our sub-committee expressed profound concern that these pathogens could potentially be so alien to human biology that they posed a biosecurity threat far greater than that of the previous pandemic.
3. In the interests of biosafety, we expressed grave concerns that security measures had not been stringent enough worldwide around these new pathogens. That there was, in fact, international competition to patent, monetise and trade in these viruses and that this had led to many international thefts of said viruses.'

Science stuff is just so dull and I was drifting away there in the 4x4. A sheep/goat thing wandered past with gross swaying boobs, while Dad's voice said one of the new viruses, CHF-4, was classified as one of the most infectious lethal pathogens on the planet.

'CHF-4 has a very slow incubation period, which means that there is a delay of around one month between the point of infection and the first symptoms. This creates viral spread multiplied to a factor of six, compared to the last known strains of SARS-CoV. Essentially, during the incubation period, contaminated people will spread the virus to everyone and everything they come close to. In today's interconnected world, a pathogen can travel around the globe to major cities in as little as thirty-six hours. By the time any government discovers and admits to a CHF-4 leak, it could already be one month too late.'

By Dad's calculations this would mean one million three hundred thousand people in fifty-two countries would already have the new virus.

Like, on that very day, while I was sitting in his SUV in the rain.

It made me shudder but it sounded like made-up sci-fi. Then Dad said, 'The CHF-4 experiments on laboratory primates had ninety-seven per cent likely correlation to humans, and the apes showed a for-ty-forty-eight per cent mortality rate. Secondary symptoms include a flesh-eating reaction that can't be stopped with any known drugs.'

Now I was listening hard.

'With alarm we noted the reported smuggling of six new pathogens, intercepted by U.S. Customs and Border Protection agents at Detroit Metro Airport in 2020. These including the "super viruses" PQ141 and CHF-4.

'We noted with greater alarm the theft of twelve vials of CHF-4, later known as Virus X, from the P4 Lab in W.H.O. Region 3. The pathogen has yet to be recovered. Using mapping programmes we predicted that, if not tracked, contained and eradicated, the stolen CHF-4 pathogen and/or its variant mutations, had an eighty-two per cent chance of infecting the world population within ten years. We recommended that this virus should not be experimented upon but should be completely destroyed.

'We submitted our report to the GHFS but it was not publicly acknowledged. They denied the existence of the report and of the exist-ence of CHF-4. Attempts by my colleagues and myself to make our findings public were then dismissed by government organisations and mainstream media as "fake news" and "conspiracy theories".

It all sounded horrible and totally possible, but then Dad said, 'Two of the scientists we worked with were disbarred from the scientific community after government intervention. My associate, J. Samuels, who attempted to self-publish an article on the inter-governmental cover-up, disappeared. Later it was announced that he had "committed suicide". I personally was hounded from my job and false accusations were made to discredit my mental health...'

I hit Stop.

It was maybe the close sound of my own breath and the

claustrophobia of the condensation on the windscreen, but I felt more trapped than before. Then a voice in my head started.

'Your dad has gone insane, the proof is there in his own words: "mental health". These are nothing but paranoid delusions from years ago. It's 2025 now and none of his predictions have come true.'

Then it became two voices, arguing.

'You will never see your friends again,' the other voice said. 'You will die here in this safe house. Your mother will die of infection, alone.'

'Bullshit,' the other voice said. 'She'll be sitting at home doing the online shopping. There's no super-virus!'

Yes, I told myself, Mother is fine, and Dad's new super-pandemic is a super-delusion, and if the GHFS even existed, they were right to fire him.

But there it was again, the old dilemma: is Dad mad, or is Mother in denial?

Two conflicting voices and one horrible choice. Which parent should I believe, and which should I betray?

Survival Tip: When you have a panic-slash-asthma attack, focus on the real-life objects around you or pinch yourself. Do not get into a paranoid cycle of worrying about not being able to exhale, as this will only make it worse.

I stared at the inhaler Dad had thrown me. What if it wasn't a real nebuliser? What if it was full of CHF-4 or some mad-making gas, and if I inhaled it I'd become infected with Dad's insanity?

What if I was already mad, like my dad, and it was genetic? Mother had said my fugues could be signs of 'dissociative disorder'.

I couldn't focus my eyes on the rain on the windscreen or the wall and wires beyond. My heart was thumping in my ears and I was panting like a dog, telling myself, oh God, what's happening to me, this isn't happening!

Maybe this entire thing was payback against Mother. In this insane safe house, he could even kill me and Ben because he thought there was no escape from the virus. He could be *that* mad. How would I even know? Like I say, I only saw the guy one day a week.

It felt like everything was sliding down into some vast magnetic hole. I couldn't exhale and my mouth was dry and the sound of my breath in my ears was so loud it sounded like an animal or something stalking me. I was staring out the windscreen but I wasn't seeing glass, rain and razor wire, I was seeing Mother in her nice car, two hundred miles away. She'd tried to call us a hundred times and she was crying on her phone. Calling out, 'Where are you, Ben? Haley, Haley, what's happened to you?'

And Mother told herself not to panic – 'The kids must just be at their dad's house' – and this was after he'd sent her on a wild goose chase to Nando's, and all the time she was trying really, really hard not to think me and Ben had been in a road accident. But how would she know with zero replies from Dad's phone or mine?

She wouldn't have watched the news or surfed the net that morning because she'd be too panicked to sit still. She'd have taken a beta-blocker. She'd be driving over to Dad's house to get us back and she'd be scanning the streets for me and Ben. She'd head onto the ring road, which would be at a standstill, as news of the pandemic hit and panic buyers were trying to get to the stores to stuff their cars until every shelf was stripped bare. She'd be frozen in that traffic jam all day, till her phone battery and her fuel ran out and she'd be terrified, and she'd have no idea that Dad had calculated all the steps of her wild goose chase to ensure that she was sent right into the epicentre of what would become the largest traffic jam in history, buying him even more time to get us under lock and key.

God, poor Mother!

Yes, if what Dad said was true, then he'd planned to leave Mother behind to die, all along.

And Dad had thrown my inhaler to me, because he knew exactly that I'd get into a panic over all this. He'd calculated for that, too.

I couldn't breathe. You can die of an asthma attack. I pulled off the lid and stuck the inhaler valve in my mouth. There was the usual gasping crap, like a stupid addict. Now, I guess, Dad was the keeper of the inhalers and he could determine whether I survived or not. In that moment, as the steroid spray hit my lungs, I truly feared and loathed him.

The Initial Reaction To The Truth Follows The Five Stages Of Grief

Grief is not just about family death – you can also grieve over the end of a way of life. There are five stages of grief, and they are: Denial, Anger, Depression, Negotiation and, finally, Acceptance.

According to Dad, I should have been in the Denial phase, but after an hour of sitting alone in the jeep, I seemed to have accelerated beyond Anger, and I was already in Depression and heading well into Negotiation.

Sometimes you just have to admit that even though you have four hundred Snapchat chums and you've had two semesters of Sex-Ed and have secretly drunk an entire bottle of gin and become adept at menstruation, you're still just a kid who needs to clean animal poop off themselves and have a sleep and ask the horrible scary grown-ups for a towel. Please.

Pathetic, but that's what I did. So after the towel rub and my apologies, Hippie Meg was leading me with my sore, bandaged hand and my pigged-out half-asleep sibling up the cold wooden stairs to that weird prison cell that Dad had called 'you and your brother's room'. She flicked on a lethal-looking electric fire and it started filling the place with this stench of burning dust and mould. And it was pointless anyway because the curtainless windows had this huge crack where the wind whistled in. There were twelve identical plastic storage boxes stacked high against one wall – all labelled with random things like *Candles*, *NP5 Filters*, *Isopropanol* and something called *Lint*. The beds had those grey, itchy-scratchy army covers. Meg asked who wanted the top bunk and Ben pounced on it, 'Me, me, me!'

'Wow, Ben,' I said wearily, 'you finally got to live inside *Call of*

Duty 3, huh?'

'Now,' Meg said, 'I'll get you some proper clothes. Your dad put some in storage for you.'

'Proper'? What would a hippie survivalist know about 'proper' anything? Or maybe she said 'prepper'.

She showed me to the shower and left me alone to undress. I stared at the grime and the old, cracked tiles. I turned the tap thing and the pipes rattled, then a solitary brown drip came, like a metaphor or something.

Meg stuck her head through the doorway, as if the sheer force of her smiling could make the world a better place. 'Here's those clothes, love,' she said and took my Diesels away. In their place, with a thump, landed a pair of military slacks. Wow, these losers were totally into all this, all the way down to their matching camouflage-print fashions. Did they get them all in one batch from Argos? There was also a big Arran sweater, mountaineering socks and huge dirty rubber boots. 'Is there anything else I can get you, love?' she asked me. 'A big T-shirt to sleep in?'

I shuddered to think of the vast, boob-stretched hippie garment she'd offer me, no doubt emblazoned with a long-faded picture of Bob Marley or Bob Dylan or one of the other great dead Bobs of her bygone era.

She put two brand new toothbrushes in a cup for me and Ben and I was utterly covering up my practically naked self and shivering but she seemed not to have even noticed. 'Oh, the water valve!' she said. 'Silly me, forget my head if it weren't screwed on – we're conserving water, see.' The pipes groaned as she bashed the valve. There was nowhere to run and no shower curtain, so I tried to shield myself. A spray of freezing rusty water shot out and she said, 'Make sure to keep your bandage out of the water, love.'

Love! What gave her the right to call me that?

On her way out, Meg turned. 'Silly me, you'll need a painkiller too for your hand,' and she went into this old wooden cupboard as high as the roof and awkwardly tried to hide what was inside. I pretended not to peek and just made sore noises till she came back with a big white pill and some water.

'Here, throw this back in a one-er, it'll make you feel better,' she said, and I wondered if she'd been a nurse or a junkie. She was too chunky for a junkie.

'Once you've had a rest and some dinner we can all sit down and we'll fill you in on our plans for lockdown,' she said, just like this was a totally normal day for her. 'Best not to tell your brother about the pandemic, though, it might upset him.'

Yeah, right. So, by Meg and Dad's twisted logic, me and them were on the same side, protecting Ben. Jesus, these people!

I put the pill in my mouth, and again it was a choice, like swallow their version of the truth, or not.

I usually postpone choice until I faint or things get into such a mess that someone else is forced to take control and make the choice for me. The pill tasted sour and I was saved when Ben called out from down the corridor. Meg ran out, like her booby-baby-detectors had been activated by Ben's poor-me voice. 'It's OK, honey, Auntie Meg's coming.'

I gagged up the pill and spat it out into my hand. I checked to see if she was coming back because I was dead curious about that weird wardrobe thingy. I tippy-toed over to it and opened the door, trying not to make the hinge creak.

The first shelf was toilet rolls, Band-Aids, tampons and regular crap. But then the shelf above had ten packs of my inhalers, that's ten times twenty. Weirder still, the bottom bit had a wooden door and inside it was a freezer, stacked with bags of what looked like frozen blood. In a thin drawer I found the packet Meg had taken the pill from and it said, *Morphine 30mg*. There were other packs with 60mg and 120mg, and in the drawer above that there were neat rows of scalpels, medical scissors and forceps, or something. And these things, so close to my dripping wet naked skin, made me totally shudder.

I could hear Meg cooing over Ben from down the corridor, so I picked up one of the scalpels. To be honest, I didn't know what to do with it but I went over to my gross army trousers and hid it in the big leg pocket. I don't know why, probs just cos it's the kind of shit you see abducted teenage girls do in movies.

Then I thought, well, I should probably take this shower properly, cos I was majorly still reeking of that aforementioned animal crap.

It was hard to wash while sticking my stupid bandaged hand out of the freezing water. When I was pretty sure the last of the stink was scrubbed off with that practically wire brush, I attempted to dry myself. Then I felt this weird presence, like a cold draft, like eyes were spying on me round the edge of the door. I covered my lady-bits fast, fearing it was Ray.

'Wait, no! Please. I didn't mean to ... I just ... have something to tell you,' the voice said, and it was the redneck, Danny.

I grabbed one of my muddy sneakers and threw it at him, yelling, 'Get out! You ... you perverted freak!' or some such. My sneaker turned slo-mo circles in the air and sprayed that exact same animal poop all over my arms, chest and my mouth. Danny utterly stared at my boobs when my towel fell to the floor. My nipples were sticky-outy because of the freezing water and he probably even saw my ass when I turned to pick up the towel! I concentrated on not puking as I leapt back into the shower and began the entire process of scrubbing again, mortified that, on top of it all, I had now become the porno fantasy of a redneck psycho.

So, I'd sort of gone from Denial to Anger to Negotiation and back to Anger again, or maybe I was experiencing all of the five stages of grief all at once. But one thing was for sure: me and Ben had to get the hell out of there.

What Not To Do In The Rations Bunker

As if Dad had read my scheming mind, he decided that me and Ben needed a rapid induction into our new lives. We were, he said, the luckiest people in the world because we were already in a safe house, but there were these Dos and Don'ts me and Ben had to learn about the rations bunker.

Then he picked the person I disliked the most to show us round his delusion: that bright beam of military sunlight called Ray.

Just at the farmhouse entrance, Ray pulled up the rug from the ground, and underneath was a hidden wooden trap door. 'Long-term food storage,' he grunted. 'Best way you can make yourself useful is by fetching food and things we need, but only when we say,' he barked. 'Otherwise, don't get under our feet.' Charming.

Ray yanked the trap door open and underneath was what looked exactly like a submarine hatch with one of those circular hand-bars on the top. He strained and spun the lock and the circular lid opened with a hiss. 'Awesome!' Ben said, and I peered into the incredulously vast hole with its metal ladder vanishing into blackness.

I looked up and spotted Danny spying on me again from the doorway, like he really was trying to warn me about something. Maybe Ray was a serial killer and the subterranean storage unit was really a huge fridge filled with dead teenage girls! I gave Danny the finger, anyway, which kind of hurt with my bandaged hand.

Ray was climbing down, telling us it was just like a ship's ladder and to copy him: toes in, heels out. I just got on with it. But it was hard to climb down with my cut hand. By the time I got down the twenty steps Ray was already rolling his eyes at my girly whimpers.

I helped the massively over-excited Ben down the ladder, and then Ray raised a hand and activated a row of fluorescent lights.

'Wow! Spaceship!' Ben gasped, and I must confess it was pretty amazing.

Down there, eight or twelve feet below the farmhouse, was a pristine metal-walled storeroom. The bunker was semi-circular, like one of those nuclear hiding-holes with corrugated walls. There were big tanks of air or chemicals and pipes and levers and something like a huge aluminium air-conditioning system, plus a sign that said, *DANGER AIRLOCK* and a big sign that said, *Emergency*

First Aid Kit. Ben had the big-eyed look of a kid that suddenly realises that things in war movies are for real.

Ray gestured for us to follow and he strode between the rows of metal shelves stacked with boxes and cans and huge plastic storage vats, growling the names of everything he touched. 'Wheat flour, corn flour, oats, fats, oils, powdered milk, soy milk, canned fruit, canned veg, canned meat, canned rice, dried fruit, dried rice…'

Survival Fact: Canned food lasts for three years before expiry.

I used to get major choice-induced-paralysis in supermarkets due to there being too many brands of shampoo to choose from, but here there was only one kind of soap, one kind of jam, one kind of everything. Zero choice. I guess we weren't going to be nipping down to Tesco, like, ever again.

Ray vanished, his gruff voice echoed from what must have been a second aisle. 'Water sterilising tabs, heavy-duty gloves, fuses, cables, copper-wire, aluminium foil, paper plates, bleach, hand sanitiser, soap, aloe vera.'

I figured, like for most army-ish males, lists made Ray feel safe.

I looked round and Ben had vanished. I went back and found him staring at a shelf. Peanut butter. 'Wow,' he said, and it was true, I too had never seen such an amassment of our favourite quality foodstuff.

Ray's voice boomed from the other side of the metal shelves: 'You got to keep up, I'm only showing you this the once. You'll be on storeroom duty day after tomorrow.' Ben and me ran to catch up. '…tampons, maxi-pads, bandages, erythromycin, penicillin…' There was something macho and DIY about the stash that made Ray's barrel chest swell with pride. And I guess Meg, being a hippie, thought hoarding was kind of anti-consumerist or something.

We found Ray at the end of one of the five corridors of shelves and I reminded myself that, a couple of hundred miles away, poor Mother was most likely having a nervous breakdown over me and Ben. I had to find some way to get in touch with her, but given that Dad and his cronies had dug this vast bunker, my chances of stumbling upon an overlooked landline were slim.

Ray raised his hand and another sensor made a neon light flicker on to reveal a hidden corridor. The place was immense and L-shaped. They must have dug out the foundations of the whole farm and Dad must have squirrelled away a ton of dosh to do it over the years, which explained why our Xmas presents were always so crappy and why he never paid Mother alimony and child support.

Ray marched on, shouting, 'The whole lot is itemised and rationed. You take something for the communal meals each day, you fill out the chart, exact quantity and time. No treats. No extras ... Next aisle: face masks, surgical spirit, gauze, burn cream, hydrochloric acid.'

Ben saw something, gasped, sprinted underneath Ray's arms, and jumped headlong into a vast wall of toilet rolls, like it was a bouncy castle. I told him to behave and apologised to Ray as I pulled my silly sibling away and tried in vain to restack the packets.

Ray shook his shiny head and just went on. 'A family of four uses six rolls a week. You run out, you have a lot of contagious diseases, bacteriological. Your rations are two pieces of toilet roll per day, max ...'

I tried to act Mother-ish. 'So,' I asked, 'how long is this mountain of bum-paper supposed to last?'

He snapped back, 'Three years exactly, according to your father's calculations.'

Which led to the million-dollar question: What, exactly, happens after three years?

'The die-off,' Ray said.

'The what?'

'In three years' time, six billion people will have died,' he said, matter of factly, quoting Dad.

I hadn't got to that bit of Dad's recording, so it seemed totally over the top, cos there are, like, only seven billion people in the world anyway. 'Yeah, right,' I said.

Ray shot me a look and I shivered, and not just because it was really cold down there. He then informed us that the way to store food longest is at low temperatures with almost zero oxygen, and that was what the air lock and oxygen extractor were for.

Ray barked to hurry up and climb back up. 'Don't touch any switches, this whole place is vacuum-sealed when you exit. You don't ever want to get locked in down here.'

That was when I saw the hazmat suits hanging in the corner. One, two, three ... seven, in total. One was small and it had to be for Ben. I didn't know about Kane at that point, so I naïvely hoped that one of them was for Mother.

We climbed back up and Ray secured the hissing airlock and hid the storeroom entrance beneath the trap door and the rug. Just like it wasn't there. Ray gave me a forced smile that was maybe his way of saying, 'We could make you vanish under the floor too, madam! And no one would ever know.'

I had this multiplying awareness of the power my dad exercised over the weaker-minded Ray and Meg. It was like the bunker itself, huge and cold and dark and hidden beneath our feet all the time.

Keep Confidential Planning Meetings Beyond The Hearing Distance Of Your Abductees

You'd think big boss Dad would have prepped for where to have secret planning meetings and calculated exactly what his abductees should hear, but he'd overlooked two factors:

1. The stairs are like an echo chamber that amplify the sounds from the kitchen downstairs.
2. I am nosy and never to be trusted.

I didn't plan to spy on them but Meg, Dad, Ray and Danny were in a big pow-wow and I guess I picked up some skills from sneaking to hear Mother and Dad's arguments when I was little.

So I heard something pretty much like this:

'Sorry, Ed,' Ray said, 'but I think your daughter is having trouble adapting. I reckon she'll keep trying to bail on us and that could compromise our operation.'

There was the sound of a whistling kettle and then I heard Dad say, 'No, no, once we're past the point of no return and Haley sees the number of deaths, the cities burning, she'll have no choice but to accept. If she doesn't, then there's always Bunker Two, but I'd rather we exhausted all options before that.'

Jesus. I clamped my hand to my mouth. My lovely dad was actually considering locking me in a bunker? And how many frickin bunkers did they have?

Then I heard a pouring noise and Meg said, 'She'll come round. She's a good kid. Don't worry about her for today, that morphine I gave her should be kicking in by now. What about the boy? I was thinking a little sedative, five milligrams of diazepam should do it?'

Then there was a chair scraping on the floor, and Dad said, 'The intention is to save them, not put them in a coma, Meg. Just something to keep them calm while we wait for Kane to return and complete the lockdown.'

So, there were even more of these freaks?

Then it was quiet for a bit and I had to watch out because I had sort of crept down the creaky stairs quite a bit, and I heard Ray say, 'I have to ask this, but are we one hundred per cent sure that this isn't another false alarm?'

That weirded me out, totally. Because it was more proof that Dad had got everything all wrong, and it sort of implied there had been other attempts to kidnap me and Ben over the last few years that we didn't even know about.

'I wish it was,' Dad said, 'but we know the signs. We know the pathogen, it's bio-profile and the lab it leaked from. This was confirmed two hours ago, by our people inside the W.H.O. There'll be nothing but government lies and cover-up in the media now until it's too late. This pandemic is exactly what we most feared.

No more trial runs, this is it.'

'God save us,' Meg said.

I gasped then, and the floorboards creaked under me, and I had to leg it up the stairs on tip-toes and hope to hell no one caught me.

Old Technology Can Slip Under The Radar

Our society has become too dependent on the latest tech updates, Dad once said, so we overlook out-of-date tech, which can be salvaged and used against our enemies.

I was in the weird prison-bedroom, and Ben was lying there hugging this ancient dinosaur, called Rex, which Dad must have salvaged as well. My little bro was playing this seriously developmentally challenged computer game from like the last century, making 'peeooow, peoow' noises, while I was staring out the dirty, cracked window. I could see these icy mountain-tops beyond the slate roof and they looked like something from *Lord of The Rings*. I put my face to the glass and peered as far as I could to the right, and I saw the mountains run in like a horseshoe shape around us. So depressing. Then I looked in the other direction and there was a wire dangling down from an old satellite dish and, squeezing my head even tighter to the left, I could make out a sort of attic window, above and to the left of us.

'Peooow, peeooow,' Ben said. 'Neeeooow. Crassshhhh.'

And I was like, 'Ben, could you just turn that crap off for one frickin minute so I can hear myself think here!'

I was super weirded out, but also I'd just gone through many, many hours without any phone contact with anybody. Not Shanna, or Jason, or Peeve, let alone Mother. Nada. All that stuff Dad had said about smartphones being the opium of the masses must have been true because I was getting these drug-like withdrawal symptoms. I knew my phone was dead, but I could feel this vibration in my pocket and hear a buzzing in my head.

I shouted at Ben, 'You hear that? It's vibrating. There's a phone somewhere. Where is it?' I tore the sheets off my stinky lower bunk and looked underneath among the balls of dust, like a junkie or something. I stood there twitching, itching, like allergically, feeling like it was vibrating all over me. I took a puff of my inhaler and yelled, 'Shut it, doofus, with that stupid frickin game. Someone's trying to call me!'

'Maybe it's a ghost phone,' Ben said.

And I shouted at him, 'This is an actual crisis. I haven't messaged Shanna or Mother in a whole day, they'll have texted me hundreds.' Then I realised Ben still had no idea what was going on and I had to protect him from the truth.

Just how pathetic we truly were had begun to sink in. I gave up on humanity-without-a-phone and lay back on the lower bunk staring up at Ben's big ass through the mesh. His computer game was attempting to give me a migraine.

'Ben, please,' I shouted, 'what the hell is that stupid game anyway?' I stood up and snatched the damned thing away from him. To my astonishment it turned out not to be a game console but a phone, of an ugly and ancient kind. 'Where the hell did you get this?'

'Danny gave it to me,' he said. 'He's so cool. He got thrown out of school when he was eight and it's got this old game called *Snakepit* on it. You're in this pit and there are snakes chasing you and...'

But I wasn't listening and ran out of the room as fast as I could on tip-toes.

Wait, actually ... Actually, that's not quite right. Ben whined when I took the ancient phone off him, and so I had to barter. Bartering for optimum personal gain is another major divorced-kid skill. By the time we'd finished I'd promised him fifty quid plus twelve Mars bars, and I said to him, 'OK, I'll be back soon, and if anyone asks you where I am, tell them I'm in the shower, OK? Oh, and if that weird Meg woman comes and tries to give you a sleeping pill, don't take it, just keep on pretending you're asleep. OK? So, on your marks, get set, sleep!'

Sometimes I could just die with how cuddly and naïve he is. Literally.

How To Turn An Entire House Into A Transceiver

One of the dangers of having partially prepped kids is that they may have picked up some survival skills that they could then use against you. When I was ten, Dad had secretly trained me all about signals and transceivers and this gave me a massive idea.

I was out in the corridor, holding Danny's Palaeolithic phone up as high as I could, searching for a signal. But after five minutes of my creeping about, the old phone revealed that it was sadly loner -ish and would never be able to connect with anyone. Then I remembered the attic place I'd seen from the window.

The adults were still debating their paranoid crap downstairs and I had to be super careful creeping past the top of the stairwell. I found the door that I hoped led up to the attic and opened it super slowly cos it was creaky.

There was this tiny stairway, all cracked and dust-balled and for-gotten and I had to take two blasts of my Ventolin to even get onto the third step. I checked and there was half a bar of phone signal in the scratched old screen, wavering.

I wasn't even thinking of the virus at this point, only about Mother.

I felt bad even about calling her 'Mother'. It all started as a wind-up, since she referred to Dad as 'your father' or 'that father of yours' and never 'your dad'. I thought it only fair to return the favour. I couldn't bear the thought of never calling her 'Mum' again.

At the top, the attic room was like a storage space with lots of Dad's failed inventions in it – the bike fan and the solar kettle – and millions of wires, rivets and screws lying around, and some broken glass. The phone had lost its signal again and I tip-toed round every inch of the attic looking for the spot, but it was no good. I went to the spidery window to be all poetic and sorry for myself, and next to the chimney was the ancient satellite dish I'd seen before.

Not a lot of people know this trick, but Dad, to his merit, dedicated a whole chapter to this. And he must have done his first experiments with me and Ben, because I totally remember him getting a phone signal from a fence in a forest when I was little.

Anyway, here's how you do it:

1. Locate a satellite dish or TV aerial.
2. You can greatly improve your phone signal by hotwiring it to said dish or aerial – or to a frying pan, or even to the phone wires that line the walls of most houses.
3. Every house has a lot of wiring in it. There's the electrics, but there's also old TVs and lots of forgotten phone wires that never got stripped out.

So, here's what I did:

I pushed the old broken chair against the door, just in case, and I looked at what I had around me. I thought, use cables to reach cables, cos the rusty old satellite dish had some wires dangling from it.

I had the scalpel that I'd stolen so I used it to cut the electric cables off Dad's failed inventions, as quick as I could.

4. Copper wires from any electrical appliance can be used to amplify a signal.
5. Take care when cutting them because the bare copper wires are sharp.
6. Make absolutely sure none of these cables are plugged into the mains or you will electrocute yourself when you strip the plastic coating off.

There was a broken lamp cable and half a fridge that had about four foot of cables, so I sliced them off as well. My hand was shooting pain from the razor wire cuts and my bandage was dripping blood, which made stripping the wire casings even trickier, but I worked fast as hell. I probably only had a few minutes till Mad Meg worked out I was missing and found Ben pretending to be asleep, then came hunting for me. I twisted all the ends of the electrical wires together till my fingertips bled, but I didn't care.

That gave me about fifteen feet of electrical cable, and the satellite dish was about ten feet away.

If this is all too geeky or tomboy-ish for you, blame my dad – he made me like this.

7. You will need to connect the cabling to the interior of your phone. Without taking your phone apart, the simplest way is through the phono-jack socket.
8. To do this you may have to sacrifice a set of headphones.

I had to get the wires into the Paleolithic phone, and I always keep my headphones on my person anyway, so I took a breath and tore off the ear bits and stripped the tiny wires and joined them to the end of the electrical wires. Thankfully, because Dad's entire life is held together with duct tape, I found some up there.

So, the next thing was getting my wires to connect to the satellite dish, but the window wouldn't open more than an inch, and even if it did I wouldn't want to risk falling cos it looked a longish way down to the stone and mud.

So, how to get the wires out to the satellite dish?

9. To throw a length of wire over a distance, attach the throwing end to a heavy object. Ideally, it should have a hole so that the wires can be looped in and fastened securely.

I scanned around for a heavy thing that would fit through the window gap and found the base of the lamp. But it was too wide. Then I found a rusty old toolbox, and inside were screwdrivers and ratchets.

Screwdriver or ratchet?

It just seemed so unfair to me that Dad had made a decision about our lives without negotiating with Mother, so I had to get through to her.

I remember explaining to Mother that the reason I hated making choices was that someone always got rejected and hurt. She said that was cowardly and passive-aggressive, and I couldn't go through my entire life making zero choices and forcing everyone else to chose for me, then blaming them when things went wrong. She said if I could make up my mind, just for once, and take responsibility, I'd be less miserable and quit moaning all the time.

So, there I was, about to make the first real choice of my life with a heavy metal object.

Ratchets are slim and they have a hole in the top, so I fastened the wire through it with bloody fingers. We're talking cheese wire through cheese. Yelping as quietly as I could, I finally got my good hand out the window with the fifteen foot of cable and the ratchet at the end. I figured I probably only had one go at throwing it and looping it round the satellite dish, cos if I failed and the ratchet swung back it would most likely smash the window below and the game would be majorly over.

The wind covered the noise of my first failed attempt, and at least the window didn't break. My second overshot, but when I pulled it back, it got tangled at the base of the satellite dish. Bingo.

It's not like the whole house suddenly lit up with electromagnetic power, but after all that I got one solid bar of phone signal, and as far as I could tell, no one had heard me bashing about, cos of the wind and the general house creakiness. It was an actual miracle. I went close to the window and stared hard at the phone screen. Then I realised – Shit, of course! It belonged to Danny so it didn't have any of my numbers saved on it. Duh! And I hadn't ever memorised Mother's number. Or anyone else's I knew, for that matter.

Why the heck would I? Isn't that what a phone's memory card is for?

Always Keep A Paper Copy Back-Up List Of Important Contacts

I had to think massively hard to get anything close to what I thought Mother's number might be. I held my breath and dialled it. A robot voice said, 'Due to unexpected caller volume, the number you are dialling cannot be connected.' Even if it was the wrong number it gave me hope, so I thought even harder and typed in another possible Mother number with a different ending.

I couldn't bring myself to actually press the Dial button. Cold ran up my legs from my bare feet and I shuddered. I was hit by this sudden wall of shame. Because part of the reason we got abducted was my selfish fault. And would Mother be crying or massively furious at me.

Finally, I pressed Dial and a woman said, 'Hello, who is this?'

I whispered, 'Sorry, is this my mother's phone? Justine? Justine Cooper?'

'You've got the wrong number, don't call here again!' the voice snapped and hung up.

Shit, so then I was like, five seven nine zero … five seven nine eight zero … there was a five one one at the end, I was pretty damn sure of it.

But what if it just rang out cos Mother wasn't there? That would mean Dad was right and the panic shopping had already begun and Mother was out scouring the streets for us in the mass crowds and getting infected. If I dialled and she never picked up, that ringing sound could be the last I ever heard of her.

I started to wheeze and dropped the phone. It hit the floor and the plastic back broke off it. I thought that was it then, decided, fate had smashed it for me. I was seriously screwed.

I stared out of the window at the mountains and told myself, 'Damn your Hamlet-ish procrastinations, Haley Crowe.' But then

I heard a 'Hello, hello, who is this?' from the floor.

Mother!

The Dial button must have been hit on impact.

I picked it up and started apologising in whispers. I told her Ben and me were safe, but she was gasping. 'Oh my God, my darlings, I've been so scared. Where are you? Are you in the city?'

I asked her to shh, please, and stop panicking. Her tears were intense and I'd never heard her like this before, so then I was actually crying too.

'Where are you, darling?' she pleaded. 'What town is it near? Any signs? A road number, for God's sake.'

All I was able to give her was a hill, a fence, a kind of river. Up north, somewhere.

Then she was shouting, 'Go to Maps, the Google Map app! Tell me your postcode!'

I heard some movement downstairs and really had to whisper. 'Mum, listen, shh, it's this farmhouse … I don't know where, it's all very landscape-y and maybe Scotland, but we're safe-ish. I'm more worried about you and the pandemic!'

'Haley Crowe, put your father on the phone right now!' she shouted.

I held the phone away from my ear but heard 'coward' and 'liar' and some very un-her swearwords. I begged her to please, please, please not get angry about Dad, and I asked if people were coughing and wheezing, and what did it say on the news? Because I really needed to know that Dad had made a silly mistake and how I was pretty sure the man with the gun downstairs was just a regular farmer.

'A gun?' She started screaming. 'Did you say "gun"?'

A knock at the door. 'Haley, who you talking to?' It was Dad and it was not his happy voice. The door handle rattled. 'Open this door, Haley! Now!' I whispered to Mum that I had to go, and sorry for freaking her out. But yes, up north, about five hours away, in a ring of mountains, so please come and rescue us, like now. Please.

I'd called her 'Mum', not 'Mother'.

The door burst in and the chair against the handle smashed to pieces. I dropped the phone and it skidded over the floor. Dad lurched in and snatched up the phone and held it to his ear. Even from across the room I could hear Mother screaming my name down the line. Dad ended the call and let the phone fall from his fingers.

'Dad, I…' was all I managed because his eyes swung round to me with such pain and rage in them. He made a fist and raised it above me and I cowered.

But then something crumbled in him. He fell to his knees and put his head in his hands, letting out a kind of helpless groan I've never heard before and never want to hear again.

How To Deal With Mother

How The Police Will Find You

In the event that Plan A and B are discovered by someone outside the group, measures must be taken to protect the safe house.

Dad frog-marched me downstairs and then I was forced to stand there, red-faced, in the big room with the freaky deer and badger heads on the wall and the rack of crossbows, while Dad, Meg, Ray and Danny sat in an emergency meeting round the old wooden table, their angry faces flickering in the light of the log fire.

Dad started interrogating me, like, 'Tell me everything you said. Did you tell her where we are?'

'I don't even know where we are, Dad, sorry.'

So the main problems, Dad said, were:

1. All phones contain SIM cards.
2. The SIM card would have sent a location signal, and when Mother called the police after – and she totally would have – and reported the number of Danny's phone, they would easily be able to track the location within a day or two.
3. This being because of a thing called GPS signal tower triangulation.

'Five hard years of planning wasted,' Ray said, as he smacked the back of Danny's head.

Danny muttered, 'Sorry, it was my fault, sorry, I shouldn't have given the phone to the little kid.'

Ray yelled, 'Get out of my sight!'

I kind of exchanged a glance of fellow traitor-dom with Danny, and I felt guilty cos it wasn't his fault that I used his phone.

I stood there receiving more interrogations and silences as they discussed my fate. Danny sat silent by the fire, his broad back to everyone, stoking the flames. 'The poor darlings,' Meg said, 'they weren't to know any better.'

Dad ignored her and laid out what would most likely happen now. The cops wouldn't be overwhelmed by the pandemic panic for roughly another four days, so they'd have enough time to investigate Mother's claims before the roads got locked down. Just enough time for the police to get to the safe house with a warrant, and then, what with Dad's cache of illegal weapons, the illegal bunker and the abduction charges, Dad, Meg and Ray would most likely be arrested.

Seeing all the adults in total agreement struck a panic in me. Cos how could the pandemic be delusion if all four so solemnly believed it? But also, in the other side of my head, I thought, well, at least if they're arrested I'll get to go home.

'You're our leader and you have our trust, Ed,' Ray said, 'but we should never have agreed to take your kids. This is no place for silly little girls. I say we eject them both and move to Plan C: Drop them off near the roads, close enough for the police to find them. That'd give us a head start on arming the perimeter.'

'No, we need to stay calm. De-escalate. This is my problem. I'll deal with it,' Dad said, as he spun a knife round and round on the rough wooden table. 'There's no other option now. I'll have to take them back to their mother.'

'Out of the question, none of this was in our plans. This place needs you to function!' shouted Ray. 'And the cities are death traps. No way.'

Dad looked through me to the cold stone wall behind my back. 'I could meet her halfway.' He was talking about Mother. 'There's no way she'd make it all the way here, over the river, so halfway. It makes sense.' And he mentioned some locations ... a mountain, a car park, the names escaped me.

'Right, but if you meet her, she'll have the police waiting to arrest you,' Ray said, 'and then they'd be onto us as well.'

'Even if that happened,' Dad said, 'I'd say I acted alone. What does it matter? The rule of law will break down within nine days anyway. The most important thing is to protect the safe house.'

'But you'd be trapped in a police cell during the pandemic!' Ray said. 'No, no fucking way. You said it yourself, prisons and hospitals are the biggest breeding centres for the virus. You'd be walking into your own death!'

According to Dad and Ray, after one little phone call to Mother to ask her what to do, I'd endangered not just Dad, Ray, Meg, Danny and Ben, but also my Mother, which is a very good reason for never making any choices ever again.

I mumbled, 'I'm really sorry,' a few times more, because of the twisting guilt in my belly, but they weren't even listening to me anymore.

'Look,' Meg said, suddenly looking over at me with sort of kind eyes, 'what if I was to drive Haley and Ben to some drop-off point, somewhere neutral. Your ex has never seen me before, so she wouldn't recognise me. I could have the kids lying down in the back of the car, then let them out half a mile down the road from her. By the time the kids walked to meet their mum, I'd be well away. Even if the police caught me, I could say I found the kids on the roadside. If the drop-off point was sixty miles away, that'd be three hundred square miles for the pigs to search. Anyway, d'you really think they'd even bother? Surely, they'll be far too busy to get involved with domestic squabbles.'

Dad muttered, 'The panic won't hit for another two days yet. It'll be a week till police are taken off regular duties and armed. Three weeks till martial law. Plenty of time for the State to round us up.'

Danny suddenly spoke. 'It was my phone. It's my fault, not hers.' He emerged from the fireplace, his dark eyes flickering with the flames. He looked straight through me as he spoke to the others. 'I'll take the girl to the village on the quad bike and come back for the boy.'

The girl!

Meg shouted, 'No, no, no. We're not risking your life as well! Go and make yourself useful: fix up the Toyota. Make a start on it now.'

Danny shot me a glance as he went, to say sorry, but something more, like a secret.

Dad shook his head. 'Look, this is all academic if my ex has already called the police and given them Danny's number. They could be on their way here already.' And he stroked his forehead.

I wanted to tell them Meg's plan was fine and Ben and me would keep schtum and not tell Mother or the police any names or anything. I'd say it had all been a mistake – mine. After all, it was my fault. I'm a postponer, a traitor, a cowardly, Libran, insincere, superficial, two-faced, time-wasting double-crosser and it served me right.

I must have had my eyes closed and maybe muttered something, because when I opened them they were all staring at me. There was a long silence and the crackling of the fire. The cut in my hand was really aching and I was fiddling with the bandage. Then Dad turned to me and his eyes were distant and his voice was low and slow, and he said, 'Haley, do have any idea what you've just done?'

There's only so many times I could say sorry without feeling like a total fake.

He raised his hand. 'Go to your room, now.' He said it in a voice I'd never heard before. And I did, but slowly. I stepped on the first two stairs and made fake climbing-the-stairs noises, but crept back to the shadowed edge of the door, craning back to hear more. I leaned in and heard Dad whisper, 'If I let their mother take them back to the city, you know only too well what'll happen to them. No one in the cities will survive the pandemic. It'd be like killing my own kids.'

There was silence then and the crackling fire and I heard him say, 'If they die, there's no point in me continuing to live.'

I shuddered and wanted to hold my dad, but I was stuck in my stupid creeping space on the creaky stairs. I heard Ray's chair scrape and he made a stretching sound and he said, 'Kane's still out there, and Kane's armed. Kane could take care of the mother herself.'

'Sorry, is that Plan D or E or X?' Meg said, sounding scared.

'No!' Dad shouted. 'I won't permit it. I told you, I'll take care of this myself.'

Protect The Young From The Truth

Worrying will not help. This is in Dad's survival handbook in the chapter called 'Live for This'. He quotes someone dead famous, saying, 'Who, by worrying, can add a single year to his life?' Or maybe it's an hour. Anyway, instead of getting frazzled with angst about Mother and Dad it's best to:

1. Focus on something small you can actually change and...
2. Have something bigger than yourself to set as your goal.

For me, in every case, this is Ben – him being both smaller and wider. My life is pointless so it's just a whole lot easier to live for the sake of my little bro. It's kind of pathetic but who gives.

Anyway, it would have been really shitty for me to dump all my worries on his chubby little shoulders and totally selfish, so I had to be all grown-up and do what grown ups do best – lie.

There he was, totally breaking my heart, sitting there in his bunk bed whimpering in the murky dark. Meg had locked us inside with a big clunky key 'for your own protection, darlings', so we were totally trapped, but I didn't want to bang on the door and scream and make Ben even more terrified. He wanted his mummy and his computer games, and his sheets were too scratchy. He wanted his five dinosaurs and his bedtime superhero story.

There were no books anywhere in sight so he asked for his old favourite, the made-up one that Dad had drummed it into my head since I was Ben's age. Dad called it 'The Guardian of Last Things'. It had been another secret Dad had asked us to keep from Mother. I could remember nearly all of it so I started whispering it to Ben, as I stroked his head.

'Once upon a time, near the end of time, there were these special people, and they were called the Guardians of Last Things.'

'Yayyy, the Guardians!' Ben shouted.

'Shh,' I said, 'just let me tell it. The Guardians of Last Things never set out to be heroes, but they had to be. It was their task, when everything was disappearing, to save the last things, the special things, the things that would help them survive and that humankind could be remembered by forever. They were a mum, a dad, and the two kids called Neb and Yelah and they travelled round in a spaceship made of junk, and they went to all the junk-piles in all the world to search for things to save, the things that were the most precious, and they put them in their magic bag that stretched to all proportions.'

It really helped me stop panicking about Mother.

The story was a kind of interactive one, ever changing, cos Dad would ask us to think of all the objects in the world and to decide what the last things were, so we could hold them tight in our thoughts before we went to sleep. Ben really loved the story. I guess I did, too. 'Which things will we put on the list?' Dad used to say in his singsong voice. Snickers bars were very tasty, but were they important enough to be on the list of last things? They didn't want to pick the wrong things, did they?

So I told Ben that Yelah and Neb and their parents flew to a junk-pile in the North Pole and they ran off to search and Yelah found an old guitar and Neb found a box of CDs.

'And their dad said, "Which shall we chose between, what will give us more music?" And the kids answered, "The CDs, the CDs!" But the mother Guardian said, "Ah, CDs might have hundreds of songs but how many can a guitar have?" And the kids were confused, so the father Guardian said, "As many songs as you can write or remember all your life." And then he said, "So which will give you more songs, the guitar or the CD when there is no electricity?" And the children answered, "The guitar, the guitar!" And that was the right answer, so they took the guitar and placed it among the last things.'

Ben was getting sleepy as I kept on, and something was winding its way into me, making emotions break in my voice and I hoped Ben hadn't noticed. So, I made up some more and told him that Yelah and Neb rummaged around and found some old cans of peaches and the girl found some packets of seeds in a box.

'And the mother Guardian asked, "So, children, which shall we keep, the cans of food or the seeds?" And little Neb answered, "The cans, the cans, yum!" because he was very hungry and the picture of peaches made his belly rumble. But the little girl said, "The seeds, Mother, because we can't grow plants from cans of food, and besides the cans are dented and they might be rusted inside or pierced and then we would get food poisoning." And the mother and father Guardian praised her for her wisdom and they discarded the cans and placed the seeds in the collection bag of the last things. Then the family of Guardians flew off to search for more of the last things, the important things that needed to be rescued and passed on if humankind was to survive.'

I was weeping and I couldn't help it, because for the first time ever I fathomed what Dad's whispered story was really about.

'What's wrong, Haley?' Ben wasn't asleep at all.

I rubbed my tears away and put on a smile, and told him, 'It's nothing, just me being a silly billy.'

'Neb is really Ben, isn't he?' Ben said.

And I nodded. 'Yeah, and I'm Yaleh.'

'Wow,' Ben said. Then he titled his head to the side and scrunched up his eyes, thinking for a bit. Then he said something wise, because he does that sometimes, 'Are we the last of all the last things?' he said.

Tears sort of burst out of me, and I said, 'Yeah, I think we might be.' And I hugged him tight, as my shaking body set him off and he was saying, 'I want Mummy,' and I was saying, 'Shh, I know, Benji, I want her too.' And we were both shaking and weeping together, with me kissing his head, locked in our little prison room.

I heard something beyond our locked door then, a creak of a floorboard and a breath or a sniff. Most likely it was Mad Meg spying on us, or pervy Danny, but I got this feeling of sadness coming from the door as I stared at it, like this strong sense that it had been Dad, stuck on the other side, listening to me telling Ben our story, and too afraid to knock or interrupt us. Like, even after he'd kidnapped us, he was still forever locked on the other side of our lives.

Later, when Ben and me were in our beds, I could hear noises from downstairs, like a door opening, like something heavy being dragged, then the bonnet of Dad's SUV being slammed shut. I got up and went to the window, telling Ben, 'Shh, go back to sleep.'

I saw Danny opening the big iron gates, and Meg in tears, giving Dad a big goodbye hug, then Dad got into the SUV and started the engine and Ray came forward and army-hugged Dad and handed him something. Through the greasy glass it was hard to see, but it fitted into Dad's hand and looked heavy. And Dad shook his head at first but then accepted the object.

I figured Dad had made his decision and was on his way to see Mother.

Ben tugged my hand and wanted to be lifted up to see. I distracted him throughout the noise of Dad's SUV tearing out the gate and into No Man's Land, till I couldn't hear it anymore and it was just wind.

It triggered something in me, like a hundred flashbacks and all of them were the same. Me at my window, watching Dad get into his car and drive away from our house after we'd seen him for our one day a week. From the age of eight, always that same feeling like something was wrenched from inside of me, then the coldness filling the emptiness.

I used to think that Dad used the divorce as an excuse to run from my total need for him, and I utterly hated him at times, because he didn't once stand up to Mother.

He didn't fight for me. Not in court, or in the weekly schedule. He didn't defy Mother micro-managing his schedule for seeing us, reducing him to something with less status than a baby-sitter or taxi driver. I thought he was like me, a pathetic avoider who ran from all conflict.

I thought I knew what he did every time he left. Mother had implied that Dad drank alone and maybe shagged some slut and wept in her arms in his shitty bachelor pad. I didn't know that every week he drove to this safe house, or that he gave himself five years of online training in stocks, derivatives, hacking and gambling, to make millions to prepare for the coming cataclysm.

The sight of Dad just leaving like that, without saying goodbye, hurt me. It hurt me just as much as the fact that I was pretty sure the thing Dad had taken with him, in his hand, on his way to meet Mother, was an actual gun.

How To Survive A
Worst-Case Scenario

Prepare For The Worst

Worrying yourself into a tizzy is not productive and you will not sleep a wink. Instead, plan for the worst-case scenario then get some rest.

Lying on my bunk, I repeated this mantra to myself while Ben snored, and I had to majorly suck on my inhaler to calm the hell down. But I kept seeing this thing in my head, over and over:

Dad drives slowly towards the hand-over point in the hills. It's an area with deep valley drops and he lies in wait for Mother's car to arrive through the mist. Dad shoots Mother's tyres out and her car spins out of control, breaks the barrier and plunges over the edge bursting into flames.

And I woke bolt upright.

I squeezed my eyes tight and swore at myself to make the damn dream go away but then there was another one starting:

Dad drives through the night and makes it all the way back to the city. Dad knocks on the door of our house. Mother starts panicking; she's trying to call the police. Dad kicks her door in and she runs but can't escape. Dad shoots her in the head.

I turned my hot pillow over to make it all go away, but the movement made the cut in my hand really ache. But I must have drifted off, because another one started:

Dad drives to an abandoned car park to reason with Mother, but the police ambush him and when they see he has a gun, they shoot him in the chest and head before he can even speak. Dad is dead.

Then another:

Dad meets Mother at the hand-over point. He tries to reason with her but she's furious that he's not brought Ben and me. A struggle starts and Mother grabs the gun and shoots Dad. Dad dies.

Then the same as before, with a twist:

A struggle, Mother grabs the gun off Dad, but it misfires and Mother is shot in the stomach and she starts bleeding out. Dad drags her body over an abandoned field and dumps her in a ditch. He drives off, leaving her for dead. Then he comes back here and tells Ben and me that she never showed up.

Another:

Dad can't face Mother. He's on his way to meet her but realises she'll snatch me and Ben back. Dad parks the car somewhere in the mountains and whispers Ben's name and mine, then he puts the gun in his mouth, the metal rattles against his teeth as his hand shakes, then he pulls the trigger.

I choked awake. The whole night I struggled against panic dreams and every time, while Ben snored zombie-like above me in the bunk, I woke to the same thought:

Dad is on his way to kill Mother.

I forced myself back to sleep but then it was another half-dream from another time:

I'm alone in my bed and I hear crying. I walk through the house, but it's not the safe house, it's Mother's house and I find a light on in the bathroom. I push open the door and there's a naked man on the floor. He has blood on his hands and he reaches out for me and I hear Mother scream. She picks me up and throws me out of the way. The man's eyes flash and then the door slams and I can't breathe.

It was that old nightmare again, the one I had over and over since I was little and I was suffocating and falling and then I gasped awake.

I stared into the dark and found my inhaler and took a blast of it and told myself over and over – stop frickin panicking, no one is going to die, OK! Then I heard a rustle. I rolled over and saw a piece of paper shoved under the door. I got out of bed, quietly so as not to wake Ben, and went over. It had *HALEY* written on it, and was folded in half, inside it said:

ARE YOU AWAKE? I HAVE TO SHOW
YOU SOMETHING. DANNY.

I stood sleepy-staring at it. Danny was the last person I wanted to speak to on God's earth. And show me? Was he totally deranged and thought a moment of vulnerability was the perfect time to show a female his dick? But then I realised, he was probably standing there on the other side of the door.

I went and whispered something random like, 'Is that you?'

There was a 'Shhh' from the other side, then another bit of paper came through. It said:

I WILL UNLOCK THE DOOR IF YOU PROMISE
NOT TO SCREAM OR BE ANGRY.

'Oh-frickin-K,' I whispered. 'Make like Nike and just do it.'

I listened for the key in the lock but then another cringey bit of paper came under the door:

OK, I'LL UNLOCK IT. THEN YOU WAIT TWO
MINUTES. THEN MEET ME AT THE ATTIC.
BE VERY QUIET. RAY IS AWAKE.

His instructions were creepy and maybe pervy but it took my mind off the bigger shits that were hitting the fans.

The lock turned and the door swung open a smidge. I did like he said and waited for a few minutes. I got my inhaler and pulled the minging camouflage pants on, just in case. Ben was still snoring and was fine, so I tip-toed out.

In Times Of Crisis, Accurate Information Is All-Important

When you're in a life or death situation, you will come across many interpretations of any feared event. Many versions of the truth. And like Dad says, if you act on false information or fake news, you're going to really fucking screw up.

I tip-toed down the dark corridor. The floorboards seemed even creakier and I should have put on socks because I got a splinter of wood in a toe.

I practically jumped out of my skin cos Danny was lurking there in the shadows and he seemed taller than before. I thought all this was potentially rapey, but he didn't grab me, just put his finger to his mouth to made the 'Shh' sign, then turned and led me down the corridor. His shoulders were very wide and he walked like a cat. He led me past what could only have been Meg's door because of the female snoring, then at the end of the farmhouse there were some stairs down into a really narrow corridor that was painted white. I whispered, 'Where the fuck are you...?' But he turned with an angry face and made that same 'Shh' sign again.

He opened a door really carefully, and inside it was weird. It was totally my dad's mad inventor's cubbyhole cos it had dozens of TVs, CB radios, maps, soldering irons, survivalist magazines, gun magazines, motherboards and SIM cards, and drawers lying open full of dead phones and hard-drives and micro screwdrivers. A total mess, just like the inside of Dad's brilliant, mad head.

I whispered questions at Danny, like, 'What is this? Where did Dad go? Is my mother OK? Why did you let me out of my room? Is this what you had to show me? Why are we whispering?'

He gestured for me to sit. 'I know you don't like me and you hate being here and I'm sorry for your mum, but...'

I went to speak but he put his hand up. 'Please just let me tell you, then you can ask questions, we don't have much time and we have to be very quiet.'

Usually such bossiness and mystery from a guy would have me giving them the finger, but he was quite refreshingly not full of shit, and he had some mud on his cheek and his curly hair was all off to one side and he gave zero fucks.

'Your dad's a genius,' he whispered. 'He taught me how to hack computers.'

Wow, well this was news to me.

'Just listen,' he said. 'Your dad records everything, he hacked your mum's phone years ago. Your dad called her last night.'

'Right, right, yes, and so what's happening…' I was just so confused and my head was spinning and I got that hot feeling.

I felt Danny's hand on my shoulder and he whispered, 'You got your inhaler?'

I nodded and took a squirt and I guess I must have thanked him. 'What's my dad going to do?'

Danny shook his head, slowly. 'To be honest, your dad's a really nice guy – if it wasn't for him, I'd be in a foster home. But your mum has kind of messed with everyone's plans.'

'What's he going to do to her? Just tell me!'

'My guess is,' Danny said, 'your dad's actually going to try to persuade her to join us. Like, face to face.'

'Pathetic,' I said. 'So what happens when she says no? Cos she will. Is that why he took a gun?'

Danny looked surprised that I knew that. He nodded and breathed out loudly. 'Look,' he said, 'there's something else. Ray freaked out last night after your dad left and he called Kane.'

'What the fuck is this Kane thing people keep talking about?'

'Not what. Who. Kane does the outer perimeter patrol. She's pretty intense, sort of religious, I think. There's this back-up plan for when things go wrong and that's what Kane is for.'

He stood up, saying, 'It's in here,' as he went into Dad's cubbyhole desk and handed me this well-thumbed stack of paper.

This was the first time I'd ever seen Dad's survival manual. Danny led me to the page that said, *PLAN G*.

Plan G

Any safe house is only as strong as its weakest link.

For some group members, this may be addiction to substances. For others, it may be emotional attachments to people beyond the perimeter enclosure who could be dying from the virus or from starvation. For others, it may be 'cabin fever' in lockdown. In each case, some all-too-human weakness may lead one member of the group to leave the safe house and potentially compromise the secrecy that must surround it, jeopardising all within it.

The incubation period of the virus is approximately one month. There is no way to know who is carrying the contamination, and people will not know that they are infected. Each incubator will contaminate fifty people. All outsiders therefore must be treated as contaminated and potentially lethal.

No people, be they neighbours, starving groups or relatives can be admitted to the safe house after Day One. Any such people who know of the whereabouts of the safe house are to be considered contaminated and therefore terminated.

Human pity and compassion is the greatest weakness, and if left unchecked it will lead to the safe house being overrun by the infected.

This is why Plan G has been created.

In the eventuality that the group leader should violate his own rules and permit an un-planned person to enter the compound, then the leader must be terminated.

In the eventuality that the leader demands that the rules be rewritten to accommodate that need, the leader must be terminated.

In the eventuality that the leader issues new orders which contradicts and invalidates all prior plans, making demands that his/her authority overrides all, the leader must be terminated.

The security of the safe house is paramount.

I finished reading it and then I guess I was panic-breathing. I said to Danny, 'Wait, so my dad's going to be … terminated?'

'Only if Kane finds him first and follows Plan G.'

'Who wrote this stupid fucking plan?'

'Your dad did,' Danny said. 'He knew he couldn't be trusted when it came to your family, I guess. He said he was the weakest link. He said it lots of times.' Danny touched my hand. 'I'm really sorry, Haley.' Then he said, 'But don't worry, your dad's really smart, I'm sure he'll work out a way.'

And part of me was thinking this is just grown-ups playing make-believe soldiers, but then if they did think the pandemic was for real, like Danny clearly did, then what was to stop them killing each other for real?

My head was spinning and I was sucking on my inhaler and I don't know how it happened but Danny was sort of hugging me and saying, 'Don't worry,' and 'It's OK,' and I shuddered, well, just because I have a thing about my neck getting touched unexpectedly. Then I totally froze and he was embarrassed and we kind of separated, but that's not the point.

How Not To Prepare The Inner Area For Decontamination

Dawn seeped through the cracked window and down the corridor came the crackle of a walkie-talkie. I bolted awake. I'd been sitting at the cubbyhole window staring out, and I must have dozed off. Actually, I'd put my hands together at one point and made a prayer with some made-up words about saving everyone.

I ran downstairs to discover Ray at the table, walkie-talkie in hand. I asked if Dad was OK.

He gestured for me to get the hell away and shut up. He grunted into his walkie-talkie, 'Got your copy, Kane, 10-19, your package confirmed. What's your ETA?'

What the hell?

Ray wouldn't explain. He yelled at me to go and help Meg with 'decontamination procedures'.

Ben was behind me then, all sleepy-eyed and yawny, and asking about breakfast and if Mummy was here.

I asked him to shush, because I was trying to decipher Ray's walkie-talkie speak, but it was impossible, unless you know what a 10-17 or a 10-34 is.

'But if Mum comes here it'll be a bummer...' Ben said randomly, '...cos she'll make us eat tofu again.'

He amazes me, the superpower that is his imperviousness to reality.

I ushered Ben back upstairs and helped him pull on his muddy little jeans and still-wet socks, and I couldn't stop picturing this weird picture of Mother grabbing Ben's arm and Dad grabbing the other and both accidentally tearing Ben in half.

Then I heard feet running. Meg was bashing about yelling, 'Kids, kids, come now, come and help me get the bleach and masks ready.'

And Ben was jumping around yelling, 'Yay! Is Mummy coming? Yay, Mummy!'

But this whole decontamination thing sounded scary, and 'package' was a pretty ominous word if it referred to a human.

I ran back downstairs and there was Meg with her rubber gloves on, filling huge buckets full of water and bleach. 'Here, quick! Get one for your brother too!' she shouted, and threw me a heavy-duty face mask. Meg's voice went all muffled behind the filter and she was far too busy making the bleach sprays and wipes to answer my really simple, annoying question, like, 'OK, so is one or both of my parents coming back *and* are they actually alive?'

All Contaminated Objects Must Be Placed In Quarantine Or Destroyed

What would you do if one or both of your parents were contaminated? What would you do if one or both were dead and still contaminated?

Ray slung the big rifle over his shoulder, readjusted his face mask and unlocked the heavy iron gates. Danny looked over at me and made some cryptic hand sign, then revved his quad bike and, with a nod from Ray, tore off through the gateway into No Man's Land.

Ben was jumping around. He wanted to go on my shoulders, like he goes on Dad's, and it's pretty cute the way he gets the words 'shoulders' and 'soldiers' mixed up, but he's way too heavy and I say all this because I was absolutely shitting it and Ben being annoying was actually a good distraction from the mounting dread.

Who is alive, Mother or Dad? Which one is 'the parcel'?

Ray looked through his heavy binoculars, while Me and Ben shivered with our masks and rubber gloves on and waited. The walkie-talkie hissed and the voice of this distant Kane person said, '10-19, prepare for decon, over.' I gazed out at the yellow dusk light looking for a trace of the approaching vehicle, but saw only doofus Danny's quad bike dust cloud.

I heard the engine before I saw it. I hadn't put two and two together yet. The noise wasn't Dad's crummy old 4x4, but a bigger thing that I would soon learn was Kane's Range Rover. Slowly it took shape, with Danny's quad bike skidding behind it, and then I saw the Range Rover was towing Dad's 4x4. There was no sign of Mother's car at all.

My heart sank and my chest ached. Kane didn't find Mother. The package is Dad. Kane shot Dad.

Ray glanced back at me, his eyes tight and anxious over his blue mask.

It all happened too fast and bits of it come back to me in slo-mo. I saw Kane first through her windshield as she accelerated up the dirt track straight towards the gate. Her head was shorn to the skull and she was deathly thin, with a muscly neck and arms. I could see no one in the back seat, or anything or anyone in Dad's 4x4, because of the cloud of dust. Kane seemed to be alone.

How could this person I'd never met shoot my dad?

The Range Rover cleared the gate and skidded to a halt. I

covered Ben's eyes from the dust and from whatever was to come. Please, God, I told myself, please make it that Mother got away. Please.

Meg screamed at me and Ben, 'Keep back! Contamination!'

The Kane woman stepped out. Her face was tight and furious. She was tall and her creepy buzzcut and black army clothes made her look more like a Buddhist monk than a woman. She threw this huge rifle to Ray and barked out with this really posh voice, 'No police, she didn't call them – I checked her memory card. I went the longest route and doubled back. No trace of police.' The Kane woman then nodded and Meg ran towards her and dowsed her with the first bucket of bleach water. She barely even flinched.

But where was Mother then? Flashes of Mother left dead or dying in a ditch.

I took huge puffs from my inhaler as I tried to restrain Ben from running up to the cars. Out of the dust clouds behind them, Dad stepped out. He was limping pretty badly and looked blood-drained, and there was a dark stain down one trouser leg. 'Kids,' he yelled and opened his arms. Ben ran from my hands into the dust and jumped into Dad's arms.

'No contact!' Kane yelled. 'We could be contaminated!'

Dad ignored her and kissed Ben's head, ruffling up his hair. He nodded then to Kane and Ray, and following his instruction they went into the back seat of the Range Rover and pulled out 'the package'.

It was Mother. She was massively bound with duct tape round her feet and chest and arms, and her mouth was taped shut. Mother was struggling, kicking and very much alive.

'Mummmy!' yelled Ben.

My heart leapt. 'Thank God!'

Ben jumped from Dad's arms and ran towards her, but recoiled, probably from seeing the rage in her eyes. Kane grabbed Ben by the arm and threw him back. 'Stay back! Contamination!' she yelled.

She was like a purity fascist or something.

Kane grabbed another one of Meg's buckets of bleach and threw it over Mother, who squirmed and shuddered. Kane eyed my poor, dripping mother from her head to her heels, like she was calculating the exact number of meals that Mother's continued survival would subtract from our rations. It was pretty clear that Kane had not agreed to Mother coming here.

Mother lay gagged and taped and squirming in the mud. Screaming through duct tape makes a very specific sound. I said something weird and guilty-sounding like, 'Hi, Mother. Please don't be mad at Dad, OK, please?' but that only made her eyes more furious still.

I was massively happy to see her alive but totally crapping it because the last time I saw Mother that livid was during the much aforementioned divorce proceedings. It was all too much. My emotions got overloaded, then shut down, and so I just stood there sucking on my inhaler as I watched Ben, Dad and Kane getting sprayed with anti-virals, and I realised that the dark stain on Dad's leg was actually blood.

I may never know the full truth of what happened that night, because now there would be two sides to every story. And my worst nightmare of all was that I'd have to choose one side, once and for all. Mother versus father, unto death.

Dad nodded to Ray. 'Woodshed.'

Ray said, 'Affirmative,' and picked up Mother like she was a bag of potatoes and slung her over his big pink Incredible Hulk shoulders. And Ray grinned, like it actually gave his entire life meaning to obey orders.

Mother tried to punch him, kick him and scream, but without the benefit of having free hands, legs or mouth.

Dad called over to me, 'Come on, Haley, let's get you and Ben washed and geared up. You'll see your mother later, she's a little tired and emotional after her long journey.'

So this was it, our family reunion. I looked up and Danny was sitting on his quad bike, staring at us, as if Mother, Dad, Ben and me were a natural history programme on weird animals.

'Wow,' I thought, as I watched Ray set Mother down inside the stone-walled wood shed beside the razor wire bales. 'Just don't remove that tape, Mister,' I muttered secretly to myself. 'Not yet.'

But he did and the cursing began, and I started to feel all breathless and dizzy.

'You fucking beast! Take your filthy hands off me!' Mother screamed. 'You're going to be spending a lot of time in jail! All of you!'

Yes, Mother was in full health and on top form. Wow. Happy families, I thought, as I sucked on my nebuliser. And then I fainted.

The best thing about fainting is that all your problems vanish. Then, when you wake up, everyone is around you and whispering and looking down on you and they're holding you and stroking your face and it's all dreamy and lovely, and you have this sense of being taken care of and you don't know where you are.

But then you remember.

How To Live In Lockdown

Denial Is A Very Human Reaction

Human beings are habit-based and circular in their thinking. This is proven by the fact that in a pandemic the majority of the population deny it's actually happening.

It was pretty amazing how long Mother screamed for. Cursed, too. I remember thinking, wow, it's day four and everyone who's tried to bring her food in the woodshed, or loosen her duct tape, has had the aforementioned food thrown in their face. Ray even got kicked in the balls by Mother who, it must be said, was still wearing her Chloé court shoes with the pointy toes.

Kane also attempted to take food to mother and I witnessed the ordeal. When I say 'food', it was like some grey, vegan, protein goop made from packets of powder that was the only thing I ever saw Kane eat. There was something weird about food and Kane – she never joined the rest of us round the table for Meg's dead-animal pig-outs, but always hovered at the back of the room, like a long shadow of a monk, and always silently spooning this grey goop, like eating was a vile bodily ordeal to get through and she was in flavour-pleasure denial. And the speed she ate at, like she had to constantly be on guard, not just against the virus. And that nervous spasm thing she had with her head jolting to the side. I had this theory that she was a runaway from a super-rich family and had major body paranoia issues, probably cos she'd been abused as kid.

Anyway, Kane went to Mother's wood hut with the bowl of goop, and I tried to warn her but she ignored everything me and Ben said anyway, like she wished all kids didn't exist.

Kane unlocked the door and Mother sprang out wielding a

plastic spoon and cut a deep scratch under Kane's eye. For real. Kane moved super-fast with some kind of martial arts moves and locked Mother back in.

Then Kane yelled at herself, cos she has super-high personal standards, I guess. She manically covered her hands, arms, neck and face with decontamination gel from her utility belt, rubbing herself like she'd just caught bubonic plague or middle-class values from Mother. Then she saw me standing there, totally jaw-dropped, staring. She marched past me, super-stern, muttering, '1,200 calories a day.'

And I was like, random! But she was gone, leaving me to wonder if she meant how many calories Mother had just wasted, or if it was the number of calories Kane felt Mother's life was worth.

Kane gave me the shudders.

Day in, day out, Ben kept whimpering, 'Why can't I see Mum? Is she decontaminated yet? Can I show her my drawing of the T-Rex? Please, Dad?' etc.

Dad told Ben he should stay away 'just in case your mum's got a nasty bug'. But I knew what he meant: just in case Mother grabs you and the aforementioned tug-of-war ensues, with one parent yanking each of your arms till you're torn in half.

Dad was also recovering from a Mother-inflicted wound, or so I suspected, as he walked around in shorts with a bandage on his leg from the bullet wound that he wouldn't discuss. The truth was in major lockdown.

Mother's nocturnal yells from the woodshed mixed with the wind noises and kept me awake at night. I wanted to calm her, but Dad said, 'There's no point even trying to get through to her while she's in denial. Don't worry, she's being fed and watered and she's in no danger. The only thing that's been hurt is her pride.'

He said I shouldn't feel hurt if Mother behaved irrationally towards me. Like any unprepared middle-class consumer, she would have to wake up to 'the greater reality'. These were the five stages of grief that I was banging on about earlier, and, according to Dad, Mother was still in the Denial phase.

He was right. One time, when guilt forced me to creep out to Mother's woodshed, I heard her on the other side of the door, literally chanting exactly what Dad had said, 'This isn't happening, this isn't happening, this isn't happening.'

In Chapter Three of Dad's book he explains how 'Denialism' made Virus X inevitable. He said there should've been serious scientific investigation into how close we came to a terminal pandemic last time, but instead the governments of the world heaved a sigh of relief and said, 'Well, that's over and done with,' and went into major denial as they secretly snuck off to search for new, even more lethal viruses.

Nations could have told themselves that they had to make sure their food and drug supplies were entirely self-sufficient and manufactured in their own country, so they never made this mistake again, but they didn't. In the rush to rebuild their wealth, with businesses aching to make back the billions they'd lost, they became ever more dependent on food and drugs from other countries, exploiting the cheap labour of poorer nations.

They could have admitted that the spread of the virus last time was caused by international flights, and they could have cut those back by ninety per cent but they didn't. Why? Because they wanted to celebrate with one big, happy, global party. The mainstream media shot down anyone who questioned the 'It'll-never-happen-again-so-let's-spend-spend-spend' mentality.

Dad's section on 'optimism bias' is alarmingly like our previous lifestyle with Mother.

No one listened to people like Dad who said, 'Destroy the pathogens, all of them.' Dad warned that the most deadly pathogen yet discovered will be leaked during the global struggle for its possession. But governments were living in Denialism. Other nations will have laboratory leaks, they all thought, but not us.

The most deadly form of Denialism is denying all the rest of the world any information when the pathogen leaks out. This was what a certain government did last time around, and even though the world decided there needed to be one hundred per cent transparency on all future epidemics, this certain government was so ashamed that they'd leaked the brand new lethal pathogen, that they went into full Denialism. Mass mobilised Denialism. They made scientists who knew the truth vanish. They destroyed all evidence of their lab experiments. They killed journalists. This was how, Dad said, the speed of this pandemic would be nine times faster and more virulent than last time. One quarter of the world's population would die from the virus, but two quarters more would die from the total collapse of civilisation, that the governments of the world would keep on denying, even as it was happening.

This time around, the masses would be furious, after having lived in so much denial. There would not just be panic buying and hoarding – this time, there would be looting, rioting, theft, arson, opportunistic gang violence and rapes, neighbours attacking each other for the food and PPE supplies they didn't get in time... because they were in denial.

This time around, the health service, police and government would each collapse like dominos, through infections and staff walking away from their posts to protect their infected families.

Dad's book said that the food supply would break down around Day Seven and the power grid would fail around Day Twelve. If the power grid went down, and did not come back in two days, it signalled structural collapse that could only be remedied by governments taking total military control. The army would seize all food, all medicine, all property.

Governments would shut their borders and plunder other countries' supplies. A nuclear attack against the country that spawned Virus X would be th likely, according to Dad's calculations.

All this from living in denial.

Dad said I'd been in this state too, when I first got there, so I had a sort of head start and I could really be a massive help by talking Mother through everything.

'Your mother has to be more pitied than feared,' he said.

He also said, 'I don't think she realises how lucky she is that I managed to convince the group to take her in. I promise, she'll be out as soon as she's ready. Don't worry, there's a bunk bed in there and a stove and fresh water in her shed. She can be perfectly comfortable if she just accepts her quarantine. She might hate me now but she'll thank me for it in the long run.'

Actually, what he really meant was: Please persuade your mum to stop cursing and attacking us, before Kane flips out, marches into the woodshed and shoots her.

Talking of Denialism, Dad always avoided confrontations with Mother and it was kind of weird that even as 'Group Leader' he couldn't brave up to dealing with her himself. So, like usual, he was dumping her on me.

That night, I had this dream about Mother. It's not the nightmare, the recurring one where I walk through a dark corridor and find a naked man bleeding in a bathroom, and sometimes it's my dad and sometimes it's men from movies. No, not that recurring dream, but the really nice one.

It goes like this.

Fingers are touching my hair and someone is singing. She has a beautiful voice, so soft and whispery. I open my eyes and Mother is there behind me and she is so young and beautiful in the mirror and I am just a little scrawny kid. 'Sit still!' she says. I feel a tug, not hard, just the right amount, cos she is braiding my hair. 'There,' she says, 'you're all done.' And she spins me round to see my plaits.

Then Dad comes in and throws down his bag and puts his arm round Mother's waist and lifts her off the ground, kissing her for a long time on the mouth, and she girly-giggles, 'Eddie, Stop!' and I blush majorly but it's a ticklish kind of happy.

Then Dad touches my hair and says, 'Hey, you turned my tomboy into a girlie-girl!' And Mother says, 'But she's so pretty, isn't she?'

'Wonder who she gets that from,' Dad jokes. And they both put their faces next to mine in the mirror, to compare, and I can see that my eyes are Dad's and my nose is Mother's. There's some debate about whose mouth I have, then they both kiss my cheeks, Mother on one side and Dad on the other, and then their fingers tickle me, at exactly the same moment on both sides. And when I laugh I have no front teeth, and we all laugh at that too in the mirror.

Then I woke up and my face was wet, I guess from crying.

I heard Mother yelling from the woodshed. I kept picturing her, alone in there, shivering in the spidery dark, sleeping in the clothes she'd arrived in, curled up on some cold, mildewed army mattress amongst the logs and slugs. How could they do this to her?

Unless Dad, Ray, Kane and Meg were all insane sadists, there was only one possible explanation: they actually believed they'd saved her life from the apocalypse and that she'd eventually thank them.

How To Help Others Adapt To The New Reality

If you don't adapt to your new eco-bio-living situation, you will go extinct, like the woolly rhinoceros and the dodo.

Mother was on, like, day six of her hunger strike and I was worried. So, I found myself with a random make-peace-sandwich Meg had prepared, tip-toeing cautiously towards the woodshed door. Mother was yelling from the other side, weird, newly invented phrases like 'bastarding coward'. I waited for a gap, crept closer and knocked. That silenced her.

'Hi, Mother,' I said in my try-hard-smiley voice. 'I'm dead sorry about all this. They sort of tricked me, too. Look, I've got a nice sandwich here and I'm just going to slide it through the dog-flap thingy, OK?'

She didn't reply, so I set it down before the hatch. It was like a weirdly back-to-front fairy tale: Ben and me were Hansel and Gretel, and I was feeding the witch. There was no way I was actually going to pass the sandwich inside, as Mother could grab my hand, or hit my fingers with a big log, like she did to Ray, two days before.

'Haley Cooper Crowe,' Mother said, 'I swear, if you don't let me out, this very minute, so help me God, I will ground you for a month.'

I stared at the bolted door and thought, that's kind of ironic.

She didn't know if I was still there because she said, 'Wait, please, don't leave me alone, OK? I need to...' Then her voice changed. 'Oh, Haley, I don't know how this happened. I'm not blaming you ... we just need to...' She said to come closer, and asked if I was alone, because this was for my ears only.

I told her, 'Yes, sure, on you go, knock yourself out.' But not literally.

'Listen,' she whispered through the door, 'could you scout around, work out the layout? How many of these nutters are there? Are they all armed? Are there any maps or computers, yes? Are there any other ways out, doors, passages? Is there a landline even? OK, Haley?'

I mumbled, 'OK.'

'Oh,' she added, 'and please don't say a word to your father. You've no idea how much it hurts to know you went behind my back and let this happen, and I'm not blaming you, but please do what I say, darling. Promise me?'

So it was a kind of interrogate-him-but-don't-say-a-word-to-him deal. Yet another classic, contradictory, passive-aggressive Mother demand. Why couldn't she be like a normal mother locked in a shed? I had to ask myself, hold on, what's my motivation here? Plus an even bigger question had to be asked:

'Mother?'

'What now?'

'What was it like in the city, like ... when you left?'

'What on earth do you mean?'

'Well, was there panic buying, like, at the supermarkets?'

'Please, don't start talking like your father, he's absolutely insane and a liar. He tricked me, and he tricked his therapist too. Your father was terrified by the last pandemic and now he sees pandemics everywhere.'

'But were people dying? Like, of the virus? Didn't you watch the news?'

'Darling, how on earth would I have time for the news? I was trying to find you and your little brother.'

Not exactly informative. Maybe, like Dad said, Mother had picked a comforting lie over facing a horrific truth, and drove around with her eyes shut. On the subject of lies, I really had to ask her, 'Dad said you have a boyfriend, is that true?' but I couldn't bring myself to.

'Haley, are you still there? Please don't walk away on me, darling,' she called out, sounding strangely vulnerable. 'I know you're cross with me about something, but ... could you please try to focus and help me get out of here? OK? OK, are you still there? Why aren't you speaking? Haley? Haley, come back!'

When conflict happens, I zone out. It's a defence mechanism, a bit like Denialism, apparently. I sucked on my inhaler and stared at the padlock and the razor wire bundles that Danny and Kane had unwound all the way round the inside walls over the last few days, and the cut in my hand ached.

I heard a sigh and Mother said, 'I can see you're clearly on your father's side in all this.'

That set me off. 'What? No way! Why do you always make me take sides, anyway? It's not fair! Why can't we be like a normal mother and daughter? Why is nothing I do ever good enough for you? Why do you always blame me? It wasn't my fault that you and Dad got divorced! Stop making me suffer for how miserable you are!'

She went silent then, so I was shouting, basically, at a bolted door, which was metaphoric or something. But at least I'd told the door things I'd been wanting to yell at Mother for years.

It's hard to believe but Mother used to hold Dad's hand everywhere, which had been pretty embarrassing when I was six, like, in actual supermarkets.

Maybe, in my tweenage divorceling years, I still clung to the dream that Mother and Dad would get back together one day, and that the reason Mother really had to regiment her exposure to Dad, and limit the handover time to nanoseconds, was that she was actually still suffering from the breaking of a vast and beautiful togetherness. Like, you know, to hate someone, it really helps if you really loved them like hell first of all, cos everything else is just middling and average.

Some part of me always thought the secret reason why Mother had become this neurotic, micro-managerial monster endlessly filling up our lives with play-dates, extra lessons, sporting events, schedules, rules, timings, more schedules, her always trying to keep Ben and me busy, was so we wouldn't have to confront the gaping hole in HER life.

'I'm sorry that I'm such a disappointment to you, Haley,' she sighed from the other side of the locked door. Her hand slid out of the cat-hatch thing, looking weirdly vulnerable, her peach lustre nail varnish bitten down to stumps, and I recoiled. Her fingers assessed the texture of the sandwich I'd set there, a bit like a dog's nose sniffing, then pushed it away. 'I don't want this, and don't you eat their food either, it might be poisoned. And tell Benjamin too,' she said. 'You won't need to eat it anyway – we're going to get out of here in no time, if you do what I say. Now go and check for phone lines and a ladder, I need to contact the police. Please, Haley. Run! Don't waste any more time! I have to get back to work tomorrow.'

Dad was right, total Denialism.

I recalled once joking with Shanna that if Mother was up to her neck in a tank of steaming shit, she'd tell herself it was a rejuvenating mud-bath.

I tip-toed away, the recruited spy of a mad witch locked in the woodcutter's hut. I knew there was no point looking for phone lines and I'd already injured myself on the razor wire. I watched a bird flying over the top of our enclosure, and the clouds passing, until all I could think of was the pain in my hand. Conflicted people never make good spies.

How To Make Power

There is electrical power and interpersonal power. Both are dangerous and have to be contained or you'll get a shock.

My snooping for Mother's escape plan got off to a pretty bad start. I checked for ladders to climb over the wall. Nada. Hidden doors? Nada. So I had to crack on with Mother's 'pretend you're one of them' act.

So, I volunteered me and Ben to 'learn how to use the emergency manual battery charger' with Mister-muscle-head Ray. It was basically this old exercise bike that Dad had hauled off the street years before. You know, one of those things wannabe female adulterers buy to tone their butts at home. It didn't have a front wheel, so Mother couldn't pedal to freedom on it.

It was in this dark, dingy barn room with no windows, and there were tons of cables and a stack of phone rechargeable batteries in this custom-built rack that went to the ceiling. There were about fifty batteries, all with flashing lights.

Ray and Danny showed us how Dad had somehow retrofitted the bike with a fanbelt and wired it to this chunky engine thingy. It was pretty hard not to mouth-fart when Ray explained with utter seriousness that 'this invention is going to be your chief supply of energy when the power grid goes down. One hour of cycling per person each day, mandatory.'

Well, at least I'll have a firm butt for the apocalypse, I thought.

Danny climbed on the bike to demonstrate. I felt icky being in the same room as him after our sort of hug-thing and he was doing his brain-dead best to show off, like he wanted me to be impressed by his crazy muscles or something.

Ben thought the sun shone out of Danny's aforementioned ass and he was jumping up and down, yelling 'Wooohoo!' as Danny pedalled faster. Then the 'invention' made a grating noise, so

Danny changed gear and started panting. Ray flicked a switch and this light bulb they'd soldered onto the top of the battery-charging box started glowing. Ben yelled, 'Cool!'

'That's a variable DC current, for batteries only – not for complex electronics,' announced Ray.

In the strange light I noticed that Ray's face was covered in tiny scars that looked like they came from fights or many accidents with random tools. Also, one of his fingers had been lopped off at the top joint. He had a thin, narrow mouth and always barked instructions. I figured he had Gulf War Syndrome, or maybe life in general had been the battle he'd lost.

Ben was shouting, 'Wow, please, gimme a shot,' and 'My turn next!' getting more wound up with every turn of Danny's bike wheel, his eyes wide at the surging bulb. I guess he'd never fathomed what power actually was, and thought it came from God or the air, like YouTube.

Danny plonked Ben on the bike seat. I wanted to yell, 'Take your hands off my brother, you muscle-bound brother-stealer!' but I just sighed.

Danny re-adjusted the seat for my short-assed sibling, then Ben was peddling and shouting, 'Look, look,' at the light. 'Me-Power! Me-Power!'

Then Ben tried to make a grab for the light bulb and started falling and his fingers were just inches from the speeding chain. Danny jumped in.

'Hey, little fella, you gotta be careful,' Danny said. He turned to me. 'Watch out for the little guy, OK, there's lots of dangerous things here for city folk.'

'City folk? Get real!' I puffed. 'It's you that nearly killed Ben on that ape-shit quad bike of yours!'

Danny looked like I'd slapped him. I don't think he'd ever had back-chat with a city girl before.

Note for survivalist, home-reared males: just because you held a city girl in your big survivalist arms a few days before, doesn't mean she'll reciprocate anytime later. She might even resent you for it.

Ray told us the geek facts:

1. The generator is made of a spinning magnet within a coil of wire. As the magnet spins, electricity flows through the coil.
2. The energy can be used straightaway or can be stored.
3. If you pedal for two hours then you should produce around four hundred watt-hours of power. Enough to power a one hundred-watt light bulb for four hours. Or a twenty-watt laptop for twenty hours.

Ray barked, 'We're heading into a post-electrical-grid future, so every battery counts.'

Jeez, I thought, what a totally deluded waste of time and energy. Anyway, Ben needed a hug after his little fright, but he wouldn't come to me, even though I had my arms wide open. He hugged Danny's legs instead.

Danny offered me a shot of the bike and actually touched my lower back and this bolt shot through me. He recoiled, too. 'Wow,' he laughed, 'static!' I must have muttered something like 'shit', because Ray snapped, 'What did you say?'

'It,' I mumbled, pointing at the bike. 'Can't wait to get started on "it".'

There was a noise like a cat from outside then, and I remembered, to my shame, that it was Mother yelling from the woodshed. She'd be disappointed in me. All I had to report so far was bad news: that my father's preparations were hardcore and that me and her and Ben were, metaphorically, a lot like that the bike welded to the floor – wasting our energy, going nowhere.

How To Milk A Goat

Mother's plan to 'act interested' backfired when I had to go on the little military man's tour of smelly beasts and learn how to milk a goat.

'These are working animals, not playthings,' Ray said, 'essential for survival, and stay well away from the guard dog. I feed it. I walk it. Best if you never see it.'

I was standing in the barn with Ben before two skinny, smelly, bony creatures, which looked like anorexic sheep. They stank of toilets and had big, bulging, stare-y eyes like junkies. I could tell that super-macho Ray didn't really want to spend any time with us either.

Here is what he forced us to learn:

1. Never approach a goat from behind or it will kick you. Come from the front with carrots and a bag of oats.
2. You need three buckets. One to sit on and one to milk into, and one to save your first batch in when you move onto the next goat.
3. Don't risk using the same bucket for two goats as they take devilish pride in kicking over buckets with milk in them.
4. You've got to keep the milking bucket sterile. There's always faeces around goats and if you get it in the milk, the whole batch is ruined.

I heard a shout behind me. 'No, watch out!' Ben had been trying to stroke the goats, and Danny had 'saved him', apparently.

'That beast can chew through electric cable, it could have had his finger off in seconds,' he said.

'What a hero!' I muttered.

The more Ben liked Danny, the more he annoyed me. And that 'rugged good looks' thing? I was so over it already.

'Show them how it's done, Danny,' Ray said, and Danny, having another chance to show off, sat before the goat, reached underneath and pulled out – the thing.

I sort of screamed. It looked like a shrivelled penis. Danny seemed to enjoy how grossed out he was making me, but then Ray barked, 'Get on with it, stop giggling like stupid girls!'

Danny squirted the disgusting 'teat' and the stink of goat's milk was puke-making. He turned to me and asked, 'Fancy a shot, city girl? Here, I'll show you.' He aimed and squeezed, for a joke, at my shoes – which, BTW, were my sneakers. This gross, whitey, gluey liquid splashed me and I reeled back and my elbow hit something metal. It was sore and I swore. There was this clunk and rush and I felt this warm wet down the back of my neck and this total stench hit me. Ray shouted, 'Shit, shit. Keep her away from the milk!' and, 'Stay still! DON'T MOVE!' and I was dripping with something that stank like every crap in the world mixed with Thai fish sauce.

Sometimes you just have to shriek 'Euww!' and panic. Which is what I did, knocking Danny over and spilling all the milk, in the process. Ray yelled orders and Ben giggled and Meg ran round the corner yelling 'God almighty!' and I was begging for them to please do something as I watched the milk and toxic brown contaminant intermingle around my feet and felt it creep cold down my back. Danny started laughing at me.

'What?' I yelled. 'You should see your face – you're covered in crap too, asshole!'

Meg quarantined me away by the side of the house and hosed me down. Apparently, I'd upset the barrel of fermented organic fertiliser. It was mostly chicken shit and straw with biodegraded leaf mulch and dead veg. 'It's brilliant for the potatoes,' Meg said. 'It's our own mixture ... with a secret ingredient to activate fermentation.'

I just wanted to get those horrid, pissy camouflage clothes off and never go near any animal ever again, but she rabbited on. 'Male urine,' she said, 'it's the enzymes – doesn't work with female pee. I tried but no luck. Funny that, isn't it?'

So I was covered in chicken shit and Ray's piss?

'Yeah, and Danny's too,' she said with a smile, and I barfed into my own mouth.

Then Danny came round to get hosed and saw me soaked and my nipples all sticky-outy through my T-shirt and he said, 'Look, there's something I have to warn you about!' and I yelled, 'Stay away, piss man!'

Then Meg pushed me inside to get changed. 'Not to worry,' she kept saying, 'what's natural can't be nasty. No use crying over spilt milk.'

In the shower, I stood shivering under the freezing cold trickle and gazed forlornly at the last of my city clothes, in their putrefying pile. No amount of chanting 'it's not fair' made it any fairer, like Mother had already worked out.

It was no good, I wasn't going to make it. I'd never be able to adapt and we were trapped here. Then I had this weird flash of Danny in the shower with me as the cold water trickled over my body and I screamed, 'Euwww!' or something equally futile.

Locate The Truth

It's not always true that the truth is out there somewhere, but if all else fails, you might as well search for it.

Re-dressed in mortifying Meg-ish hippie hiking clothes, my fact-finding for Mother had achieved nada, so I re-traced my tip-toeing steps to Dad's cubbyhole, thinking if anywhere had a phone connection to the outside world, it had to be there.

The door was ajar and I jumped when I found Dad inside.

'So you found my control room already,' he said, almost smiling. 'Thought you might have.'

Caught in the act, I shrugged.

But he just said, 'Well, come in, then.'

The room didn't have a window and his workbench was jam-packed with computers from the Stone Age, and millions of wires and motherboards. He was in his element with his soldering iron and this ancient pair of duct-taped headphones on. He turned the dials on this big CB radio thing and I heard static and voices.

He turned to me and accidentally bashed his wounded leg, scattering his crazy pages of calculations everywhere. I apologised sheepishly and tried not to look like Mother's two-faced, fact-finding spy.

He said sorry for being so busy and asked me how I liked Danny and Meg and apologised that Ray could be a bit gruff at times. 'Don't be afraid of Kane,' he added, 'you won't see much of her, she a solitary type.'

'Psycho-type', more like, I thought, but I said, 'Dad, don't you think it's kind of a bit inhuman to have my actual mother locked up like an animal? I mean, it doesn't show you in a very good light, to be honest. Can't you just let her out?'

He smiled and shook his head. 'All in good time.'

I stared at him and the bandage on his leg with way too many questions, and my head was already spinning a bit.

'You OK, Haley?' he asked.

And I said, 'The end of the world doesn't happen every day, in case you hadn't noticed, Dad. I'm just adjusting, OK?'

He said, 'OK,' then there was silence and I said, 'Dad?'

'You want to ask me about what happened that night we got your mother? Right?' he said, like reading my mind was that easy.

'Yeah,' I mumbled, 'so like, how did you get shot and why did Mother get tied up and ...'

'Your mother will no doubt have her own version of events,' he said calmly, leaning forward to his messy desk. He flicked some switches and handed me his headphones. 'Here, best to let you hear for yourself.'

I hesitantly put them on, then he went through some files on his big computer and I was thinking, so, he totally lied to me about an internet connection because he had, like, five computers on and some had video feeds from different countries playing.

He clicked an audio file and – I couldn't believe it – I heard Mother and Dad on their phone call from that fateful night. And I was like, 'Dad, what the hell? Why did you record Mother?'

He nodded and said, 'I've recorded all of our interactions for years.'

Freaky. There was the ringing noise and Mother picked up and said her name and asked who was there, then Dad, in the recording, said, 'Justine, this is Ed. Please stay calm.' Dad's phone voice was really chill and Mother's really wasn't.

'You bastard!' she yelled. 'Where are my kids? What have you done with them? Where the hell are you?'

'They're safe, Justine. Try to listen and stay calm. But first I need you to confirm that you've not called the police.'

'How fucking dare you! I'm going to have you arrested this time, you lying piece of shit!'

For real, I'd never heard Mother cursing like this before – it was kind of amazing. Dad didn't react beside me, he just stared at the wave form of Mother's screaming and nodded for me to keep on listening, then wheeled his chair back to give me more privacy.

'Dad, why are you letting me hear this?' I asked, cos it was private and spooky, but all he said was, 'If you hear the truth for yourself, maybe it'll help you trust me a little more.'

It was so creepy, Dad sitting behind me silent and his disembodied voice from five days ago in my ears.

Dad's phone voice said, 'Every time you shout at me, Justine, I will hang up. I will then wait for three minutes and redial your number again. The more you shout, the more times you force me to hang up, the longer this will take. I am not here to argue, but to give you information. My number will appear as a different number each time on your phone because it's scrambled by an encoder. You will not be able to trace the number. Do you understand?'

'You fucking coward, when I . . .' Mother began, but then I heard the click of Dad hanging up.

Dad leaned over and moved the mouse to the next audio file. I stared at Dad's big screen and saw other folders with tiny thumbnails of photos. I looked closer and realised the photos were actually from my own phone. What the actual fuck? Dad must have hacked it and downloaded all my personal pics. And the other folders too: I looked at their names and there was Justine, Ben and three of my friend's names.

I was freaking out, but Dad super calmly just clicked on another phone recording.

Mother's voice was different this time, like she'd spent three whole minutes screaming at the walls of our lovely home and got it out of her system. 'Ed,' she said, 'I know things feel very intense for you just now, and something's triggered you, something in the news, maybe, but let's try to de-escalate this, OK?'

She was like the Mother I knew once again. The refined, self-controlled, passive-aggressive skillset.

'Have you called the police yet?' Dad's phone voice asked.

Mother ignored the question. 'You're not feeling yourself just now, Ed, whether it's a change in medication or something else, I understand. If you can just tell me where you are, I can come and help you.'

Dad's phone voice was having none of it. 'It's the last time I'll ask this, Justine. Have you spoken to the police from your landline or visited a police station?'

Mother sighed and growled. 'No, I have not called the fucking police. Believe you me, I tried, but the lines were busy, you lying swine. When I...'

And once again I heard Dad hang up on her.

Dad just kept on playing the clips for me and explaining jack shit, and it was majorly unnerving, him watching me listening. In three more clips, he tried really hard to reason with Mother. In one call Dad said, 'I can make a place for you here, Justine. You can live with our kids safely, securely, until the pandemic is over.'

Then I couldn't believe it, Mother actually laughed. Like sneering.

But Dad kept on and it was heart-breaking to listen to. He said, 'It's begun, Justine, just like I warned you it would. What you've seen in the news today is just the beginning. Listen, we can save our kids, we can save our family.'

Then there was this silence and Mother said, 'You're so deluded. Nothing's happening. There's some flu thing in Asia, it's under control. You're freaking out about fake news again. Listen, Ed, if you can recall, I had to take the kids away from you for their own safety. You weren't well, you're clearly still not well.'

Dad sighed down the phone and said, 'Justine, can you just trust me for once?' and he sounded kind of pathetic, like he still loved her or something. 'What would it take to come, try to live here for a week, a month? You can see how the pandemic develops for yourself, in safety.'

'I have work, unlike you, and kids to feed,' she snapped. 'You know who I did speak to today? Doctor Marshall. Yes, your so-called shrink, and you know what he said, Edward? When I called him, worried for the life of my kids, he said you signed yourself out of therapy two years ago. He said you were a disruptive influence in the group sessions and that when you left you took a bunch of patients with you.'

'Justine, please,' Dad's voice pleaded, 'do we have to go through this again?'

'No, no you listen to me, you liar. Doctor Marshall told me told that any paperwork I'd received about your therapy progress was fake, because...'

And Dad hung up again. There was just dead tone on the recording.

I turned round and Dad was looking at me with eyes like someone who's used to taking a beating. He whispered, 'Just one more to get through, Hale-Bopp.'

On the last recording, Dad's voice was slow and tired, and he said, 'I can see we're going in our usual circles, Justine. OK, you win. Have it your way. I'll return the kids to you. I am going to give you the GPS of a hand-over location. It's near Loch Etrie in Scotland. It'll be a five-hour drive. I'll meet you there in six hours' time with Ben and Haley and I'll hand them over to you. If you come with the police, there may be conflict and you could endanger the children, so please come alone and tell no one. Understood? I'm sending you the co-ordinates now, then I'll hang up and that will be the last you hear from me till you see me tomorrow morning.'

And then he hung up.

I sat there, cold to my bones.

'Any questions?' Dad asked.

I turned and tried to read his face. 'Yeah,' I said, 'so what happened, you used me and Ben as bait, lied, and met Mother in the middle of nowhere so you could kidnap her?'

He shook his head. 'I tried to reason with her.'

'But how did you get shot? Was it her?'

He shook his head. 'No, I don't like weapons. Your mother's never seen one before. But Kane was there, and she's very handy with a rifle, perhaps a little too handy. I saw that she was going to shoot your mother, following prior orders, so I jumped in the way. After that, well, Kane saw she'd injured me, and that made her see sense, and your mother was in shock, so we decided to bring her here to you and Ben, and tied her up so she couldn't hurt herself. And that's it.'

My head was spinning. I just kept saying, 'Jesus, Dad, Jesus, Jesus Christ, Dad,' and so on. He was, like, such a total hero. Risking his life for Mother, and twice. I felt completely guilty about being Mother's little spy.

'Any more questions?' Dad asked. 'Perhaps about the virus?'

He totally floored me, like he was reading my mind and three steps ahead. I nodded.

'You'd like some proof,' he said, 'that everything is happening like I say it is, so that you'll know for sure I'm not psychotically deluded, like your mother thinks I am.'

And I blushed and nodded and said, 'Sorry, yeah, if that's OK?'

'It's fine, Haley, I'm glad. You're a smart, deductive person, and it's only rational that you'd want evidence.' He turned back to his computer and said, 'Took me three hours to upload this, the cell towers are melting down with the mass panic.' He hit a button and bit of footage came up. It was of some woman and two kids in separate oxygen tents, all wired to about three machines each. Their bodies were spasming. Doctors in hazmat suits were panicking around them. 'That was Japan at 0800 hours this morning,' Dad said. 'Fifteen thousand cases overnight.'

The footage changed and there was footage of a child coughing inside a ventilator helmet, with this horrible wheezing noise, then this spray of blood plastering the inside of it. And I was like, 'Jesus!' Dad hit a switch and it vanished. 'Sorry,' he said, 'that's all the clear pictures we have. There's only a sketchy terrestrial TV signal due to the mountains and I'm afraid there's no fibre optics for sixty miles, so we only get internet on dial-up and the phone lines are jammed.

He gestured to a screen with a snowy fuzz of what looked like the BBC newsdesk, with crackling audio. 'We get some broken-up government media,' he said, 'but it's solid propaganda, telling us all to remain calm because it's a false alarm.'

'Denialism,' I said.

'That's my girl!' He grinned, then became sombre again. 'Satellite and long-wave radio are our best options,' he said, 'and that's exactly what I'm working on right now.' And he showed me how he welded together something that looked like a wok with cables and an old computer keyboard. He handed me the headphones with a smile and said, 'You any good at deciphering Russian or Morse code? That's the strongest signal I'm getting right now. There's information lockdown in China and Russia. This is someone in Ukraine. The virus is bad there, thirty-two thousand cases with forty-eight per cent mortality in six days, the contaminated doubling every three days. There's been rioting, their power grid went down almost immediately.'

I put the headphones on and there was static and beeping and a foreign person shouting far away.

'Wait,' Dad said, 'listen to this.' He flicked a dial and a posh robotic voice came on. It said, 'This is a test, this is only a test, this is a test of the emergency broadcast system.' Dad raised an eyebrow and I had to concur.

'Spooky,' I said.

'Yes, but even spookier is that the signal is exactly where the World Service used to be. See,' and he pointed to the dial. 'What does that tell you, Hale-Bopp?'

I was freaked. I thought about Jason and Shanna at lunch-break trying to listen to 1Xtra and getting 'this is a test of the emergency broadcast system,' followed by a loud shrieking tone.

'Don't worry, Haley, you're safe here, we just have to convince your mother.' He went into a drawer then handed me his manual, which I had to pretend I was just seeing for the first time. 'You could really help me by reading your mother some of that to help her adapt. Chapter Three is all about pandemic acceptance and cognitive re-adjustment. But best if you hide that from Ben, though – there's some pretty scary pictures in it. Keep it to yourself, eh?'

I nodded, in shock. Dad stretched and said he'd find a better internet dial-up by hook or by crook, just for me. 'This time tomorrow, we'll find out how bad the cities have been hit, then we'll know our timeline for sure. It could be that what hits this region first is panic overspill from millions trying to get out of the cities. I'll know tomorrow how far the virus is from us. OK, Hale-Bopp? Trust me. OK?'

Did I trust him? I guess I did. And that could only mean that I no longer trusted a single damn thing Mother thought, believed or had possibly ever said.

Everyone In The Safe House Must Believe The Same Facts

If you have differing analyses, differing narratives, differing facts, then you will not be able to act with unified action. Dad must have told me this a hundred times. And I knew it was my major failing. If someone tells me red is red, I always have to check that it's not actually orange, or maybe purple.

Like Dad said, in life-or-death situations, procrastinators like me are actually really dangerous people to have around. We can massively slow down reaction times when it comes to shooting or fleeing, for example. Indecision is like being on both sides of a wall and that means contamination.

So, I was back at Mother's woodshed.

She'd thrown some paper plates out through the dog flap and was doing her whispering thing, superfast. 'What did you find out, Haley? Is there a phone, can we get out of the main gate? Who has the keys for this lock?'

I did my Hamlet-ish ruminations, as I stared at her door. 'But why do you want to escape?' I asked her. 'Like, thousands or millions of people are contaminated already.'

'Oh, don't tell me he's brainwashed you already, Haley Cooper!' Mother sighed from the other side. 'I expected better of you.'

Wow, I thought, it was totally amazing how Mother could be locked up for six days and still totally manage to control people. It made me kind of angry. 'Dad told me what happened,' I said. 'You were horrible to him and you didn't give him a chance. If I were you, I'd be grateful to him for saving your life.'

There was a silence, then Mother muttered to herself on the other side, 'Saved my life, saved my life? That's what you think, is it? Well, let me tell you what happened.'

And so she did, giving me what they used to call 'an earful'.

'Did you know, Haley, that on the day your father abducted you, he sent me three different messages saying, *Meet me and the kids at mall*, *Meet us at the park* and *Sorry, pick up the kids at my house*. Why do you think he'd do that, hmm?'

I mumbled dunno.

'Because he needed to keep me busy and he's a psycho. Did you know, Haley, that on the day he kidnapped you and Ben, I called his therapist in tears and do you know what he told me? Doctor Marshall said that he'd filed a report on your father because his delusions were on the increase and he was borderline psychotic.'

It all sounded a bit too anti-Dad for me, so I said, 'OK, you're talking, I'm listening. Can we skip the opening titles and go to the rousing finale?'

'Don't be so rude,' she said. 'The doctor had mailed this letter to me two years ago, to warn me. But it turns out your father had changed my address on the medical records so I would never get that warning. He tricked me and the doctor. He's been wandering around, clinically insane for years, and covering it up.'

'Yeah, right, and now a word from our sponsors,' I said.

'There's no need to be sarcastic,' she snapped. 'I'm just trying to tell you the truth about your father's mental illness. Has your father ever explained it to you?'

I mumbled, and she said, 'What was that?'

'No, Mother.'

I was feeling short of breath and went through my pockets for my inhaler but I couldn't find it.

'So, what has he told you? No doubt he said this new pandemic began with the theft of a super-virus from a lab and he calls it Virus X?'

I shuddered and muttered, 'Yes.' Once again, I didn't know who to believe.

'And did he show you some horrible pictures of people spewing blood?' she said.

'How do you know all this?' I asked her, my head spinning, the choking feeling getting worse.

'Oh, Haley, I'm sorry. I should have warned you about all this before. I just didn't want to scare you. This is exactly the same delusion your father had last time he had a nervous breakdown. He thought the last pandemic was the end of the world, too. Six billion would die, he said, the population would return to...'

'The medieval plague era?' I asked.

'Exactly,' she said. 'I'm so sorry.'

It took the breath from me.

'Your father was diagnosed with what they call borderline

personality disorder, Haley. He gets paranoid persecution fanta-
sies, delusional episodes. I lived with it for as long as I could. God
knows how he managed to fool us into thinking he was healthy
again, but he's managed to rope these other folk into his delusion.
There's no point trying to convince them otherwise, he'll have
brainwashed them all. He can be very convincing, making you feel
special, like you and him are the only people who matter and all
the world is against you.'

'So nothing ... nothing's happening in the outside world?' I
asked.

'It was just a scare, some fake news. I can assure you that back
home people are going around shopping, walking in parks, eating,
drinking. Believe you me, they're still playing horrible pop songs
on the radio. Everything's just like normal.'

'There's no new pandemic?'

'No, of course not, and we need to get back home so you and
Ben can get to school. All your friends will be worrying about you.'

My heart had shattered. It couldn't be true. 'But Dad said there's
mass infections. He showed me some video.'

'He used to collect video clips obsessively,' she said. 'He once
showed me some horrific footage of teenagers setting cars on fire.
He said it was spreading through the country. I looked closer and
it was from the LA riots, twenty years before.'

Everything was spinning. 'I don't know,' I said, 'you're twisting
it all up. Why didn't you tell me all this about Dad before? It's like
my whole life is just one big lie now, and you hid all this from me,
to what? Protect me? That's so fucked up! I'm so confused, just
stop talking, stop talking!'

She was silent then she said, 'Oh, Haley.' Like, gently. It sounded
like she was weeping on the other side of the door. 'I should have
warned you,' she said. 'I'm sorry, I'm so sorry.'

Hearing her cry made me choke even more. I finally found my
inhaler in the army pants and I deflated down onto a log pile and
sucked on the steroids, feeling that dizzy emptiness that I escape

into when it all gets too much.

'Did your father tell you that he tried to shoot me?' Mother said from inside.

I gave myself another blast and sucked it in.

'He said he was going to hand you over to me in this car park, in the middle of bloody nowhere. He snuck up behind me and pointed the stupid gun at me. But he's so damn clumsy, he tripped and shot his own leg.'

I was in eternal Haley hell, again. Who to believe? Mother? Dad? Which version of reality to choose and which to betray? I sucked steroids till I felt high.

'OK, Haley, listen up,' she said, 'I need you to be my eyes. I need you to assess and record every inch of this place for our escape.'

But I'd already done that and already knew this place was a fortress, so what was the point in even trying? Like with everything. I was just so confused.

What To Do When Attacked By A Large Prey Animal

People who engage in actions without focus are a danger to themselves and others. I was about to learn this lesson. You see, every safe house contains lethal elements and these are necessary for protection against external threats. The last thing survivalist groups need are new members wandering around aimlessly – like me. Lost and dreamy and stressed, in a 'fugue state' – and unleashing lethal shit.

So basically, I slunk around, worried that even if Dad was wrong about the pandemic, these nutcases could kill Ben, Mother and me anyway. I had to ask Dad what to do. No! No! Believe Mother instead. Ask her.

Analysis paralysis had kicked in. Where am I going? What am I doing? Who do I believe? Why? Why? I was just drifting round the barns trying to escape myself, like Ophelia or something, and I came across this little stone shed, hidden behind a mouldy sheet of plastic and with a bolted and padlocked door. When I peeked through a crack, it seemed to be full of massive rifles and bigger things.

I drifted on, tripping out, nowhere to go because I couldn't settle in 'our bedroom' and I really wanted to shake off creepy Danny.

I came across an enclosure inside one of the barns with a rusty old sign saying, *Keep Out*. I peered in and it seemed empty apart from some straw bales and chains, so I climbed in, thinking it a perfect place to be alone and think about what the hell I was going to do.

There was this stink like rotten meat, then this snarling came from the darkness behind me and this vast animal with cold eyes emerged from the dark, snarling. A huge, police-looking dog. It was easily my size and it seemed pretty hungry and bred to kill and there were big chewed bones beneath its claws.

'Good dog, nice doggy,' I said, backing away, but it was sniffing my bloody hand-bandage and drooling.

Important tip: When confronted by a lethal prey animal...

1. Don't scream.
2. Don't break eye contact and don't run. Both of these actions increase adrenaline in the prey animal.
3. Back away very slowly.
4. Ideally throw it a meaty snack to distract it.

I screamed and turned to run, but the monster leapt and I slid in the straw and its huge claws pinned me down. Its face inches from mine, dripping spit, its jaws creaking wide open, its tiny eyes bloody and cold.

Your life doesn't flash before your eyes. Massive teeth and dog breath do.

There was a sudden thud and the vast beast fell from me. I scrambled up and Danny was in the mud wrestling with the beast, its teeth round his arm. It moved too fast to even see, in a snarling blood frenzy. Danny screamed at it and punched it in the ear, the jaw, the eye, hit it with a stick.

'Run,' he yelled. 'Get help! NOW!'

But I was frozen to the spot. Danny pulled the dog's legs from under it, but it went for his throat. He punched its teeth and screamed.

Tip: If attacked by a large prey animal, what you should do is grab each of its front legs and yank them apart. This, with any luck, will break its ribs and puncture its lungs or heart. The problem is, you have to be very strong and this is hard to do when it is trying to rip your face off.

'Get Ray!' Danny screamed.

But Ray had already burst in with his shotgun and was upon us. Ray tried to take aim at the dog, but Danny's body kept getting in the way. I whimpered, 'Don't shoot, please, please!' cos he might hit Danny.

Danny screamed as the dog tore at the arm he'd put up to protect his face. Ray swung the gun one way, then the next, then he spun the gun handle round and beat the dog with it like a club. The dog yelped and went jaws for his jugular. Ray swung and bashed the dog over the skull with the gun handle. It made a sickening crack noise and the dog fell with a howl and lay in the mud next to Danny. Ray kicked the dog in the ribs five times and dragged Danny and me away, yelling.

'What the hell! You fucking idiots! Fasten the fucking thing back up again and let's hope it lives!' He kicked Danny in the leg and stormed off.

I stood there stupefied, staring at the dog's chest rising and falling. It was unconscious. Danny's arm was bleeding from many places. He hid his face, got to his feet and whispered, 'Maxi, poor Maxi.' He stumbled to his knees in the mud and took the dog's head in his hands, stroking it. It was such a sad sight; I wanted to apologise and I edged closer. 'Sorry, Maxi boy,' Danny said.

He heard me behind him and turned. 'What the hell were you

thinking?' he yelled. 'Maxi doesn't know any better. Get out of here!'

I stepped back in shame. I reached the corner of the barn and stared back at Danny and his comatose prey animal. Danny was kind of weeping. I guess I'd never heard a man cry before.

'You'll be OK, Maxi,' Danny kept saying. 'I won't let Ray shoot you.'

The noise had brought Meg and Dad out. They ran past me to Danny. Ben came out and hugged my leg in fear.

'Danny.' I said his name to myself and it seemed somehow noble. 'Danny,' I repeated, as Dad led me and Ben back inside.

I wanted to say sorry. I guess, corny as it sounds, he'd just saved my life, but I really wasn't cut out for all this intense crap.

If Disunity Spreads Within A Safe House, Mutiny Can Develop

If you take new people into your safe house then the following become problems:

1. You have extra mouths to feed and this depletes rations faster, throwing out all previous ration calculations.
2. If you break your original plans early into lockdown, it's bad for morale and bad for faith in the survival plan itself.
3. Any new person can spread dissent like a virus.
4. What is to stop other people in the group all demanding that their friends and relatives should be allowed into the safe house too?

These were basically the arguments that I over-heard among the adults in whispering conspiracy voices, in the eating room downstairs. 'She's been nothing but trouble!' Ray said, and this meant either me or Mother.

I snuck a peek. Meg and Ray were sat round the old oak table, the fire roaring behind them. There was a long shadow that must have been Kane. Dad wasn't there, and Meg dabbed some of that lint stuff on Ray's arm where he'd been bitten.

I ducked back and just listened. They seemed to be whispering behind Dad's back about me and Mother.

Ray growled, 'The dog today, what'll it be tomorrow? We can't go on like this. Total chaos. Might as well invite their aunties and grannies, then half the bloody city'll be here...'

'They'll come round, love,' Meg said. 'They just need a little time, we all did at first.'

There was a sound of a bottle being tipped and Ray hissed in pain.

Then Kane spoke, slowly, as if calculating an equation. 'I say put the mother back out, let her fend for herself, and the daughter too.'

'To where, the village?'

'The hills.'

'Don't be friggin' daft, they wouldn't last a night!' Meg said.

'I'm with Kane, no point being sentimental,' Ray said. 'What did Ed's book say? Eh? We've all left relatives behind. Danny won't see his granny again. We've all made sacrifices.'

It hit me then that I'd never see Nana and Papa Cooper or Nan Crowe again. And also that Kane really hated us. Actually, Kane maybe had some bigger issue about families, full stop, and she probably really resented being the third wheel caught between our family and Meg's.

'We're not fucking baby-sitters,' I heard her say. 'They've thrown the survival plan six days behind schedule.'

'Give me another day with their mum. I'll make her co-operate,' Meg said, trying to be the peace-maker. 'And the girl, yeah, she's a nightmare, but maybe this has done her some good, bit of a wake-up call, eh? We'll manage.'

I must have made a creaking noise then. Feet fumbled then Ray's voice was shouting, 'It's her! Bloody spying on us!' He leapt round into the stairwell and actually grabbed me with his huge stumpy hands, yanking my bandaged hand and I yelped in pain.

'Leave her alone, ya big oaf!' Meg yelled, and she pushed in-between us. 'Are you alright, love?' she said, her arms open to me. 'Poor lamb got a fright.'

'I was just looking for some water,' I stammered, totally lying, and they could tell.

'Maybe it would like to sleep in the wood shed with its mother?' Kane barked.

And I got this sense that she'd been one of those furious shaven-headed protesters who screamed in the streets that the nuclear family and babies were destroying the planet.

Anyway, so I kind of felt bad. Like I'd landed Dad in the shit, cos he was supposed to be their leader but had shown he was majorly weak when it came to us and Mother. His weakest links.

I went and got my glass of pretend water and they were all just silent staring at me, apart from Kane who was stroking her bald head with this huge commando knife and doing that involuntary tick of hers with her jaw. Then I walked back upstairs and I felt there was a major mutiny brewing. I pictured Kane slipping out in the night and slashing Mother's throat and disposing of the body and, like, not even telling us.

Accepting Your Weakness Can Make You Stronger

I never understood how recognising your weak points could make you tougher – generally, strong people just trample all over you. I was so messed up and I had to apologise to Danny for the shit with the dog. I figured if I didn't then that weird thing would happen where someone makes you feel guilty, and then you start to feel bad about yourself, and then you start to hate them for it.

I couldn't find him outside or in Dad's control room, or in any of the bedrooms I snuck round. I was about to give up when I noticed a stepladder leading up to a hole in the roof. I called his name. There was no reply so I climbed up.

It was a crazy little loft: you could see all the timbers and it had a V-shaped roof. There were dozens of aeroplanes hanging from threads, like in a kid's bedroom, but when I got up and bumped into one, I saw it was made of hand-carved wood not plastic. I may have said, 'Wow!'

Danny was in a corner, fastening a big bandage on his arm and he didn't turn to face me. He didn't tell me to fuck off, either, which I took as a plus.

I asked him, 'You OK? Were you hurt bad?' And I said some sorries, too.

There were lots of pictures of jets and guns pulled out from magazines, pinned to the wooden beams, and majorly sexist centrefolds of girls holding rifles, in bikinis with very large boobs. He bit the end off the bandage with his teeth and pinned it. He turned and said nothing, just stared at me.

'Cool place. You carve all these planes yourself? They're awesome.'

He shrugged. Keeping his distance. Flexing his mauled arm. He turned and his face was shy and I saw his cheek was cut.

'God, I'm really, really sorry,' I said. 'I know that sounds so crap but I'll just have to keep repeating it till it sounds better.'

He stared at me as if to say, your city life is a million miles away from my life.

'What was that thing you wanted to warn me about?' I asked.

He shook his head. 'Doesn't matter now.'

'No, tell me.'

'I just wanted to show you round, warn you about the dog and stuff,' he said, staring at the floor. 'Ray forgets how dangerous this place is for new folk. There's mantraps, too, snares and battery acid. That was all. But I guess you kind of found Maxi by yourself.'

'Oh! Sorry. Did the dog bite you really hard?' I asked, like a total doofus. 'It looks so sore!' I could see blood seeping through the gauze.

'I'll live,' he said.

How do you thank a guy for saving your life? I mean, seriously, without sounding like a lame damsel in distress. I had to try harder.

'Is Maxi your pet?' I asked.

He shook his head. 'Saved it from the Pet Rescue. They were going to put him to sleep anyway. He's from the military base where Ray used to work. Maxi's for emergencies – Ray has one command he can say and it'll rip your throat out.'

'Nice!' I said, then felt totally guilty for having sarcasm as a default setting. I edged in a bit and suddenly wanted to ask all these questions. Is there really a pandemic out there? Do you think my dad is insane? I grabbed one and asked, 'Why did your dad kick you?'

'Ray's not my dad.'

That was news to me. 'So what is he then?'

'A dick,' Danny said.

'My mother's a dick too, if it's any consolation,' I said.

When he smiled, it was with his eyes not his mouth. And he had that blood-smear on his cheek and that shy-but-strong look. Maybe I'd got him all wrong.

'My dad is a bit DC,' I added.

'You mean like electrics?' Danny asked. 'Or the rock band?'

And I was like, 'What? No. You never heard of DC before?'

And Danny shook his head in a way that made it clear that he was genuinely not winding me up.

'Wow,' I said. 'It's kind of embarrassing now, but it means "developmentally challenged". I know, it's a horrible thing to say and I was kind of just joking. You must think I'm a total knob.'

'Sorry? Like a door handle?' Danny said with massive degrees of total sincerity.

I guess I was blushing then and I couldn't work out if he was being 'post-cynical' or if he was, like, a 'noble savage'. 'How come you never heard words like that at school?' I asked. Then it dawned on me: 'Wait, didn't you go to school?'

'Nuh,' he said. 'They threw me out. Way back. Anyway, school's just State brainwashing.'

The way he looked at me made me feel fake and shallow and I had this weird urge to touch his bandaged forearm and ask him what it felt like to be a real person but that would have sounded mean.

'Shit. What's wrong with me?' I asked. My head was spinning with stupid feelings, and I suddenly had to cry, but I couldn't, so I just yelled, 'FUCK!' Then I yelled it again, at his pictures of booby women with guns, at my crazy mother in the woodshed, at the end of the world, at my insane father and at Danny's killer dog.

FUCK!

There was touch. I flinched. He led me to sit on the edge of his bed. 'You're going to be OK,' he said. 'This must all be really hard to adapt to.' And he put his arm round me and I let go to the warm strength of it. I stared at him through my semi-tears, right there sitting on his actual man-bed.

'Am I?' I asked. 'Going to be OK, I mean. Like, how the hell would you know?'

'I dunno,' he shrugged. 'You're stronger than you think.'

I was staring at his lips and was suddenly sick of being cynical. 'No, no, no, you don't know me,' I said. 'I'm about as strong as a … as a seriously not strong thing, and I have practically no friends in school and not even a boyfriend.'

Why did I say that?

His dark eyes widened and then he got up. 'You can stay here for a bit,' he said. 'Just pull the ladder up and no one'll bother you. I've got to go and get ready for night patrol.'

He didn't try to take advantage or make a smart-assed jibe like the boys at school would've. He left without another word. The hole in the floor was almost too small for his shoulders as he climbed down.

I sat on his random bed staring at his poster of this Barbie bitch with a vast assault rifle. Then I sort of lay down and there was something soothing about the smell of his pillow, like animals and candles. I couldn't help it but I closed my eyes and had this weird mini-dream where he came back into the room and didn't even notice that I was there and got undressed and climbed into the bed, beside me. And I felt his warmth right there and his hand on my hip, and I woke feeling hot and bothered and guilty and icky because only a few hours before I had utterly hated him.

Man! I climbed down the ladder and told myself I was screwed up, like my parents. Maybe sick with cabin fever or Stockholm syndrome, or some such.

At least I'd discovered one thing: if Mother tried to escape, she'd have to kill a lethal dog first. That was something.

The Point Of No Return

How To Tell When The Tipping Point Arrives

In every crisis there is a tipping point at which things will either swing back to normal or swing into cataclysm. There's a whole chapter on this in Dad's survival guide. Basically, the tipping point is the power grid.

If contaminated people can be contained and the power grid stays on in the first two weeks of pandemic panic, there is still hope for society to hold together. But if the power grid goes down and stays down then that's the mother of all feedback loops and the pandemic will spiral out of control.

Dad said we came super-close to grid failure and martial law during the last pandemic, but we drew back from the edge and the government hid the evidence on how close we'd come.

But, this time around, Dad thought the pandemic-panic would be so much larger, because:

1. No one would be able to endure the lockdowns, shortages and curfews that happened last time.
2. They would not trust or follow their government's laws anymore.

There would be an insane rush, every man for themselves, and in this hysteria the supply chains of food and electricity would break down. With no power, mob hysteria would vastly increase and, with it, contamination. We're talking panic-hoarding and people fighting each other in supermarkets and petrol stations. And this happening in every town, in every city, in every country, spreading contagion. With the grid down the following problems would arise:

1. There would be no power for cooking or heating.

2. Elevators wouldn't work, water pumps at reservoirs would shut down, and all hospitals would be forced to close, as they have back-up generators but only enough emergency fuel for two days.
3. Roads would be blocked because of carjacking and siphoning of fuel. Fuel supplies would not be able to get through, which leads to another feedback loop resulting in hospital closures.
4. Hospitals closures then increase infection rates and mob panic, riots and fires, which in turn cause more destruction of the power grid.

Without power, the nation descends into a bloody chaos that, in turn, ensures the spread of the virus. In this way, the extreme fear-reaction to the virus is the very thing that ensures its exponential growth. It's all about power.

How To Tell if Your Mother Is Still Contaminated

I wasn't so much scared of Mother having the virus, as I was that she was going to contaminate everyone with her anger.

Fingers woke me, a whisper in my ear: 'Shh, you'd better come.' It was Meg, and I was in a daze. Dad's survival guide fell from my bunk bed, throwing pages everywhere. I asked her what was wrong: had the electricity grid gone down?

'What? No, no, no,' she said. 'It's your mum.'

I touched Benji in his bunk to see if he was OK, cos I was worried he might have been infected, but he squirmed and seemed fine. I was cold and ache-y from my cuts and bruises, and what I'd read the night before followed me like a lonely ghost as I pulled on Meg's big boob-stretched woolly jumper in the freezing air.

Meg rushed me down the stairs and out into the Arctic wind. It was a dull grey dawn and as she led me through sucking mud to the woodshed I had my second psychic paranoia that something horrible had happened to Mother in the night. I thought of the tools in the woodshed. Maybe she'd tried to get out with an axe and cut herself and bled out all night.

Meg told me to shh and made a sign for me to listen. 'Hear that?'

And from inside the shed came this weird sound of Mother singing. Like, a goofy old pop song from the last century. Meg's face said, insane?

I called out, 'Mother, you OK in there?'

Just then Danny arrived. 'Hey, your mum OK?' he asked.

Meg said, 'Shh, she's singing!'

'What song?' Danny asked.

'That's not the frickin point,' I shouted, and Meg waved him away.

'Mother, Mother,' I called out, knocking. 'Can you hear me? Are you sick? You're seriously freaking us out!'

Meg fished out her keys from her vast hippie cleavage. 'Tell her we're going to open the door, but no funny business this time.'

I repeated this word-for-word and added, 'Please don't hit anyone this time. Please, Mother.'

Meg undid the lock and there was no smash-of-door-into-face or log-bashed-onto-fingers. Meg lifted her torch. 'You OK, love? You look awfully cold.'

Mother stepped out, dishevelled, with woodchips in her hair and stains all over her formerly lovely designer clothes, this hippie blanket round her shoulders. Her usual Kate Winslet-y good looks were scrunched up as she squinted in the pale light. She stretched and walked straight past me and Meg, through the mud, toward the farmhouse. She shot me a withering glance and put her finger to her mouth to 'Shh' me before I could even speak. Then, completely unfazed, and to no one in particular, her teeth chattering, she said, 'I need a hot shower, a proper bed and some clean clothes. I think I'm done with quarantine now.'

Hippie Meg immediately scurried off, subserviently, saying, 'Yes, of course, I'll take care of it all.'

Up ahead, Dad came to the farmhouse door and propped his tall frame up within it. He was measuring Mother, assessing degrees of damage limitation. Another massive cringe moment was upon us.

'Oh God,' I whispered to no one but the wind, 'please let there not be fighting again!'

Dad filled the doorway and didn't move as Mother approached. She stopped before him and raised a hand. I closed my eyes, waiting for the sound of her slapping his face, but I heard nothing. She raised one finger and shook it, to communicate 'no talking', then her hand made the sign of 'let me pass'.

Some silent territorial dominance ritual was enacted. Dad stepped out of her way and, with that, the negotiation of our new life had taken place in no language I could understand. From inside I heard little fast feet and Ben's excited voice shouting, 'Mummy! Mummy's not contaminated anymore. Yay!' Even as he jumped into her arms and she held him tight, Mother still didn't say a word.

She shot me a look then, in the doorway, loaded with recriminations. Like she'd read my mind and knew I'd totally failed to commit in any way to her plan to escape.

How To Spot The Weakest Link

Mother showered and was shown to our room, and I was set to the task of pumping up an inflatable bed as an act of penance while she lay on my bottom bunk. This was to be hers from now on, I insisted, as a token sacrifice. I was overdosed with guilt and didn't know where to start with my apologies.

Her silence was ominous and Ben kept obliviously bouncing on the inflatable bed, like a doofus, as I struggled with the foot pump. I yelled at him to stop but Mother silenced me with that same cold hand gesture.

I waited for a classic judgement from her, but she didn't comment on the lack of a rug on the bare wooden floor, on the spider-webbed window or the bare light bulb and the army surplus beds. I suspected maybe even just a critique of my pumping skills as a way of communicating that I was a worthless, weak-willed, two-faced traitor. But she'd left her repertoire of put-downs in the woodshed.

Mother let Ben witter on about how Danny was going to teach him how to shoot birds with a slingshot, and how you can make one with elastic from your underpants. She massaged her temples. 'Benjamin, go to the bathroom and brush your teeth,' she said suddenly. 'Your breath is stinky.'

Ben ran off, attempting to sniff his own mouth. Mother had these astute techniques to get people out of rooms before a character assassination and I cowered.

'I tried to get you out,' I pled. 'I really tried, but they wouldn't listen to me.'

'Quiet,' she said. 'I'm going to say one thing to you and one thing only.'

'OK, sorry.'

'The weakest link,' she pronounced, and I repeated the name of the TV show as a question and added that there was no TV signal here.

'Don't be idiotic, Haley. We pretend to fit in with these nutcases, to be nice, very grateful and interested in how it all works. Work out where all the keys are kept and where the alarms are. If there are any traps. And please try to find my phone, the morons took it off me.' She took a breath to compose herself. 'We pretend to be helpful little eager-beavers and that's how we find the weakest link. It might be that horrid hippie or that schizo woman or the smelly young man.'

'Danny?'

She turned and scrutinised me. 'Yes, maybe we can trick him into getting us the keys for one of the vehicles and maybe a weapon. Do I have your promise that you'll help, properly this time, that you won't be a tell-tale-tit and go running to your father?'

I shrugged and said, 'Your wish is my command,' but it came across as sarcastic, so I said sorry about that too.

But now I was more conflicted than ever because if her plan was to escape back home and Dad and was right, then she'd be leading us back into the heart of the pandemic. And she wanted me to deceive Danny and we'd only just started being friends. How come she always ruined all my friendships?

'They're clearly not very bright,' she said. 'And don't worry about your father, I can wind him round my finger. But don't tell Benjamin. And Haley…?'

'Yes, mother?'

'Don't disappoint me this time,' she muttered.

I realised then that I'd actually forgotten to say one thing to her. Like, 'Oh my God, Mother, you're OK, I'm so glad to see you.' And how I hadn't even hugged her.

Mother closed her eyes and did that hand movement again that meant to leave her in silence. Like, now.

Then I heard a gunshot beyond the wall, like it was another metaphor or something.

How To Face A Fresh Kill

Learning about killing, skinning and butchering was, unfortunately, the only thing I could think of to express 'taking an interest' in the workings of the safe house, while I gathered mother's secret intel.

Ray had shot a deer that morning and I saw him return with the carcass. It was brown-skinned, with a lovely white tail, and its neck all floppy and bobbing on the back of the quad bike as he drove past the window I was staring out of. It was a little Bambi and the brute males Ray and Danny laughed and applauded each other on their carnage. I didn't want to watch but I was morbidly drawn to it and thought I could pick up some useful escape information for Mother.

Ray hauled the dead Bambi out, tied its back legs with metal twine, then hung it upside down by its hoofs from a vast hook in the barn doorway. The poor Bambi's head swung by Ray's feet, inches from the ground, and he shouted instructions to Danny, who came back with a metal bucket and what looked like a box cutter. Ray nodded for Danny to proceed and held the head for him.

Survival Tip: Usual city-girl levels of squeamishness are no longer any use to you in a safe house. Getting used to gore is part of learning about the cycle of death and life. So if you're mega-girly, probably skip to the next section.

I couldn't believe it but Danny actually sliced through the Bambi's neck in one big swipe and the blood fell like a sudden sheet into the bucket and all over his feet. For some reason him and redneck Ray were patting each other on the back and in that moment I don't think I've ever hated anyone more.

Then Danny covered his nose and gagged as Ray took the box cutters and sliced down the length of the body. A white sort of bag appeared through the brown hair, then he sliced through bag, and then – oh my actual God. Ray reached in with his hands and tore the sides of the chest apart and there were what I guess you'd call the innards. It's majorly not what you'd think. He pulled out what looked like yellow, pink and greyish purple bags and severed them from their attaching stringy stuff with the knife. I was set to barf but I couldn't take my eyes off it because there were miles and impossible miles of what looked like sausages and a white thing in there the size of a tennis ball, and hardly any blood.

Who knew organs were all colour coded?

The macho brutes left the deer shell hanging to drip and I was in a state of shock as I stared at the steam rising from the bucket. Deer had only been a lovely landscape-y screensaver for me before.

When I was sure the male brutes weren't coming back, I crept out and looked at its upside down face. It was so pretty with these long eyelashes, like a Sixties supermodel. And I had to tell myself that the deer wasn't hung there on purpose to warn me, Ben and Mother what would happen to us if we ever tried to escape.

There was the crackle of a walkie-talkie from Ray's quad bike and Kane's voice said, 'Rover 2 to Sierra Hotel. Security, Zone 4 secure, over and out.' And I shuddered, thinking that if we ever did escape from the farmhouse, we'd still have to get past Kane at the perimeter fence with her gun.

The huge dark eyes of the deer drew me in and I saw myself reflected upside down.

Conflict Avoidance Does Not Resolve Conflicts

In the small space of safe houses, it's impossible to hide conflicts for long. They are like dirt in a wound, and it is better to be cut out than left festering inside.

I was pretty fearful of the coming cat 'n' dog fight between Mother and Dad and I was hoping they'd keep eluding each other indefinitely. Dad had been doing a pretty fine job of it, hiding himself away in his cubbyhole, claiming he was 'gathering evidence on the spread of the pandemic'. He actually seemed scared of bumping into Mother. He was scurrying around, practically whispering, 'Is the coast clear?' The farmhouse was small though, so the confrontation of the century was inevitable.

Two hours later it began.

Dad sat at the head of the table, with his back against the stone wall, like some clan chief. Next to him sat Ray – he and Dad were deep in discussion about the failing wind turbine or something. Next to Ray was Danny, and across from Danny was Ben, because Ben was now semi-officially Danny's younger sibling or something. Danny was telling Ben about bird-killing catapults and was throwing me these sidelong 'concerned' glances. Meg sat at the bottom, so she was the clan queen, and I sat next to Ben on the newcomers' side, on this orange school chair. I had my back to the door, so I couldn't see why things had suddenly gone silent.

'Justine,' Meg said, 'come on in. I hope you're feeling better. Have a seat, and some stew.'

I turned and saw Mother's silent shadow approach. She was wearing another one of Meg's vast hippie sweaters and camouflage fatigue trousers, plus she had zero make-up on, and her post-teary panda make-up streaks had gone which made her eyes look small and wary. She stood just behind me and waited, silent. Dad's fork screeched on his plate. I waited for the moment when Mother would scream at him.

But she was weirdly cool. Dad stopped eating and lowered his eyes. Awkwardnesses multiplied in the dusty air. Mother was an expert – she could sit out any humiliating situation calmly.

'Oh, sorry,' Meg said, 'you need a seat! Silly me,' and she made to get up and offer Mother her own. But that would have been hellish, Mother at the other end of the table from Dad, like a king and queen in a showdown!

'Take my seat,' I said to Mother, 'and my stew, I'm not really hungry.'

'I don't need to sit,' Mother said with massive composure.

'Danny, get Justine a seat. Go and fetch one from upstairs,' Meg said. Nervousness was infecting her every muscle. Danny got to his feet and Meg said, 'Sorry, we should have got another chair for you, Justine. Sorry, caught me on the hop.'

'I'd rather not sit,' Mother repeated.

Danny shot me a look and left and Meg was tongue-tied. 'Danny,' she shouted, 'the foldable chair! I'm really awfully sorry,' she said to Mother. 'Please, I feel so bad, take my seat, I insist,' and she got to her feet. 'Are you warm enough, is there anything I can get you? It's venison hotpot … Are you a vegetarian? God… I could get you some mash and beans. Sorry.'

'It's OK,' Mother replied. 'Really. I'm not hungry.'

I was cringing so bad my teeth were grinding. I put my head in my hands and stared up at Dad through my fingers. He was rubbing his temples and pushing his food round his plate. The fear of impending humiliation spread faster.

'Danny, for God's sake!' shouted Meg. 'The collapsible one in the back room! Don't take all day. Sorry,' she said, 'didn't mean to swear in front of the little one.'

Ray got up suddenly, scraping his chair. 'Right,' he said, 'that engine won't fix itself.'

My father's hand shot out and tried to hold Ray back. He must have been scared that Mother would sit next to him in Ray's empty space. Ray whispered something to Dad and left the table.

'Where is that boy?' Meg said. 'He'd forget his head if it weren't screwed on!' And she went off too, supposedly to search for Danny and the chair.

That just left me and Ben and Dad seated, and Mother still standing with three empty seats she could have taken. The others gone, leaving the nuclear family alone to have its explosion.

Still Mother did not move or speak.

I stared at Dad. He was wringing his hands. I wanted to run, too, but I had no excuse.

'Look, Justine,' Dad blurted out, 'I can sense that you're angry and I know you don't want to talk about the pandemic right now and I'm sorry that things…'

'What's that you're eating, darling?' Mother said to Ben, totally ignoring Dad.

Dad tried again. 'It must be very hard for you and … but I think it's important that we move beyond blame. And like you always say, be practical and…'

'Is that really deer you're eating?' Mother asked Ben, blanking Dad. Ben launched off on how yummy venison was with jam and Mother sat down beside him in Meg's seat. She was now at the opposite end of the table from Dad.

He pushed his plate away and scraped his chair back. 'Look, if we have to have this stupid argument, I'd rather it wasn't in front of the children…' He was twitching with anxiety and I blushed so hard I thought I'd choke. For the record, I live for the avoidance of awkwardnesses.

'Are there any greens?' Mother asked Ben and she took his fork and poked around.

'For God's sake, you're impossible!' Dad roared and stormed off.

I had to marvel at Mother's toxic genius. She had some high-level Zen bitchiness that didn't even require words. Some feminine power mystique that I so lacked.

There we were, the three of us, at a kitchen table. Ben gorging himself, me sick with nervous tummy and Mother poking at food, critically. Just like home.

'The weakest link,' she whispered to herself. And some other medical-sounding words.

'What do you mean?'

But she was silent, pondering, staring at the empty seats.

It was all getting me panicky so I cleared away the plates and scooted Ben up to bed. When I came back, Mother was still staring at the table and chairs.

'What? Tell me. Stop being so mysterious!'

'Your father is the weakest link,' she said. 'We'll deal with him first. It's good. Very good.'

She was smiling to herself and I didn't know what to say or think.

'Shh,' she hissed, 'someone's coming. Remember our plan, look for weaknesses!'

Danny stepped out of the stairwell and stood there holding this collapsible chair, wondering, no doubt, why the hell everyone else had run away.

How To Deceive People By Showing An Interest In Them

These are Mother's strategies for how to win your enemies over:

1. Show a huge interest in their really boring shit. Like:
    a. The composting toilet, which turns human crap into plant food.
    b. The rainwater filter made of oil drums and sand.
    c. The seesaw that used the up and down motion to saw through huge logs.
2. Tell the people you are tricking that everything they say is 'fascinating', 'amazing' and 'really interesting'. Vary this with

'I had no idea' and 'tell me more'.

3. Get them to do all the talking by asking them questions. 'How does this work?' etc. then repeat with praise from Number 2. People will generally think you're a great person if you encourage them to talk about their unique selves and their passions for infinitely boring shit.

4. When they're talking, they will invariably let slip some procedural fact that could be your key out.

Already, Mother was putting phase one of her escape plan into action. It was excruciating watching her being so phoney with Meg, Ray and Danny and them being taken in by her. You could see on their faces that they thought they'd got her all wrong. Marvelling at how adaptable and friendly and sensible she actually was. What a nice woman!

Mother was impressively skilled when it came to kill-or-be-killed. Her smile showed no trace of the scheme going on behind her eyes.

Meg was the initial sucker. Mother stood next to her, enquiring about the large metal tank by the outer wall of the stable, peering inside, asking, 'So, what's this?'

'It's our mains water storage tank,' Meg said proudly. 'In a day or so, if the power goes off, this'll be all the mains water we have for drinking.'

'How fascinating,' Mother said, without any apparent hint of irony. 'How so?'

Meg grinned, happy to educate. 'The tap water gets pumped from the reservoir, forty miles out. When the electric goes down there'll be no more pumping.'

I heard Danny's booming laughter. He was ten feet away with a large collection of bottles lined up by the wall, showing Ben how to fill them with the hose. 'Tell them about the sewage, Mum,' Danny called over.

Mother acted 'very interested'.

'Well,' Meg said, scratching her mass of matted ginger hair, 'when the electricity stops the sewage from the city starts backing up in the pipes, then flows backwards polluting the reservoirs.'

Danny shouted, 'Pee coming out your taps!'

Ben giggled. 'Euuuw! Is there poo, too?'

For a second Danny blushed and I flashed back to my little secret snooze-dream in his bed. Meg snapped me out off it. 'You wouldn't be laughing if you got the virus from a contaminated water supply! Think of all those poor souls out there.'

I really wondered if Meg had once been a nurse. She looked like the type who 'cared for other people'. Maybe she'd seen too much horror in the last pandemic and that was why she joined with Dad.

'What happens when this barrel runs dry?' Mother asked. I could practically hear her wheels of deception turning.

'We ration it,' Meg said. 'Plus that's why Danny's bottling all we can get from the water system before it goes down. After that, we have the rain-harvesting tanks.'

And she pointed out the system of buckets, wires and hoses that ran round the roof gutters. Rainwater then had to be filtered to remove bugs and bacteria, Meg said, and she told us the stages:

1. First, filter it through sand buckets.
2. Boil it.
3. Pass it through the UV light source in the dark shed.

'Amazing … Ingenious!' Mother declared, and Meg was so pleased that Mother had learned something. 'But don't most farms have water wells somewhere on the property?' Mother asked.

'There's a stream about half a mile out, by the perimeter fence.'

Bingo, a spark ignited in Mother's eye. 'Really, could you show me?' she asked. 'In case of emergencies. Don't want the children to be dehydrated.'

Meg seemed amazingly unaware of Mother's manipulations. A trip to the perimeter fence might be all it would take to escape. But what would Mother do about Meg once we got there? Beat her up? Tie her up? I groaned and Mother silenced me.

Meg led the way to the big iron gates. I checked over my shoulder, totally gobsmacked that Dad hadn't caught us red-handed and that Meg could be so seriously dumb. Where was Dad hiding anyway? Meg pulled out her big bunch of keys from her camouflage dungarees and Mother's eyeballs lit up. There were about ten keys in the bunch, all shapes and sizes. I was silently praying, 'Jesus, Mother, don't snatch them now, please, you'll get beaten up, they'll lock you in the shed again, or worse!'

Meg reached for the lock and sighed. 'Oh, I'd forget my head if it wasn't screwed on!' She called back to Danny, who was now chasing Ben with the hose to screams of giggles. 'Danny! Stop playing silly buggers, and go and ask Ray for the big double keys, would ya?' Meg turned to Mother and said, 'Ray must have them after being out on night patrol last night. He'll still be having a nap.'

Then Mother called out to Danny, but her over-familiar tone betrayed her. 'Yes, Danny, go and get the keys, please.'

Meg stood back and scanned Mother up and down. She'd blown it. 'Actually, love,' Meg called to Danny, 'let Ray sleep, we'll do this another day.'

Danny just stood there in the mud, looking ruggedly oblivious to Mother's mind games. He wasn't super-cynical, like everyone else I knew in the city. You could tell it in his moves: like his body had to tell the truth.

So, I guess I was staring at him again.

I felt eyes on me and turned. Mother was observing me and Danny. Like, in her mind, my only interest in him was that he was the weakest link and so he deserved to be deceived to further her plans for freedom. That made me feel pretty unclean, actually.

How And Why To Save Water
Fresh, uncontaminated and purified water is very important. Here is water advice:

1. Hoard as many glass bottles and jars as you can before the pandemic.
2. Save and store as much tap water as you can, as the mains supply can quickly become contaminated and will be cut off.
3. Take care handling any water containment objects made of glass. If you break them, you will never be able to replace them.

Danny, Ben and me filled a hundred bottles with the tap water from a hose, as Mother watched over me, scheming. I was conflicted, watching Danny be so brotherly to my little Ben. For a second I thought, he'll be a good dad for some kid, someday. And then, where the hell did that come from?

I was getting the melancholies. Some bottles were old wine ones, some for soda, all kinds with their labels still on. Coca Cola, Fanta, Pinot Grigio, Rioja. So, yeah, it gave me the melancholies about all the things I was missing.

Converse, manga, Gummy Bears, Lorde, Nivea, *To Kill a Mockingbird*, YouTube, Philadelphia cheese, putting my toes in the cold sea, the smell of really old books, hugging Shanna. Bitching together and pointing at boys, garage sales with boxes of junk that was once cool, like Cabbage Patch dolls and fluorescent hot pants and rollerblades, Sylvia Plath and the sound of traffic outside my window, that old lady in the neighbourhood in the electric wheelchair who smoked as she sped along and so looked like a steam train, the spooky silence in libraries, National Geographic vids about Neptune and other planets, stroking Jason's dog, Pavlov, and hearing Mother sing ancient songs while she stacked the dishwasher, like she used to when I was tiny.

I heard a voice. 'Pass me the green ones, would you?'

'What?' I looked up and I was back in reality again and it was Danny. I said sorry and handed him some bottles and our fingers touched and I felt a shudder.

'You OK?' he asked.

I felt pretty desolate as I helped put the corks into the recycled bottles lined up on the mossy concrete by the farmhouse wall, refilled with tap water that would stop one day soon. I looked up at Danny, so deftly hitting the corks into the bottle tops. His movements were strangely swift and accurate, as if he owned his actions, as if it didn't matter to him that the world was possibly ending. The bandage started falling off his arm and I saw the red swollen tooth marks from the guard dog. I hissed, 'Ouch!' and felt a pain in my own bandaged hand.

'What's wrong?' he asked, and he was on his feet beside me.

'No,' I said, 'not me – you!' I pointed, and he saw his loose bandage and fastened it tighter again. He said thanks and smiled at me, then he got back to corking the bottles.

'Can we smash them now?' a little voice said. Ben was holding two filled bottles above his head, with a devilish face. 'Hey, put that down!' Danny laughed, like a big brother. 'You could knock your big sister out with that!' Ben giggled and I realised my poor little bro really did think he was still on a vaventure.

Get Reliable Intel Before It's Too Late

In a pandemic, it's important to ask: Where is my intelligence coming from and do I trust the source? Because so many governments lied and covered up last time around.

I didn't know who to believe, on my puny little family level. It felt like I was being pulled into two pieces, and my chest pain was worse than the usual asthma allergies stuff. So I returned to Dad's cubbyhole later that night.

He had a very big rifle, lying against one of his busted TVs and he said, 'I've asked Kane to train me for perimeter duty, and I have to rush.' I could tell he was using it as a way to stay as far away from Mother as possible. And maybe even away from me, too. Maybe Mother was right and he was a coward.

'Dad?' I stood there staring at him fastening his military boots with long laces. A pistol sat beside his dead TV. 'Dad?' Then it was like he'd read my mind again.

'I know, Hale-Bopp,' he said, 'and you're right to ask. I did promise you your evidence, but I'm sorry, we've been so busy, I couldn't find a decent signal. Not yet. Just fragments of talk, wire-buzz, panic speculation. It's mostly market speak. Governments blaming each other as a way to distract attention away from their lack of a pandemic survival plan. I managed to get online for few minutes on dial-up, and got some text, but no audio. The US is threatening to attack China, Russia is threatening the US – you know, the blame-game, the circular firing squad.'

He showed me a page of computer data but it was way over my particular head.

'What about riots? You said there'd be riots. Like, is our house OK? Are there strangers in it? I'd rather know, I'm not a stupid kid.'

'I'm going to go out to the perimeter fence,' he said, 'to check the telephone wires, OK?' He touched my chin and smiled. 'Believe me, this bothers me even more than you. I should have planned better for the internet breakdown, and the government information blackout is much worse than I thought. Still, we can't put our plan into action until we know exactly the state of play out there.'

He grabbed a hokey-looking radio with a wind-up handle and an old laptop, and stuck them into his army bag along with some more tools and a spaghetti mess of cables. He asked me to carry his mini-satellite dish for him and I helped him lug it all out to the quad bike. The dish had a handle he'd welded on from a frying pan. For an instant he was back to being my dad the madcap inventor.

I'd asked for hard evidence but he gave me a soft smile. 'Believe me' was one of his alternative versions of 'trust me'. Then Meg opened the gate for him, and he was out into No Man's Land.

How To Turn Everyday Domestic Objects Into Escape Tools And Weapons

I was tormenting myself in my bunk and heard Mother creeping in. I pretended to be asleep and out of my fake-closed eye I watched her pull a tool from the front of her trousers.

She whispered, 'I found a pair of secateurs, we'll use them as fence-cutters.' Then she took other clunky things out of her clothes and stashed them under the bunkbed. One looked like a little kitchen peeling knife and the other was a bit of broom handle.

Wow, I thought, innate IKEA survivalist drive.

'And I found a map,' she said. 'If I'm right then we're not as far from a main road as I thought. Haley, you asleep?'

I squeezed my eyes tight and tried to block out her schemes.

I was more lost than ever. Was she totally deluded, or was Dad? Couldn't she just be sad about all this for a moment? Was she actually hiding from the horrors of the pandemic by just doing what she always did and keeping herself mega-busy? Like – what did Dad call it? – re-arranging the deckchairs on the *Titanic*.

Mother shook my shoulder. 'Haley, wake up, I've been thinking about that deer, it must have got in somehow. So there must be a hole in the outer fence, if we could just find out where.'

I mumbled to leave me alone but she wouldn't.

'And that boy, Danny,' she said. 'After your dad, he's definitely the next weakest link. I've seen the way he looks at you.'

I was like, 'What the actual fuck?'

'Oh don't be so naïve, Haley, and don't swear,' she said. 'Boys his age are all the same. It's good. We can exploit that.'

'Mother!'

'Shh,' she hissed, 'don't wake Benjamin. OK, so here's the plan, I need you to lead Danny on, so that he can help us escape.'

'What?!' I whispered. 'Are you my pimp now?'

'You're going to trick him into showing us where the weapons are. Offer him a kiss and maybe he'll even join us.'

'Christ, Mother, no way!' I told her. 'Just stop talking, stop talking!'

I was disgusted with her. I told her I needed a pee, a walk, some fresh air, whatever. I told her to take my bunk and go to sleep. I didn't wait for her to reply, I just had to get away from her manic scheming. Out. Well, as far as out was.

You Must Believe In One Single Plan For Survival, Not Two

Everyone needs to believe in one story-for-life. Because if you don't, you'll be adrift, with no belief and no goal. This state of aimlessness, Dad says, began with the collapse of our faith in religion, but it's been exploited by consumerism. Most of us wander around bedazzled and blind, unable to make the most basic choices. This, Dad said, made the pandemic inevitable.

I stared at the moon through the bathroom skylight. My feet were cold on the tiles. I peed in the dark. I drew a house in condensation on the window. I couldn't get the big question out of my head. Who to believe?

I crept along the corridors and stood before Danny's ladder and there was a light on above. I waited, and thought twice about climbing. I ascended and found him lying on the floor and gave him a fright. 'Shh, everyone's sleeping, come up,' he said and threw a shirt on his bare chest. He'd been doing pull-ups on this cringe-y bike handlebar fastened to his attic beams and his veins were all standy-outy.

I plonked myself down on the edge of his bed with a deflated sigh.

'You're struggling,' he said.

'Yeah, it's my 'rents,' I said and he looked baffled. 'I mean my parents. Soz.'

Danny hung his towel over the handlebar, not like he was embarrassed by it, more in a totally Zen way. 'You want a Coke?' he said. 'I have a secret stash.'

'Wow, hard drugs,' I said. 'Sure.' I was trying to work him out. He had a big book called *Zen* and another said *Nietzsche and Nihilism* on this one solitary shelf and a bunch of what looked like diaries.

He was literally from another era.

'Don't you have any music?' I asked and he mumbled, 'Not any recordings if that's what you mean, but I have a banjo.' He rummaged around under his bed and I had to lift my feet to make way for his huge back.

'Maybe we shouldn't,' he said from underneath. 'I mean, the Coke … the caffeine'll probably keep you up all night.'

'Wow,' I said sarcastically, 'you're a real party animal!'

He decided we should share the aforementioned carbonised sugar drink, because of rations, and we sat there for a bit sharing sips, and me staring at his banjo. How could he be a Zen hillbilly? He made no sense. I wondered how he could be so comfortable with silence and just stare into space, and I felt my stupid head wanting to say a thousand totally trivial things to him, then telling itself to shut up. Then I remembered 'the world'.

'It's just not fair,' I said to him. 'Now it's not just "choose my mother over my dad", it's "choose her version of reality over his". I mean is the world collapsing out there, or not? Mother wants me to believe her, but I can't bring myself to betray Dad. It's like she's saying to me, "And when you choose my side, Haley, you also have to never ever see your dad ever again!"'

Danny somehow seemed the only person in the world I could talk to. He coiled his legs into a Buddha pose, and his leg muscles were massive and I found myself staring at them while I went on.

'I mean, how do I choose what's real and not? Do I agree with Mother just because I like the sound of her world better than … than this…'

Danny was playing with the bandage on his arm and watching me carefully. I passed him the Coke and he took it and set it on the side unit.

'I mean, is it a personality contest? Do I just do what Ben does and choose the parent who promises ice cream? Maybe the one that's telling me the truth is the one who's less fun to be with, right? Right?'

'Do you … want to know my opinion?' Danny said, and I realised that yes, I really did, but first I needed to get more off my chest.

'You know, this started way back. I'm talking, forget the pandemic; I mean, who had the comfiest sofa? Who made the best soup? Who had the best jokes? Who made the best Lego animals? Who had the most channels on TV? Who gave the best hugs? Mother versus Dad. I mean, why bother even trying to love if you're going to have to cut it into two pieces and spend all your life comparing the size of the portions?'

This surge of rage went through me and his hand touched mine and it felt OK, so I let him hold my hand and he was strong and gentle, all at once. I had some primal need and let my head fall into the hollow between his chest and shoulder.

Then, somehow, I was sobbing and saying, 'It's not fair, why do I have to choose? Why, why? You're the only person I can talk to in the whole world, and is the frickin world even there anymore?'

It was all pretty melodramatic, actually. He stroked my hair and I felt his stubble on my forehead and I did the whole hetero shivers routine. I curled into him and he moved his hand from my shoulder to the small of my back and I could feel this strength moving through my skin as his fingers spread across my spine. I had this total urge: kiss him!

'Wait, wait, wait,' I said, pulling away. 'Sorry, Jesus!' Was Mother actually controlling me with psychic powers? I stood and straightened my clothes, which I only then realised were merely a very long hippie Meg T-shirt and my undies. 'How old are you?' I asked, randomly, to hide my embarrassment, and I made myself stare at him really hard.

'Seventeen,' he said. 'What's that got to do with anything?'

'Well,' I said, 'I'm not even sixteen and everything is so messed up and people are dying from the virus and rioting and you don't seem very upset about it.' I was pacing. 'Look,' I said, 'I need you to tell me straight up, like, is this apocalypse total horseshit?'

I realised it was a dumb-ass question because his eyes already had the answer. 'Your father is a great man,' he said calmly. 'You should trust him. If it wasn't for Ed, my mum would probably have died of a drug overdose or I'd have been taken away from her.'

'What? For real? How come?' I was utterly confused and he was silent. 'Never mind, look,' I said, 'thanks for your advice, I'm sorry about barging in and unloading and the kiss and everything but …'

'The kiss?' he said, with a wry smile. 'What kiss?'

I stepped out of the room blushing and cringing. 'Forget I said that – none of this happened, OK? Sorry, I hope I didn't wake anyone. Sorry for disturbing you and about your dog and my mother and yours and everything.'

I climbed down his ladder, fast.

'Goodnight, Haley,' he said in a low slow voice, and a shudder ran through me and my pants felt cold because they were actually moist. God, I hate that word.

Even after I'd tiptoed back along the corridor to my bedroom and onto the squeaking blow-up mattress, taking care not to wake Mother, I could still feel his voice, and it didn't seem to come from the past. It was as if, one day, years from now, Danny and me would be the last ones and he'd say those same words to me as we lay together. 'Goodnight, Haley.'

Weird.

How To Plan An Escape

Deceive People Who Care for You

Mother's master plan went like this:

1. She would 'thin out the numbers' by sending Dad off on an errand.
2. Then distract and disorientate Meg and Ray, while...
3. She used me as a 'honey trap' with Danny, and tricked him into helping us escape.
4. Kane was an unknown element. To mix a metaphor, Mother would cross that bridge when it pointed a rifle in our faces.

Mother was seriously on my tail all morning. Like in the absence of her calendar app, her brain had rewired itself to mega-planning mode.

Danny was out in No Man's Land shooting targets, and Ray had given me and Ben the idiot-proof task of pulling up potatoes in the raised beds in the quad. It was hard on the back and I broke my nails. Ben started yanking out beetroots and carrots. Meg treated him like a challenged child of her very own, gently showing him how to tell the different plants by their leaves.

I was deep in dirt when Mother nudged me. 'Look,' she whispered, 'look at him sneaking around.' I followed her dirty-gloved finger and saw Dad taking boxes off the back of the quad bike. He looked over his shoulder to see if anyone noticed. 'He's hiding something, keep an eye on him,' she whispered. 'We'll be out of here sooner than I thought – I've got a plan to get rid of him.'

'When you whisper,' I whispered, 'it makes you look like a witch.'

I used the excuse of carrying the potatoes into the barn to get away, but she followed me and grabbed my wrist, 'Where d'you think you're sneaking off to? To yabber and tell tales to Daddy?'

She was using her old shaming strategy to get me to do something. I waited a second and there it was: 'I need you to deliver this message to your father,' she said.

And she handed me this bit of paper. And it said:

I need the following from my car:
1. Beta blockers, in passenger-side glove compartment.
2. Anti-depressants in handbag, back seat.
3. Mobile phone charger, in handbag or the boot.
4. Benjamin's cholesterol tablets and sugar-substitutes, in handbag.
5. My trainers, in the boot.
6. My reading glasses and regular glasses and contact lenses – handbag or glove compartment.
7. My Climagest. HRT treatment, blue packet – handbag.

'Deliver it yourself,' I said. 'I'm not your slave.' But then I felt bad and asked, 'Wait, since when were you on hormones and anti-frickin-depressants anyway?'

'Never mind that,' she said, 'I need your father to go and get these things. The car is about sixty miles away, just lying there.'

'No chance,' I said. 'He won't do it.'

'Well, maybe you can tell him that I'll have to go through withdrawal from all my medications then. That could be unpleasant, not just for me.'

'Best if you ask him yourself,' I mumbled, lugging the heavy bag of manky potatoes away, not wanting to be a pawn yet again.

It was no good, she caught up with me at the potato stack. She brandished the bit of paper and looked furtively over her shoulder. 'Young lady, this is not just about you, there's your brother's health to think about too. Ben needs his tablets. Give this list to your father, immediately! He'll listen to you.'

'Here we go again,' I said. 'Piggy in the middle.'

'And I won't put up with you back-chatting and wasting our pre-cious time.' She grabbed my bandaged hand and I yelped, 'Ow!' with some exaggeration.

Then Meg passed by with some veggie bags, and Mother and me had to pretend we were talking about potatoes. As soon as Meg was out of sight, Mother said, 'Haley, I'm sorry. Please, sit with me.' She led me into an alcove with a bench. Her eyes kind of shamed me into it. 'You're right. I should have told you more before. I've been on anti-depressants for years, since your father left, in fact. I'm sorry if they make me a bit distant sometimes,' and she sighed. 'Your father's been on a lot of medication, too, antip-sychotics, anticonvulsants, lithium. Oh, they tried everything. He had to be very heavily medicated.'

All I picked up was the word 'psychotic'.

'It all started back when he lost his job at the newspaper. He became obsessed with conspiracy theories on the internet, all day and night. He was in a panic, I think, about me having to be the breadwinner and him stuck at home all day with a very small child to take care of, so he developed these paranoid delusions. Your father used to imagine spies everywhere.' She was whispering. 'It was a worldwide conspiracy and they were all out to silence him. One time, he broke apart my computer because he said there were surveillance cameras inside. Then there was his suicide attempt.'

'His what?'

She said she'd tried so hard to protect me and Ben from the truth and this was during the first pandemic. There was, she said, a night after Dad had been deeply depressed for many months, and she'd found him on the floor in the bathroom after he'd taken many tranquillizers and he'd shattered the glass medicine cabinet and passed out and was lying in the shards.

I froze. It was my recurring dream: the naked man on the floor, the blood and her trying to wake him. She kicked the door in my face so I couldn't see. My dream wasn't a dream at all. Everything was falling apart.

'So this whole thing…' I stammered.

'I'm so sorry,' she said, and there was no trace of deception in her face. 'But, you know, the sickest thing of all is that I'm pretty sure your father really wants the end of the world to come. Before all this, he was convinced nuclear war was coming. Why, I don't know – so he could save us and feel like a hero, maybe? Then he got terribly depressed when it didn't happen.'

She rubbed my back and told me to take a deep breath and let it out. 'I'm so sorry you had to find out like this, darling. I thought it was a small mercy that you'd forgotten all the horrible stuff that went on when you were younger. But maybe I should've been more open about it, maybe I tried to protect you too much.'

The look on my face must have made her feel guilty because she snapped back into organisational mode. 'I should've placed a restraining order on him years ago. He seemed well the last few years, but I should never have trusted him. It's all my fault.' She got to her feet, with that forced smile of hers, and said, 'Once we're back home we can get your father the professional help he really needs.'

Her voice seemed to echo. I felt my senses separating.

'Please don't tell your little brother any of this,' she whispered, 'it would only scare him.'

And I was like, 'So, what am I supposed to tell Ben? You want me to lie to him forever?'

'Not lie,' Mother said, 'just … just till we're out of here.'

My head was spinning again. Dad was lying to me and to himself, and he wanted me to lie to Ben, and now Mother wanted me to do the same!

'How do I know you're not lying to me, too?' I asked, feeling pretty desperate.

'Well, you're going to have to trust me,' she said.

Oh great, I thought, that one again!

Mother touched my shoulder and with the other hand smoothed out my clenched bandaged fist and placed her piece of paper within it. 'Now, we all have to put on a brave face. I need you to go and ask your father to fetch the things on the list. I haven't got time to explain why, but I'm hoping that when your father drives out there, past the mountains, and sees that everything in the world is perfectly normal and there's no pandemic, he might even let us go.'

She hugged me tight and said, 'Poor you. I know it's confusing, but it's all going to be OK.' Just like she did when I had my nightmares when I was nine, only they hadn't been nightmares at all. And that had been a lie, too.

Poor, stupid me. And poor Mother – I'd blamed her for forcing Dad to leave us. But maybe she'd been right all along in trying to protect us from him. How could I undo the damage I'd done through five years of resenting her?

So, I agreed to give her piece of paper to Dad.

I'd made another actual choice.

But before I did the deed, I had to have a bit of a lie down.

Make Sure You Have Your Apocalypse Date Right

There have been a whole bunch of end-of-the-worlds that were supposed to happen but didn't. Some sort of started then just petered out, then other ones didn't happen at all. So there was:

1. 2020 – Covid-19 pandemic
2. 2018 – All major coastal cities flooded due to climate change
3. 2014 – Collision with planet Nibiru
4. 2012 – Collision with comet
5. 1990s – Y2K bug
6. 1980s – AIDS pandemic
7. 1970s – Global freezing ecological catastrophe
8. 1960s – Overpopulation leading to mass starvation by 1990
9. 1950s–80s – Nuclear war

I was upstairs in my bunk-bed having a weep about how insane Dad had been, and I guess I started to pity him. I'd never really thought of it before, but what would it be like to kidnap your kids when there was actually no pandemic, after all?

Like, what would you do the day after you realised?

Like, you'd made the biggest, stupidest mistake a parent could ever make.

Mother was right: there were probably tens of thousands of divorced deadbeat dads who dreamed of the end of the world so they could feel like heroes. Rather than do the daily housework and all that 'compromised' sell-out shit that mums do, rather than admitting they were career failures and actually sticking around and getting their hands dirty and paying the bills, they dreamed of rescuing the family they'd probably walked out on. It was all deluded grandiose crap made up to hide the fact that, deep down, men would rather that the world ended than they had to change a nappy.

And just think of Dad, having to face the fact that he'd abducted us for no reason at all. No apocalypse would redeem him. He'd trashed his marriage and was an unemployed guy with mental illness, and not a visionary of the end times at all. He'd realise he was pretty much just a washed-up loser who needed to find a job and stick with his medication.

So, yes, I had a good cry about Dad. And worried about him and his guns.

So then I went looking for him, to do Mother's dirty deed with the list.

When Something Unpleasant Needs Doing, Do It Swiftly And Decisively

There's a chapter in Dad's survival book about the necessity of cutting grit out of a deep wound and cauterising it, immediately, to prevent greater pain later. This is like a metaphor for what I had to do to Dad.

I found Dad carrying crates of beans from Kane's Range Rover to the opening hatch of the bunker. 'Hey, soldier,' he said, and that made me feel bad. He chatted away as he spun the wheel handle of the air lock and it hissed open. And I felt hurt that he couldn't tell that I'd actually been picking my cut hand and crying for quite a bit.

'Haley, can you do me a favour and pass that box down to me?' he asked and touched my arm, smiling.

I flinched. It was too late for him to be nice now, and it'd only make betraying him more awful. I tried to prep myself and touched Mother's bit of paper in my pocket. I stared at him as he climbed down into this bunker he'd built secretly through most of my childhood. Who was Dad, really? If he'd been living a delusion all this time, then I knew the delusion and not the man himself.

I tried to map his happy energy onto this picture of a naked man, overdosed, bleeding and insane in a bathroom. What was that old phrase Dad had said? 'To be well adapted to an insane world, is the greatest insanity of all.'

'Dad?'

'Yup, what's up, Hales?' he said, from the middle of the ladder.

I told myself that if I didn't go through with Mother's vile deed now, we'd be trapped here till something nasty happened, maybe to Ben. That when we escaped, like Mother said, we could send a really good psychiatric doctor for Dad.

'Mother asked me … she asked me to give you this.'

I handed the paper down to him. It was smeared with a tiny bit of blood from my bandage. He read over it quickly then scanned my face.

I wanted to grab him and shout, 'Dad, please tell me the truth, did you go mad and try to kill yourself? Please tell me, because that's so fucked up, because that means you didn't want to be our dad anymore and you would've destroyed my life and Ben's!'

But I just bit my lips and wheezed a bit.

He folded up the page. His breath was all steamy in the cold bunker air. 'OK, well, I know your Mother's angry and trying to boss me about,' he said. 'Nothing new there, but she's right, she's really going to need these things. I can't bring her car over the river, but she'll need those pills, and the glasses too, fair point. We don't have any contact lenses here.' He sighed.

If he'd climbed back up to me then and said, 'But, Haley, what is your mother really up to?' I'm pretty sure I would have melted and blurted that she wanted him out of the picture so she could trick the weakest links. But I'd started the lie and had to keep going. I pointed at the list and repeated the words Mother had told me to say. 'She says her glasses are in the glove compartment and the pills too. Ben's pills and boots are in the boot. Oh, and she wants the car charger for her iPhone … and a newspaper … from the corner shop. *The Guardian.*'

He shook his head, smiling darkly. 'Maybe she'd like me to fetch some champagne and truffles while I'm at it?'

I told him it wasn't my fault she was like that. 'I know, I know,' he said. 'I won't shoot the messenger.' He climbed back up out of the bunker and put his hand on my head and asked again if I was OK. I shrugged and tried to hide my face from him, so emotions wouldn't come.

'OK,' he said, 'tell your mother that if there's no roadblocks I might be able to get it done tonight. And, by the way, in future she can deliver her own messages. OK?'

'OK,' I mumbled.

'You always were the smartest one in this family,' he said randomly.

I felt so drained.

Reasons Not To Leave

There are good reasons why no one should make such excursions beyond the perimeter fence during a pandemic. These include:

1. Risk of coming into contact with contaminated persons, most probably refugees fleeing the cities.

2. Risk of being caught and questioned by police.
3. Risk of leading police or contaminated persons back to the safe house.

Dad was in a heated debate with Ray, Meg and Kane, who were all dead against it. I heard Kane yell at Dad, 'I thought you were our leader, not a delivery boy for your ex-wife. I can't believe you're risking infection for all of us, for the sake of that selfish, bourgeois bitch!'

Then it was weird, cos dad was sticking up for Mother. A major first. But I guess it was just more evidence for Kane that Dad had betrayed the survival plan for the sake of his beloved fam.

Kane stormed off to patrol the perimeter fence and I got this sense, spying on her picking out her huge assault rifle, that mere survival wasn't what it was all about for her. Like, actually, her real goal was to be out there at the perimeter fence, offing wheezers with her assault rifle, one by one. Like, maybe this whole pandemic was a Godsend to her, like a massive revenge thing against the society that rejected her.

She turned as she got into her Range Rover and nearly caught me spying. She had majorly murderous eyes and I shat it, but not literally. And I thought, maybe that thing about Dad finding his prepper buddies in his therapy group was true, i.e. maybe Kane was actually dangerously mental.

Half an hour later and Dad was stacking the old SUV. Meg and Ray tried to convince him not to go, one more time, but came out to help him anyway. The things he took with him and which are essential for trips into possibly contaminated areas included: binoculars, a carry bag, bin-bags, duct tape, hand sanitizer, a box of rubber gloves, three face masks, a helmet, a chainsaw, a can of diesel, a walkie-talkie, a spade, his toolkit, a rifle and other random shit.

Ray silently helped Dad stack it all inside, cos I guess Ray is a mister fix-it, a do-er always doing, and not a planner like Dad. And maybe Ray would be totally lost without Dad giving him orders, even for just one day.

There was solemn silence then Meg shouted, 'Go on then, Ed. You're breaking my heart! Just, please, God, be careful. Don't come back contaminated!' And she gave Dad a massive booby hug.

I was standing at the gate, watching him, taking hits of my nebuliser. I could have yelled, 'STOP, Dad! Don't go! It's a trick!' Once. Ten times. Twenty.

There was this dread thing hanging over me, just like the big dark mountain clouds falling into the sunset beyond.

Dad climbed inside his SUV and turned the ignition. It roared and belched out fumes and it magically worked again. And I was feeling like an evil, traitor-ish person, but I had to remind myself it was like Mother said – tricking Dad was the kindest thing for him.

He drove the ten feet to the gate, stopped and unlocked it. 'I'll be back in five hours, max. Get some rest and I'll see you in the morning,' he said to me. 'Tomorrow's when the hard stuff starts. OK, Hales?'

He seemed almost chirpy as he pulled the iron gates open. Maybe he was just happy to get a few hours away from the sniping gaze of Mother, like a chided husband heading out for a secret pint. But how the hell could he be happy about tomorrow if he believed that the numbers of infections were supposed to double every three days, if the power lines were supposed to go down any day now, if he was driving miles closer to the pandemic?

But then I had to remind myself that Mother's car was near a village, and maybe there'd be smiley tourists and pensioners out shopping. And not a single person with any masks or hazmat suits on. No virus, and just the possibility that he'd realise he'd been wrong.

So Mother was right to send him out.

I followed him to the open gateway. The mountainous wind blasted through and it was all falling darkness and *Lord of The Rings*-ish.

'Don't worry, Hale-Bopp,' he said. 'We're ahead of the viral curve. The rural areas will be low risk for another week. And let's face it,' he grinned, 'your mother's not going to give us any peace till I get that stuff for her, is she? I'll see what I can do. If it's safe, I might be able to pick up some of the last of the diesel, too.'

He drove through, parked and came back to lock up. But then I thought, crap, what if when he finds out there's no pandemic, he has another nervous breakdown? Out there all alone, and we never see him again.

'Chin up,' he said. 'Oh, and don't go taking what your mum says seriously. If she starts on about how mad I am, just ask her about my Section 3.'

'What do you mean, Section 3? Dad, wait,' I called over the engine.

'What? You want to come with me?'

I took one step towards him, then recoiled. I looked back at the farmhouse, then at the gate.

He was twirling his set of gate keys. 'If you want to come, you'll need protective clothing, a hair net, a hood, a mask and gloves from Meg.' And he fastened the medical face mask over his mouth.

Maybe I was scared. Maybe I was lazy.

'OK, stay safe here. I'm going to have to lock you in,' he said, his voice muffled. 'It's nothing personal.' And he kissed his fingers through his mask, and touched my forehead with his fingertips. 'Take care of your little brother for me. OK? I'm proud of you.'

Proud of me? A two-faced traitor like me? What the hell?

In the last moments before the two sides of the iron gate slid together and hid him from me, he pulled a goofy face, like we both used to do before he put the lights out at bedtime. I heard his keys turn in the lock.

'By the way,' he shouted over. 'I got you that footage. News broadcast. Midday. The old satellite dish.' He opened up the throttle and yelled over the engine. The last thing he said sounded like, 'Left. For you. Desk. In case. Don't come. Back.'

That freaked me out and I yelled for him to get the hell back inside right now and forget Mother's bossy list, but my voice was drowned out and he was already tearing away on the other side. I tried to climb the gate and fell back on my ass. I found a tiny hole in the rusted iron and watched my father's red tail lights vanish to dots in the darkness.

Missing Person Protocol

M.I.A

If someone beyond the safe perimeter falls out of contact and is missing in action:

1. Do not panic.
2. Continue trying to contact them on all frequencies.
3. Continue with lockdown procedures.
4. Do not send anyone looking for them.

Dad hadn't made it back, like he'd promised. We were awoken at 05:30am to the sound of Ray's walkie-talkie. 'Alpha Charlie, this is Alpha Charlie three, calling Delta Foxtrot one-niner. Do you read me, over?'

Mother dragged herself up and with her first waking words she was already frantic, asking me over and over, 'What time did your father leave?' 'Did he agree to get everything on the list?' 'What was his mood like?' 'Did he say when he'd be back?'

I'd screwed up, apparently, by sending Dad off so late at night, and Mother had screwed up by falling asleep from exhaustion. Hours had been wasted.

I watched Ray by the wall. He was holding up the walkie-talkie above his head, trying to get a better signal. 'Delta Foxtrot one-niner, Ed, pick up for Christ's sake man.' No reply. He cursed, then strode over to the quad-bike and tried the walkie-talkie sitting there.

Mother and me were supposed to be on goat-milking duty, but Mother was only using the foul beasts as an alibi to get planning time with me. 'OK, we're one down,' Mother whispered to me. 'If

Ray goes looking for Ed then that just leaves Meg and her son and that crazy Kane woman.'

'But what's happened to Dad?' I whimpered. 'He said he'd be back by now.'

'I told you, he probably realised that everything's perfectly normal out there, and he's driven off to find a village pub to drown his sorrows.'

That made me feel pretty bad. 'Anyway,' she said, 'have you made any progress on the keys with the big dumb kid?'

'He's not dumb,' I snapped. 'He's just not city smart. He reads books on philosophy, actually.'

'Really! So you've been in his room, have you? Excellent. Well, we can twist that to our advantage.'

I gasped.

'Don't pretend to be so naïve, Haley,' she said. 'Let's not forget I caught you watching porn, more than once.'

'Jesus, Mother!' I gagged.

'Has the boy told you where they keep the weapons?' she snapped.

'No,' I said, 'and his name is Danny, by the way. But I saw some guns in a shed and, anyway, shouldn't we just wait and see what's happened to Dad? I mean, he's totally vanished, seriously, like in a bad way.'

'He's gone, just as planned,' she said. 'But we have to move fast, your father could be very, very angry when he returns, given that half the things on my list aren't actually in my car at all.'

And she snatched the goat bucket from my hands, spilling some of the rank milk on my feet. 'And put on some make-up, for God's sake, Haley,' she snapped. 'And find out where the mother of that Romeo of yours hides the gate keys! And I'll get to work on the weapons.'

'Mother!' I shouted, but she'd already marched off to begin the next phase of her cunning scheme.

I watched as Meg walked past, holding a fluffy bunny upside

down by the feet, and Ray barked into his walkie-talkie, 'This is Alpha Charlie three, calling Delta Foxtrot one-niner, over. Do you read me, Ed?'

Mother tried to pass by him but he grabbed her by the arm. 'You didn't send Ed off to get something else we don't know about, did you?' he grunted. 'He's gone M.I.A.'

Mother shook off his grip. 'What on earth do you mean?' She smiled, the picture of fake innocence. 'If you're so worried, why don't you go and look for him yourself? I'm sure two grown men with walkie-talkies should be able to find each other anywhere.'

Ray narrowed his eyes. He called over to Danny, gesturing at Mother. 'Danny, get this lot on BB duty. Every battery in the house charged, every bucket filled.'

'Affirmative,' Danny said.

S.H.T.F

When the shit hits the fan (S.H.T.F.), universal ethics no longer apply. There is only 'us' and 'them'. This, unfortunately, made Danny and Meg 'them'.

Danny used all the power sockets in the kitchen and wired up racks of battery chargers, all sizes and shapes. Meg skinned her gruesome, freshly killed bunny in the sink while she sang. She had a good strong 'fat-lady-sings' kind of voice and did some jiggy moves with her big bottom. It was a song called *No Woman No Cry* and it had a bit in it about a government or something in Trenchtown and how everything was gonna be alright.

I was overcome with dread, staring at Meg's fast hands pulling the rabbit skin off, like it was another ominous sign.

Mother waited for a break in Meg's song then asked her about what other wild animals they killed.

'Squirrels, they're perfectly edible,' Meg said. 'Birds, a lot of pheasants this time of year. I'm a pacifist myself, vegan for ten years, but actually you have to cull a lot of beasts round here, otherwise they just overbreed and starve to death anyway. We have to use what fresh meat we can to conserve our rations.'

'And you shoot them with … ?' Mother asked cunningly.

'Well, it's snares, mostly, and crossbows.'

'Really, could I see one?' Mother asked and I cringed.

Meg eyed Mother with semi-suspicion, so Mother picked on Danny instead.

'Danny?' she said smiling, 'Haley says you're quite a whiz with a crossbow. You know, I don't even know what they look like.'

Danny was bored from battery charge duty and itching for something better to do and he wanted to get back into my good books, I guess. He smiled over at me and asked Meg, 'Can I show them, Mum?'

Ben started in on the same routine. 'Can I see a crossbow, Mum? Can I, please, please, please?'

Meg and Mother exchanged a glance as if to say, 'Boys, eh, what can you do?' which was utterly fake in Mother's case because she likes to call herself a feminist when it suits her ends.

'No, boys, sorry, you know I don't like weapons,' Meg said. 'And there's work to be done in the kitchen!'

Mother tried a new strategy. 'So the women do the cooking and the men do the hunting and shooting. Not exactly gender equality, is it?'

Meg stopped the gruesome skinning and stared at Mother, knife in hand.

Mother kept on: 'You know, I hate the very idea of weapons too, but now that we're here, I suppose it does make sense. I mean, why grow all this beautiful food and rear these lovely animals if any evil contaminated man can just jump over that wall and … my God, well, if they had knives, guns even, it just doesn't seem right that we women wouldn't have the tools to defend ourselves.'

It was a classic. Mother had used the Girl Power card to over-power another woman. Meg threw down her apron and said, 'Right! Come on then.'

Mother secretly squeezed my hand and dragged me out.

A Weapon Is Only As Smart As Its Handler

Weapons don't have intelligence, but they're not stupid either. Don't do anything dumb around weapons.

At the far end of the farmhouse was that weird place I'd spotted before. Meg pulled back the mouldy plastic sheet, took out her vast key ring and unlocked it. Danny kept shooting me glances, as if to say, what's going on?

What could I say: Mother intends to grab a gun and blast her way out of here?

I sighed and shrugged and lurked behind as Danny showed us his crossbow and he became his redneck-self, talking about gauges and speeds and distances. I could see Mother's eyes focused on the darker corner over his shoulder, where the guns hung. Two pistols and six rifles glinted ominously. I wondered what her first line would be.

'Oh, is that one of those night-vision thingummy-bobs?' she said. 'I saw them on telly.'

I groaned. 'Good grief!' But Danny's inner redneck had taken over.

'Yeah, that's the Armalite, with the Ultra-Fire night system.'

'Wow,' Mother and Ben said together. 'And are you allowed to...?'

'Yeah,' he said, and without realising it he was tricked by my smiling Mother into taking the automatic weapon off the rack. 'I'm goin' on night duty, by myself. Tonight,' Danny said. 'Round the perimeter.' Then he wasn't sure. 'Is it tonight or tomorrow, Mum?'

'You're not taking that damn thing with you, that's for sure,' Meg said from behind me.

'It looks really heavy,' Mother said. 'Could I just ... I've never held one of these things before.'

I looked over my shoulder. I couldn't believe Mother would be so brazen as to actually snatch a machine gun, and, like, now.

'Mother, no!' I whispered.

'Could I?' she asked. 'It looks very heavy, you must be very strong,' and she elbowed me to make me stop cringing. I tried to get Danny's attention with my eyes, but he handed Mother the big black gun. Ben tried to grab for it.

'No, Benjamin!' Mother shouted. 'Don't touch, it might be loaded! Is it loaded?' she enquired, smiling, and I had visions of her turning it on Danny and Meg if they said yes.

There was a violent rush beside me and I was thrown into the door. Ray tore through us and knocked Danny to the ground.

'Ya fuckin idiot!'

Danny tried to explain himself, but Ray was already strapping the gun back in place. 'Fun and games over. Out of bounds.' He pushed us all back, super roughly and bolted the door, muttering to himself.

Danny protested and Ray kicked him in the ass and sent him sprawling through the mud. Danny looked at me and a surge of white rage went through him – he seemed to grow to twice his height. Suddenly, he lurched at Ray and pushed him hard, sent him flying. My legs turned to jelly. Ray's face turned red and for a second he looked scared, as he picked himself up out of the mud.

'Bring it on!' Danny yelled and raised his fists.

I screamed in a weird, scary way and both men froze. But if it wasn't for Meg calming Ray and her leading him away like he was a mad dog, I'm sure Ray and Danny would have strangled each other to death. Danny stood there trembling.

'Are you nuts?' I said to him. 'Why did you do that?'

'He pushed you.'

'Woah,' I said, 'don't go all heroic on me.'

Danny marched away without looking back, and all the hairs on my body stood up, like I'd got too close to the electric fence or something.

I was pleased with one thing though, at least Mother's ill-considered scheme had ended up in the dirt with Ray. She grabbed my arm and led me away. When we were out of earshot she whispered, 'The brute had a second set of keys, did you see? Good, now go and get back to work on the boy. They'll never trust me with the keys, that's clear, but the boy will do anything you say now. He's clearly crazy about you.'

I flushed with embarrassment and rage. 'Fuck off! Do your own dirty work!'

'Suit yourself. Do nothing then,' she said. 'Stay here.'

'Fine, I will!'

'You're weak,' Mother said, 'just like your father.'

She stormed off and left me alone. She must have known that, at that point, being like my father terrified me and I would do anything to prove that insanity was not my fate. I would, in fact, do exactly what she wanted.

Being A Double Agent Messes With Your Head

When you have to trick someone but you care for them at the same time and you feel guilty, this will get you into a major emotional mess. Double-crossing equals double standards equals double trouble.

I found Danny lurking behind a tarp, stroking the goats. He flinched when he heard footsteps. Maybe he thought I was Ray come to beat him up properly this time. He blushed when he saw me and told me to go away and wiped his cheek with his muddy sleeve, trailing dirt up his face.

'Hey, majorly sorry about that,' I said. 'Mother is kind of weird.'

'I could take him on, I could beat him,' Danny muttered.

'Forget it,' I said, 'Ray's just a short-ass bully. You're bigger than that.' I didn't mean to make a pun but I hoped it would break the tension.

'Hey, so … what do you think happened to my dad?' I asked. 'He's been away, like, way too long, don't you think?'

'Maybe he came across a gang, you know, stealing fuel. Or the police, they might have started rounding civilians up.'

'Jesus! Put my mind at rest, why don't you! You believe that stuff?'

Danny shrugged. 'Most likely he just forgot to turn his walkie-talkie on.'

'Yeah, he's such a ...'

'A DC?' Danny said and a light came back to his eye.

I laughed and Danny stood up and stretched and I felt this weird impulse to touch his bicep. I dunno why, maybe it was one of those dodgy primordial pheromone situations, like 'female apes get aroused by displays of male aggression.' I shook myself out of it. More than anything I wanted to prove to Danny that I wasn't part of Mother's secret plan and that I'd never exploit him.

To be chirpy, I asked, 'So, can I come with you? On your night duty thing? We could go to the perimeter and see if my dad's coming?'

He looked at me quizzically and I felt devious and bad.

'To be honest ... my mother keeps using me, like her slave or something.' Then I almost said, she thinks you're the weakest link and you'll let us escape if I snog you. But I caught myself just in time and so instead I said, 'I just wanna get away from her for a bit. She's driving me nuts.' Then I worried that I sounded like I wanted 'a date'. I blushed and shrugged. 'Nah, forget it, Ray won't let you take me, anyway.'

'Screw him,' Danny said. 'Yeah, you can come, you'll have to sneak out with me though. The perimeter is pretty amazing. There's a stream and a marsh and hawks.'

Don't ask me why, but his smile made my skin tingle.

We walked on together, sort of flirting, I guess, past the barns. And something got stronger with each step. I don't know, like maybe I thought, I *could* actually run away with him and leave everyone. Our fingers brushed and I suddenly had to grab his thumb with my fingers. So I did. He stopped.

'Oh my God,' I said. 'I just have to kiss you. Or would that be too weird?'

He just stared.

'Shit, sorry, I'm really embarrassed now. I guess it must be cabin fever or...'

He bent down to my level and we did that hesitation thing with the eyes before the lunge, then our lips locked and it was warm and ticklish at first and our teeth bashed. OK, well, I screwed that up, I thought. But then his dark eyes sort of opened and his hand brushed my cheek, and then he stroked my neck and went down my side to hold my waist and I practically lost the ability to stand. We kissed deeper and faster, our lips moving in this rhythm all by themselves. My brain was dizzy with nervousness and my knees sort of trembled and we fell backwards in the mud and he practically lifted me up and laid me against the barn wall. But it was like our bodies knew exactly what to do, like on auto-pilot. His hand slipped under the hem of my T-shirt and I didn't want him to stop. Our tongues were spiralling and I could hear myself gasping, but not in an asthma way, and I was suddenly worried that someone would see us, but either he didn't hear me or he didn't care, because he pulled me hard against him with one of his huge hands and his other one moved up inside my T, and I quivered but I didn't pull my shirt down even when I felt the cold air on my belly. My God, I thought, so THIS is what everyone's so excited about. The stupid fucking movies were right! His fingers cupped my breast and Danny whispered my name and his lips scraped my neck and power jolted through my spine and, I guess, my pelvis. 'Wow!' I gasped and pulled away. 'Wait!'

I suddenly remembered that I was supposed to be snogging Danny to trick him for Mother's escape plan and I felt awful. Was this the way Mother kissed Dad before she had him thrown out of our house? Was Mother making me do this by mind control? Or was I just doing it to rebel against her? Was this the kind of kiss Italian mafia give you before they shoot you?

'You ... you OK?' Danny said, his eyes so wide they could have just sucked me back in for more.

'I'm fine,' I said, tucking my T-shirt back in, with rippling waves of awkwardness. 'Yeah, yeah, no, I don't know. Actually, no offence, but I feel pretty bad.'

This is the problem with being two-faced: you end up not knowing whether you're coming or going and then you can't even trust your own impulses anymore. And then everyone gets hurt.

'Look, sorry,' I said, 'I don't think this is such a good idea.'

And I ran off and he must have thought I meant 'him and me', but I meant me exploiting him to get the keys.

'Wait, Haley!' he shouted, but I seriously had to run and it was hard because my legs were absolute jelly.

The Five Scenarios In The Event That The Leader Does Not Return

I splashed my face with cold water and told myself. 'Time out!' Then I formulated my own solution: there would be no mad dash for freedom, like Mother planned. No two-faced treachery of Danny. No, we'd wait until Dad came back, then he'd confess that he'd made a silly mistake and he'd let us all go back to civilisation. Simple.

I snuck away to Dad's cubbyhole, thinking how he told me he'd left something there for me. Part of me was thinking, Dad never messes up – he can't have had an accident or something, vanishing like this must be part of some plan we don't know about, that's all.

Just like he said, there was an envelope on his desk with *For Haley* written on it in big letters, and it had a little hard drive inside. I sat there amidst his masses of cables and ancient old CDs and calculations, playing with the hard drive in my hand, worrying about it, and staring at the fuzzy TV screen that had images of people throwing things and flames, all snowy and broken up, cos of the bad signal.

I had only a few minutes alone before Mother would be on my tail again, so I stuck the drive in this laptop Dad had left lying there, selected the file and clicked. There was Dad on screen, sitting exactly where I was sitting, like some weird mirror of myself.

He must have recorded it the night before, just before he left.

'Haley,' he said, '*I'm recording this for you, just in case I don't make it back. It struck me that I don't know exactly what I'm heading into and that's my own fault, for not prepping more for the breakdown in telecommunications that has occurred.*'

I stared at his bony face and thought, the way he talks, it really is like he believes one hundred per cent in the pandemic and he's just being one hundred per cent honest.

'*Most of what I'm about to tell you is in my survival guide,*' he said, '*and has been adapted from material I stole from classified government pandemic survival information.*'

I stared at his face and watched him say all this stuff from memory.

'*If you don't hear from me within a day, one of five things may have happened to me and you will have to help the team make plans accordingly:*

1. *I'm out of range and communications are down. The walkie -talkie has a range of three miles but your mother's car is thirty-two miles away. I have a mobile phone with me and a long-wave radio, but the comms towers may have melted down, like in the last pandemic. I told you about this before. If millions of people try to make calls at the same time, then the network collapses. In the eventuality that Ray can't get through to me, just sit and stay put, wait it out until I'm back within walkie-talkie range. Most of all, don't panic and don't make your little brother panic.*
2. *The second possibility is that I've hit a roadblock. We saw these in the last pandemic, but this may have started sooner this time, due to mass looting and the more aggressive spread of the virus. It's possible that I've had to elude police or military, by taking a different route, and that this has delayed me. Again, don't panic.*
3. *The other possibility is that a mass refugee flight from the*

cities has begun, with millions of people trying to get away from the contagion epicentres – London, Manchester, Birmingham, Glasgow – and all these people will be heading north to try to get to rural areas, where there's less contamination and, they hope, more food. These hungry, angry mobs are highly dangerous. They think they're fleeing the virus but they're carrying it with them. If they have made it this far north already and I encounter them on the roads then I will have to: (a) flee them to escape contamination; (b) flee them so that I don't get rounded up when the military attempts to contain contaminated gangs; or (c) flee from battles between police and gangs. Again, wait for further information.'

I was getting pretty freaked out. Just the fact that Dad could tell me all this, like it was a shopping list, with zero emotion.

On he went:

4. *'It's also possible that I've been caught by the police. If this is the case then I will have had to destroy my communications systems so that I can't be tracked back to the safe house. The police and military are already mapping the movements of the entire population and they are on the look-out for any stashes of food or weapons.*
5. *The other possibility, Haley, is that I suspect I've become contaminated. So I'll have to self-quarantine away from the safe house for a month. We don't know what the quarantine period is for this virus yet, perhaps as long as a month. I have brought a tent and some rudimentary supplies.'*

I was in total shock, thinking of him out there, all alone and sick.

'I know this is hard to process, Haley, harder to accept,' he said, *'but the mission your mother sent me on is much more dangerous than she realised. If I don't return, it is protocol that no one comes looking*

for me. Not Ray, not Kane. I have to make that one hundred per cent clear. Do not put pressure on anyone else in the safe house to come looking for me. The worst-case scenario is if I become contaminated and, out of weakness, return to the safe house, because I want to see you or say goodbye to you. In such a situation, even if I am dying, even if I am showing no symptoms, I am to be treated exactly like a hostile, as described in Chapter Seven. If I become contaminated and appear at the perimeter gate, I am to no longer be treated as your father but as a source of contagion. In such an event, Ray or Kane will deal with me accordingly.'

I was weeping there in his cubbyhole. How could he be mad and wrong, when I could see the love in his eyes when he said my name?

'I'm telling you all this now so that you're prepared, and as the next part of your training. When I return, there will be no more excursions beyond the perimeter, and the only people we will ever see at the fence will be starving, contaminated survivors, armed and roving in mobs, who we will have to drive away or destroy. Prepare for the worst-case scenario. But, all being well, I will see you for breakfast tomorrow morning. In which case, don't tell anyone else about this recording.' He paused and said, *'Take care of your little brother. I love you, Haley-Boo.'*

Then he reached over and turned off his webcam and it all went to black.

Signs Of The Coming Collapse

Even without TV and internet there are specific signs that the point-of-no-return has begun.

It was late in the day and Ray, Meg and Kane were deeply distressed about Dad being out of touch for so long. And I couldn't face the dinner of boiled bunny or the glances that Danny was now shooting me.

Kane stood in her usual place in the window frame, as if she was a soldier who couldn't ever sit or eat. Like the Terminator. She was listening to the crackling long-wave radio for any trace of Dad.

It was hot, smelly and loud in the kitchen. Twelve sets of large batteries were beeping as they charged and the washing machine was on full spin. Danny was showing Ben all of the scars on his arm and telling the stories behind them. This was a chainsaw and that was a chisel and that was a glass window from before he got chucked out of school. Danny's eyes shot to me. He wanted to talk, really badly. Or touch.

Ray pushed his plate of rabbit ribcage away. He kept checking the walkie-talkie every twenty seconds, cursing, trying another channel. 'I should go and look for Ed,' he said. 'It's not like him at all. What if the looters are at the village already? He's no good in a fight ... if I could get to the outer fields ...'

Mother shot me a glance, as if she was pleased.

Ben pleaded, 'Mum, can I have Haley's rabbit?'

I scraped my gross carcass onto Ben's plate and took my plate to the sink. Danny came up behind me and pretended to clean his plate. He whispered. 'Hey, why do you keep running away? I didn't mean to touch you like that, if that's what you're worried about, I ...'

The lights flickered, off and on, twice, then went out. The washing machine died. All electronics just stopped. Sudden, total silence. Thick, mute blackness. Mother screamed. A plate smashed on the stones and I realised I'd dropped it.

In the dark Danny's hand reached for mine. I pushed him away.

'Don't panic!' Ray yelled, and I heard him flick a switch. But nothing happened.

In The Event Of The Grid Going Down

If you suspect the power grid has failed, there are procedures you must go through to double check.

Ray was hunched at the fuse-box in the hall, with all of us around him. 'Give me some fucking room!' he yelled. Meg was in a fluster and wittering on. 'Keep that torch still!' he yelled at her.

Ray pulled the old fuses out with a hard, tight ping, blew on them, scrutinised them closely then put them back in, one by one.

'Let's not jump to conclusions. It might be something local,' Meg twittered, as if sharing the contents of her panicked brain would keep our panic at bay. 'Or maybe it's the battery chargers that blew the fuses.'

Ray flicked the trip switch, once, twice. He turned the handle. Nothing. He got to his feet. 'Stay calm,' he said, 'we know the procedure.'

'So, it's the grid,' Meg said, and she exhaled loudly. 'God.'

'There's one more thing I have to check before we know for sure,' Ray mumbled as he went to the door.

Mother dragged me upstairs to our room, her voice in conspiratorial whispers.

I asked her if this was this part of her plan, too.

But shit, didn't this prove that Dad was right?

She told me not to be such an idiot: these back-of-beyond shacks had power cuts all the time. 'They're probably just too embarrassed to admit they've got faulty wiring.' She grabbed me firmly and shook me because I was getting all breathless. 'Stop worrying about your dad! I told you, he's probably in a pub somewhere on the other side of those mountains, watching the news and having a beer, too damn embarrassed to come back after leading these fools up the garden path.'

I tried to get away, but she kept hold of my arm, 'Don't you see?' she said, 'This is good, very good. Things have swung in our favour. If I can just get Ray and that Kane monster out of the way, and you can take care of the boy and the hippie…'

I heard the cough and splutter of a diesel generator kick starting, and Danny's voice shouted up the stairs. 'Emergency meeting, everyone … bunker!' He was trying to sound full of authority, but his voice broke halfway through a word and I could tell that, for the first time, he sounded scared.

Initiate Back-Up Power Plan

In the event of grid down, the following procedures must be gone through:

1. Frozen food supplies must not defrost. To this end, all generator power must be diverted to the deep freezers. All other uses of power are now considered a luxury and wasteful.
2. An inventory of fuel supplies and battery power must be made to calculate how long the generator can last.
3. All other forms of back-up power must immediately be put into effect. These include wind, solar and human-generated power.
4. Listen to the pre-recorded instructions and do not deviate from them.

Meg was freaking out down in the bunker, worrying over the meat in the deep freezers. The generator had kicked in but there had been forty-five minutes of thawing. 'Do we have to cook it, now? I don't know, I don't know!'

Kane stayed at the top of the bunker hatch while we were all down below. She shouted down her 'info report' at us, and said it was 'imperative' that back-up electricity be kept running, otherwise all our contact with the outside world would end. She reported that radio, TV and internet were down and only battery-powered long-wave radio was feasible, but it was 'imperative' that we map the spread of the virus and the path of the infected. For that reason, she said, she was going beyond the fence on 'information reconnaissance'. I wanted to ask her to look for Dad as well, but I was too scared. I stared up at her sharp face with her newly applied camouflage make-up and got this weird sense that she totally loved this.

The rest of us sat down there in the cold, beneath the surging light of a bare 100-watt bulb, feeling freaked. The generator made the light come in waves. Ray had a metal box and a bound stack of paper before him on the tin-covered collapsible table. He lifted out this battery-operated tape player and put it in the middle. Meg stopped fussing over the meat and sat beside Ray, stroking his arms. Ben cuddled into Mother, who was doing her best to hide her smile.

I got that salty taste in my mouth as I watched them all staring obsessively at the tape player. Ray hit Play. Dad's voice crackled out.

'*You are listening to this recording because the tipping point has been reached, and I am not with you.*'

Meg clutched Ray's arm and gulped back a sob or a bit of snot.

'*Once the grid goes down, Phase Two begins. Without food, water or power, and in terror of becoming infected, the masses attempt to flee the cities. Armed mobs ransack the countryside for food. The military attempt to contain the masses, while they too scour villages and farms, requisitioning livestock, crops, fuel, machinery, vehicles and weapons. This is under emergency laws similar to those enacted during the last pandemic in the US and during Hurricane Katrina. It means that, under martial law, all property rights cease to exist. You no longer own your homes, your cars, your food, your medical supplies. Everything is, from that moment, the property of the State. You will be arrested for being in your own house. Arrested for looting by holding onto your own possessions. This is another feedback loop that will only increase the number of contaminated gangs scouring the country, searching for food, and carrying weapons to fight the police and military.*'

Dad's voice sounded kind of slow and ghostly, like maybe he was emotional or the batteries were wonky.

'*Running battles between roving gangs and the police-military will destroy what remaining societal infrastructure there is and destroy all chance of social distancing or isolation from the virus. Civilians will either be herded by the military, or attacked by gangs. All forms of contact will spread the virus. At this point it is paramount that lockdown is total, that the safe house becomes invisible to all outside eyes. That any person seen near the perimeter fence be eliminated.*'

Ray's quivering finger hit the Stop button. 'We had plans in place, Ed's plans, but we've changed so much already this last week and since he's not here…' He shook his head, his nerves getting the better of him. 'I just don't know.'

Ray's trembling made me shudder. It was like, until now, the collapse had just been these plans and numbers for him, but now he'd woken to something too horrible to even tell us about.

Another voice came from inside the bunker then, a metallic -sounding woman. 'The air-lock is not secured. Warning. The air-lock is not secured.'

Ray swore at it and told Danny to pull the lid shut. 'Not too tight, and jam that stick in it, it's a bugger to open again.'

Danny pulled the hatch shut cautiously and stood behind us as we sat at the table. I felt bad because Danny had totally misinterpreted my 'go away, don't touch' signs, but that was the least of our worries.

All sound in the bunker was unexpectedly muffled. Without the breeze and the distraction of the diesel fumes from the generator, we were all suddenly too tightly packed, like sardines in one of the thousands of cans stacked down there. The bunker smelled of new carpets and superglue and bleach. I was utterly shivering and felt woozy, sitting next to Mother and sensing her silent gloating. She was intermittently covering Ben's ears and trying to distract him, by bouncing him on her knee, so he didn't grasp what was being said.

Ray rubbed his temples. 'I have to admit, I'd hoped it wouldn't come to this. Like Ed said, it's not a drill this time, it's fucking irreversible now.' He took a deep breath. 'Ed was going to be reading this out, not me.'

Meg massaged Ray's shoulders, and I thought how odd it felt, like a distant memory, to watch two grown adults, a man and a woman 'touching' and 'working as a team'. *Stand By Your Man*, and all that ancient jazz.

'You're doing fine, love,' Meg said.

Ray passed round a piece of paper covered in complex diagrams and schedules. Mother studied it, hungrily.

'All the procedures are in this file. As you know, Ed's been out of contact for over twenty-four hours. So we have to decide: do we start final lockdown procedures without him? In which case, he would become a hostile body if and when he returns.'

Ray stopped, cleared his throat. Meg sniffed.

'Or...' Ray stammered, 'should I ignore all his plans and go and try to find him, and risk our defences being breached? Or me and him becoming contaminated.'

Mother looked at me, gave the tiniest hint of a wink. 'Well, we should vote for it, shouldn't we?' she said with a burst of confidence. 'It's something that affects us all, isn't it?'

I had my foot poised to nudge her under the table. Ray eyed her with suspicion. Meg clung to his arm and said, 'No, Ray, like Ed said, we have to stay put. Ed's a grown man, he can make his own way back.'

'But what if he's been injured?' Mother snapped, and she snatched up the paper and did her best impersonation of a concerned fellow human, reading out loud, '"...by the marauding hordes fleeing from the city seeking medicine, food, shelter, fuel."' Ben clung to her arm. 'You said yourself, Ray, security can't work without two men. I vote that one of us goes to find him.' Mother paused and turned to Ben, with her coercive voice on. 'Children, should someone go and find your poor father?'

Ben nodded and, as if on cue, muttered, 'Where's Daddy? I want my daddy!'

Then Mother turned to me. 'Haley? Is that a yes? To go and find your father?' Speak up, stop mumbling, make up your mind for once.'

I really didn't know, and I said as such, but then Mother kicked me under the table, so I said, 'Yeah. I suppose so. Sorry.'

'Well,' she announced, looking accusatorily at Ray, 'that's three for you going to find Ed, against two for you staying, so that just leaves you, Danny.' And she said this with the most appalling, flirty smile. Then I couldn't believe it, but she said, 'Haley, what do you think Danny should do?' All eyes turned to me and Danny, and Mother kicked me harder, to suppress the flurry of OMGs that I was whispering.

Ray butted in. 'Now, I never said I was staying, and I never said nothing about a vote, so leave the boy out of it. We'll ask Kane.'

'It's a dictatorship, is it, then?' Mother snapped. 'One man commands and women obey?' Then she sweetly smiled again at Danny. 'Danny, what do you think? Should Ray leave the children's father in jeopardy?'

Ben asked what jeopardy meant. 'Shh, shh, not now. Don't worry, darling,' Mother said, 'I'm sure Ray or Danny or a brave woman like Kane will go and find your daddy.'

The generator made a growling noise and the lights flickered out for a second. I held my breath. Mother kept the pressure up. 'What would you do, Danny? Would you rather stay here ... hiding in fear?'

Danny stepped into the light and stared at me and Ben. 'I'll go and find their dad,' he said.

Ray stood and blurted out, 'No, you will fucking not! Alright, alright, I'll go!'

Mother did her best to conceal her growing grin.

When Leaving Quickly, Follow A Pre-Planned Checklist Of Actions

'Two down, two to go,' Mother whispered from the doorway, as we spied on Meg hugging Ray goodbye and passing him his shotgun and torch. Kane had already headed out on the quad bike.

Ray climbed into his jeep, handed his big bunch of keys to Danny and ruffled his hair, saying something about 'being the man of the house now'. Ray revved the engine and the headlights illuminated Danny heaving open the iron gate.

'But what if Dad really is in trouble?' I whispered to Mother.

'Bugger,' she said, talking to herself. 'Of course he's taking the stupid jeep. Why didn't I think of that?'

Ray drove out, Meg waved and Danny slammed the gate behind him. Mother muttered to herself, 'The bunker, the storeroom, no, the woodshed...' Then she turned to me. 'Go and put all your clothing on, in layers,' she whispered, 'and the same with Benjamin ... shh, mum's the word!'

I set off to do as she instructed but then she told me to wait, she had a better plan. It went like this. Benjamin was to pretend to be sick with a sore tummy. I had to tell him to get into bed and moan and groan. He was to have his clothes on under the covers for maximum readiness. Mother would not explain to me why this helped her plan of action.

'But Mummy said I shouldn't tell fibs,' Ben said as I tucked him in and put a bit of water on his head to make him look sweaty.

'This isn't a fib, this is more like a ... pretend,' I told him.

He sensed something wrong, so bargained with me. 'I'll only do it if you give me your chocolate rations.'

'OK, a whole bar, but this'll be the last time ever. Just do what Mother said, OK?'

After watching him for a minute I decided Ben's whimpering sick-boy routine was a bit over the top, so I told him, 'Just lie there totally still and silent, like that zombie in *Zombie Mall*.'

'Skull Crusher or Bone Breath?'

'The one that doesn't move! But don't do the zombie noise, OK? Just stare at the floor. Got that?'

Ben nodded. Mother had only given me part of her plan and I was getting that guts-churning feeling, because she'd overlooked one essential thing ... If the power is out, it proves that Dad was right and the pandemic is real – so then why, Mother, are you still planning to escape?

However, there are strong, rational people who calculate all the options and act rationally, then there are weak, indecisive people like me, who when we get into a panic lose all sense of reason and become the powerless servants of supposedly more rational people. Aka, Mother.

The next of Mother's instructions was for me to get my shoulder bag and sequester as much food and as many torch batteries as I could carry. Plus, any major-sized, nasty kitchen knife I could find, cos the one she'd stolen was too puny.

Survival Tip: Asking someone to swiftly do three things at once only causes confusion. Mother would have done better to ask me to get just a knife, just the food, or just the batteries, as I failed on two fronts anyway. Mother should have been:

1. Collecting the objects she needed me to get, by herself, over a number of days.
2. Breaking down a list of what was most essential and could be carried, rather than this mad scramble at the last and most dangerous minute.

Meg and Danny were busy outside with the generator, which was chugging in bad ways, so I ran round the kitchen stuffing things into my little rucksack. I got a box of cereal and I shone the torch into the fridge and grabbed some randoms. There were tons of batteries but I didn't know how to get them out of the chargers, so that was a major fail. The one thing I did right was to get the knife, which was lying by the sink. It was about as long as my arm and covered in something brown, but I didn't have time to wash it or to question what life-threatening use this could be put to. I heard voices, so I scurried out with it.

And that is How Not To Prepare For Escaping From A Safe House.

You Can Use People's Good Intentions Against Them

Nice people with good intentions are the most vulnerable to manipulation. Don't get all ethical about it, just get on with it.

Ben lay moaning in his bunk, with Mother's candle beside his face. Meg and Danny looked on and it was seriously like something out of a Renaissance painting. The 'Dying Zombie Jesus', or some such. For a moment I thought God had played a nasty trick and truly made Ben sick to spite us. Mother was wittering, a real Oscar-winning performance of maternal distress, while Meg took Ben's temperature and called him 'poor lamb'.

Mother said, 'I told him to wash his hands before eating. Look at those fingernails. And he was playing near the chickens in the dirt. It's probably Salmonella.'

Ben groaned, as if Mother had prepped him to emote on certain key words.

'Doesn't have a temperature,' Meg said. 'Do you feel sick, love? It might just be nerves, worried about his dad. Do you feel you need to go poo-poos, angel?'

I expected Ben to burst up at any moment and shout, 'Surprise!' but he just lay there because I'd done such an excellent job prepping him. I wanted to have just one moment with Danny to whisper, 'Look, we're kind of tricking you, but it's not because I don't like you, because I really do.' But I couldn't.

'He's got bad diarrhoea,' Mother said to Meg. 'Can I see what medicines you've got? Ben's got such a sensitive tummy, so nothing too strong.'

Meg nodded and went searching.

Then Mother played her next trump card. 'Danny,' she said, 'could you be a hero and stay here with Ben? He's scared of the dark.'

Maybe Danny did what she asked just for my sake, or maybe he stayed because he was genuinely worried about Ben. The sight of Danny there with his hand on my little brother's head made me think, he's such an amazingly nice guy. This was my last chance to warn Danny what Mother really had planned, but I just stared open-mouthed at him and was too ashamed.

'Hurry up, Haley!' Mother shouted to me from outside the bedroom door.

Prior Experience of Handling The Weapons You Intend To Use For Your Escape Is Probably A Good Idea

To be fair, the Jamie Oliver five-piece kitchen knife set was about as close as Mother had ever come to holding a weapon. Mother and me followed Meg through the darkness of the farmhouse, and I worried about what use Mother had planned for the big carving knife.

Meg was oblivious. 'Let's pray it's not the virus,' she said, staggering onwards, stumbling down the stairs. 'But if Ben's got it, that'll mean we've all been infected. Oh my Lord!' And Meg was practically crying and muttering to herself. 'Now, we've got kaolin and morphine in the storeroom but that might be too strong for a little one. Or some Pepto-Bismol, that would maybe do it ...'

'I'm pretty sure I saw some sauerkraut in the bunker,' Mother interjected. 'That's a good probiotic and usually calms his stomach.'

'Right you are,' Meg said, and changed her direction towards the bunker.

'Do you need the keys?' Mother said, and I thought she'd been too brazen.

'Danny's got them,' Meg replied, thinking for a second. 'Anyway, the bunker's got that stupid air-lock.'

'Mother, NO!' I whispered and tried to pull her to a stop but she pushed my arm away.

Meg didn't see anything, she was too busy stooping over before the bunker hatch, trying to grip the circular rim of steel. 'Give us a hand, would ya?' she said, 'Damn thing's so bloody heavy.' She handed me back the torch. 'Take that, would ya, love?' she asked. 'Oh, I hope the electricity comes back. If only Ed was here, he'd know what to do ...' as she strained to lift the heavy lid.

Mother helped and when it was open, Meg said, 'Hold it steady, eh, use your leg to take the weight. Whatever you do, don't drop the lid on my fingers!' Without thinking, Meg climbed down the ladder, jabbering as she went. 'I've an irritable bowel myself ... You're quite right, a bit of sauerkraut will do the job, saves me trawling through all those medical boxes in the storeroom.'

Meg reached the bottom and called up, 'Pass us down that

torch, would ya? Can't see a bloody thing.' I was about to do it when Mother pushed me aside. She nudged the lid with her hip and released her fingers. The last we saw of Meg was her startled face staring up at us, a flash of confusion in her eyes, her yelling voice cut short by the clang of the metal lid and the whistle of air fleeing from the air-lock.

Mother was already putting her whole weight on the turning wheel. 'Help me, for God sake!' she shouted, and I did and became complicit. Mother jammed a broomstick in the wheel handle and said, 'Shit, what if we just locked her in there with the keys? I wouldn't want to have to go down there and get them off her now.'

Meg's yelling and pounding on the other side sounded muffled. We hadn't considered how she might breathe in there in the airtight shelter without electricity to fuel the air pump. Mother whisked me on before the guilt could catch up with me.

I don't know if it was part of her plan, but Mother picked up a boulder and carried it over to the diesel generator. Maybe all the noise and fumes had just been bugging her. She raised it and threw it down hard onto the spinning chain wheel. She pushed me back and threw her arm across her eyes as the chain gadget thing snapped and flew and the last of the lights went out.

I heard a noise and my torch found Danny in the doorway. 'Haley, what's going on? Where's my mum?' I felt totally torn.

'Meg's off to get the tools to fix the generator,' Mother said, before I could screw it up. 'She said to tell you you're the boss now till Ray gets back. And you need to get your weapon for perimeter patrol.'

'Isn't that cancelled? I thought Kane was ...'

'No, no,' Mother said, 'your mother said you'll need to patrol the fence, right now, with a gun. Oh, do you still have the keys for the gate?'

'Yeah, of course,' Danny said. And he flashed me a smile that made me feel even more guilty. Sometimes when you're involved in a lie, the only way out is to see it through.

Mother pushed me to walk ahead with Danny. He whispered to me, 'Hey, why are you being so weird? Did I kiss you too hard? Sorry, I really like you. I've never...'

Oh, Danny. If only I could just have told him that what Mother was doing would make him hate me forever. I had this feeling of fate and falling, like I had no power to stop it.

At the door to the weapons store, I held the torch while Danny sorted through the keys. Mother flooded him with words, so he wouldn't have a second to think. 'Must be hard to remember which key is for what?'

'Yeah,' Danny said, 'the blue one's for the weapons, the red one's for the food. I put labels on them myself, with duct tape.'

Danny put the key in the lock. He handed me the torch and his fingers glanced off mine. He smiled and asked, 'Did Mum say a crossbow, or a rifle?' I wanted to shout out, Stop! This is all a horrible trick!

As if sensing my potential screw-up, Mother butted in. 'A gun, definitely, the one you had before, please.'

He stepped inside and under the torchlight I watched him proudly pick up the rifle. It had a dull dark weight about it and it gave me the belly-ache.

'Oh, Meg said to make sure it's loaded.'

'They're all loaded all the time,' he said. Then something clicked. 'But Mum knows that...'

With sudden violence, Mother pushed past me and I fell to the ground, dropping the torch. I heard shouts and scrambling in the dark, a sound like a slap and click of metal. My hands panicked over the concrete floor to grab the light.

'Give me the keys,' Mother was screaming. 'Do it! Now!'

I lifted the torch and she had the rifle pointed at Danny. He raised his hands before himself, and told her to be careful, she didn't know what she was doing. Mother fiddled with something on the gun and yelled, 'I don't know if this is the safety catch but get on the GROUND now!'

Danny lowered himself, saying, 'OK, OK,' trying to unhook the keys from his jeans.

A deafening blast threw Mother backwards and I raised the torch.

'Danny, Danny! Oh my God! Mother, you shot him!'

'I'm OK, I'm OK!' came his voice from inside. His eyes were horror-struck, but there was no sign of blood and he threw me the keys. 'Take them, take them, put the gun down, please.'

Mother bore down on us both. 'Pick up the damned keys, Haley. Don't be stupid. I need both my hands, do it now!'

'I'm really, really sorry,' I whispered to Danny, but it felt lame, like, 'I'm really sorry you can't come to our party,' not, 'I'm really sorry we nearly tore a hole in your face with an assault rifle.' I picked up the keys and I really wanted to say, 'I really like you. A whole lot. Like, tons. This wasn't my idea at all. She tricked me too and when I kissed you it was because I really wanted to, not because she made me.' But Mother shrieked before I could say a thing.

'This is not the time for sweet nothings! Lock it now!' and she kicked the door between me and Danny shut. I didn't even get to see his eyes to see if he forgave me. 'Get that lock on! Bolt it,' she yelled. 'And don't try anything, young man, or I'll shoot you through the door!'

I got the lock on and Mother and I stood there in the dark, one torch and one gun between us, both shaking with nerves, both staring at the lethal weapon, horrified at the power she held. What would we do if Ray came back now?

'What about the perimeter fence?' I asked. 'Are we going to walk all that way? How far? And this late?' It was so dark and cold.

She stared into the night, the torchlight made her face look haunted. 'Go and fetch your brother,' she said, 'and bring the food bag and blanket. Hurry!'

I wanted to shout, 'Sorry, sorry, this really wasn't my idea,' to

Meg and Danny and the whole world. But Mother grabbed my arm and shook me roughly: 'Haley, focus, for God's sake. We have to move fast, we're now in very great danger!'

I bundled Ben's sheets into my rucksack and got him out the door, with the promise of a multi-pack of his favourite cheesy crisps once we got to the end of our new vaventure.

We found Mother in major meltdown at the gate. Ben was giving it, 'Where's Danny?' 'Where's Dad?' and 'Where's my chocolate? You promised!' I was freaking that Danny might shoot the lock off the gun store at any second. I'd witnessed his rage against Ray before. I checked over my shoulder while Mother tried key after key in the big metal gate. She dropped them in the mud. 'I've been through them all!' she groaned. 'Which bloody key is it?'

Her hands were trembling like crazy with adrenaline.

'Where are we going? Can Danny come?' Ben whined. Mother snapped, stepped back and glared at the razor wire, sizing up whether we could climb over.

'No fucking way!' I said, and grabbed the keys off her. I tried one after another till there was a loud clunk, then a creak of hinges and the gates swung open on their own weight. Mother yelled, victorious, and picked Ben up. The metal moved past me and I saw the vast expanse of black wilderness open up before us. Mother pushed past me and the cold mountain wind hit me. I turned and stared back at the farmhouse. I looked at the razor wire and its glints of moonlight, and the tracks in the mud where Dad's SUV had been.

'Bloody hell, Haley! Come on with that torch, it's dark as hell,' Mother shouted. She had already marched over the threshold and vanished into the blackness beyond with Ben in her arms. I pulled my collar tight and tried not to think of the dark mountains and the chill wind waiting for us.

'Hurry up, Haley!' Mother shouted. 'Or stay there if you like, but give me that damn torch!'

Choice kills me.

How To Survive In A Wilderness

Be Prepared

To survive in a mountain range, you will need the following:

protein bars	paper map	compass
tin cup	duct tape	waterproof (WP) tent
WP sleeping bag	extra socks	GPS locator
flare gun & flares	camping stove	ignition materials
heavy gloves	hat	hunting knife
Swiss army knife	marker pen	superglue
30ft of rope	bandages	air-horn or rape alarm
1 litre of fresh water for every four hours		
outdoor survival manual		sturdy boots w/ ankle support

We were seriously in shit, to say the least, having only three of the twenty-four things required to survive.

We ran down the dirt track as fast as Ben could move without actually dragging his little blob bod. To make it seem like 'fun' for Ben, and to make him speed the hell up, Mother started singing, 'Five little monkeys jumping on the bed, one fell down and bumped his head.'

I ran ahead down the dirt track through No Man's Land and my torchlight hit the ghostly shapes of abandoned refrigerators and broken TVs dumped in gullies. Suddenly, there was a man crouching with a gun.

'Ray! No!' I gasped.

But it was just one of Danny's stupid soldier targets.

Mother shouted, 'Hey, over here! Keep pointing the torch at the track, dummy!'

It couldn't be more then half a mile to the perimeter fence. I shouted back to Mother, 'What do we even do after the big gate?'

'We'll be free,' Mother said, doing her 'positivity' thing and adding, 'No more monkeys jumping on the bed!'

I was pretty sure I'd heard Dad say it was thirty miles to the nearest village. I tried not to think about Ray and his rifle or the fog or the temperature, which was falling fast. Can human beings actually walk thirty miles in one night, and with Ben in tow? I shouldn't have mumbled any of these things because Ben ground to a halt.

'Are we there yet? Can you carry me?'

Mother glared at me. 'Now why did you say that, Haley? We were doing just great and you had to open your mouth and...'

'Carry me,' Ben said. 'On your soldiers.' Because I think he deliberately gets soldiers and shoulders mixed up so as to manipulate us with cuteness.

'No, Ben,' Mother groaned, 'if I start carrying you now, we'll never get there. I can barely even lift you as it is. Anyway, aren't you big and strong? I bet you are. I bet you can beat me in a race.' She put her hands on her knees, her face right next to his. Really, you had to marvel. 'OK, on your marks, wait for it ... get set ... GO!'

Ben sprinted on down the dirt track, but looked over his shoulder and tripped in his outsized rubber boots. He went face down into a rocky puddle and started howling. Mother tried to clean him up with her sleeve and she checked for 'boo boos' with the torch, but he'd torn a hole in his little jeans and his knee was bleeding. We had no bandages. We had no antibacterial cream. If the cut was deep, we could have used superglue on the wound, as per Dad's survival guide.

Mother kissed Ben's sore knee and dragged him on with another chorus of 'Five Little Monkeys'. My head was numb with fear and freezing fog. I pictured Danny, shooting the lock off the weapons shed and running after us, furious, vengeful, his rifle pointed at us.

I turned to look back and the safe house had vanished.

'C'mon, c'mon, keep going,' I told myself, foot after freezing foot.

Mother's torchlight vanished into nothingness a hundred yards ahead of me, then suddenly a light flashed back at us. 'Mother, run! Hide!' I yelled, but she ran straight towards it. The light had a vertical shape, shiny and metallic. We'd reached the perimeter fence.

Mother dropped the keys. She was pretending it wasn't from terror – her fingers were just cold, she said. She handed me the keys and lifted Ben up, but she was worried then about having him in her arms and the assault rifle over her shoulder, so she pulled it over her head and handed it to me. 'Take it, just for a minute, please.'

I told her I wasn't touching that damned thing. It looked like it had killed people in some war already. She untangled herself from it, set it down in the mud, and we both stared at it in the torchlight, like it was some deadly snake. She nudged it with her foot into the ditch beside the track. I flinched as it hit the bottom, but it didn't explode. 'Euuuww, good riddance,' Mother said.

In a wilderness survival situation, a gun can serve a triple function, not just for self-defence or for hunting for food, but to act as a signal, to alert rescue teams to your location. Gunshots can be heard for miles.

We had literally just ditched our best source of food and rescue.

I unlocked the gate and Mother tried to distract shivering, beloved Benster from his bleeding knee. The gate shuddered and creaked open. It was a deer fence, two or three meters high and topped with older, rusted razor wire. Mother yelled, 'We did it! Benjamin, we're free. Yay, Benji!'

I said it was maybe not such a brilliant idea to be making such a damn noise. I seriously didn't want to be a total killjoy, but on the other side of the fence I felt the presence of the black mountains against the black sky, invisibly hanging over us, and the only lifeline back to home was the dirt track.

'Stop, Mother,' I said, 'we can't go on the track. It's the way Ray'll come if he comes back, and Kane and Dad.'

'Smart thinking!' Mother announced. 'Fine, we'll walk over the hills then.'

Her big idea was, we'd use the dirt track as our guide but we'd stay about two hundred yards away from it, following it at a safe distance.

Mother grabbed the torch from my hand. 'C'mon then, we haven't got all night. What song shall we sing next?' And she dragged Ben away into the squelching mud and heather. In seconds the torchlight looked tiny, bouncing into a black void. There were no stars to guide us, and who the hell knows how to read stars anyway?

'One little, two little, three little aeroplanes,' Mother's voice came as her light vanished. 'Four little, five little, six little...'

How To Navigate With Nothing

As Dad's survival guide says, fifty people die each year in the exact same mountain range we were heading into, and most of these are experienced hillwalkers and mountaineers, with a full kit. If you do not have a GPS system, a map, a fully charged phone and signal, or you've never studied stellar navigation, then, for God sake, do not lose sight of the tracks or riverbeds you are using to navigating with.

I must have been stumbling around in a daze for an hour, because when I jarred my ankle and screamed in pain, I realised we'd lost the track completely and were in some random open marshland.

I yelled at them, 'STOP! Look! We're lost, for frick's sake!'

Mother snatched the torch from me, hissing, 'Shhhh!' and she made signs to say, 'not in front of your little brother'.

Ben was on a loop, whimpering and moaning, 'I'm hungry,' 'I'm sleepy,' 'I have a boo boo,' 'Carry me!' Poor kid, it must have been, like, five hours past his bedtime, but truth be told, I could have utterly strangled him. Plus, the stupid torch was giving up on us.

'I know exactly where we're going,' Mother declared. 'I'll lead the way and you can carry Ben.'

Then I saw a single bright star in the sky right above where Mother was headed, and my head said, North Star. But if we were walking north, north was more mountainous and 'sub-Arctic tundra', and totally not the way home.

The torch went out. I heard Mother hitting it, then it flickered back to life for a bit, then off. There in the dark, I suddenly felt really ashamed.

'Mother, why did we have to do that to Danny?' I said. 'It was totally crappy. Why couldn't we have taken him with us?'

Ben immediately started moaning and shuddering, 'I want Danny, I want Danny!'

Mother snapped, 'God, Haley! Why did you have to start that?!'

'We could have at least asked Danny to help us. We could have waited a day,' I said, 'and I could have explained it all to him. He's smart, he'd totally have understood. He thinks Ray's a dick, too.'

Mother bashed the torch but it stayed dead. 'Haley, sometimes you can be so naïve!'

'But Danny'll blame me now … he'll hate me! He'll think I'm a two-faced … prostitute.'

'Look, I'm sorry that I took you away from your new boyfriend.'

'He's not my boyfriend. God!'

'But what does it matter what he thinks?' she shouted. 'You'll never see him again!' Jesus, was that the way she treated all men?

She punched the torch and it re-lit again. She trudged onward, declaring, 'Come on, lazy bones, it's this way!'

Ben's little frozen hand gripped mine. 'Where's Danny?' 'Haley, I'm hungry,' 'I'm sleepy,' 'I have a boo boo,' 'I'm freezing,' 'Can you carry me?'

How To Recognise The Symptoms Of Hypothermia

The onset of hypothermia has the following symptoms:

1. Cold and blue skin.
2. Enlarged pupils.
3. Slurred speech or mumbling.
4. A headache that makes you want to close your eyes.
5. A desire to 'just have a little rest' by lying down.
6. A sudden, inexplicable feeling of being warm.

We stumbled through bracken, heather, thistles, gorse, bog moss and all the other pointless freezing crap in this stupid mountain range. Mother had totally lost the dirt track, and the plot. She kept saying, 'Keep up, children. It's just over the next hill!' But it never was. Basically, Mother was creating her own guide on How To Kill Your Kids By Accident.

My ears and forehead were migraine-ish. My lungs ached with stabbing pains. My muscles were getting heavier and slo-mo. Ben's weight grew on my back and I sensed that he'd nodded off. I wanted to give up and lie down and sleep. I pictured my brain in a skull full of frozen water and I thought of my dad's madness.

I staggered behind Mother's single shaking spot of light and I realised how she'd survived after Dad and her split. She'd turned herself into a forward pushing force, head down, forging on alone, against the wind. She was fifty feet ahead of us, fighting her own exhaustion. Her strategy was always, 'Don't ask questions, don't doubt, just put one foot after the other, be practical, don't think about the bigger picture. You'll never keep the kids going if you don't believe in yourself. Never look back.' She couldn't admit, ever, that she'd made a mistake.

I stopped. Mother hadn't even turned to see if me and Ben were following. In this foggy darkness she wouldn't have heard our calls to stop and wait. She could've left us three miles behind before even realising.

'Mother!' I called out, 'Wait, Please!'

I heard a breaking twig, and I froze. It shook me awake. I couldn't see a damn thing. My skin was prickling and I felt eyes upon me. We were being circled. Mother stumbled back towards us, yelling, 'What? What is it? What's wrong?'

I grabbed her torch and whispered, 'Shh, I think it's Kane. Kill the light!' I led her to a boulder to hide. She took Ben from me, her movements all clumsy and frozen-ish. My teeth chattered and I whispered, 'I think she's stalking us. What do we do?'

The sound of creeping footsteps moved closer through the heather. A dozen tiny snappings under the weight of one foot then another, coming round us from the other side. Mother gasped, 'God!' and whispered, 'Give me the gun.' But we'd left the damn thing behind.

A sound like an old man clearing his throat behind me. I gasped.

'Kane! Ray! Whoever the hell you are! Stay back!' Mother yelled. 'I have a weapon!'

She swung the torch round and two red eyes glowed back through the blackness. I screamed. Mother screamed. Ben screamed as Mother dropped him. This thing let out a high-pitched snort. Legs bolted and Mother swept the torch after it and we heard the thunder of many others.

Deer. Everywhere around us. Huge and hairy and muscular and perfect and terrified.

Mother burst into laughter. 'Deer, darling, it was only deer.'

But Ben was wailing in the mud. I picked him up and he was soaked and shuddering.

Mother chortled, 'Scared us half to death! Stupid deer!'

I'd had enough. I stomped deeper into the heather. I shouted that it was no bloody joke, and next time it would be Ray for real and he'd most likely shoot us and throw us in the quagmire and no one would find our bodies for a thousand years, like peat-bog-man.

'Shh, you're upsetting Benjamin,' Mother said, and she turned to him. 'It's OK, darling, Haley's being a silly billy, everything's fine, we'll be home in our lovely house soon.'

'OK? Everything is not OK, have you even heard of the word "hypothermia"?' I yelled at her. 'It's not fair, Mother. You say, for the sake of Ben, let's not tell him … but I'm sick of it. So we just keep telling him lies all the time, do we? Telling him everything's hunky dory? Jesus, Mother. Everything is not OK. We're going to fucking die out here!'

'Language!' she snapped.

'You think language is our primary problem in this location?'

'Mummy, Haley said the Fuh-word,' Ben said.

Then the rain began. It pounded at us from every direction.

'Fuh this!' I yelled. 'Fuh you! Fuh both of you!'

And I stomped off, heading most likely even further away from the stupid track in pointless circles, deeper into wet, furious, totally lethal darkness.

Beware Of Peat Bogs

Peat bogs behave like quicksand. Peat bogs and quicksand kill, on average, two hundred people a year.

'I'm sinking, oh God,' Mother called out from the dark, making me drop the torch. 'You moron, Haley! You led us into a peat bog. Help me, for God's sake!'

'Where are you? I can't find the torch!' I screamed back, my mouth numb with cold. And I squelched into exactly the same mire that she, twenty feet from me, was sinking into.

'Quick. It's got my boot,' she yelled. 'God, God, it's sucking my leg down. Euwww!'

Ben started wailing, 'Mummy where are you? Where's Mummy?'

I was sinking up to my knee but I grabbed a rock and pulled myself out. I searched the gross slime for the torch, but found nothing but twigs. 'Ben, quick, help me find it,' I shouted, and he slumped forward beside me.

'Stay where you are, Ben, don't move! You might get sucked in too!' Mother screamed. 'My God, it's got both my legs now! HELP!'

I'm not proud to admit it but I was scared that if I went to help her I'd get pulled under as well.

Ben found the torch and I aimed it at where I could hear Mother struggling. She was sinking fast, up to her waist in the bog and thrashing about. 'For God's sake, get over here and HELP ME!' she yelled. 'Do something!' Mother fell to one side. The bog had both her legs and one of her arms now, sucking her in like a huge mouth.

At this point, I should have used my thirty feet of rope, and got her to fasten it round her waist and pulled her out. But we didn't have any aforementioned rope, or anything. All we had were the literal clothes I was wearing.

Her screams made me think of something Dad taught us years ago on one of our woodland vaventures.

To save someone from a peat bog, here is what you must do:

1. If you don't have any rope, you must take off your jacket and your jumper and tie them together in a knot.
2. Standing there in your bra in the rain, you must then find the edge of the bog, and make sure you don't fall in, too.
3. Grab one end and throw the other end to the sinking person.
4. You must, through yelling, convince the sinking person to lower herself flat into the peat slime, so that she is not in a vertical position sinking downwards, but horizontal, like someone swimming. This is counter-intuitive as most people will automatically want to keep their face as far away from the stinking bog as possible.
5. The sinking person must grab the improvised rope and let you pull them out, very slowly, inch-by-inch, not wriggling and not trying to stand.

Many minutes of yelling and grunting and muscle agony and primordial farting suction sounds later, I pulled Mother out and we collapsed together breathless and covered in black slime. I tried to rescue her rubber boot, but it suddenly filled with a rush of malign goop and was sucked under, and I had a major 'that could have been you' moment. And Ben said, 'Wow!' then he started crying.

I helped Mother to stand. Ben shivered and pointed fearfully at Mother's bare foot in the flickering light. It looked like a ghost limb.

She leaned on my shoulder and tested her weight. 'Thank God,' she said, 'I thought I'd sprained it.' Somehow, she laughed. 'Well, I'll just have to hop home,' she said. 'Can I rest on your shoulder, Benji-Boo? Oooh, the squelchy slime's going between my toes ... Yuk, it's so cold and gooey.'

I wiped the black goop from the torch glass and it flickered again. I noticed that Mother's lips looked blue-ish and she was trembling all over. She and Ben limped on ahead of me in the failing torch beam, adult led by child. Mother's one bare foot and calf were shining white and disembodied in the darkness, like a lost limb from some Greek sculpture.

And I got a flash of how it would end for us. Not with the virus or the marauding mobs or with a bullet from Ray's gun, but by a silly mistake. The strongest person sprains her ankle from walking barefoot and she's too heavy to be carried by her children, so she says, 'Go on without me, get help and come back, I'll stay right here.' The kids wander for a night and day and get hopelessly lost. They argue and separate.

According to Dad's manual, rescue teams often find two bodies dead from hypothermia, half a mile from each other. In our case, it would be three.

Before You Reach The End Of Your Energy, Find Shelter

Rain fell in sheets on us. Ben's wails went exponential and my teeth chattered. No shelter, anywhere. The wet bog clothes and

Ben's dead weight on my back threw me off-centre. My foot jarred and my balance went. I let myself fall into it, like the marshland wanted me to. It had been whispering to me for miles, 'Lie down with us, close your eyes.'

I woke, limbs twisted, face down in icy-mud-water. Ben upside down on top of me, wailing. Mother pulled us up, in a panic.

I could barely get the words past my chattering teeth. 'Have to go … back … no good … Mother.'

Ben chuntered, 'I want to go home! I want muh … ma … my … daddy.'

Mother yelled, 'We ARE going home, if you could just keep up!'

'No, back to the farm!' I said. If we could even find it. 'Please, just admit failure, Mother, you know? We'll die out here, if we keep on. Please.'

'I want my daddy. Daddy. Daddy,' Ben whined.

'Daddy, Daddy, Daddy!' she exploded. 'How do you think that makes me feel? My God, you two are so selfish.'

So Mother marched off. Actually marched off, over a hill.

Ben screamed after her, 'I want Daddy! I want Daddy!' and I felt like joining in, replacing 'Daddy' with 'Danny'.

My torch was dead. I hit it and nothing happened. I undid the top and water poured out. From over the hill, I heard a yell. OK, I give in, I thought, Mother has broken her stupid leg or some shit. We're dead.

'There it is!' she was shouting. 'Come, quick!'

I dragged Ben over the hill and in the moonlight I saw the puddles of Ray's dirt track. My heart sank. Christ, we'd walked in circles all night.

But then, further on, the track broke into two.

Just great, I thought. My total favourite thing in the world. A crossroads. A frickin choice.

'Which one do we take?' Mother asked me, trying to hide her chattering teeth.

'Don't you remember, Haley, when your father drove you here?

Didn't you watch where you were going?'

In both directions, the barely moonlit landscape was frozen and featureless.

'This way or that?' Mother barked. Her lips were definitely blue and Ben's eyes looked wide and weird. 'If we wait for the sun to come up,' she shuddered, 'that would be east. Oh, Haley, please concentrate! Quick. Choose! Which way?'

'No way,' I said. 'If I choose wrong ... you'll scream at me ... make my life hell forever.' She was doing that thing she always accused me of: trying to get someone else to make the decision so that when it all went tits up, she could blame them.

'Well, choose the right one then!' she yelled.

Haley, Haley, quite contrary – give me a choice between a rock and hard place and I'll choose both. Neither.

I must have made a prayer to the non-existent God, because an answer appeared through the downpour. About three hundred yards into the peat bog was a tumbledown old barn thing.

I pointed. 'Look ... rest ... there ... need ... lie down ... can't go further. Ben ... freezing ... really ... freezing.'

Mother's teeth were properly chattering now, too. 'Typical, what's wrong ... with you, Haley? ... Any decision and you're totally ... If you hadn't dilly ... dallied back at the ... farm, none of ... this would have ... Well ... enough! I've had ... enough!'

'Screw you!' I yelled and I dragged my hypothermic sibling through the heather to the ruined stoned shell of a thing.

Fire And Food Are Essential For Outdoor Night-Time Survival. Failing That, Use Shared Bodily Warmth

We didn't have matches or any other ignition materials. What we did have, if we didn't get warm and dry, was a forty-two per cent chance of going to sleep and not waking up again.

I felt my way into the barn with hands outstretched and my frozen nose on alert. There was hay and little balls of dung. Some farmer, aeons ago, must have used it for sheep or something. I let my shoulder bag fall and Ben was shivering worse than me so I gave him my wet jumper and kissed his little head. I told him everything would be OK, just to try to fool myself, like Mother always did.

Mother surrendered and stumbled dripping through the doorway.

She capsized down and took Ben's boots off for him. Water poured out and she rubbed his toes to try to get his circulation going.

Survival Tip: In nineteenth century Scottish fishing culture, fisher-wives used to bring their half-drowned, frozen fisher-husbands back to life by placing the aforementioned men's feet under their armpits and between their warm breasts.

There was no way I could see Mother doing this.

I emptied my bag, searching for anything to make a fire with, but all we had was the half-box of breakfast cereal, the carrots and the huge kitchen knife. If all else fails, calories can generate body heat.

Ben dived into the cereal. I couldn't face food but Mother nibbled a carrot. They chewed like goats, without saying a word, teeth chattering. Ben grinned then he started whining, 'I'm thirsty, I'm so thirsty.'

Survival Tip: The dangers of dehydration are as follows:

1. Fresh water is more important than food. You can die of dehydration in a wet country.
2. By walking in mountainous terrain for three hours, you can lose half a litre of water through sweating.
3. If you lose more than a litre of water from your body, you will become dehydrated and your abilities will decline. Your organs are most essential, your muscles less so, so your body will send all fluid to your organs, depriving your muscles of the ability to move.
4. You can become sick from bacterial infections from

drinking rainwater or stream water that has not been boiled or sterilised.

5. Many mountain deaths are caused by giardia and norovirus, which cause vomiting and diarrhoea, both of which accelerate dehydration.

Ben randomly asked, 'Mum, do you have any elderflower cordial?'

Mother was clutching her head in pain and didn't reply, so then Ben found a puddle and was about to lap at it, dog-style, but I remembered Dad's instructions and snapped at him, 'No, Ben, it's not safe!'

Survival Tip: It is actually safer to drink your own urine or that of your fellow survivors than it is to drink untested, un-purified ground water.

My eyes were adjusting; maybe the sun was rising a little. Mother undid her coat and let Ben put his head inside. She closed her eyes and I stared at the hormonal happiness on her face, as Ben sucked his thumb. Like, for want of actual water, they were both pretending he was breastfeeding again. Gross.

Mother put an arm around me and squeezed me tight. She told me she was sorry we'd got lost and argued and that shared bodily warmth was natural. She admitted I'd been right to get shelter, and if we could just rest for a bit, the sun would come up and then we'd know which way was which. 'Snuggle in tight,' Mother said, 'and we'll be alright, through the night.'

Mother had never read dad's chapter on the hypothermia plus dehydration double whammy.

Her fingertips were definitely purplish, and her lips and Ben's too were grey-looking, but I couldn't stop them from dozing. My whole body ached and I felt myself tumbling into sleep. 'Mother!' I woke with a jolt and nudged her. 'We have to stay awake, all of us. Dad said that about the cold! He said you have to keep talking.'

'Shh,' she grumbled. 'Ben's sleeping.'

I had to ask her the question, the big one.

'Mother, what if we even get back to the city and there's thousands of people dying from the virus?'

'Don't be insane.' She shivered.

I stared at the mouldy walls, covered in random markings maybe made by a human. And I thought about my dad and madness. I got up and stood in the doorway, staring out at the peaks as they glowed a grey orange. The rising sun was behind me, which meant we had been walking north all night and further away from civilisation.

I was crying, I guess, but not just because we were going to die.

I heard a noise then.

It was the wind, but it had some kind of echoing distant growl like an engine within it.

I shook Mother. 'Something's coming, we have to hide!'

Mother jumped up, perplexed, but then she heard it too. A buzz getting louder, but because of the echoing mountains it was impossible to tell which direction it was coming from.

'Maybe it's a plane?' I suggested.

She listened and said, 'No, it's a farm vehicle. Farmers have phones ... Benjamin, wake up!'

Then we both saw it. 'There it is,' she shouted, pointing at the headlights that had appeared. 'Haley, wake Benjamin. I knew someone would come, I knew it!' She ran towards the growing lights and I yelled, 'No! Stop!' It could only be Ray, and he probably hadn't found Dad, and he'd be murderously pissed when he found us. Plus, Ray would be contaminated.

'Hide, Mother. Fuck sake!' I screamed, but she kept on walking closer to it. What should I do? Drag Mother away or run and hide with Ben?

The two lights became a jeep but I couldn't see the driver's face. The engine growled and the lights were skidding everywhere and the driver was in a frenzy. Mother stood in the middle of the track, waving her arms in the air, jumping, calling out against the snarling engine. Some gut instinct forced me towards her, screaming, 'Get down!'

I hit her hard and threw both of us to the ground, our faces just feet from the track. The jeep roared towards us and I was terrified it would skid and hit us. The speeding wheels threw mud over us, barely a foot from our faces.

It was Ray at the wheel, I saw him, but he hadn't seen us and wasn't stopping. As the back wheel cleared, a heavy thing of metal spun and bounced in its wake. It was Dad's SUV, stained and damaged.

I got to my feet then, not caring anymore about being seen. Through the back window, speeding away from us, I caught sight of a human body entirely covered by a sheet.

Keep A Safe Distance Of Three Metres From Potentially Contaminated People

If a person has been retrieved from an area contaminated with Virus X, even if that person is dead, they will remain highly infectious for over a week.

My aching guts told me this body was my dad.

'Stop! Where I can see you!' Ray jumped out of the jeep with his rifle trained on me, a medical mask over his face, blue rubber gloves on. 'How the hell did you get here?' he yelled. 'Don't come any closer! Where's your mother?'

I ran to the back door of the jeep, trying to unlock it. I'd been lucky Ray had seen me in his rear-view mirror, screaming at him to stop.

'Dad, Jesus, is that you? Dad!' I banged on the windows. I couldn't bear to even think the thought. 'Is he ... OK?'

'Yes, it's your father,' Ray said. The 'it' was motionless, the sheet covered its entire face. Ray yelled at me to step back, told me to be calm, prepare myself. 'Don't go inside the vehicle!' he shouted. 'He's probably infected.'

I yanked the door open and I fell inside, wanting to touch Dad but the stillness of the body repelled me. I was sort of wailing the word 'Dad' on repeat.

'Get a mask on,' Ray yelled. 'He's alive, but in a hell of a state.'

Ray threw me a surgical mask and gloves. I put them on and watched as he pulled the sheet from Dad's face. His cheek was burned, his mouth blistered, one of his eyes was caked with blood, the other was distant with pain. Alive. 'Dad!' I recoiled and called for Mother and Ben.

Ray raised his gun to the landscape. 'Is your mother armed? Did you see anyone else? A mob with weapons?'

'No, no one.'

My dad moved a hand from beneath the blanket. His mouth was cracked and dry, and he was struggling to speak. His blackened, blistered fingertips reached for my face and I was hit by this stench, like a burned frying pan, and I couldn't breathe. His one good eye struggled towards me. 'Hale,' he whispered, or it might have been 'hell'. Ray yelled, 'Get back! Don't let him touch you!'

But how could I not? Dad touched my cheek and everything spun and went dark.

What To Do In A
Massive Medical Emergency

**Worst-Case Scenario: Many Group Members Will Become
Contaminated In The Attempt To Save One Life**

The diesel fumes hit me and my eyes opened. The jeep threw me
around, woozy and seasick, and for a second I had that lovely
post-fainting feeling before realising I was staring straight up at
Mother's chin. She had a medical mask on and I worked out my
head was resting on her lap and I recoiled away from her.

Across from me lay this gasping, wheezing, burned creature
that I couldn't believe was my actual dad. Then I remembered
everything.

Mother was sat on one of the jeep benches and she didn't look
at Dad or out the windows or at me. She was wearing blue surgical
gloves, like Ray, and she was trying to get Ben to keep his mask on.
Medical boxes lay scattered all around the jeep floor and Mother's
eyes were catatonic in terror.

Ray yelled back from the steering wheel, 'No one touch him!
If he's infected then we're probably all contaminated already, but
don't take any risks!'

I sat beside Dad's body. Every movement of the jeep caused
him to gasp in pain. I stared at the red welts on his eyelids. The hair
was burned off one side of his face. I couldn't take his hand in case
it caused him more pain. I whispered, 'Dad, oh Dad,' and tried to
summon his old face, as if that would save him.

Ray was driving like mad and I was confused, because Ray was
one of the good guys, after all. He was strong and he'd found Dad,
and there really was a deadly virus and people were rioting and

dying out there. I wanted to know why Dad was burned, what had happened – would Dad survive? – but Ray was driving to save Dad's life and couldn't be interrupted.

'It's a four-one-seven, base five-niner, one man down, do you read me?' he shouted into his walkie-talkie. 'Need full decontamination procedure. Over.'

I sat and stared. On the two bench seats facing each other were my two opposing worlds. To my right, Mother was rubbing Ben's arms to get his circulation back. 'But is that really Dad?' Ben said and pointed, and Mother whispered, 'Shh, shh, it's going to be OK,' as she tried to cover his eyes.

It was like this was their eternally frozen pose, like her whole life was about surgically removing all truth from Ben, denying that one day he'd grow up and leave her and hate her, like I did now. I could have just sat there wailing, 'Dad, oh Dad,' as I watched his burned face gasping for breath, but I couldn't cry, I was just too furious.

'Mother, listen to me,' I shouted over the noise of the engine. 'Dad said to ask you about Section 3. What does it mean?'

She did not reply or raise her eyes to me or Dad.

'What does it mean?'

'Haley … this is neither the time nor the place,' she snapped. Then she stroked Ben's brow, trying to get him to stop staring at Dad's burned body in its shroud-like sheet.

I felt Dad's leg shivering against my back as the jeep skidded, and I stared at mother's frozen face. She was utterly hiding something. 'What does it mean?' I continued, relentless. 'Three sections of a book? Sections of what … a pie, a brain, a fucking what?' Then it hit me: that time Dad took the pills in the bathroom. 'Jesus, Mother! Did you have Dad sectioned?'

She was so drained and not fully in control of her usual self-censorship, so the truth started slipping out. 'It wasn't just me, Haley. The doctor and … another responsible person … decided he had to be taken to hospital for a while. They said the third level of security was best for his own protection.'

'You mean like … locked in … like, a madhouse?'

'They don't have madhouses anymore, Haley. Please, you're scaring Ben.'

'Wait, wait,' I said, 'but if they don't have madhouses anymore then why couldn't Dad just walk out? Like a regular hospital.'

She closed her eyes and shook her head. 'He had to stay in, until he was well, by law,' she said. The jeep was throwing her about and I knew she was hiding something really huge and hearing Dad's wheezing breath fuelled me.

'How long was he in the hospital for?'

'I didn't know it would be so long, Haley. I thought he'd be in for a month, but then it was six and they had to re-evaluate him and the doctors kept him in for another three.'

It was getting lighter now and I saw the huge blisters on Dad's face. I said, 'Wait, did you just say that you, personally, locked Dad up for nine months?'

'Haley, please calm down and sit down!'

But hold on, no, no, there was other information coming at me now and this didn't match up. I was back at the age of ten and she was telling me, 'Your dad's gone on a little holiday.' And that had really hurt my feelings at the time because I thought he'd gone away all by himself and that was selfish and I'd wanted to go too. And he hadn't even taken any photos of his beach or brought me back a snow globe. And I'd been furious with him because he wouldn't even tell me anything about his selfish adventure. I was ten, for God's sake.

I was crying now as all the hidden pieces finally clicked together, and I stared at this burned creature that was my dad gasping for life. 'You told me Dad wanted to live alone after his "holiday"!'

And Mother's silence was more proof of guilt.

'You said he didn't want to live with us anymore, like he didn't love us anymore. Like it was his choice!'

Mother's eyes narrowed, like a cornered animal. Ben cowered

from me but I couldn't stop.

'Oh, how inconvenient it must have been to have a mentally ill husband, how impractical. You couldn't possibly take care of him yourself, in our house, could you? And we must always be practical, mustn't we, Mother?'

'Haley, shut up!'

'You liar,' I shouted. 'No wonder Dad did this. He wasn't crazy till you drove him crazy. He was just sick and he needed us, and you locked him up! Then you lied to me and Ben!'

Her face was furious.

I stared at Dad's closed eyes, his left side seemed burned to the bone. 'Then you divorced him, like a punishment for being sick!' I screamed. 'You tricked him. You didn't love him!'

Mother rose swiftly in the jeep and Ben fell from her lap.

'You're so blind!' I yelled. 'We could have died out there tonight, but oh no, you had to prove you were right. But you're wrong, wrong, wrong! If we ever got back to the city, there would be thousands of people dying from the virus! And me and Ben would get infected. Would you admit you were wrong then? Huh? No! Would you hell! You'd still insist Dad was mad. Look what you've done to him! Are you happy now? You self-righteous, stupid fucking bitch!'

Her eyes flashed and my head was thrown back by the impact. Waves of hot anger rushed to my cheek, where she'd slapped me. I glared back at her.

'I fucking hate you!' I yelled.

The jeep was thrown violently by a pothole and a plastic bag suddenly fell from beneath Dad's sheet. It was transparent but its surface was muddied and bloodied. Inside I could see some packets of pills, a pair of reading glasses, a pair of kiddie shoes, and the phone charger from Mother's car. They spilled onto the ground.

I wanted to scream some more at Mother, but I just sat fuming as we tore through the landscape. A red sunrise was colouring everything and I stared at this woman who could not raise her eyes to her former husband and now former daughter. The polari-sation that began at their divorce was now complete and I was no longer caught in the middle, swithering and indecisive. I chose, finally, and it filled me with a surge of energy I'd never felt before. Finally, everything was simple and clear. I didn't give a damn if we were all contaminated.

Dad had to live and Mother could die for all I cared.

Emergency Safe House Decontamination Protocol

If anyone from the group is potentially contaminated beyond the perimeter fence:

1. Do not permit entry, until 31-day self-isolation has been completed.
2. Build a small camp beyond the perimeter with one tent for each person, and each person must remain three metres away from others.
3. Water, food and medical supplies must be brought to the decontamination camp by one person in a hazmat suit.
4. Dispose of any bodies to prevent further contamination.

People in a panic and people who love each other are really crap at protocol, so Ray broke every one of Dad's rules and drove us through the perimeter gates, towards the farmhouse.

I was shitting it over what we'd meet when we got there. Over and above the fear of Dad dying, there was the very real possibility that Meg had suffocated in the bunker and that Danny was going ape-shit, searching for us with a gun.

In the last mile, I tried to explain and apologise to Ray about what Mother and me had done to escape. To my surprise, he didn't shout, but focused on accelerating up the twisting dirt track. He had a way of dealing with anger that I now understand. He didn't put it in a box and hide it away, like Mother did. He let anger fuel his actions. No time to waste on blame.

We skidded to a halt before the gates. I took the keys from Mother and ran to the locks, Ray's engine growling behind me. I opened the gates and a crossbow was suddenly in my face. Danny's eyes, full of fury.

'Stay back or I'll shoot.' Then he saw Ray and took a better look at me, and he was shitting it now as he realised we all had medical masks on. 'Jesus, you're contaminated! Get back! Fuck, fuck!!'

'Please, I'm sorry, Danny,' I yelled. 'Please, please. Help my dad!'

All hell was totally let loose. There was no sign of Meg, and Danny was yelling that she was trapped, that he couldn't get the hatch open. I went practically hysterical begging him to help carry my dad inside, but he yelled, 'Traitor! You tricked me. My mum could be dead!'

My own mother was useless, frozen and clinging to Ben in the back of the jeep. She was struggling to get the blue rubber gloves on my hysterical brother's tight little fists. And she herself, in terror, clinging to her N95 virus-proof face mask. I guess that was the moment, right there, that she accepted that Dad's pandemic was maybe not a deluded lie after all.

Ray grabbed Danny by the neck and threw his crossbow to the ground. 'Put your differences behind you, you little prick. We need to do this NOW!' He threw Danny a mask and rubber gloves. 'Put those on! It'll take three of us to carry Ed inside.'

The three of us staggered, carrying Dad, shrouded in the sheet, through the mud to the farmhouse door. Dad's weight was too much and I slipped, nearly dropping him. Danny refused to look at me. Ray kicked the door in and led us to the kitchen table, he scattered the pans and laid Dad down flat upon it.

Dad tried to speak, his blackened hands flailing around his scorched face.

'What is it, Dad, what are you saying?'

But Ray was shouting instructions. 'Right, now, try to calm your dad and get him some water. Danny, help me get your mother out!'

Dad was trying to speak but the effort was too great. I tried to give him some water but he just choked on it because he couldn't raise his head. His trembling hand was like burned plastic, brittle and crusted. I overcame my nausea and held it in my rubber-gloved fingers. His words were strangled, dry breaths, but they sounded like 'car' … 'fire'.

'Oh, Dad,' and I was crying, stupid guilty tears. 'Who did this to you? How did you get so burned? I'm sorry, so sorry, I should never have sent you off on that stupid fucking trip. This is all my fault.' And on I went saying sorry, sorry, as if it would be any stupid help. As much as I wanted to close my eyes to hide from the horror, I couldn't. I told myself I'd never let him out of my sight again.

Meg burst in, shouting at me, breathless. 'Silly bloody cow… never lock anyone … ever ever ever … the air-lock … I could have suffocated, for God's sake!' She stopped when she saw Dad. Her hand went to her mouth. 'God … Oh, Ed, what have they done to you, poor love?'

Then she was holding me tight in her big arms as her body shook with tears. She didn't have a mask or gloves on or anything. And this was something Dad warned about in his survival guide, that compassion and love can be the most lethal things in a pandemic. The desire to share touch with another suffering person.

Immediate Burn Measures

Survival Fact: With burn victims, the greatest danger is that the body goes into shock and the patient dies of a heart attack. So even before treating the burns, the blood pressure and pain levels must be taken down.

You will need: atropine, morphine, amoxicillin or another antibiotic, a cannula, an IV drip, a line and drip stand, purified water and disinfectant, sterile wipes, iodine.

Meg yelled out the list to Danny. 'And blood type O negative, a syringe and 08 needle. It's all labelled.' She threw Danny the keys and set down the big medical book next to Dad. 'You can save your sorries for later, madam,' she said, 'and I'll save beating the living shit out of you for later as well. But now we have work to do!'

Ben appeared at the door, wailing for his Daddy and randomly asking for a sandwich. 'Danny, take the little one with you,' Meg shouted, 'I don't want to be tripping over him, and it's best if he doesn't see.'

Danny led Ben out and my dad's good eye trembled open. He tried to speak, but Meg interrupted him: 'Save your breath, love, this is going to hurt.' She slowly pulled the sheet off Dad's body.

I turned my head away at first but when I saw the horror on Meg's face, I peered. I can't describe it, but it looked like his leg and his rubber boot had sort of melted into each other.

'Jesus Christ,' Meg whispered, and she told me to run and find Mother but I refused. She lifted the blanket higher. I gagged. It wasn't just the sight but the smell. 'Third-degree burns,' Meg said. 'Doesn't get any worse than this. You'd really best go, love.'

I told her I was staying, that I had to help.

Meg exposed Dad's feet. They looked chargrilled and dead already and, on one foot, not all of his toes were there. He lay there, trembling, grasping for breath in tiny spasms. Focus on his eyes, I told myself, as Meg took the scissors and cut away what was left of his jeans. I had to keep telling myself that this charred molten thing was actually my dad. Most of his leg was just as bad. Black and bubbling to the knee.

Dad's voice was a hiss, his tongue clicking, throat tight.

'He's choking,' I said, 'he's passing out. What if he doesn't wake up again?' Some inner animal sense told me then that Dad was going to die.

Meg put her hand on my shoulder. 'Go and help Danny, your dad needs morphine and fluids, really badly. Go help Danny, now!'

I couldn't face Danny's anger, but Dad came first so I ran off to find him. In the doorway I was stopped by a sub-human form cowering there. Mother was holding the bloodied bag of things – the pills, the trainers and her phone charger – in her blue-gloved hand. Her eyes to the ground, too scared to enter. Hanging there like a guilty ghost in her medical mask. In her other hand she held the kitchen knife we'd stolen.

'Go away!' I shouted, 'And stay away!'

She backed off and I ran.

If You're Not Part Of The Emergency Plan Then Get Out Of The Way

I had such huge guilt over what we'd done to Danny that I just had to apologise. I found him in the storage bunker, going through the boxes of medical supplies and putting on the surgical gloves in a hurry.

He spun round and snapped at me, 'What the hell do you want?'

That hurt. His tone, his eyes. 'I came to help you get the drugs and...' I muttered. Any normal decent person would have realised that this was no time for apologies.

'I'm taking care of it, I don't need your help.' He went through the fridge unit, checking the labels on bags of frozen blood.

'Can you just let me say sorry?' I finally ventured. 'I really like you, for real, I do, I really do.'

'Hold this,' he said and I shivered, seeing it was a bag of blood with Dad's name on it. 'And get a stand,' he said. But I didn't know what a stand was.

'Fine, don't help,' he said. And snatched the blood back. He went into another container and pulled out bags of fluids. 'Should never have let you come here,' he said. 'Stupid, stupid.' And he wouldn't meet my eye. He got a long pole with wheels and this was a drip stand.

'I know I did something bad,' I sniffed, 'but why are you being so horrible to me, Danny?'

'This isn't about you and your unique and wonderful feelings, Haley. In case you haven't noticed, Ed is dying!'

'He's my dad! MY DAD!' I cracked into tears and I thought he was going to hold me or slap me, and either would have been better than this coldness. I moved closer, but he stepped aside and went into a box full of pill packets.

'Don't touch me. I mean it,' he said. 'We've all got to stop being so soft. Toughen up.' He fastened the drip bag to the drip stand. 'If I hadn't been so sappy, none of this would have happened. Stupid, stupid.'

I held my arms out for him. 'Danny, please, just…'

'No!' he said. 'You're just a little clingy kid, and the people who attacked your dad are still out there.' He reached his hand over my head and held the edge of the ladder. 'They're coming for us next. You best start learning how to defend yourself. Now. If you want to make yourself useful, learn how to shoot.'

It was only yesterday we were kissing.

'Otherwise you're just in everyone's way,' he said.

I just stood there at the bottom rung as he held the fluids, the morphine and everything.

'Get out of my way!' And he pushed past me, his shoulder bashing my head.

He despised me. It left me hollow and gasping. I stood there watching his back vanish up the ladder and realised that this must have meant I was in love with him, or something.

Never Put Ice On Burns

To treat a severe burn injury, you must:

1. Never put ice on third-degree burns. The heat contrast will end up causing more damage to the burnt skin.
2. Apply cool water, not creams.
3. Remove dead skin.
4. Cover with a thin gauze to let the burns breathe.

Meg had me reading from the home doctor manual. It freed up the use of both of her hands and it was educational, she said. Plus, it kept me out of the way of her scalpel and syringe and stopped me and her from panicking.

She gave my dad a shot of morphine and hooked him to the drip, telling me that he needed to sleep, that it was a miracle he was still alive. Then she was weeping, and she muttered that she could handle the rest of the bandages herself and that I should have a rest too.

But I couldn't. Mother and Ben were up in the bedroom self-quarantining, which amounted to Ben wailing for Dad and Mother, most likely running out of distracting lies to tell him. I read on, '*In such cases, do not attempt to treat at home but seek immediate medical attention.*'

Ray stepped in from the shadows, shook his head. 'No hospitals,' he said.

'But why can't we take him?' I asked. 'Why?'

'Death traps,' Ray said. 'Every contaminated person in the country will be heading to a hospital right now.'

Survival Fact: One of the most overlooked things by preppers is non-virus related safety. Because if you cut yourself or break your leg, you'll have to go to hospital, and if you go to hospital you'll get contaminated, like forty-nine per cent of patients did in the last pandemic.

'We've got all the medical provisions we need here,' Ray said. 'Your dad prepared us for everything.' He motioned for me to sit by the fireplace with him. I wanted to stay beside Dad, but he insisted Meg was doing all she could.

'Is Meg a nurse?' I asked. 'I mean, was she in the past? She knows a lot of stuff.'

Ray shook his head and spoke in a sort of whisper. Something was bothering him, he said, and he was silent for a bit as he stared into the flames. 'I found your dad's car about five miles beyond the fence. Crashed in a ditch. Couldn't find him at first. He was passed out in a bog, way off the road. God knows where he thought he was crawling to.'

I asked who did this to my dad. Why would anyone burn someone?

Ray said he reckoned it was a gang. 'Fuel,' he said. 'Remember that thing your dad said, how a gallon would have more value than a whole car? Maybe your dad got into a fight over your mother's car, or someone tried to steal his 4x4.' Ray shook his head. 'If he could just speak, we'd know how close they are. One thing's for sure though: fire, that's mob behaviour, angry mob. A riot, most likely. And Molotovs … but that would mean…' He stopped and rubbed his stubble. 'Your dad was saying the same things over and over. He said, "car" and "fire" then "kids" and something about the "road" and "hide".'

'D'you think Dad went all the way back, like, to the city?' I asked. 'But how the heck could he have got back?'

Ray put his head in his hands. 'Jesus. I don't know, I really don't know. How could they burn a man like that? Kane's vanished as well. No reply from her radio. Possible she's contaminated or the mobs got her, too. But that would mean they're close.'

He was battling, I could see it. Ray the hard man fighting tears. 'Bastards,' he said. 'The evil bastards.'

It's true what they say about men crying. It sounds like something hollow, like a deep bowl breaking, and then it's over really quickly. I awkwardly tried to pat Ray's back but he stood up quickly to hide his face. I'd never seen real love between two men before, only hipster Jason pretending to be gay. I thought maybe my dad was like a father to Ray as well.

'If Dad made it back to the city,' I asked, 'does that mean, he's contaminated?'

'If he is, he won't survive,' Ray said, straight out. 'And we'll all be contaminated too, so half of us will die.'

I stared at Meg wiping my dad's skin with the water and cloth, like she was preparing a corpse. My dad had risked his life to prove to me that the world out there was burning. Guilt was crushing my chest. I couldn't breathe. He'd been right all along and this never would have happened if I'd just trusted him.

Later, something weird happened to Ray. I saw him near the

gate with the razor wire. He was fussing around with it, untangling another bale of it, and he cut himself. Then he was carrying over a bucket of goat milk and he stopped, like he'd suddenly forgotten what the point was, and he abandoned the bucket and it fell over and spilled on the ground, all that white flowing into the dirt. Then he went and got a bone for the lethal dog, but then he just sort of stopped again and leaned against the wall, like he was totally lost. Then he started hitting himself in the chest and the face. It was all weird and to do with Dad. Like Dad probably always told him when to go to bed, what work to do, when to take a shower, what seeds to plant, what weapons to use, otherwise Ray just found it all pointless.

I felt really sorry for the horrible little muscle-man, like he was a faithful dog who'd lost his master. Then I realised I could lose Dad, too.

Fluids, More Fluids And Antibiotics

Meg woke me. I'd sort of fallen asleep with my head on Dad's chest, feeling the raspy risings and fallings. The home doctor manual was face down on the floor. I'd been halfway through alternative burn treatments, which included washing the wound with milk and applying maggots to dead skin.

'Come on, love, I'll watch over him now,' Meg said. 'You go and get some kip.' I seriously didn't want to go upstairs because Mother was there. 'Try and have some pity for her,' Meg said. 'She's been in a hell of a state, had to knock her out with Valium.'

'I'll stay here, thanks,' I said. 'I'd rather suffocate in my own vomit than bump into that bitch.' I figured that our half-assed self-quarantining was a good excuse to stay away from her, and that staying right next to Dad was best.

Meg brought over a candle and lit its end from the flame of a dying one. 'Your mother's not so bad,' she said, 'she apologised to me. And now that I understand her position, you know, she wasn't aware of the whole picture. If I was in her shoes, I'd probably have done the same thing. Now that we're all probably contaminated, we're all equal. So, let bygones be bygones, eh? She'd really like to say sorry to you, too.'

I was in no mood and I'd already made up my mind.

'Now, how can she say sorry to you, if you won't even let her stay in the same room as you? Go on, don't be nasty.'

'I thought we were supposed to be keeping a distance of two or three metres from each other?' I snapped.

Meg sat down beside me. 'Bit late for that,' she said and sighed. She handed me a protein bar from within her camouflage pants, breaking it in half to share. 'You're just like me when I was your age,' she said. 'God, I hated my mother, all girls do at a certain stage, but no, I despised her. She let my dad beat us up, you see.'

This was all very random and troubling and heartwarmingly honest, but it had nothing to do with my dying dad. I was deeply drained by all these emotions, like I'd had more than a lifetime's worth already.

Meg checked Dad's pulse and I told her his lips looked seriously dry and asked if it was OK him sleeping like this. She said morphine in big doses always knocks you out, so not to worry, she didn't think he was in a coma or anything. She said diamorphine was sort of just the posh name for heroin, and now Dad was 'on the nod'.

She fetched the next bag of fluids. I stared at my dad's sweating brow and felt that ache again. It spread from my chest to my stomach and through my guts, this hollowing-out feeling. Maybe it was the virus, but I didn't care. Oh, Dad.

Meg brought the half-litre bag over and emptied a different kind of syringe into it. 'Erythromycin,' she said, 'a strong antibiotic. Come here, give us a hand. I'll show you what to do, so you can do it next time, if I get sick.'

Meg showed me where the valve was in the good arm and I gagged thinking of the metal spike deep in the vein, but I thought about how Dad really needed all that moisture because he'd gone through three bags already. She showed me how to unscrew the used bag and fit the new one. 'Make sure there's no air bubbles in the IV tube,' she said. 'An air bubble in your veins can kill you.'

When it was fastened in, I opened the tap to let my dad get his water and drugs and his eyes were moving behind his eyelids, as if he was running, fast, in his sleep.

Meg took his pulse again and nodded. I told her Ray said she hadn't been a nurse, so how come she was so excellent at all this stuff? She laughed a little. 'Do you really want to know?' and before I could say yes or no, she said, 'Put it this way, I know quite a lot about drugs, for all the wrong reasons.'

Well, that hooked me. She smiled and rolled up her sleeve. 'See that,' she said, almost proudly, 'that was the razor wire at the nuclear base.' I must have looked baffled. 'I was a peace protestor,' she said. 'Me and the others used to climb over the wire into the military base to sabotage the nuclear submarines. I thought there was going to be a nuclear war. Then I was obsessed with global overpopulation. Then I thought the world would end with global flooding, then I thought all the oil would run out and that would be the end for mankind. And then it was the planet getting hit by a meteor. I was always out on protests and got myself arrested a lot and took a lot of drugs, thought it was rebellious at first...' She stopped, then said, 'Wait, not like that,' and took the drip bag from me, hung it on the stand. 'Fluids can't move upwards now, can they? Gravity!'

I could tell she was changing the subject, though, and I had some itchy kind of hunch that Meg's many apocalypses were deeply connected with Dad, so I asked how she first met him.

'I shouldn't really tell you.'

But she totally wanted to.

'I'm rubbish at keeping secrets,' she said, so I said 'Go on' a few times.

'Well, put it this way, I met your dad at Narcotics Anonymous. You know what that is?

'Dad was a junkie?'

'No, no, no,' she said. 'I was, but he wasn't. He'd got himself addicted to benzodiazepam. It's something the doctors give you when you're very sad. Nasty addiction.'

I looked at Dad hooked up to the drip and thought that, for all I knew, he could have been a crack addict six days a week. I watched the rise and fall of his chest and they were like little stabs, irregular.

'Your dad said the government was keeping everyone drugged up and locked up to cover it all up,' Meg said. 'He said it wasn't the nuclear bomb or the coming pandemic that was the problem, it was worse: the apocalypse was inside us all. There were no bad men and no good men, the system infected us all, no point blaming anyone. "We're all junkies, with the TV on and the curtains drawn," he said.'

I'd heard that line of Dad's before.

'Your dad got me off drugs. I'd be dead if it wasn't for your dad. God bless him.'

'Well how did Dad … you know, help you?' I asked.

Meg told me that her and Ray were supposed to be doing the Twelve Steps but he used to hit the bottle and she'd been addicted to smack and then they'd fight, and one time the police came and that was when they took Danny away.

'Wow,' I said. 'Poor Danny.' And I saw that Danny and I had even more in common.

'Well, your dad was our sponsor at NA. He took personal responsibility for getting us both dry. Your dad did all the paperwork for me with the social services, just in time, and got me a good lawyer, because they were going to give Danny to foster parents, because of my addiction. I remember, your dad cornered me and Ray, and he said, "You've fucked up your lives, but don't waste any more time worrying about your past, no more fantasising about the end of the world. A pandemic is coming for real, the final one, and when you wake up to it, you'll have to throw your wasted life away and start again from zero. I can show you how."'

Meg stroked Dad's blistered head with half the hair burned off and wept. It was majorly exhausting seeing all this love folks had for Dad and feeling like my tear ducts had already dried out. I looked at his burned face and still couldn't believe it.

Meg tidied up the syringes and sterile kits and I didn't know what to say, so I started flicking through the home doctor manual.

Meg fastened a bin bag and started randomly singing. I guess women with big boobs also have big lungs. It was some old reggae song about prophets and books and redemption songs.

I turned the page and there were pictures of a leg with gangrene. It said, *Gangrene is a life-threatening condition that arises when a considerable mass of body tissue dies (necrosis). This may occur after severe injury or burn or among people with circulatory disorders.* The black creased skin and yellowy green-crusted toenails in the illustration looked exactly like my dad's. I called out for Meg to come and look.

'Meg, I think Dad's got gangrene,' I said in a panic.

But she was singing her lungs out. 'Redemption songs, redemptions songs.'

More Signs Of The Coming Collapse

I heard gunshots out there in No Man's Land and I crapped it. Meg told me it was just Danny doing target practice and the damn fool should have been using a silencer because anyone could hear him for miles.

'I think it's my fault,' I said. 'He's really pissed off at me.'

It was true. Danny had even gone without the supper of pigeon pie and pellets when he saw I was at the dining table.

Meg gave me a hug and said, 'Don't worry about that grumpy bugger, there's bigger fish to fry.' She told me to get some rest, she'd take care of Dad through the night and wake me up if he got worse. 'And take a shower, you stink, love,' she said. 'You can't touch your dad if you're dirty, he could get an infection.'

I should have gone and scrubbed, but first I had to be alone to try to work out what had happened to Dad out there. I went back to his cubbyhole to watch more of the video he'd left for me. It was ghostly in there, with all his tools and wires, his inventions lying around, abandoned halfway through being finished.

Then I was watching his normal, unburned face on the laptop screen and hearing him talk, like normal, while knowing that the real Dad was a dying wreck on the other side of the farmhouse.

Dad's recorded face said, '*With the power grid down, millions of people will have to light fires to cook and keep warm. The result is an unintended consequence of the pandemic. Many houses will go up in flames and the fire departments will not be able to get through due to the abandoned vehicles in the streets. Entire neighbourhoods will burn, forcing thousands more onto the infected streets.*'

I sped through Dad's horrific video and there was footage he'd edited into it for me. There were flashes of pictures amidst black at first, but then through the fuzz I made out lines and these were streets. The streets were bright with flames and smoke. I could hear the sound of a helicopter and a news reporter, but the words were all scrambled. There was a sudden surge, it looked like water flowing through the streets, then the camera zoomed in and it was people, hundreds, running away from something. '*An eighteen-wheeler supply truck,*' the voice said, '*strewn over the road...*' Fifty riot police in hazmat suits were advancing on a ton of people, and they were throwing rocks and Molotovs and stuff as they tried to loot this overturned supermarket truck. And the voice said, '*... lost their homes ... lack of protection ... authorities ... contaminated.*'

Then riot cops were being beaten by a mob with pipes and there was tear gas, and this shopping trolley on flames crashed into the riot police. Then the footage spun and I saw a row of over-turned buses, all in flames, and a big cluster of police under shields who were hit by fire bombs and fell, burning. Dozens swarmed and attacked them, stealing their shields and helmets. A gang of little kids dragged a TV through a street on a blanket and one of them wore a police helmet and the other a hazmat mask. There were random shopping trolleys just lying everywhere, abandoned, some packed full of stolen stuff.

And Dad's voice said over the top, '...*under martial law it becomes a capital offence to protect your own home and possessions. All food and medicine that the military find is seized by force. The entire population are treated as if they are already contaminated and a threat to the State.*'

It was like fuzzy footage you'd see from any riot anywhere. There were graphics at the bottom, scrambled, but the word in the box wasn't Ukraine or Egypt, it was London.

Through the digital crackle I saw a line of men in white hazmat suits with guns trained on screaming, dying people in their hundreds, all piled up against these huge fences like ants. Mothers with blood-soaked face masks handing their babies to the army over the wires, begging soldiers for pity. Helicopters circling with guns.

And all of these incidents had occurred across different countries during the last pandemic, Dad said, but the video evidence had been destroyed in the cover-up.

I saw footage of thousands of people on beds in a stadium. It seemed familiar, but bigger. '*The populace are herded by the military into "containment centres", just as they were in Hurricane Katrina and the last pandemic,*' Dad said. '*These are football stadiums, gymnasiums, hospitals. Although they may carry the logos of charities, they are too overcrowded and under-resourced to feed and care for the survivors. No one can escape from them and all people within them become infected. All who attempt to escape from containment centres have to be eradicated.*'

And there was footage of people in Hazmat suits with flame-throwers. Then I saw this woman, running, clutching something to her chest, and her body was in flames and I thought, my God, is this what happened to Dad?

I heard faster gunshots from outside and thought, please, please, don't let it be here already. I paused Dad's video and listened. But it was just Danny, still doing target practice, like a total knob. Who knew what the hell he was even shooting at? Maybe nothing, maybe his own rage.

The Uncontaminated Should Share Human Touch While They Still Can

I wanted to wash everything I'd seen out of my head and have that shower, like Meg said. I wanted to scrub the fear of contamination and loneliness and dying out of my skin. I wanted to cry and be held. I was a total mess.

There was no more water coming through the pipes, and that, Ray said, was more proof that the electric problem was grid-wide, cos the pumps at the reservoir must have stopped. Meg gave me a bucket of rainwater from the outdoor tank, and there were bits of leaf floating in it and some creepy-crawly things, but she told me to recycle it with the second bucket she gave me.

I counted to three then hauled the bucket over my head. The cold water punched the air out of me. I frantically scrubbed myself with the grim carbolic soap and stood there shuddering, realising I'd screwed up. All the water had missed the bucket between my feet and gone down the frickin drain. I'd used up all my water rations and now I was covered in stupid soap. I had no idea how to get another bucket without getting dressed and going outside to refill it. And other people needed that water, not just me.

I admit I had a bit of a scream. Like, the shower was a metaphor, and if I couldn't even wash my stupid body properly, then what frickin chance did any of us have of surviving? I scrubbed all the soap off with the freezing towel and on the way back from the bathroom, I don't know why, but I kind of found myself under the ladder to Danny's attic. He was still shooting his stupid gun outside so I knew he wasn't in there. I stood there in the dark for a bit, cursing him, then I thought, fuck you, redneck, and climbed up.

He'd taken down all the posters off the walls, all the model aeroplanes, and all the pics of bimbos with the big boobs lay torn up in a box, alongside old comics and some toy soldiers. The moonlight made the empty room haunted-looking and I sat on his bed, staring out at the sad old moon and hearing his asshole gunshots echoing.

I'd only seen his back, all day, turning away from me. Here's what was going through my selfish little mind: maybe Danny never even liked me, maybe he thinks I'm a cynical manipulator and so I'll never have any hugs again or hope or anything to look forward to, apart from us getting infected too, one by one.

Maybe the only reason he kissed me was he was bored or he was practising for some other future female. Maybe I only imagined he liked me because I was weak and needy and because there's literally no other male hominids to dry hump, and all these feelings were just a displaced helplessness about the world and we were just two scared monkeys clinging together in a lab experiment.

I'd never know now how he really felt because I'd ruined it all. I could have refused to go with Mother, refused to lock Danny in the shed, refused even to send Dad off on the stupid errand, but I had been weak and let other people decide for me and now everything had gone to shit.

A month ago, I thought love was for losers, but now, as I stood there by the window in his room hearing Danny's gunshots ring out, I felt this aching hole in my chest. And this love-feeling meant Danny, but it also meant Dad, and just plain old life. I realised that maybe Danny would die, too, from the infection I brought in.

I watched my own breath steam against the window.

We could all be infected already and die here, in this farm.

I don't know why I did it, but I lay on Danny's bed and smelled his sweat from the duvet. I stared at the torn images of blonde bimbos with machine guns. It was freezing, so I climbed inside the sheets, pulling them over my head. The smell of him was more like the sea and bleach, and it was like he was next to me. I pictured his hand at the base of my spine and moved it in my mind to the warm centre of where it wanted to be. I kissed my own arm and imagined it was his mouth. My thumb became his tongue and we circled and probed deeper, and it made the whole world go away, then I shuddered. But then I was crying and reality was back again and I needed a pee.

Idiot, I told myself, psycho skank. Stupid city girl with your oh-so-important little emotions and your clever-clever words, get back downstairs and do something useful for once in your pointless life. Your dad is actually dying! Get it? And it's all your fault!

To Amputate Or Not To Amputate

How To Confirm The Symptoms Of Necrosis

Gangrene is a kind of tissue death caused by lack of blood supply to the cells. It is a type of necrosis, which means 'a becoming dead' or 'a state of dead'.

I came downstairs to see Dad and I saw a flickering female figure in candlelight sitting beside his body, holding his blackened hand in her long white fingers. Her dark hair hung over his face, she wore a shirt that looked like a shroud, and she was whispering to him, like a magic spell or a curse.

'Stay away from him, or I swear I'll kill you!' I yelled.

The evil form got up and vanished into the shadows. If it wasn't Death then it was my mother.

Either way, I woke up. The weird thing was, I wasn't in my bed. I was actually sitting beside my dad and I had no memory of how I got there.

I kissed Dad's head through my surgical mask, then, when Meg came down to check on him, I showed her the bit I'd been worried about in the big medical book: *The following are the possible outcomes: delirium, stupor, jaundice, liver damage, kidney failure, blood poisoning, toxic shock and coma.* The last four were totally fatal and said, *emergency surgery required.*

'Calm down,' Meg said, 'I've given him a double dose of antibiotics, we just have to wait for them to do their job.' Meg examined Dad's horrific foot again. 'The rest of him is healing fine, but it's that one leg – it looks like it was cooked on a bonfire.' I gagged at the rotting smell and the sight of the black oozing stumps where his toes had once been. She asked, 'Do you think it's spreading?' and she was meaning the blackness. I told her it really wasn't up to me: could she take responsibility, please?

'Now, it could be gangrene,' she said, 'or it could be vasculitis, or just a very bad surface burn. That's the problem with these manuals, you look up any page and you convince yourself you've got the disease. I had strep throat once and I thought I had bloody tongue cancer!' She told me to put the book down and put some more water on the stove to keep steam in the room, because burn victims need steam to help them breathe, and she went off to get more morphine from the store.

Her strength and faith gave me something like a bit of both. More than could be said for the boiling of the water. Since the power had gone down, the stove was totally powered by wood and it was a major task to stoke it and keep its temperature high enough to do jack shit. Ray said it was because the logs were wet and he blamed himself for not having planned for that, plus he was in serious glooms about Dad and was always running off alone to the perimeter with his gun to watch for signs of infected mobs.

I heard a gasp beside me and turned. A sort of electric shot ran through Dad and he was awake, shivering, gasping, trying to speak, his throat making these cracking sounds. 'No ... haw ... pow ... cah...'

I ran over and told him, 'Dad, Dad, it's OK, it's me, Haley. Dad.'

But his eyes stared through me, like he was seeing some horror in another world. He clawed at his chest, like he was trying to tear a hole through his skin so his lungs could get air. His teeth gritted in a snarl. I was panicking, too, then another screaming bolt of pain laid him flat, and his lungs screeched and I thought his heart had stopped. 'Dad, Dad!' I kept yelling, but he was like a scary dying animal and not like my dad at all, and I was alone and I couldn't help him and I really couldn't bear it. So, I screamed for Meg.

She came running and went to Dad's side. She took his hand and told him to be calm, and just breathe, breathe, in, out, slow, there you go, as she got his arm ready. 'Don't try to speak, love, you're safe here.' Meg plunged the needle into Dad's arm with a ton of drugs and Dad went slack.

'He's in so much pain, love, that's as much as I can give him without risking an overdose,' Meg said. 'He'll heal better if he sleeps through the worst of it. When he wakes up, he just gets hit by a wall of pain. Can you even imagine it? It does him more damage to be like that. Don't worry, that diamorphine's the dog's bollocks.'

'But we can't just keep filling him up with drugs!' I whined. 'Please, can we just break your rules and get him to hospital, please?' I pleaded and I whispered the next bit in case Dad could hear. 'He's dying.'

'Bollocks,' she said, 'don't you ever say that again, and anyway the roads are so bad and it's so far, he'd never make it. Plus, you should bloody well know by now, go and read your dad's book on contagion in hospitals!'

Meg took Dad's pulse and told me to calm the hell down. I said it wasn't me I was frickin worried about and I showed her the medical book page again: *Blood poisoning from gangrene.*

'I'm no doctor and neither are you,' Meg said.

'But touch his leg. Try it. He can't feel anything. It's like what it says in the book.' I poked at the leg with my pen. 'Dad, sorry if this hurts, but can you feel that? Can you?'

Dad seriously didn't flinch.

'See? It's dead already.' I told her the book said Dad could totally die of gangrene in twenty-four hours without surgery.

Meg grabbed me by the arms. 'Look! We can't rush a decision like that. If it's septicaemia, we'll only make it worse by amputating.'

'Amputate, as in, seriously, like, cut his leg off?'

'What the bloody hell else do you think surgery means?' she snapped.

She got the book and showed me the page: *Surgical removal (amputation) of an arm or leg is required immediately to control the spread of necrosis. If this is delayed, the patient will enter toxic shock or coma.*

Then she showed me the page on septicaemia, and it strongly

recommended the total opposite: *No further blood loss, the patient needs all the healthy blood cells they have. Amputation can kill someone with septicaemia.*

How do you choose? Septicaemia or necrosis? Toss a coin? Hope for the best? All the stupid webpages that could have helped were gone. All the knowledge that we could access in the whole stupid world was on that one frickin page, in that one scrawny book, on my knee.

Just then, Danny appeared in the doorway and shot me a hard-faced glance. He was carrying a huge crossbow and Ben was behind him, holding some arrows. Meg covered up Dad's legs and yelled, 'I said no kids in here, Danny, keep that boy busy! We need more wood, more water. Get to it!'

I yelled out, 'It's OK, Ben, nothing to see here! Go and muck out the rabbits, too. Scoot!'

Meg turned to me and whispered, 'Let's give your dad another few hours, OK? See if the drugs start working, then we'll see.'

'See what?' I asked, frantic. 'And how'll we know what the hell getting better even looks like?'

Survival Tip: How to check for necrosis:

1. Draw a line round the limb at the limit of the area of blackened flesh.
2. Check regularly to see if the blackening has grown past the line.

This is what Meg did on Dad's leg just above the knee, and she said we'd know in a matter of hours if it was necrosis spreading upwards. Which basically means part of you is dead, and it's spreading death through you. I kind of pictured this black mouth eating its way through his body till it reached his heart.

'The best way you can help right now, love,' Meg said, 'is by lightening my load. There's eggs to gather and, for God's sake, go and make peace with your poor mother.'

I sighed. I couldn't face Mother, maybe ever.

'Well, shit. Go and get Ray or Danny to give you some weapons lessons. God knows you'll need it when the mob that did this to your dad find us!'

There is nothing slower than waiting for your very own flesh and blood to decide whether it will live or die. I couldn't do Dad's healing for him.

I had time to kill and I wanted to kill something. Or someone.

How To Shoot A Crossbow

I was out in No Man's Land, standing in front of Danny's shooting target – the one with the picture of the soldier running and yelling. Danny had filled its face full of arrows.

'I don't care if you're not speaking to me, like a major chicken,' I shouted. 'Just drop the crossbow and leave it here and I'll teach myself.'

He lowered the crossbow from his eye and stared up at me with a 'get real' expression.

'You said I was weak and soft and I couldn't defend myself,' I shouted, 'so I'm here to learn!'

'Look, I know you're angry about your dad,' he said, 'but don't come here accusing me of…'

'Oh shut up,' I interrupted, 'and stop being in the huff about me locking you up, or kissing you or whatever, just get over it and be a man or something! Just teach me how to shoot and then you can go back to huffing.'

He looked baffled and alarmed. I guess I was itching for a fight.

'Hand me the stupid crossbow,' I said. 'I want to kill those infected sons of bitches who did this to my dad!'

Danny studied me carefully, then slowly, distrustfully, handed me the crossbow. It was much heavier than I thought, and I practically dropped it.

'Careful!' he shouted. 'It's loaded!'

I took a deep breath and turned it towards the target. I raised the crossbow and aimed. Well, sort of. My hand was shaking like daft under the weight.

Danny sighed. 'OK, don't even think of firing it like that. Lower it, safely. Then let's try again.'

'I didn't even get a shot!' I snapped.

But he already had his hands on it and he was stronger, so I couldn't lift it again. 'You can't shoot it till you can hold the bow steady. That's a rule. You have to respect your weapon. OK, tell me, what are the advantages of a crossbow over a gun?'

God, he was being such a bossy geek. Maybe I did loathe him.

He answered his own question: 'Silence and stealth.'

'OK, great, whatever. Let me try again!'

'No. This is called a Ghost 350,' he said, looking down the sights. 'Do you know why?'

'Because you're a moron?'

'No, because it's discreet and delivers 350 feet per second.'

'Delivers?' I said. 'What is it? A Chinese takeaway?'

'If you're not going to take this seriously, Haley, then get back inside,' he said. 'This weapon is very powerful.'

And so I mumbled a minimal apology with some stuff about bossy males and their rules. He showed me the foot stirrup and how to use my weight to pull the wire back into the 'cocked position'. And we were both silent.

'Oh come on,' I said, 'do you really think I'm going to make a dick joke at a time like this?'

Then he showed me how to get the taut string clicked into the safety latch and this was called 'cocked and locked'. He said if your fingers were in the way of the mechanism when it fired, the wire would tear the finger off in a sixtieth of a second.

It was all pretty impressive and I studied him carefully. He was doing that man-thing of being able to talk technically with zero emotion to a woman who'd broken his heart. He fitted the arrow and helped me lift the crossbow so I could see through the sights.

'Take the weight, focus, and then release,' he said. 'The longer you wait, the heavier the bow gets, the more chance you have of misfiring.'

Every word he said felt like criticism in advance. The more I tried to raise it, the more the bow shook and made me feel like an utter failure. The trigger was so stiff, and I was such a wimp, that I practically had to use two fingers to pull it. When I did, I was so focused on the trigger that I was barely even looking at the target. The stupid arrow pranged and flew off into a clump of heather. The screaming soldier looked like he was laughing and the wind whistled at what a loser I was.

'Try again,' said Danny.

I was pretty habituated to giving up, but I thought of Dad lying there, and the mob that did this to him made me want to shoot that wooden soldier right in the frickin eye.

'Ready and steady?' Danny asked. I moaned that it was getting even heavier and he said I needed to do some push-ups and weights, to get the strength to hold it properly. 'Now try again.'

I understood something about Danny then. He had ways to control his rage, but he was like the crossbow itself: if you didn't treat it with respect, it could explode in your face.

I guess I dropped it.

'Woah, no, never let it down with a thud, it could go off into your foot,' he snapped. 'Never let the weapon out of your control. It's primed to kill! Put it down slowly, breathe, take its weight, then up again and aim again.'

I groaned. 'For God's sake, just demonstrate, OK!'

He stepped behind me then and put his arms around my arms to hold the bow steady. 'Like this,' he said, then he put his head beside mine to show me how to look down the sights at the same time. I could have bitten his ear or yelled, 'I HATE YOU!' or utterly snogged him. I felt his resistance as I pushed myself back tighter into his body and I savoured the weird revenge feeling of forcing him to touch me, because I was making him feel really nervous.

'And take aim,' he said, 'and finger steady on the trigger.'

'Wait,' I said, 'are you, like, rubbing your actual dick against my ass?'

'Jesus!' he yelled and backed off and I guffawed. 'God damn it, Haley! If you're not going to take this seriously!'

Then I heard a voice calling across No Man's Land. It was Meg running, waving her arms. Danny screamed at me, 'NO! Don't turn and face her with the weapon in your hand!' This was exactly what I'd done, like a doofus. 'Stop! You could shoot her by accident!' I could actually see Meg in the sights. 'Haley! Put it down, put it down, you idiot! NOW!'

Danny snatched the bow from me and I ran towards Meg, feeling even more of a failure for having left Dad's side for a single second.

Planning-Based Preppers Can Be Inflexible

This happening to Dad was never part of any plan. Especially not his.

Dad was drenched and in a fever. He'd been calling out for me, Meg said, but when I got there he was totally unconscious and sort of shuddering. 'God, I wish he'd wake up and tell us what to do!' Meg said.

She showed me where the black skin had crawled past the pen mark she'd made. 'It's bad, look! See for yourself,' she said. 'Necrosis,' and she didn't like to admit it, but…

'Tell me.'

'You were right, the manual says your dad has an eighty-nine per cent chance of dying if we don't amputate.'

'We?'

I stared at Dad lying on the kitchen table. My actual dad. Half his face looked like roast meat. His lips were whitish grey. A whistling wheeze made every lungful sound pained and it was too emotional. I kept saying, 'Oh, Dad,' but he couldn't hear me.

Meg was already going through the drawers with the manual

in her hand. 'Tourniquet, surgical spirits, naked flame, sharp meat knife … now, where's the hack saw?' I heard the clunk of metal and she held up one of the kitchen knives. 'Damn it,' she said. 'Go and get your mother,' she shouted at me, 'go and prepare her for the worst and tell her I need her down here to help me decide. I won't tell you again. Go, Haley!'

'Wait, wait, wait, I thought you said, the drugs might work … the …' I whined.

She shook her head, showed the page in the book: *toxic shock*. 'That leg isn't your dad, it's not part of him anymore, it's dead,' she said. 'See the black in the veins, that's poisoned blood creeping up inside him.'

I felt sick to my soul.

'We need to put it to a vote then, so go get your mum,' said Meg.

'Justine!' she called out. 'Come downstairs! We need to vote, love, on Ed's leg!' But Mother did not respond.

Meg sent me upstairs to get Mother and to fetch as many towels as I could. I was making weird noises, like panic and crying and wheezing all at once and I was sucking on my asthma inhaler to try to get a grip. I came across Mother's shadowy figure in the bathroom. It was pathetic and excruciating and I told her if Dad died I would never forgive her, that even if he didn't I would still never forgive her. Which I guess wasn't very helpful.

But Mother had guts: she crept down the stairs after me and took a seat beside Dad. She was acting weird and took off her surgical mask, right next to Dad.

I couldn't even look at her, so I focused on Meg. She was laying out the plan, telling Mother how we had to vote for or against the amputation.

Mother seemed not to hear. She took my dad's burned hand in her own, even though she wasn't wearing the blue gloves either, and she rocked back and forwards releasing these whispered sorry-sobs and stroking his head.

'Jesus, Mother,' I shouted, 'he's not dead yet. Can you at least frickin wait till he is before you start mourning!'

'Right, well, she's no use,' Meg said. 'Now, where's that hacksaw, and where the hell is that bloody Ray when you need him?'

I found Ray under the rainwater tank, a spanner in hand. He said it was leaking. 'I have to fix this now, or we'll all be dying of dehydration.'

He was utterly scared of Meg's whole home-surgery plan and that surprised me. Things had got way too real for him. I knew I couldn't trust him, and if Dad did die under Meg's kitchen knife, I worried Ray would have his revenge on Mother and me. He was still furious with us and Meg had come out to try to convince him. She was literally standing in the mud, waving around a kitchen knife.

'For the last time, I'm not playing doctors and nurses,' he shouted at us. 'We're not going to be cutting him up. What do we do about arteries? Tie them up? You don't have a clue, Meg, and neither do I.'

'He'll die if we don't try!' Meg shouted.

'What does your mother say?' he yelled at me.

Meg shook her head and answered for me. 'No chance, she's out of her box on Valium.'

'Well, I vote we wait and see,' Ray said. 'So that's a NO, and that's my final word. Now let me get on with fixing this bloody water tank!'

Meg reached into the shed and pulled a hacksaw off the wall. 'There it is,' she announced. 'Haley, are you a yes or a no?' Her and Ray turned and looked at me.

'Can we ask Danny?'

They shook their heads in disappointment.

'Or Ben?'

'No. Absolutely not.'

So that was it, the final bloody decision rested with me.

How To Choose In Matters Of Life And Death

There's really nothing in modern life that prepares us for the big decisions. Most of our choices are just these coercive games with consumer goods. Like, in the old days, Mother would say to Ben, 'Would you like to go to your father's house this weekend, or would you prefer to go shopping with me for that new PlayStation you wanted?'

And that was so unfair. He's a kid, so he chooses PlayStation over Dad. Every time Mother tried that stunt, it meant she was going to reward us for choosing her over her opponent.

And anytime there was a conflict, like Dad is there at the door, saying, 'It's my turn to have the kids, why aren't they ready to go?' Mother would hold Ben tight and say, 'Actually, the children are both a bit tired today. Why don't we let them choose?' And then she'd say, 'Ben, do you want to drive over in the rain and hang out with your dad in his cold little apartment or stay here and bake a chocolate cake with Mummy?'

So Ben always picked Mother, and that meant I had to as well.

This is called 'passive-aggressive manipulation'.

But then Dad had to beat her at her own game. So he'd be at the front door at hand-over time, and Mother would be saying, 'Kids, what do you want to do?' and Dad would say, 'Well, Haley and Ben, I was going to take you both for Tex Mex, or you could stay here and have veggie salad with your mother,' because Dad knows Benji kills for Tex Mex. So Dad would win, by becoming more coercive than Mother.

When Dad used to give us his lectures while we were driving round, staring out at the shops, he said no one really chooses anything these days, they just think they do. The one thing about consumerism, he said, is that it says it offers you infinite choice. 'Never before has there been so much choice', but it's all just an illusion to keep you buying shit you don't need.

'Consumer choice is a myth that oppresses us all,' Dad said. 'Try choosing to recycle your phones or fix them and they'll lock you up in the funny farm. I say, let's refuse to take part in the waste machine. Let's choose not to choose one kind of shiny fake disposable crap over another.' Then, he said proudly, 'One day we'll all be saved from fake consumer choice because the only choice left will be life or death!'

Dad said that when billions died, the survivors would be forced to live 'on the knife-edge of pure necessity'. No more coercion. No more lies. No more passive-aggressive manipulation.

I realised that actually I'd spent most of my life caught in the middle of this non-believing mess. The land of: I dunno, and please just leave me alone and decide for me, so then when it all fucks up it it's your fault, not mine.

I guess I blame Mother and Dad for making choices totally toxic for me, and maybe millions of divorcelings are just like me. But always seeing both sides and never being able to decide is a lonely life, because how can anyone trust a person who never commits to anything or anyone? How can you trust a two-faced, fence-sitter like me? But now my procrastination was becoming deadly.

I had to make a choice. Which story of the future to believe in? Which to reject? Which person to sign up with and which to betray? Amputate or not? What if we accidentally killed Dad by trying to save him? What if my inability to choose killed him?

I mean, how would you choose? Toss a coin or something?

Right Or Wrong, Stick To Your Decision

I went to Dad's manual to help me decide, and in his chapter on 'Right and Wrong' I came across his prediction of what was happening out there beyond the fence. It said:

By the end of the second week, the government realises that there is no possibility of viral containment. As violence, infection and fires now rage in the cities, the military complete the work that was started by gangs and looters. What was previously a Level Five lockdown now becomes a state of absolute martial law. Army platoons now scour the streets, going from door to door, forcing entry. All 'survivors' in cities, towns and villages are herded into centralised containment centres to be 'processed'. Those who refuse to be processed are arrested. Those who resist arrest are shot, or hunted down as is now 'legal' under the state of emergency.

I pictured Dad escaping, through gunfire and flame, crawling in his burned, gasping state through miles of pain. I ran back to his side. His breath came in jolting bursts, and his eyes rolled back up into themselves, like stained sheets hanging over his irises.

Mother was weeping. 'Listen,' she whispered, 'it's the death rattle.'

'Jesus, Mother,' I yelled, 'you really are a witch!'

Meg took Dad's pulse and shook her head. She said his heart was really struggling. I thought he was awake, because his eyes kept twitching and I'd been asking him things, but Meg said she'd seen this before with her own father and his terminal cancer and that Dad was in this other place that wasn't sleep or waking and there was no real name for it.

Mother totally freaked me out. She kissed Dad's forehead and said, 'Goodbye Edward, I'm sorry,' a few times in a kind of morbid meditation.

This kissing business was terrifying.

'Don't ask me to decide,' Mother muttered, 'he's not mine anymore,' or something random and psycho like that, and she drifted over to the stove where the water was failing to boil. Meg shook her head.

Mother was in bereavement for more than just my dad, Meg whispered. 'Think about it, love, the things your mum's lost this week, eh? Her house, her job, her furniture, her friends, all those lovely things she thought were her life. The pandemic's taken them all. She's in a state of shock, so she thinks he's going to die too.' She winked. 'But don't worry, with or without her, we're going to do our very best to save your poor old dad. You made up your mind, Haley?'

Was my name Haley Crowe or Haley Cooper? Or Cooper Crowe. Sit on the fence. Choosing not to choose was a choice in itself.

Plus, I'm really squeamish, blood makes me faint.

'Is that a no then?' Meg asked. 'You have to decide now. Ray's voted no, I vote yes, and I'm not letting Danny vote and your mum's out of it, so it's all up to you.'

I stared at my dad fighting for breath and the black veins had grown a whole inch past the pen line. This life was not what I signed up for. I could have cried or screamed or just run away.

'No, I mean, no, not no,' I stammered. 'I mean, that's a no to no. But not a yes to yes. But can you just give me a little bit of time? Please? I need to do some solitary shit to work this out, for just five minutes, please.'

But pacing around didn't help and I'm shit at 'alone'. I am weaker and more needy than I realised.

I climbed up Danny's ladder and stared at his back. He was working at his desk with a knife, carving arrowheads by candle-light. The ladder creaked under my foot and he turned round with an angry flash, knife in hand.

'I'm a total failure and I hate myself,' I said. 'Can you help me decide?' I just stood there, half in and half out of the roof hole.

'I can't decide for you,' he mumbled. 'And I didn't mean to call you an idiot, by the way. Come up.' He came over to the hole, but didn't help me as I climbed in. He just rested against a beam and stared at me. 'Is he dying?'

'Wow, you're so sensitive,' I said sarcastically. Then I felt bad, so I said, 'He'll die if we do nothing, and if we try to help and screw it up, it might kill him. They've forced me to choose, no one else wants to. Great choice, huh!'

'I'm sorry.'

'You've really got to stop saying that or I will seriously bitch-slap you.'

Danny shook his head. 'It's your call, Haley,' he said. And his eyes were dark with tiny points of light, like a candle in a chasm.

I was randomly staring at the veins on his forearms. I thought, I could upset him and make him strangle me to death. I'd seen the way his rage could flare up. That could be one way out of making the wrong choice about Dad.

His fingertip touched mine and then it happened. Like all my strength passed into him, then rebounded back. I sort of staggered and it was like he was waiting to catch me. I buried my head into his chest and felt his stubble brushing my forehead as he squeezed me tighter and whispered my name.

I lost all control and reached up to find his mouth. It was the only thing that mattered in the whole unfair world. Like I'd always wanted this, like it was what my stupid body was actually meant for.

His hand ran from my shoulders to my waist, fitting to the bend of my curves, and I shuddered all over. Everything else vanished and the world became just the warmth and wetness of our lips and this pulling urge to get closer and closer and vanish inside each other. The same pulse was beating through both of us. He kissed my neck and his hand went inside my shirt and touched my belly, my breasts. I pulled his vest over his head and his hand slid inside my jeans and gripped my buttocks and I put my hand inside his jeans and felt him hard.

'OK', he said, 'Wow.' Then we just separated and both said 'Wow' for a bit and stood there facing each other, sort of panting like dumb animals.

'Where did that come from?' I said. I was really spoiling it all. I just wanted to silence myself with his mouth again. I wanted to tell him, make me stop talking like an idiot, just kiss me hard again and make the world go away. But it was too late. He was backing off.

He sat on the bed and put his head in his hands. 'I'm sorry, I shouldn't have. What with your dad. It's not right. We're here and he's lying down there dying and...'

He was right, I had to make my choice and I was making out to take my mind off it. I was being fucking immoral.

'Look,' I said, 'I should go.' And so I climbed down the ladder and left him.

I made it to the bathroom and splashed my face with the cold, dirty water. I stared at myself in the candlelight in the broken mirror, and the face that looked back didn't look like me. It was panting, its chest was rising and falling. This thing in the mirror looked like a hungry creature.

Life is a force, and this force can grip you or it can leave you, but if you do nothing it can wither. There is real choice – it exists in our bodies even if our brains are tied in knots, and if we make no choice then death will decide for us.

I ran back downstairs, to Meg and Mother, to tell them.

I voted yes.

Home Surgery For Beginners

What You Will Need For An Amputation

Once you have created a sterile surgical area, everyday kitchen and work-shed implements can be used. You will need the following:

1. A marker pen.
2. A leather belt to use as a tourniquet.
3. A bowl of warm, clean water with fifteen per cent Dettol or bleach in it.
4. A large supply of absorbent towels, or kitchen towels.
5. A scalpel. If you do not have a scalpel then a box cutter or a set of kitchen carving knives may suffice.
6. A bone-saw, but failing that a sterilised hacksaw will suffice.
7. A naked flame and flat-ended tools for cauterisation. A steel pancake-flipping spatula is ideal.
8. A pulse monitor to ensure the patient is not going into cardiac arrest.
9. A home doctor manual, ideally under transparent plastic sheeting.
10. A person to observe all proceedings and to remind the surgeons to re-sterilise hands and all implements at each stage.

'You're absolutely sure you won't change your mind when the blood starts spraying, and you won't come blaming me if it all goes wrong?' Meg said.

I shivered and nodded. Meg hugged me and, since I didn't have time to change my mind again, the yes stuck.

'Well, that's final then, two votes against one,' Meg said, and she started laying out the knives and the saw on the chairs she'd put next to the table. 'You lucky man, having a brave daughter like that, Mister Ed!' she said to my dad. His breath was racing, with big gasps on the intake. His eyes rolling white.

'Right,' Meg said to me. 'You sterilise the leg and read the instructions out to me, Haley, and I'll start the cutting.' And she shook the 'negative energy' out of her arms and cracked her fingers.

'Wait, wait, wait,' I said, 'you mean, like … right now?'

Meg carried over the steaming water and poured in the disinfectant and I felt weird and dizzy. 'Of course, Haley!' she yelled. 'This minute. Now, prop that bloody manual open with something so I can see the illustrations.'

There were, like, ten images in a step-by-step array of increasing gore.

'Looks pretty straightforward,' Meg said.

'Where's Ray? You can't do this all by yourself,' I stammered, staring at the IKEA knife set. And I began whimpering, I'm not proud to admit it, things like, 'What if I change my mind? Can I?'

'No, no, no,' she said, 'we're seeing this through, just you and me.' She grabbed my arms and gave me instructions so that I could stay focused and not pass out. It really was happening.

Ray wanted nothing to do with it, Meg said, and he was on armed perimeter patrol with Danny, while Mother was keeping Ben distracted upstairs and Kane had still not returned. Meg said Kane knew the protocol – you got infected out there you didn't come back to the safe house, ever, and anyway Kane had always insisted that if she got the plague she'd kill herself, but not to worry. Dad's breathing was raspy, then slow, like he was running from someone in a dream.

Meg scanned the room and announced that we'd done everything 'ass-side foremost'. 'Silly buggers, how the hell can I cut through if his leg's on the table? I'd have to cut through the table too!' So Meg got me to push the big chair over and she lifted Dad's black leg and placed it at an angle, resting it on the back of the chair with a pillow under it. I had to turn my head away, the leathery skin cracked and her tight grip made holes in the yellow pus below. She gagged and urged me to stop ogling and get busy with the bleach wipes. Then she laid out the ominous kitchen knives, the marker pen, the belt and the hacksaw.

A marker pen is like the most important thing. Meg explained, 'We have to make sure both sides of the cut meet each other, otherwise we'll be cutting round and round and round like a corkscrew.'

Sometimes you just have to joke about things that are terrifying.

'I can't see a bloody thing,' Meg said, staring at the doctor manual with her reading glasses on her nose. And it was true, the light from three candles was no way enough and moving them closer to Dad meant they were blocking her way. 'God,' she said, 'maybe we should wait till it's daylight.'

'Can we?'

She saw my face. 'No, forget I said that.' She disinfected her hands and the tools again in the bleach water. 'Right, the pen, love. You'll have to do it, my fingers are wet. Be a good girl and draw the circle round his thigh, would ya?'

I drew a circle round Dad's knee, on the bit of dark tight skin where I was sure he wouldn't feel it, because I didn't want to tickle or hurt him.

'No, no, no,' Meg said, 'it has to be further up on the living tissue, above the knee. What's wrong with you, afraid you'll see his willy? Get a move on!'

The stench of rotting from his lower leg made me move higher, but the higher I got, the thicker his hairy leg became. By the time Meg said, 'Stop,' the bit she picked was almost twice as thick as Dad's knee and so much more muscly and meaty.

That word made me want to vomit. But actually, it helped to think of the leg as something in the deli section of the supermarket.

'Get on with it!' Meg yelled, as she put her blue gloves on.

I drew the line round the thigh and told myself that on one side of the line it was Dad, and on the other it was death.

Meg stepped in and fastened the belt round his lower thigh, pulling it seriously tight. 'Don't worry,' she said, 'he's out cold. I gave him as much diamorphine as I could.'

Dad's breath sounded like he was choking. Meg had the kitchen knife in her hand, but I had to have a word with Dad before we started. 'It won't hurt you, Dad,' I said, 'cos you're asleep. I'm sorry for sending you out, this is all my fault. I should have said no to Mother and just believed you from the…'

I was going to bubble and burst.

'Come on, you can say your sorries when he's on the mend. Hold the leg steady.' Meg carried the kitchen knife and candle over to Dad's side. She moved the blade back and forth over the flame, sterilising it. Half the problem with amputations, the book said, was avoiding infection. 'Right,' she said to herself, 'no point dithering like a silly-billy.'

'Right,' I said.

She touched the super-sharp meat knife against the marker pen line and the thigh skin singed with steam. Dad didn't flinch but I shuddered and felt my own leg twinge.

'OK, here we go, here were go,' Meg said to herself. 'Get on with it, Meg.' She started breathing heavily. 'Look,' she said, 'best if you don't watch this first bit, Haley. Can you read me the instructions, yeah?'

I did like she said, and kept my eyes on the page. And sucked on my inhaler. '*The muscle must be cut through by one sweep of the knife, with its edge turned obliquely upwards.*'

'What does that mean?' she asked. 'Obliquely.'

'At an angle,' I said. 'I think. I dunno.' And I felt my chest tighten, like my asthma was starting. I took another blast from my inhaler.

'Put that away,' Meg said. 'You haven't got bloody asthma. You just get panic attacks, that's all.'

I put the inhaler back in my pocket, thinking, how would she know?

'Right, I'm going to cut up from below. Like it says, right?' Meg announced and she put the big kitchen knife under Dad's leg and so I shut my eyes and closed my ears, like a pathetic squeamish person.

'Haley!'

I opened my eyes and Meg still hadn't started. 'Keep blooming reading,' she yelled.

I apologised and skimmed the page and told her, 'You have to cut by pulling the knife through with one clean swipe, not sawing it back and forward.'

'Right,' she said, 'just like a roast.'

I swallowed some vomit.

'Sorry,' she said. 'OK, here we go. No more dilly-dallying. No point putting off till tomorrow what we can do today. Time is of the essence. Right, here we go.' And she took a deep breath and focused on the blade and held Dad's pink thigh in her finger. 'No time like the present,' she said.

I did a sort of quick prayer to the God I don't believe in and covered my eyes. I thought I would faint and hoped I would. Then I heard the slice.

Dos and Don'ts

If you are squeamish then please skip this part. If I describe the whole thing properly, I will barf, so here instead is a list of useful things to do (and not do) just in case you ever need to amputate a major limb from the person you love most in the whole world:

Haley's Dos and Don'ts Amputation List

1. Do not cut your thumb really deeply on the first slice, as Meg did. This will result in jumping around yelling and swearing and not focusing on the job at hand.
2. Do not run around looking for Band-Aids for the afore-mentioned finger cut – as I did – while the patient is clearly bleeding massively and the virgin surgeon is staring into space, saying, 'Help me, bloody hell, fuck, it's deep. God, God, what do I do next? Keep reading, Haley!'

3. Do pull the blade, don't push it. Just as you would when carving a Sunday roast. Meg pulled out the blade and I was relieved: the leg was cooked solid, and there was no blood. But then on her next slice, there was a spray of it.
4. Do try to remain calm as the amateur surgeon gets blood in her eyes and mouth.
5. Do refasten the tourniquet much, much tighter, to stop the bleeding, further up the limb. Do not worry that you're hurting the patient as there are bigger fish to fry, like the litre of blood on the floor, which Meg then slid in while holding the meat knife.

'My God,' Meg said, 'barely even started. No going back now.'

Dad groaned then, and Meg said that was really good, cos that meant the bit she was now cutting through with deeper slices was still alive and not infected.

Then Meg was saying she didn't think she could make the next cut because her thumb cut was too deep and her left hand was rubbish. 'Haley, Haley! Listen, we have to get down to the bone, OK! Don't look at his face. When you do it. It's not your dad, just a bit of dead meat.' And she held the bloody knife out to me.

But I had already opted out of the world. I closed my eyes, trying to make the dripping sound of all the blood go away, saying, 'This isn't happening, this isn't happening.' I wondered how long Dad could bleed before that became what killed him.

Do not tell yourself it isn't happening. It is. And it won't stop.

I heard a screech and then Mother was with us. 'For God's sake,' she shouted. 'Out of the way, you two.'

Mother took the knife from Meg and, without even cleaning it, started sawing away at the leg. I told her no, not like that. Meg tried to get her to stop, but Mother pushed her away. 'Leave me alone,' she said, 'he's my husband.'

She actually said 'my' and 'husband'. And, like, in the present tense.

Her knuckles were white and her teeth clenched. She groaned with the exertion, sawing that damn knife through the bulging flesh, muttering, 'You make a choice, you see it through. When will you learn that? You start something, you have to finish it!' I couldn't tell if she was talking to me or herself.

It was like a work song, in a round. 'I'm sick of telling you,' she said, as she cut deeper and deeper, going right round the inner thigh. 'You never listen, you need something done, you do it yourself, you face the music, you make your bed, you can't undo it...'

I had never seen her so ferocious, sawing away, shouting at the leg. 'Come on, you bastard, in sickness and in health, you buggering moron.'

How-To Tip: Do not be scared that some blood looks red and some looks darker. There are veins and arteries in a major limb and the dark blood is just oxygenated, not contaminated.

Mother had cut all the way round the leg and blood was pouring now all over her feet. She started singing as she sawed and hacked at the flesh round the bone.

Do sing while you do the horrible work. People used to sing together when on chain gangs or hauling nets to help them get through hellish processes. Mother was actually singing Ben's cringey 'Five Little Monkeys' song as she sliced down to the bone. Then she hit something and got sprayed in the face, and Meg jumped in with the candle and a smaller knife. 'That's an artery! We have to – what do you call it? – cauterise it. Quick, Haley, what do we do?'

Do learn what 'cauterise' means before you start, as flicking through blood spattered pages in candlelight to locate this key information is pretty tricky.

Meg heated the blade, and her and Mother were then side by side, with Mother wiping blood away from the leg, and Meg cauterising with a hiss that made me flinch. Dad didn't move.

It's a good idea to realise that when you've gone past a certain point, you can't fix what you've done with super glue, although super glue is of use in stopping the bleeding where cauterising has failed.

Do pay attention to pulse rate. Don't let it get above 115. Meg, with her one good hand, took Dad's pulse and announced that it was way too high. She ordered me to give him one of the pills she'd laid out and to shout the next bit.

It really, really helps not to keep thinking, this is my dad, and crying, 'Dad, Dad,' and just basically getting in people's way on the slippery floor as they proceed to stage two.

Other words to look up before you start include 'ligament' and 'tibial nerve'.

'Are you at the ligaments yet, Mum?' I asked, and I had called her 'Mum' again, not 'Mother'.

'What are they like? What does it say? I can see something white.'

I told her it said ligaments looked like wires and it would be like 'cutting through rubber'.

Meg vomited. But Mum kept on cutting.

'Have you reached the tibial nerve yet?' I asked. 'It says it's pink and looks like an elastic band.' I didn't want to go close to compare the actual leg to the illustration.

'I see it!' Mother yelled. 'What now?'

'Er, slice it, then you're at the bone,' I said, 'then change to the saw.'

'Done!' Mother screeched, then she grabbed the hacksaw. 'OK,' she said, 'which one of us is going to do this?'

Dad started moaning then at regular intervals, even before the saw went in.

'We'd better hurry,' Meg said, and she wiped her mouth with the sheet, but it was already spattered in puke and so her face was worse than before. Mother held the saw in mid-air, as if she was at a dinner party offering cocktails. 'We could have drawn straws,' I said.

'Sod this,' Meg said, 'I'm the strongest, let me in.'

Meg's makeshift hand-bandage fell off as soon as she grabbed the saw. She hissed with pain as she placed the serrated blade deep into the leg wound and onto the bone. Mother went over to Dad's head and started stroking his brow, whispering, 'Shhh, shhh,' and 'Hold on, Ed, hold on.' Meg forced the blade forward. There was a sickening, grinding 'rrrrr' sound.

Do not, ever, saw in a forward direction. Saws are meant to be pulled backwards in a ripping motion. If you push them forward, the saw blade can jam and snap.

'Bollocks, it's jammed in the bloody bone!' Meg announced. 'Fuck. Where the hell is Ray?'

Mother tried to help Meg get the hacksaw blade back out, but with all the tugging Dad slid to the edge of the table. I shouted to warn them but his full weight tipped and he nearly hit the floor before all three of us managed to wrestle him back up to safety. The jolt had thrown the saw blade free, though, so Meg tried again. 'Haley, hold the leg steady, stop it wobbling about, put your weight on it, hurry!'

Do not listen to the sound of a hacksaw going through bone. It's like someone trying to hack through a metal bar with a nail file, but the metal bar is juicy and wet. Earplugs might be a good investment too.

Do not think of the word 'marrow'. Or the bright pink colour.

I shuddered with each rip of the saw and felt it in my spine. Meg stopped, drenched in sweat. She shouted that it was no good, the bone was too thick. She took her hand off the saw and it remained in place, wedged in.

It was Mother's turn to vomit.

I had been too scared to go close to Dad, but now I saw how this could end: one woman sick and the other exhausted, and him bleeding with the life dripping out of him.

Mother turned all fatalistic and emo again and was sitting stroking Dad's head. 'He's lost a lot of blood, we're losing him.'

'No, we're not,' I yelled at her.

'C'mon, then,' Meg said. 'We'll saw together, you take one end and I'll do the other. Haley!'

I stepped forward, and no choice was necessary. I looked at his face and it was ghost white, I looked at the deep red wound and the white bone at its centre. My head started to spin and I was going to faint.

'Haley, no, focus!'

Meg shook me. I reached out to steady myself. Half in dream, my hand found itself in motion with the saw – I was barely aware of what I was doing as Meg took the other end of it. Minutes later, I felt the judder and grind through the bone and worked out that, yes, Meg had released the other side and it was only me, actually sawing through my dad's leg.

Do just focus on getting the job done, not on worrying if the patient will die. That can come after. Actually, everything in the whole world can come after.

I was sawing like someone obsessed. Telling myself, I am saving his life, I am cutting his old dead self away. And there was this stink coming from the bone, like a baby's nappy. I know, I should have felt something really profound about life and death and the universe, but to be honest, all I was thinking was, don't barf!

Do not waste time thinking YOU are the victim.

Do just keep sawing.

'Stop!' Meg shouted. 'Sorry, love,' she said, 'sorry, but you're getting nowhere, you're not strong enough.'

Do not feel anti-feminist or old-fashioned if at the end of all this you have to admit that a thigh bone is a very thick thing and that this really needs the help of someone with twice the upper-body muscle mass, aka a man. Because time is running out and your father's pulse is erratic and he's breathing in choking gasps and you are just wasting even more time staring and staring and staring into the biggest wound in the world.

Do admit when you need help.

Meg said Ray should have been back from patrol by then. 'Where the bloody hell is that bastard? Ray!' she screeched. 'RAY! Help!'

Former Alcoholics Must Be Kept Away From The Surgical Alcohol

I sprinted through the dark shouting Ray's name, searching everywhere till I noticed candlelight coming from Dad's cubbyhole. I pushed the door open, expecting Ray to bark at me, but he was hunched over Dad's old tech stuff and there was a half-empty tall bottle of something in his hand. I told him he had to come now and even pulled his arm, but he brushed me off and gazed at me with his bald head all wrinkled.

'What's the point?' he slurred. He had those slow-mo moves of the rat-arsed.

'Please, please, come and help. Now!'

'Five years,' he said, 'and not a drop. How many days've we been hiding here? Eh?'

I yelled, 'Who cares, c'mon!' and tried to drag him out.

'Two weeks and we're fucked already.' And he laughed that dark way scary drunk men do, then took a swig from the bottle and grimaced. It said *Surgical Spirits* on the label. 'We're not going to make it,' he said. 'We're all contaminated already, most likely. My fault, my fault, should never have brought Ed back, should've left him out there to die. My fault.' And he took another swig.

'I don't care about your tragic-loser-man-shit,' I yelled, dragging him to his stupid feet and out through the quad, past the smelly goats and the polytunnel, into the kitchen and to my poor dad.

'Jesus fucking Christ,' he mumbled as he staggered through the doorway. It was a shock to me, too. Coming back, it all looked like some Renaissance painting, the two blood-stained women, the candlelight flickering and the body of the Jesus.

'God sake!' Meg shouted out. 'What's that in your hand, Ray?'

Ray held up the spirits bottle, shrugged. 'Medical,' he mumbled, 'in case of emergencies.'

Then Meg ranted that if he was back on the booze, we might as well all give up now. 'Alky bastard!' she cursed. He looked like he was going to hit her, but he went straight to my dad and checked out our failed amputation. Meg kept on and on at him about how he'd thrown his whole life away and now ours, too.

'Shut it, woman!' he snapped. 'Give me that candle.'

Mother passed him a candle and he looked closely into the gash, nodding and muttering to himself.

'Chainsaw have this off in seconds,' Ray muttered. 'I'll get it.'

'NO! God, you're drunk!' Meg yelled. 'There'd be splinters. Splinters'll cause infections.'

Ray grumbled and poured his alcohol over Dad's wound and told Mother to stand well back, and he yelled at Meg to hold the fucking leg still and for me to hold the candle, as he picked up the saw and wiped soft pink stuff off the blade.

Mother went to Dad's head and whispered to him and Ray apologised and made the sign of the crucifix or something on his chest. He held the blade over Dad's leg and I could see it wavering in his hand and the look on his face as he tried to focus away his massive drunkenness. He lurched forward and I thought, Christ, please no, he's going to start sawing the wrong frickin leg! He staggered then slid backwards, pulling the whole table of tools on top of himself and onto the floor.

I must have started screaming.

Danny ran in then, and Meg ran to him weeping, and Mother helped Ray up to the other chair. Meg whispered in Danny's ear and he stepped towards our operating table.

'OK,' Danny said, his face drained white. His eyes went to me. 'OK?' I didn't know what he meant till he had the saw in his hand. 'OK?' he said again. His eyes told me if we didn't see it through, if we kept messing up, Dad would die, for sure. 'You want me to?' he finally asked.

'I do,' I said, and these are the words women say when they get married.

'OK,' he said, and he took a deep breath, set the blade into the gash, put his full weight down on the blade and began sawing with long, slow movements.

I couldn't bear it and had to focus on something else. Mother. I looked at her tragic, weeping eyes and her whispering mouth. She was telling Dad something, maybe, like, 'So you finally got your just deserts,' but I don't think so. It looked more like she was remembering when she first met him, or something like that. Her mouth was so close to his ear. Her eyes were kind and her hair and face was bloodied and she kept dipping this towel in water and wiping Dad's face with it. She leaned in and kissed his forehead and his nose. I closed my eyes so as not to disturb her, or maybe to stop myself from crying because it was proof, finally, that despite all the shit she and him had done to each other, she must still kind of love him or something.

Then I heard it: Mother was singing. A song like a lullaby. Mother, singing to Dad! And I couldn't believe it. It made me weep so much and it drowned out Dad's wheezing and the sound of Danny panting and the back and forward sound of the saw.

Then I heard the blade stop and the heavy thud.

I opened my eyes and Danny was looking straight at me, his eyes like he'd been to hell and back. I stared at the others, all blood spattered, all silent and numb, and the rising and falling of my dad's chest was the only movement in the whole room, even the candlelight seemed to have stopped flickering. None of us wanted to look at that thing that had rolled off the table and fallen to the floor, that thing of death that was no longer part of my dad.

Accept That You Did All That You Could

After Meg had cauterised and dressed 'the stump', she told Mother and me to get cleaned up. 'Take a shower. Hurry up, ya dozeys,' she smiled. 'Then come back and help me clean up and work out what the hell do we do next!'

I ran and got three buckets of rainwater and we stood naked, me and my mother, kind of speechless before each other on the cold bathroom tiles. Mother lifted the bucket of rainwater and poured it over me. I scrubbed with the soap and thanked her, asked her if she thought we'd made the right choice. It was all very quiet and gentle and whispery, cos we were in shock. She poured the rest over my head and the water slopped and dripped into the bucket at my feet and I felt like we both had the same question inside us, but I whispered it first.

'Will he survive?'

'I don't know,' she whispered back. 'We did the best we could.'

It was my turn to wash her, with the bloodied, cold, soap-sudded water that had fallen from me. She didn't want to debate it. 'Just do it,' she said, nodding. She braced herself and I lifted the bucket over her head. In that instant, in that low light, with her eyes closed, her hands across her bare breasts, the veins sort of protruding on her neck and the skeleton visible through her goose-flesh skin, and just the rush of dirty pink water, she seemed to me the most sad and lovely creature I'd ever seen. Maybe it was a trick of the light, but she was like some higher species who'd lived through many centuries and seen many generations of humans live and die. Wise and sad, but so beautiful. Maybe all mothers look like this eventually.

'What you staring at?' she asked. 'Hurry up, pass me the towel, I'm freezing!'

'Sorry, Mum,' I said.

I had called her 'Mum' for a third time. Weird, but hacking off Dad's leg was like the first thing we'd done together for years, other than shopping and arguing.

'I'm sorry, too,' she said. 'For everything.'

I was crying and then I couldn't stop saying it. 'Mum, Mum, oh Mum,' like all the times I'd called her Mother to spite her had meant all these Mums had been imprisoned, and now they were free and pouring out.

And she was crying, too, and I felt her tears inside me.

Mum was back. My mum.

We shivered, clinging together tight, and our tears somehow turned into laughter as the water stained with my dad's blood dripped from our naked bodies.

How To Heal After A Loss

If Consciousness Is Not Recovered Within Forty-Two Hours...

If consciousness is not recovered within forty-two hours, it is likely that the patient has slipped into a coma. Dealing with someone in this state is a very hard thing. You must **not** do the following:

1. Run back and forwards every ten minutes to see if he's woken up.
2. Worry endlessly about what you will do if he doesn't wake up.
3. Lose sleep worrying, because then you will be no good to man nor beast.
4. Get in the way of Meg and her drugs.
5. Get impatient and angry with everyone, shouting, 'Can't you just make him wake up?!'

The week after the amputation was this dream-like blur of many things repeating.

Like this:

Meg and Mum changing Dad's huge bloodied bandages and wiping the wound with salty water and aloe vera. And repeat.

Me saying, 'Wake up, wake up, wake up,' and soon learning that trying to make someone wake up by staring at them very hard does not work.

Me following Danny everywhere and wanting him to kiss me, but him saying he's too busy now that there's one less able-bodied man. Him cutting wood with an axe to drown out everything I say. Him hunting alone. And repeat.

Ray apologising for drinking, promising he will never drink again. Saying he was starting sobriety again from Day One. Ray drinking. And repeat.

Meg changing Dad's drip. 'His vitals are fine,' she says. Me changing his drip. Me whispering, 'Wake up, Dad.' And repeat.

Meg preparing food. Ray hunting. Mum stroking Dad's face. 'Wake up, Ed.' And repeat.

I confront Danny and say, 'Why can't we talk about this huge thing that's happened between us?' and he backs away and I feel so needy and spoiled. So I resolve to change my ways.

I watch a blister on Dad's face turn from clear to yellow, then burst by itself. I say over and over, 'Stump, not leg.' I tell myself to stop staring at it, and just accept it.

In the home doctor manual, I read, *If consciousness is not recovered within forty-two hours, then blood poisoning causes coma and further amputation will be necessary to remove the source of the toxin.*

Meg takes Dad's temperature and tries to wake him by slapping his face and shouting his name. She shakes her head.

I sit in Danny's room on his bed but he doesn't come. I go over what I've done to make him run from me. Maybe the amputation traumatised him for life. Or he's afraid to show emotions. Or he's religious and thinks he's committed a major sin because I am merely fifteen.

I milk the goats. I look at Dad's face and see the burn scars healing.

We all look at the stump and it weeps, but I can't.

We look at each other and we shake our heads and we tell each other, without words, to wait, he will wake. Let nature decide. But I can't sleep.

We all decide there is no point anymore in wearing the masks and gloves because if we are contaminated we are already contaminated. I kiss Dad's head.

I watch the rise and fall of his chest and I whisper, 'Please let it not be a coma.'

I carry in logs for the fire, to keep Dad warm. More logs, more logs, to boil water, to make steam, so he can breathe.

I need to tell Danny not to be disgusted with himself. That he shouldn't feel ashamed that we made out while Dad is so sick. But as soon as our eyes meet, he turns and leaves.

I tell God, 'If you kill my dad, I will tell everybody that you don't exist.' And then I apologise.

And the problem, Meg says, was that without ECG we couldn't really tell if he was awake or not. He was in a fever and sometimes, sort of, tried to speak through his cracked lips. Did people dream-talk in comas? Did their eyes and fingertips twitch like his? We didn't have a single page on that subject and Meg cursed herself for not having stocked up with more medical textbooks and an encyclopaedia. 'Call ourselves preppers,' she says. 'How the hell did we overlook that?'

Ben and Danny and me carry down two mattresses and make a semi-proper bed for Dad on the floor of the kitchen, next to the table. We take turns sleeping beside him. To not let him out of our sight.

We eat standing up because the dining table seems wrong, and we eat from cans because cooking seems wrong, and we watch him while we eat with disposable spoons because washing up seems wrong, too.

Sleep, eat, work, return to his side. Medicine, temperature, drip. It's been days and so it has to be a coma.

I see myself in the mirror and I see my mum's face hiding behind my skin.

I rehearse this scene in my head. I corner Danny and scream at him, 'Dad is dead, please hold me!'

Danny and Mum scrub the dried blood from the kitchen table and floor.

Ben sits on my knee as we both watch Dad sleeping. Sleeping, still sleeping. Meg refuses to let Ben hear the word 'coma'.

I decide I don't want to live, if he dies.

I decide Danny doesn't love me and only snogged me because there were no other girls for a hundred miles and I had been a fool.

Days and nights blur into each other and still Dad does not wake.

Watching the drip, drip, drip of Dad's morphine and antibiotics, we are in the same horror as before, but a slower kind. Waiting, waiting, in fear that black veins will sprout from the stump and we'll have to go through the entire process again. Cut off more leg. Half awake, no sleep, not even counting the days.

I shave Dad's stubble with Meg showing me how. I don't cut him once. I wait and wait.

I decide, finally, that Danny has no more feelings for me than that deer he slaughtered. He would have just used me for sex and I have dodged a major bullet.

I change Dad's dressing. I study blue veins that look darker.

I read, *The chances of waking from a coma caused by blood poisoning are around 5%.*

Those words swirl in my head as I walk the inner walls, round and round. I tell myself that I have to prepare for the worst, that if Dad dies, for Ben's sake, we have to follow Dad's plans and survive.

How long do we have until the people who burned Dad find us? What is happening in the towns and cities right now? Dad's book said:

With 60% of the population infected and the NHS, financial and food supply systems in ruins, the cities become burned-out centres of contagion, without water, food or electricity. The vast majority of the remaining population are now in the intermediary stages of virus incubation and the later stages of starvation within city population containment centres.

Thousands of evacuees who have evaded military sweeps attempt to leave the cities on foot in the attempt to find food and safety. As with the earlier mutually reinforcing positive feedback loops, the massing of evacuees causes bottlenecks, hostilities and the exponential spread of the virus. Road blocks are set up by the military at all city exit points and civilians herded at gunpoint back to the city containment centres. Many fatalities occur on these newly created 'borders'. The military become infected from the conflict.

Militarized gangs break out and head towards rural areas in search of livestock and villages to plunder. They bring contagion with them and starving hordes in their trail.

Was our wall high enough, was there enough razor wire, was the perimeter fence secure? What if the infected mobs saw our candle-light? If we gave them food, would they go away? I couldn't picture the faces of our enemies, but I sensed their shadows slashing and burning their way across our mountains and fields. Mile by mile, getting closer. I could feel them through the ache in my muscles.

Consider What You Will Do if the Patient Dies

Actually, the last thing I wanted to do was consider what I'd do if the patient died. I had to escape all thinking.

I cornered Danny in his room to tell him how much I hated him, but when I got close my body threw a random fit and we started snogging. I pinned him to the wall, pulled his T-shirt over his head, kissed his neck, his chest. I was basically possessed.

'Woah! Woah, woah,' he said, backing away from me. 'Haley, Christ Almighty. Just stop, please!'

I stood before him panting, part-shocked and part-shamed. 'What? What did I do wrong? Why have you been avoiding me? Why am I so disgusting?'

'No, that's not it,' he said. 'This isn't really about me, is it? Think about your dad.'

But I didn't understand. 'Look,' I shouted, 'I don't even like any of this emotional stuff, OK. What's the point of caring for anyone, if everyone just gets divorced and burned. So forget it. Don't play games. If you hate me, just tell me!'

'You're in shock,' he said. 'Maybe you should be grieving instead of...'

'He's not dead!' I yelled.

'OK, let's just wait and…'

'What? Wait and see if he dies before we can kiss again? Like, at his funeral. That's so sick! You freak!'

I hit him with my fists, yelling into his face. He let me hurt him, then he slowly took my wrists in his big hands and I collapsed into full-on dog-like howling. He was right, I wanted to shatter into a million pieces and vanish. I said many sorries and I was a mess, tears and snot all dripping from me, my mouth wide open with this horrible sort of frog croak – like, probably the ugliest he'd ever seen me.

He held me firmly and whispered, 'Haley, shhh, it's OK. You're fine.'

'But … what am I going to do if he dies?' I asked, my voice breaking. 'I'm so screwed up!'

'It's the world that's screwed up, not us,' he said, wiping a tear from my stupid cheek. 'We're doing pretty well, I'd say.'

'We?'

He didn't speak for the longest time, he just held me tight like that, until my sobbing calmed into semi-pathetic, hiccupping whimpers.

'Whatever happens, I'm here for you, Haley Crowe,' he whispered.

It was such a massively corny thing to say but the best thing about Danny was that he could be a totally sincere medieval peasant and make that more cool than being cynical. I felt great weariness and I curled up in his arms and he laid me down on his bed. All angers and lusts drained from me. I went foetus-shaped and he cradled me from behind. A warm wooziness overtook me and I forgot all about our burning world and the infected wheezers clawing at our gates and poor dying Dad. I felt only his warmth around me and everything felt fine.

I don't think I'll ever understand humans.

Read To The Coma Patient

Things you can do to be useful include:

1. Help purée his food and inject it into his mouth with the turkey baster.
2. Help clean his wounds and replace his bandages and clean up his pee and poop.
3. Keep his lips moist and replace his IV fluids.
4. It may also help to read to the patient.

It was like a fairy tale all screwed up and back-to-front. Dad was both the hideous monster and the sleeping beauty. I didn't want to leave his side, in case he woke up without my being there or he stopped breathing, so what I did is that one crummy thing you're supposed to do, like, in all the movies, when someone's in a coma. I read. I read out loud to him.

I spent a whole morning trying to locate all the books in the safe house and the results were pretty disappointing, actually. Mostly, there were user operation manuals. One for Ray's jeep, one for the quad bike, ten for the wind turbines, and one for each one of the weapons and so on. Like, sixty of them, and who's going to read the *Armalite M15 Series Rifle Operations Manual* out loud?

The only novel was this thing called *Fifty Days of Black*. It was a cheap rip-off of the real *Fifty Shades* and many edges were turned over, usually on pages that featured the words 'throbbing' and 'gushing', so it had to be Meg's.

Then there was the home doctor manual and Dad's survival guide.

And that was all.

It blew me away thinking that, if we survived, we would one day disseminate the wisdom contained in these books around a ravaged planet. These, the pillars of the new world. A million years from now aliens would say that these were clearly their sacred texts for the last humans.

'*Winston thrust his throbbing manhood into Cecilia's…*'

Note for pandemic preppers: please hoard vast libraries of the most important books in the world.

It made me shiver thinking about what had happened to books out there in the real world. They'd burn well and winter was coming on and my guess was all the toilet rolls in the world had already run out.

No books would ever be printed again.

There was no way I was going to read Meg's porn book to my dad. So, I read to Dad from his own book. There was one chapter called 'Coping' and in it was a section called 'The Awakening'. I propped it up beside his head and, in the breaks between tending his wound and topping up his IV and the hundreds of other chores, I read in the hope that hearing his own words might awaken him.

This is what he wrote:

The Awakening

On the day when you have accumulated and sifted all the facts, once you have told yourself that this is the future the world faces, you will wake early and you will want to kill yourself.

I know this to be true.

Be kind to yourself, on this day. Give yourself one more day.

On this morning, go for a walk. There is no point in going to work and it is early yet, the sun has not risen. Don't bother to call in sick – why should you? When the final pandemic strikes, your job will cease to exist. No more career plan, no more glass ceiling, no more ambition or bosses or pension plan. Walk the city and let the world undo itself before your eyes.

Today, you are going to say goodbye to everything. You are going to start your 'List of Last Things'. For some, compiling this list may take weeks or months. At the end of this process you will either wish to kill yourself or you will awaken and know what you must do for you and your loved ones to survive.

Go and walk this city that you think you know. Start to compile the list as you pass things by.

Go to spaces of transit where people rarely walk. Find a forgotten pedestrian overpass, stand alone and watch the six lanes of cars rushing like a river. Rush hour is just beginning and the sun has not fully risen. The cars have their headlights on. Maybe you listen to music on your iPhone when you do this. It might help you cry. I listened to Mahler. Crying, alone, outside, is a public part of the awakening.

Look down at the cars, white lights oncoming, red receding, and tell yourself that there will be no more cars. Listen to the music and say, there will be no more MP3s, no more singles or albums or recording artists or record companies. Take the headphones out and tell yourself that there will be no more streetlights and traffic lights when the pandemic comes. There will be no more petrol, no more radio stations, no more news bulletins.

You will feel a terrible rage in your chest, against those in power who let this get to the point where the pandemic is inevitable. The immensity of the collective delusion they have created. The billions they have lied to.

Everyone who passes beneath your feet is going to die, the slow death of infection, the slower death of starvation, and the brutal death that comes to the survivors. The blood on their hands.

Picture the thousands of cars abandoned and burned beneath your feet as you stand on the overpass. Cry or shout at the cars. No one listens. Learn from this.

You have to get beyond anger, because impotent rage without outlet will kill you. It is already killing hundreds of thousands of people who also know what you know. They know the truth but it rots inside them because they believe they are powerless to do anything. The world won't listen. The truth-tellers are locked in lunatic asylums, medicated, fired, divorced, imprisoned. So they kill the truth, they pretend they don't know, they drink and take drugs and seek a way out through sex, they bury themselves in distractions, walking amnesiacs, the pre-dead, they choose the slow suicide that the world has pre-packed for them.

Keep walking. See the advertisements for alcohol on the roadsides and in the housing estates, see the adverts for sexualised products and sensory distractions everywhere. You may find yourself weeping in the car park of a shopping centre. Cry at the sight of families stuffing their branded boxes into their cars, and their children, faces smeared with ketchup, with ice cream, screaming for more. Their whole lives are mapped out like products with planned obsolescence built in.

Tell yourself, there will be no more toys. No more credit cards or credit, when the pandemic hits. No more ice cream. You pass advertising hoardings with the faces of smiling people, the exposed bodies of women. Tell yourself, there will be no more adverts for holidays, for insurance, no more desire for things of status. Stand back and watch the thousands drive out of the retail parks and join a traffic jam, and see them as rows of caged animals in a vast bio lab experiment. That is what they soon will be.

Your anger may shift. Perhaps you will feel a hollowness developing as you empty yourself of illusions. You may be overwhelmed with compassion or pity. These are useless feelings. Add these emotions to your list of last things. Pity will leave you and the ones you love defenceless.

Walk forgotten sidings and glimpse the future without humans, the weeds reclaiming the concrete architecture. Walk to a train station. Watch the young people, so attractive, so vital and hopeful. Tell yourself, there will be no more power lines, no more timetables. No more time to catch or kill.

Look at them. Sixty in the carriage, all on their smartphones, texting, playing games, making no eye contact with each other. Picture the spread of the virus in the air between them. And tell yourself, there will be no more dating apps, no more games, no more upgrades. No more memory.

Remind yourself that there are four vast conglomerates who control all news media and technology. Two of whom also fund bio-warfare laboratories.

You want to scream out what you know. Scream, save yourselves! But it is futile. No one will listen.

Today you must give up on everyone.

Walk through the city centre to the shopping precinct. Consider a world without electricity. What is the carbon imprint of six billion dead and decomposing bodies? Add ecology to your list of last things that no longer matter. Tell yourself, there will be no more recycling, no more charity.

Ask yourself why you should even try to save these people who laugh at you. They would only be competitors for the last remaining resources.

If they survive, they will take food from your children.

No democratic processes, no media revelation will change what is to come. Give up hope of that. Learn to live with your knowledge as a secret. The last thing you need is for others to know. Let the power of the secret locked inside you fuel you, like a contained explosion in a nuclear reactor.

Walk through a mall and take the elevator to the car park, go to the top floor and stand looking out at the hundreds of people far below, as small as a virus in a petri dish. Tell yourself it is too late for them – let them die in your mind. Then look out to the skyline.

You must face death now.

Kill yourself and all anxiety will end.

Or walk away and start your life again from zero. Turn your despair into action, but know that these millions will be against you, everyone will think you insane.

Feel the wind, hear the distant sounds of shoppers. See how easy it would be to jump. Feel that hollow expand within you. Look down and tell yourself your list of last things. There will be no more stores, no more fashions, no more buskers playing pop songs in the streets, no more traffic wardens, no more credit cards, no more special offers, no more debt.

Jump or don't jump.

The words blurred and I turned to Dad's face. Behind his lids his eyes were moving as if he was walking miles alone in some parallel universe. I squeezed his hand and whispered, 'Don't jump, Dad, please.'

What To Do When Waiting For Nature To Decide

You can't force nature to decide whether your loved one will live or die. Worrying never changed any outcome. Instead, take time out. Write about what you are going through. It helps give focus and perspective.

I told Ben I was doing my homework and catching up, and sometimes I did little drawings with him, so that kept him busy and stopped him whimpering for his chums and his sweets and his computer games. He filled three jotters by the candle, drawing imaginary 'weapons of mass destruction'. Mum told him he was very creative, inventing all those incredible bone-crushing machines, and I hadn't the heart to tell her he was just copying shit from *Warworld IV*.

Every day I prayed for Dad and counted my blessings.

There was this advice in his manual that said, *To get through lockdown, create a log of your daily high points, new experiences and goals for the next day.*

So, I sat beside Dad and started on that.

High Points of my Day: Dad not dying. Not being shot, raped or eaten by marauding gangs of infected, starving civilians and/or the military.

New Experiences: Dad not dying. Watching my little brother skin and gut a pheasant then watching it bobbing about in a stew pot with its feet still on. Ben and me actually eating it with jam. Unpeeling the bandage on Dad's remaining foot and his little toe falling off.

Hopes for Tomorrow: See: high points of today. And repeat.

At first I wrote to keep the fear at bay, then cos it gave me a privacy barrier. Privacy is a major problem here.

Like when I got my period and Meg shouted to Danny in the bunker, 'Danny, while you're down there can you get Haley some fanny pads?' and I'm dying from cringe, then she says, all smiley,

'What kind of flow, love?' and I give her the name of my brand but they don't have them, so she shouts down to Danny, 'Heavy Flow, please, Danny, to be on the safe side.' I could have died.

For some reason, the privacy of writing is respected. Sitting in my bunk, knees pulled up, scribbling away, it's like I was in a glass box, no one came near me, and I was no longer simply waiting for the horrific moment when Dad would die or our infected enemies would appear at the fence. I could write a word and, for a second, I was in another day, further back, a day that was safer, a day before I fully understood that one day I would die.

I secretly mulled over Dad's battle with suicide. No kid should ever know such a thing about a parent. I felt sorry for him, but it really hurt to know that he'd practically gone through with it. I felt so abandoned, and it was yet another horrible truth that I'd have to hide from Ben.

I missed Josh and Shanna and Teeny and Sean and Bo. And sometimes I thought, what if they're all dead already? And I couldn't bear it. I didn't even want to think about what the mobs would do to Shanna cos she's so pretty.

So, then I got the hollow sick feeling and I ran back to Dad again, to watch his chest, falling, rising, falling, rising, and I took a blast of my inhaler, but, truth be told, my asthma symptoms had pretty much gone away. Which was something, at least.

Then it was late and I was reading the medical manual next to Dad, the chapter on treating third-degree burns with a thing called 'de-briding' which is nothing to do with divorce but means cutting off dead skin, and it had been freezing cold so I'd put some logs in the stove. I guess I'd be been pretty exhausted from staring at Dad's face and his stump and from the fear that we'd all got the virus now. I must have got so stressed that I fell asleep, cos I started dreaming about me and Dad and Mum at a campfire when I was little and there was this lovely smell like incense burning. I woke up choking and there were flames from the top of the stove.

It was the medical manual, lying exactly where I left it. I flew up in a panic and grabbed it to try to put it out, but the more I fanned it the faster the pages burned. I was so furious at myself, just standing there holding the flaming book, staring mesmerized at these words that could save our lives getting eaten by flames. I threw it down and smothered it and burned myself a bit.

It was all charred on one side with maybe fifty pages turned to black ash, and Dad was choking but still deep in coma sleep and Meg ran downstairs, yelling, 'Bloody hell, what's all this smoke? What's on fire?'

Then Meg and me stared at the smouldering medical manual on the floor. Most of it was saved but the flames had stolen all the index and the pages from W to Z, which included How to Survive Worms, Weil's disease, West Nile Virus, Wisdom Tooth Removal, Yellow Fever and Zika virus.

I apologised, cos I could have set the whole house on fire and killed Dad, and Meg gave me a sweaty hug and said, 'No use crying over spilt milk,' which didn't make me feel any less like shit. I stared at Dad's blistered face gasping for breath and at the burned edge pages and it all seemed connected and horribly portentous.

What To Do If A Coma Patient Wakes Up

I was milking the goats and it had rained and the mud mixed with the stinky, spilled milk. The morning light hadn't yet come round to share its glare with the solar panels and I was staring at the eyes of this goat that I named Cara – on account of her resembling Cara Delevingne – and I'm not superstitious, but I heard a shout from inside.

'He's opened his eyes!'

I ran through and Mum was doing the 'weeping for joy' thing, running round saying, 'Haley, he's awake. He's awake! Get Ben, quick!'

Dad's eyes were waxy slits and his voice was this kind of cracked whisper.

'Hi, Dad, how goes it?' I said, or some inappropriate crap like that. I don't know for sure how many days he'd been under – but my God, how amazing to see him lift a hand, even though it fell again. I saw a trace of a smile, through the massive scab thing on his left cheek.

I took his hand and kissed it, which was a bit weird. I talked to him tons and Mum said, 'Don't bother him with your yabbering, Haley, let me give your dad some water.' And this amazed me, because she was literally putting her hand behind his sweat-drenched head so he could drink. Dad eyed her strangely, probably a bit freaked as to why he was even lying there and why his ex-wife wasn't being a total bitch, like usual.

Dad tried to speak to her, just a whisper, but she told him, 'Shh, save your strength, Ed,' and I wondered if, as soon as he was well, they'd go back to their usual recrimination routines.

Ben ran in then and was jumping all over the place, shouting, 'Daddee, yippee!' and Dad was trying to hold Ben but wincing in pain, and Mum told Ben, 'Give your father some room, for God's sake!'

I sat on the table edge and I discovered that it's not just corny and people really do weep for joy, aka, me. I wondered if, by some miracle, we had gone back to a time when we were an actual family again. Then I came up with this weird solution: maybe Dad could stay on the edge-of-death forever and Mum could care for him. It was sick, like ... Munchausen's syndrome, but we were already doing Stockholm syndrome, so why the hell not?

Then Ray, then Meg and then Danny all filed in to take Dad's burn-scarred hands and do their own variations of the weeping-with-joy routine. My eye turned to the edge of his makeshift floor bed and to his one good foot sticking out from under the covers.

Dad didn't know. He probably had, you know, the other syndrome – phantom limb syndrome – and thought his leg was still there.

Everyone was crowding Dad, with Mum telling them over and over to give him some space, for God's sake. Dad was awake for two whole hours but the commotion completely exhausted him, and in that time I didn't think once about the pandemic.

Then Meg had to dose Dad with diamorphine again. 'He's got a long way to go,' she said, 'and when he's better we'll have to wean him off the drugs, too.'

I was so happy and then so sad and then totally confused.

So I went off to the bathroom and put my hands in a praying shape on top of the cistern and said, 'Dear God. You make it pretty impossible to believe in you, what with you letting six billion people get infected and die and everything. But, fair's fair, you did a great job on Dad, so I will make a serious attempt to believe in you. A deal's a deal, so I guess I have to stick with it. Over and out, and thanks, BTW. Cheers. LOL. Sorry, not LOL, but you know what I mean. Amen. Xxx.'

How To Adjust To A New Disability

The wound should fully heal in five to eight weeks. However:

1. The physical and emotional adjustment to the loss of a limb can be a much longer process.
2. Patients may experience phantom pain and experience grief over the loss of the limb, in much the same way that one would grieve over a dead person.
3. Extra emotional support is required for all involved. Not just the patient.

No matter how happy we were to have Dad back there was still the ghostly memory of the massive fight Mum and me had before. I was kind of scared that our old wound would re-open.

We were in the bathroom and I was trying to get her to look at the section in the medical manual on recovering together, after the loss of a limb. But she wasn't listening. She was sorting clothes from the washing that she and Meg and Danny had done by hand. 'Damn,' she said, and she held up her blouse, the one she'd arrived in. It still had stains even after they'd pounded the living Jesus out of it in that big plastic tub with bleach and broom handles.

'How are we going to tell Dad about his leg?' I asked. I wondered if the trauma of Dad's loss of limb might have re-awoken her feelings of grief over her divorce or something.

She threw down the blouse, exasperated. 'It's no use,' she said, totally not listening to me. 'I might as well throw it out.'

And I thought, crap, she's gone back to fussing about her petty little things again to distract herself from her pain.

She sorted through the other clothes, all these non-fashion things Meg had loaned us – pants, socks, knickers. 'We can't wear these horrible things,' she said, holding up some random army fatigues.

And it really bugged me that we could go through all this and still sink back into these old habits of snooty one-upmanship. Like we'd learned nothing. I wasn't getting through to her, so I read to her from the medical manual and I said, 'Hey, don't you think we should study this? Like, about losing a leg, it says, *Adjustment to the new body image can be like learning to be a new person, from scratch.*' The words seemed to be about her, actually. '*The grief and readjustment can affect all family members.*'

Without warning, Mum kind of choked into tears. I came closer, but she did that busy-yourself-while-crying routine that grannies do – hanging the wet things, complaining that they weren't even clean. The wet trousers in her hand were the exact same bloodied ones she'd been wearing during Dad's operation. The blood had been bleached to a thin yellow grey but the outline of the stain was still there. 'We'll never … never get to buy new clothes again, will we?' she asked.

'No,' I said – and I almost added, 'duh' – 'cos I don't think capitalism will exist, Mum.' Then I hugged her and she kept crying.

It's so weird to feel like you're a parent for your own parents.

How To Help The Young To Understand Loss

Kids are like animals: they don't think much about the past or future, and they don't understand yet that we'll all die one day, or that some of us might have experienced the loss a significant part of their ambulatory body mass.

Ben clutched his leg and wailed, 'Yuk, yuk, yuk, blah, gross!'

'Ben,' I said, 'calm down, it's Dad's Goddamn leg, not yours!'

I had to talk Ben through the situation because he was allowed to sit with Dad on his makeshift bed. We didn't want Ben to be the one that broke the news to Dad, like, by accident. Like, oh by the way, everyone cut off your leg! Dad was still almost totally speechless and incapacitated, with his arms wired to drips and mostly out for the count, and Meg said she was only going to break the news to him when he was ready. She didn't want the shock to give him a heart attack, but I could tell she was putting it off.

'So, you can't tell Dad yet, OK? Promise,' I said to Ben, using a Dad-ism. 'Sometimes, Ben, we have to protect people we love from the truth. OK?'

Ben nodded. 'OK,' and he stopped clutching his leg and swung his feet from the top bunk.

'Will Dad get a new one?' Ben asked. In his teenie mind he probably thought you could grow a new one, like a lizard. I told him no, but if he and Danny wanted to make a present for Dad, like, some crutches, that would be awesome.

'Can I have a shot, too?' Ben asked.

'Well, you'll have to make them first … Oh, and keep that a secret too. OK?'

So Ben was happy and then confused again. He pulled one foot out of its boot and scrutinised his wrinkled sock. 'I'm going to kill the wheezers when they come,' he said.

'Wait, who told you about that? And that's not a nice word for infected people.'

'They're going to climb over the fence and we're going to set mantraps and shoot them.'

'Wait, wait, wait. Who told you all this?'

'Danny,' Ben grinned, proudly. 'I'm not scared. We made a hundred thousand arrows already. Peoow, peooow, peoowww!'

So, this was what had Danny had done to keep Ben busy during the operation. I had a furious elder sibling moment.

Ben jumped off the top bunk and landed with his usual mouthed explosion. He pointed at the walls and said, 'Peooow, peooow!' Then dashed off to play in his imaginary world of endless war where, when you die, you can always come back to have another go.

I found Danny out in No Man's Land on patrol. I yelled, 'What the hell were you thinking, telling Ben that stuff?'

'Someone had to tell him. Your family's pretty good at avoidance,' he said, shooting at the target. I dunno, maybe the energy in arguing and the energy in kissing are connected but a minute later we were rolling around in the heather and mud, barely hidden by the shell of the old car. We were getting majorly into it when there was a noise.

Danny grabbed his crossbow.

'Don't fucking shoot, Danny!' It was Meg. 'The birds and the bees, is it?' She smirked, and I must have blushed and made up some crap, because she said, 'I've been standing here for five minutes and you two were so busy you never even saw me! Anyway, we'll talk about your antics later – I'm a bit worried about your mum. Have you noticed anything odd, Haley?'

I shook my head and refastened the buttons on my shirt. Danny was massively blushing, too, and trying to hide his trouser-boner from his mum.

'Well,' Meg said, 'it was just … I was in the polytunnel this morning, you know, getting the last of the tomatoes in, and I'd asked your mum to take in the beetroot. If we don't get them in soon before the frost, they'll get all woody tasting. Well, she'd gone awful quiet and she was sitting there in the mud, with the trowel. And she was just … staring at it, the trowel.'

I said Mum had never been a fan of gardening and was probably worried about her nail varnish or something.

'No, but she'd been crying,' Meg said. 'I asked her if she was OK, but she wanted to be left alone, made that very clear to me. I just think … it must be really hard for her, you know. Sprung into all this. I mean, one day your whole life's there and then the next … It's easier for you kids, but when you're a grown-up, she'll be thinking about her job. You know, a powerful career woman, like your mum. I just, I know what she's going through, and it took me three years to come to terms with it all. She'll be thinking about her home and furniture and friends. She's going through all these feelings and any stupid thing can set you off. A boot or a bag or anything … It's very hard, you know, to accept that the whole world out there is dying. Messes with your head. I'm just a little bit worried about her, Haley. She wouldn't do anything to hurt herself, would she? Will you keep an eye on her for me, love?'

Now, this is what Dad calls 'worldview re-adjustment grief', but I didn't know that at the time. Plus, Dad said that some people can never adjust.

I shrugged and asked Meg if it would be OK if I focused my attention on weapons training, instead of on Mum.

I heard a noise and I looked up and I saw a silhouette in the stone arch of the gateway three hundred feet from us. At first I thought it was Ray, but the form was female. It was Mum, but dressed in army fatigues. She stopped there. This tiny figure, waving like mad and calling out.

'Haley, Haley! Get back here, it's not safe!'

Wow, this was my mum who only ten days before had led us running through that very same gate. Now she was yelling as if she'd just seen something creeping up behind us. Meg and Danny and I looked out to the perimeter and a low slow fog was coming over the land. A bird flew. Nothing more.

'Haley, run!' Mum screamed.

If You Kill Something, You Must Eat It

That night, two things happened that merged portentously in my mind – not that I'm superstitious. It started with a squawking, screaming noise from the quad. I ran out and Mum was standing there with a meat cleaver in her hand, while a chicken, bleeding and limping, ran in panic in the straw. Her eyes looked dazed.

'Mum, what in God's name are you trying to do?'

'Help me catch it, Haley.'

I watched her lurch after the terrified bird, like someone possessed. I should add that she was just wearing a T-shirt and knickers and rubber boots, like a mad slag.

'Mum, just put down that knife, eh?' I said.

'We have to put it out of its misery,' she shouted. 'Help me catch it!'

Danny appeared and she shouted, 'Danny! Help me catch this beast and show me how to kill it.' And I caught Danny staring at Mum's boobs, which were pretty much all over the place because she wasn't wearing a bra. I thought maybe it was a test or a punishment because Meg told her about me and Danny kissing.

'Are you sure?' Danny asked, and he looked to me with a 'has-your-mum-gone-nuts?' expression. Danny caught the chicken in seconds. 'Did you cut its toe off?' he asked my mum.

'Yes, yes, just get on with it, we all have to learn how to kill what we eat, even madam Haley! Show us what to do!' Mum snapped.

The chicken screeched in panic in Danny's hand and he shot me this perplexed glance. Like, how come your mum has changed so suddenly?

'Don't just stand there, Haley. Take the knife,' she said, and I thought Mum had done this to try to make me be disgusted with Danny.

'Don't you dare hurt it … You let that poor bird go!' I yelled at her.

I ran into the kitchen and there was this ominously strange silence. This is what I saw: Dad was sitting upright and Meg was holding his hand. The covers had been pulled back and his stump was exposed and he was staring at it in disbelief. Meg gave him this slo-mo hug and patted his back and she gestured for me to stay away for a minute, give him some space.

I went back out to the quad and Danny was forcing the chicken's neck down onto a wooden block. 'OK, bring the knife down fast,' he said to Mum. 'Do it quick, the bird's in distress!' She raised the cleaver-knife-thing to shoulder height. 'Watch my finger,' Danny said, but his eyes said to me, please, don't blame me! The bird's wings were flapping horribly. It was making these strangled sounds and then all was made worse by Ben's arrival.

'Cool,' Ben said randomly. 'Can I have a shot?'

'Mum!' I shouted. 'Not in front of Ben!'

'Ben has to watch too, Haley,' she said, like she was sleep-talking. 'We all have to do this, the days of fun are over. We have to get used to it!'

She raised the blade and I screamed, 'Stop!' I pushed past her and ran into the kitchen.

There by his bed, Dad was standing, leaning on Meg's arm as she took his weight. He didn't look up to me. He was staring at the stone floor next to his one good foot, transfixed by the empty space where part of himself had once been.

I ran back outside and the chicken's head was lying in the dirt, while its headless body tried to run and fly, like it hadn't learned yet that it was dead.

Ben clung to my leg, and we both stared at Mum. It was the first living thing she'd ever killed. She was panting. There was a spray of blood on her top lip and she hadn't even noticed it.

Don't Become Too Attached To People Who Might Die

You can minimise emotional pain by being Zen and trying to care less about everything, but this is not something I can pull off.

I lay on the floor with Danny, staring at the rafters, breathing heavily. We'd been making out and had gone as far as we could without going *too* far. Our faces were flushed, our fingers intermeshed in sweat. I could taste his skin on my lips and feel the cool wind on my bare belly. Joy was sort of bursting from me. Dad's terrible wounds were healing and I was in something like love. I hadn't told Danny yet. I was keeping it inside, till I was sure, kind of enjoying the secret.

'Danny?' I turned and he turned, our faces so close he was a blur. 'You think my mum's gone crazy for real?' I asked.

'City people are weird,' he said.

'No, but I think it started before. Like back home, we'd be in the lounge and she'd be on her iPad and I'd be on my phone and we actually texted each other from one side of the room to the other...'

'So?'

'I think she's scared of emotion, cos of her past,' I said.

Danny raised our held-hands to his cheek and rubbed his stubble.

'I think it was so to do with my dad cos he tried to kill himself when I was young and maybe it scarred her for life. I used to think it was a bad dream but now I know it's true. It's probably what made me weird too.'

Danny rose on his elbow and his bicep flexed. He stroked a hair from my face – one of his intensities was building. I tried to fend it off.

'Close shave with your mum today,' I said. 'How much do you think she saw?'

He was silent.

'OK, you were right though, we really have to cut it out.'

Danny nodded. 'Yeah, no, you were right, I don't want to tell them about us. They've got enough to worry about,' he said. 'It's irresponsible.'

'We're just being selfish,' I said. 'OK, no more kissing for ten days.'

'OK,' he agreed, 'totally banned.'

'Right,' I said, 'let's shake on it.'

But as soon as we did the forces of nature returned. I just had to feel his skin against mine. Belly to belly. 'My God,' I moaned as I pushed him back onto the floor and climbed on top. 'This is so wrong. We're totally banned!'

I squeezed my hand inside his jeans and he put his hand inside mine and his finger slipped inside me.

'Woah, hold it! We really, really, really have to stop,' he gasped.

'You're right,' I panted. 'I mean, you shouldn't develop strong feelings for someone in a time of mass death, right? Like, what if you were to die?'

'Right, we're only going to hurt each other, right?'

We both agreed to not touch each other again and negotiated it to five days as we lay panting into each other's mouths, our eyes so close and so wide, like we were just one person.

Then, totally randomly, he said, 'Haley Crowe, will you be my girlfriend?'

'Wow. Old-fashioned. Wow.' I said all this and it sounded ironic, and he looked hurt and so cute I just had to kiss him. 'Do you mean like, "going steady, going out together"?'

'Yeah.'

I laughed and he seemed even more hurt.

'Sorry, it's just funny,' I said, ''cos it's not like we can actually GO out anywhere, you know, for a date to the movies, the mall. And it's not like we can boast about it to anyone else!'

He sat up.

'No, no, no, sorry,' I said. 'Do you mean, like, you want to tell people I'm your girlfriend? Is that what you mean? But, like, who?'

'Forget it,' he said.

'You mean, like, my parents? Why d'you want to tell them?'

He shrugged and nodded.

'No frickin way, my mum would go nuts,' I said. 'She'd totally ban us from seeing each other! Ray would literally kill you!'

He became sullen in that dark, fire-y way of his. He got up and I tried to stroke his leg but he pulled away.

'No, no, no,' I said. 'Shit, sorry, I mean, it's just … maybe we should keep it secret a teeny bit longer, you know, just until Dad's utterly well.'

'Well, maybe we shouldn't touch till then, like zero,' he said, and he walked to the door in the floor. 'No more fooling around. It's kind of wrong, anyway.'

And this seemed to be our first argument.

'For Christ sake, Danny, wait! You think I'm ashamed of you?' I shouted. 'I'm not, I totally … I … I …' But I couldn't get the 'I love you' part out.

'It's obscene,' he said, 'being happy when so many people are infected and dying. They can't touch each other, can they? And what the hell happened to Kane? She went out and she's probably dead now! We should be out there doing something, saving lives, not just hiding here, pawing each other.'

'Fuck you!' I said. 'You're just frustrated cos I won't let you go all the way!'

'Jesus, Haley,' he said, 'people are dying out there!'

'Yeah, right,' I said, 'so now you're not going to touch me because *other* people are contaminated? Shit!'

'I could be contaminated!' he yelled. 'I don't want to hurt you.'

'Well, maybe I'm contaminated already!' I shouted, and he wasn't getting it, so I shrieked, 'Why are you men so frickin stupid? I'll bet you only snogged me cos you got bored of your chicks with guns posters and you can't get online for a wank anymore!'

He started climbing down the ladder. 'Grow up,' he muttered.

'Fuck off and die!' I yelled, and instantly regretted it.

I threw myself back onto his floor, appalled at my stupid self. Maybe he was right. I'd seriously blown it, and how the hell were we going to get through the weeks and months and years of lockdown if we hated each other? And we could be contaminated already. Dad said it could take as long as a month to show.

I lay there listening to the relentless grind of the wind turbine going round and round and round.

How To Live in the Dark

Night Is The New Day

Once you are certain that the infected and the military are on the way, you must make the following changes:

1. Perimeter patrol is now dangerous. You can't risk being seen. Patrol must be conducted from a distance with binoculars, telescopics and night vision.
2. The house must be blacked out.
3. Night must become your day.

I was sitting by the fire with Dad, listening to the crackling static of his long-wave radio, when there was a tearing sound from one end of the sky to the other.

'Spy plane!' Ray yelled. 'Military.'

I ran around shouting, 'Where's Danny? Is Danny OK?' because he was out on patrol and seriously not speaking to me.

Ray yelled that the plane was hunting for packs of refugees, probably. 'Blow out all the candles, now!'

Ray called an emergency meeting. Dad insisted he take part and sat on the mattress clutching the makeshift crutch Danny and Ben had made for him. Dad still found it hard to speak and could only whisper. I don't want to tell you about the wounds on one side of his face.

The rest of us sat round the big wooden table on which Dad lost his leg. It had reverted to a dinner table. Meg said that if we were going to moan about a few silly bloodstains, we could damn well have a go at scrubbing the table ourselves.

Ray had Dad's book before him. He read out, '*Military*

surveillance of the populace in outlying regions during pandemic.' Dad listened and nodded, and his eyes, which almost smiled, were silenced by pain. Ray skipped some pages and started reading aloud.

'Point one: *You must fear the military at the gate just as much as the gangs. If local people come looking for food, it will be a small-scale ambush. If the military come, they will requisition all of your livestock and rations. Soldiers or police are to be treated as contaminated and as hostile. Use lethal force.'*

Ben sat beside me, confused. 'Is that what happened to your leg, Dad? Did ambush men come?'

Dad placed his hand on Ben's head. Mum spoke for him. 'Your father can't remember what happened, darling, and I'm sure it's very upsetting for him to even try, so let's not bother him.'

'Made … mistake,' Dad said, and he looked over at her.

'Yes,' Mum replied. 'We all did.' But she couldn't meet his eye.

Meg was right: Mum had changed. When Dad had been unconscious she'd held his hand and kissed his brow, but now that he was out of danger she had this nervousness around him. Dad had a look on his face like the last month had just been a blank and I wanted to tell him that Mum had changed his bandages and cleaned his wound and whispered and sung to him and wept over his body.

He'd missed all of that. How romantic – like, you love someone because you think they're dying and when they don't die it's a kind of embarrassment. Like, maybe Mum was thinking, please come close to death so I can love you again.

'OK. Point two,' Ray said. '*No more fires during the day. Can't have smoke on the horizon.'*

'Great! How we going to keep warm?' Meg asked. 'Or bloody cook?'

'Don't bark at me, these are all Ed's plans. Anyone can see smoke for miles, but not in the dark. So that also means all cooking has to be done at night.'

Meg groaned. 'Might as well sleep through the day then and go into hiber-bloody-nation.'

Ray pressed on, as if being super bossy was going to erase our memory of him being a drunken coward: 'Point three. *We have to get into the habit of putting the wind turbine up at night.*'

'Can't we just leave it up?' Meg asked.

'No chance. Folk could see it from the hills, jets too. So up and down every night – it's got hinges. We're not getting enough wattage from the solar. Plus, we're all going to have to put in an extra half hour each in on the bike-charger.'

'Super muscles! Yayy!' Ben yelled, and I groaned.

Mum was silent, staring over at Dad. Danny was majorly avoiding my gaze.

'Point four,' Ray said. '*Blackout. We have to make the house light tight, no more light leakage.*'

'Bugger,' Meg said. 'Living in darkness … What's the point?'

She had meant it as a joke, but no one laughed.

A log in the fire sparked, as if to protest that it would be the last of its kind to burn in our daylight hours. Were we infected already? I worried. Would we be locking ourselves into the dark with the virus?

How To Blackout

To blackout your safe house you will need:

1. Thick black plastic bin bags.
2. A box cutter.
3. Duct tape.
4. A test candle.
5. Co-operation with one other person.

We were blacking out all the windows and it was my job to go round, pane by pane, and check for light leaks.

I stood in the quad and watched Danny cover the kitchen

windowpane with bin bags and duct tape. I blew him kisses and did a goofy dance to try to bug him and get his super serious face to talk, then I gave him the finger, but he kept on with the job until he'd blacked the window and vanished from me. He called out, 'Can you see any light?'

I told him, 'I can't see your ugly face. But I never want to, ever again.' Then I knocked on the window and whispered, 'Danny, only joking. Don't black me out, please!'

He said nothing, so he was still really pissed at me.

'OK, I'll be your girlfriend,' I said, being pathetically needy. 'Are you there? Danny?' But either he was pretending he'd walked away or was standing there giving zero fucks.

What could I do?

I moved to the next window and saw Mum sitting on the window ledge alone, her bin bags and duct tape untouched. She had a box cutter in her hand and she was staring at it for a freak-ishly long time. She didn't hear me as I knocked. Not the first time or the second.

'Come on, Mum,' I said, 'you're lagging behind.'

She looked at me through the dusty window and her face seemed like an old black-and-white photo.

I wanted to ask her if she was OK, but she'd have said, don't be so silly, I'm fine, and put on a fake smile and maybe even got cross with me for asking.

She placed the black bin bag over the windowpane and blacked me out. I stepped back and every window in the quad was black. The only light was from the moon, and it was a scrawny grey light, half-masked by low clouds.

Later on, I was reading Dad's manual by candlelight. The chapters on what was happening now in the evacuated cities. It said:

The bodies of those that have died from the virus are thrown into the streets, further contaminating public walkways and the sewage and water systems. There are no ambulance services to clear them up, and the military are too busy attempting to enforce martial law on a population that has become overrun with crime. Water and sanitation workers have abandoned their posts.

Human waste contaminates the food chain, with a plague of diseases caused by faecal contamination. These include: campylobacter, toxoplasmosis, E. coli, salmonella, norovirus, diarrhoea, acute gastroenteritis, cholera, giardia and tape worms and other parasites.

Over the next month, within the contaminated population containment centres, the number of deaths doubles every two days, before exploding exponentially as the virus and bacteriological infections become a quadruple feedback loop. The contained populations die slowly from starvation, dehydration, multiple infections, violence and lawlessness, in addition to those who succumb directly from the virus.

The government plans to manage the die-off. 'After the pandemic' it plans to rebuild civilisational structures under military rule, with a 'sustainable population' that is one-seventh the size of what it was.

I stared at the blacked-out window, in shock, and I could sense none of these horrific things that were happening so far away. Then I heard a sound of chains from beyond the window and the air tasted metallic, just the way it does before a storm. I heard a sound of, like, slapping or fighting. I jumped in fright – the infected are here!

I listened harder and it was just the stupid goats pulling against their chains, and the flapping sound was most likely just the stupid wind whipping up the polytunnels. I was just being paranoid.

But, after I snuffed my candle out, I couldn't get the image from my head, of those nameless bodies piled up in our street back home, rotting outside our actual door, which was probably kicked in. And then I thought of Granny Cooper and Granny and Grandad Crowe and I had to swallow a bit of barf, and I felt really shitty for not having texted or Zoomed them more before.

How To Rehabilitate

Long-term recovery and rehabilitation for an amputee will include:

1. Exercises to improve muscle strength and control.
2. The use and acceptance of assistive devices, such as crutches or artificial limbs.
3. The acceptance of help from others.
4. Meaningful activities to help restore the ability to carry out daily chores and to promote independence.

It had been around a month and none of us showed signs of the virus, and that meant, if his calculations were right, that Dad hadn't contaminated us after all.

His body was making quality progress, but something else was missing from his old self. I worried that he'd been brain-damaged by the whole burning thing, and I worried about how the fire thing had even happened. Like, how, and where?

I sensed some unspeakable secret that he was saving us from, about the fire and maybe about Kane and if he'd seen her murdered. I kept wondering, if he'd been burned by attackers, how close they'd been to discovering us, and where they'd gone after.

Amnesia is a kindness for those in trauma, Meg said. Dad sat there, staring out at us, and he looked like Grandad Crowe when he used to say things like, 'I went to the whatcha-call-it with what's-his-name.'

I watched Ray and Meg take turns helping Dad hop around the kitchen and stretch his limbs with the crutches. Dad had these desperate bursts of enthusiasm that then laid him so low. 'You're overdoing it, don't be an idiot,' was Meg's refrain. 'Lie down and do as you're told, for Christ's sake.' But all such barks were said with kind humour, cos she was overjoyed to have her saviour back.

Danny and Ben sat with Dad and he slowly showed them how to remake the crutches with twine to make them stronger. I came closer and sat beside Danny, but he got up and walked away.

Mum avoided touching Dad. She stayed beyond the drip stand, and he could only reach so far. You had to be careful when you hugged him so as not to brush the drip-needle out by accident and make him yelp.

Dad's speech was returning, but Meg said he should save his voice. He ruffled my hair and got me to read out loud from the medical manual. The book was right: *Setting challenges and new goals with others in a caring environment is the key to full recovery.* Dad was getting restless and he would need something to do to help him get better. It also said that keeping busy and feeling like a valuable contributor were key in fighting off depression.

I worried that Meg was right, that depression had skipped Dad and gone straight to Mum.

I went to look for Danny but he'd vanished. When I came back I saw this weird sight. Ben and Ray and Meg and Dad were all huddled round the log fire, and they were singing some old hippie-ish song I didn't know the words to. Dad mumbled along, his arm round Ben.

Mum sat at a distance, in the shadows by the blacked-out window. Like she was watching a movie about a family she wasn't part of.

Dad's eyes searched for her, tried to bring her into the circle of singing, but she was miles away. Maybe, in her mind, she was tip-toeing through our gutted city home, her feet crunching on the smashed glass of windows and old photographs.

Set Challenges And New Goals

Dad was making good progress in the month after the amputation and as he always said, strength isn't just about muscles – it comes from having beliefs, goals and challenges.

For sure, Mum was adrift and needed cheering up, and so I told Dad that she was most likely miserable due to having to do washing in a bleach-filled plastic bucket that was wrecking her hands. 'She'd probably give an arm or a leg never to have to use that stupid wringer thing again,' I said to him. 'It probably makes her feel like a medieval washer wife or something.' I regretted saying 'giving an arm or a leg' but Dad nodded anyway.

Dad made a list and got Danny and Ben to fetch him things from all over. He could say small sentences then, with lots of croaking throat noises. He asked Ray to pull the now-dead top-loading washing machine out from the wall and to help him set his one-legged ass down on the floor. Dad, it seemed, had an idea.

I never really intended for him to DO anything about the washing situation, and I had goat-duty to get through, so I kept popping in to make sure he wasn't doing himself an injury.

It started off with Meg yelling at my dad, and him surrounded by bits of metal – an old mountain bike, G-clamps, widgets and bolts, chains and wires. Meg yelled, 'How the hell am I going to use the kitchen now? Who's going to feed us? This is not a fucking work-shed!' and she stormed off.

The next time I came through, Danny had helped Dad clamp the bike to an old vice and Dad was instructing Danny on cutting into the side of the washing machine with secateurs, as if he was opening a huge tin of tuna. Meg yelled, 'Now he's going to cut his finger off! God Almighty. I've had enough!'

I mucked out the goats and next time I came in the washing machine engine was lying on the ground and threads of copper wire were on the floor in the space where Dad's leg would have been, like a cyborg. Ray tried to express Meg's great distress at having her kitchen turned into a mad inventor's junk pile, but Dad winked to Ray and in his croaky voice said, 'Trust me.'

I put down fresh straw for the goats and ran back in. Danny had bolted the back wheel of the bike to the underside of the washing machine and Dad was making gestures to show what went where. 'Crap,' he said, 'chain – too short!' Dad stared into space and I ran back out.

Meg and Ray were having a whispered debate about who would clean up the goddamn mess, and how Dad's burst of enthusiasm was all well and good but he was really overdoing it. Meg yelled, 'Don't come crying to me if you have a relapse, Ed, and have to spend the next month on your back!' But Dad kept on with his soldering irons, bolts and nuts. He, Danny and Ben had turned the entire kitchen into one vast techie-nerd workshop.

The goats gave me a mere dribble of milk and Meg said they could sense when folk argued and it made them too nervy to produce. As I was struggling with the teats, I worked out what I'd say to Dad – it was my fault, after all, that he'd set off on this invention thing, but Meg was right, he was trying to run before he could walk. Like, literally. So would he mind just stopping and admit he was an invalid, so we could all just get back to our daily misery, please?

I went back in and Ben was on the bike and pedalling and laughing like a DC person and Danny said, 'Careful, slow down, it might spin off!' I stepped in and witnessed the tub spinning round in the washing machine and how the entire impossible thing seemed held together with duct tape.

'Gears,' Dad said, and he clicked the lever on the handle and Ben's pedalling went stiffer and the washing machine actually spun faster.

Then Meg came in and her hand went to her mouth. 'Spin ... cycle!' Dad announced, and then even she was laughing.

'Fancy a shot?' Danny asked me, and his hand touched my back and I shivered. I climbed on just so I could feel his hands again. I pedalled and didn't even care about the invention; I was just staring into Danny's eyes as my legs moved faster and faster.

'Show ... Mum,' Dad croaked, and I could see then that his scarred face was really pale and he was short of breath. 'Get her ... please.'

Just then the chain came off the bike and it tipped and everything fell apart and I fell off into Danny's arms.

'Damn!' Dad growled. Then he said, 'Prototype.'

As he set me down, Danny whispered, 'I want you so bad.'

'Shh,' I whispered, 'me too.' Then I ran off to look for Mum. I wanted to see her laugh at Dad's moronic machine. OK, he was no great inventor, but something told me we were going to pull through.

I couldn't find her. She was out on perimeter patrol, Ray said. It was her first time. I was so happy to be back with Danny again that I, selfishly, didn't find anything disturbing at all in Mum walking around alone in the dark with an assault rifle, in a state of, what would turn out to be, clinical depression.

The Problem With Rationing

There are two main problems with rationing:

1. It can make people miserable and angry with each other.
2. It makes you long for a pig-out.

I don't just mean food, but snogging too.

Meg had asked me and Danny to go down to the storage bunker to get a huge bag of rice for midnight dinner, and no sooner had we climbed down the ladder and Danny had heaved the bag to the edge of the shelf, than we sensed we were alone and we pounced on each other. The rice bag fell and split and rice scattered everywhere but I gave zero fucks because he was kissing me and unfastening my fatigues, and I was biting his neck and whispering, 'Oh God, I have to touch your skin.' Then we're both stripping off and majorly tongue circling, with hands in each other's underpants and gasping.

'Right, you two!' a voice growled and we recoiled in horror.

It was Meg's face at the top of the bunker air hatch.

Danny and me fumbled to put our clothes back on as Meg climbed down the ladder.

'I was willing to turn a blind eye,' she said, 'but this has got way out of control.'

I'd only managed to get one arm into my top and my bra was showing. We stared at the floor, and the thousand bits or rice.

'I knew you were trouble when I first saw you, young lady,' she said to me. 'Sneaking around behind my back.'

I was so ashamed, I lost the ability to speak.

'And as for you,' she said to Danny, 'you've been slacking in your patrol duties and now I know why. If we're not all focused on survival then everything goes to shit. I mean, look at this rice!'

'We could sweep it up,' Danny said.

'No, you can't. There's mouse shit and rat poison on the floor. We can't eat that, can we! That's one month's rice contaminated. Throw it all out!'

'Can't we wash it or something?' I bleated. 'I'm so, so sorry.'

'Can't eat sorries, can we?' Meg snapped. 'Right' – she gave me the once-over – 'I'm going to discuss this with your mother and father.'

'No, no, please don't!' I exploded. 'Please, he's not well yet and ...' In truth I was worried more about what Mum would say. 'Please, please, please don't tell her!' I begged.

Meg sighed and strode angrily past us, muttering. She went into some plastic boxes at the end of the shelves and Danny and I stared at each other, shame-faced.

'Right,' Meg said, 'I can't stop nature and God knows I was the same when I was your age, but for God's sake, use condoms.' And she threw a packet of Durex onto the ground.

'Jesus, Mum!' Danny said. 'We're not even ...' And I blushed so hard my head felt hot.

'The last thing we need round here is another bloody mouth to feed!' Meg said and climbed the steps. 'Right, back to work, I won't tell anyone if you take precautions.'

Danny and I stared at the pack of condoms in the rice on the ground.

'And clean up that bloody mess,' she shouted back. 'Don't want the rats to start thinking they rule the place.'

For some reason, even though we were alone again, we didn't want to kiss. We were on our hands and knees picking up grains that we couldn't eat. We'd just cut short our survival rations by a whole two weeks.

Just then I heard gunshots. Two, then a third.

There was a scramble of feet upstairs.

Five minutes later we got the whole story. Mum had been out by the fence and thought she'd seen someone move out there. She hadn't been properly trained and was sure that she'd missed, but she was in a state of shock, still clutching the rifle.

Ray sat her down and gave her some water and asked her, 'You sure it was people? Maybe it was a deer?'

Mum shook her head. She looked up at me and Danny; our fingers were touching and I pulled away. 'It looked like two people,' she shivered. 'Maybe more.'

'Maybe it was Kane?' Danny suggested.

'Shut up,' Ray snapped. 'No. Well, whoever or whatever it was, they know we're here now, don't they? And they'll be back.'

How To Foretell Imminent Threat

What You Must Do When The Infected Arrive

"In phase four of the collapse, the last desperate flight from the cities begins. As document G73 reveals, government population containment centres are actually 'controlled depopulation centres', i.e. mass concentration camps for 'contained die-off'. Under martial law, decontamination from Virus X is first attempted by spraying the thousands of survivors in the stadiums with chemicals. Then, after that fails to contain the contagion, the government will herd the contaminated and the uncontaminated together and spray them with bullets.

Those who escape the cities and fight their way beyond the military checkpoints will be among the 10% of survivors. They pose the greatest threat to remote communities. Not only do they bring infection with them, they also bring military patrols seeking to round up the last of the population. Groups of such escapees will begin to appear in even the most remote areas and to challenge the staying power of even the most prepared survivalists.

It is of the utmost importance that no help is given to these refugees, that survivalists remain hidden. These refugee gangs will be the most brutal members of the population – they will have seized military and police equipment, and they will have killed already. If they become aware of your safe house, you must treat them as the military does. You must shoot to kill."

I woke from another nightmare and Dad's survival manual fell to the ground. In the dream, a woman with a blood-stained surgical mask clings to the perimeter fence and begs me to let her in. 'Please, please, some water, some milk,' she wheezes, 'my baby is dying.'

I have the keys to the fence and her face is stained with sores and tears, and I tell her I can leave a little bit of milk for her baby at the gate, but then she'll have to go away and not tell anyone else. She nods and agrees to stay back and I open the gate but then I'm surrounded by three ragged men, then six, all with knives, all coughing blood. I am pinned to the ground, the keys are taken from me, their hidden truck roars through the perimeter gates and up the dirt track to the farmhouse and three of the men put a knife to my neck and strip the clothes from me.

I wake from many dreams like this and I only feel safe again after I've reached for my crossbow.

It was, like, six weeks after Dad's operation and it was pretty clear he was going to survive, albeit with half a leg and half his sense of humour. He even managed to say a sort of three-word joke about throwing out half of all his boots, and so I guess I stopped panicking about him and thought I'd better make myself useful. The place I felt safest was out on patrol with Danny and learning to shoot. But Mum insisted she do most of the patrolling.

When she was in the farmhouse, she was on high alert. Her eyes would snap at any sound outside and she'd jump up and head back out again with the M15 rifle. I'd noticed her hands were shaky and she'd been taking pills, but she said they were just indigestion tablets. There had been some sleeping pills, too, cos we had to sleep through a lot of the daytime for the afore-mentioned blackout reasons.

Ray quizzed Dad again and again about his incident, 'Who did this to you?' 'Who's out there?' 'Gangs or the military?' 'Were they carrying guns?' 'Explosives?' 'Did they try to steal your petrol?' 'What happened to Kane?' But Dad shook his head each time and said, 'Gone … sorry,' and closed his eyes.

Ray said Dad had concussion and he did lose his balance a lot and we were forever picking him up. Meg said his old self might never return, and it was maybe a 'small mercy', as it might be too horrific for him to handle the flashbacks anyway.

'Are you just saying that to protect us from horrible things that are out there?' I asked her, when Ben was out of earshot.

Mum was spending less time with Ben too, leaving that to me and Danny, and so she was out of my sight a lot. I guess we were all so focused on helping Dad heal all his scars and on the blackout that I failed to see the danger signs with Mum.

Like how she'd turn away from me, as if my energy was draining her, and head back out to her many tasks. Weapons cleaning, surface sterilising, goat milking, armed patrol. I actually thought that her being so bossy on herself was a good thing, but maybe I was just selfishly focused on Danny.

How To Spot The Danger Signs

Clinical depression can destroy a person and so destroy a group. Signs to look out for in a group member include:

1. Irregular sleeping: sleeping more than usual, or less.
2. Appetite loss.
3. Inability to focus and being emotionally distant.
4. Hyper-tension and possible paranoia.
5. In an effort to fight a sense of pointlessness, they cling to routines and schedules, burying themselves in hard work.
6. But they are listless, as if everything is a great burden.
7. They are short-tempered and say things like, 'What's the point?'
8. They spend more and more time alone and are unable to join in group conversations or activities.
9. They abuse medication or alcohol.

Another week went by and my one-legged dad invented an amazing new wind-powered water-pump that involved every hose we had but would save us tons of work lugging buckets. I ran around calling, 'Mum, Mum, come and see!' She'd taken to patrolling all through the night then sleeping all day and all evening, but she wasn't on her camp bed and I couldn't find her.

There was only one place left she could be.

The bathroom door was locked. I knocked and there was no reply. I knocked again and again, then I fetched Meg and she banged and shouted, 'Justine, you in there? What's wrong? Come on out now, love.' I listened, my face to the wood, and could just make out the sound of Dad's voice, like he was in there talking to Mum – but Dad was downstairs, so it had to be Mum listening to one of Dad's recordings. 'Open up, Mum!' I shouted. 'You're freaking us out here!'

Ear to the door, I heard my recorded Dad say, '...*armed gangs loot and burn their way across the countryside...*'

I tried the door handle again. It made no sense, as the lock had broken ages ago, so that meant there was a weight against the door.

'Do you think she would...? Is she the kind of person...' Meg asked, and I shook my head but banged on the wood in total fear. 'Mum, open up, stop being a moron, Ben's busting for a wee, so let us in!'

Still no reply, and Meg put her shoulder to the door.

It was Mum's body that had been blocking our way. She lay half naked on the floor and there were white pills scattered amongst clothes and the contents of her purse, like money and credit cards. I screamed and Meg bent over Mum, speaking then shouting, shaking her, slapping her in the face. Mum didn't respond and I couldn't move from the doorway. Meg tried to look at Mum's pupils, and then she picked up a pill container and groaned when she read the label. I stood frozen, staring at Dad's laptop on the window ledge above Mum's head, hearing Dad's voice say, '*After that day there will be no way to stop the spread of the virus. Parents, thinking they are saving their children by taking them to hospitals, will instead be contaminating them...*'

Meg shouted, 'Quick! Help me lift her!' She put her hands under Mum's armpits. 'For Christ's sake, gimme a hand, Haley!' she shouted. 'Get her head over the toilet! It's alright, I know what I'm doing.'

I wanted to help, I really did, but I was frozen by Dad's laptop voice. '*…mass starvation is under way. Dogs roam in packs and devour the dead. The number of suicides increases dramatically. Families chose to end their lives intentionally while they are still together, rather than face…*'

Meg yelled, 'Turn that fucking thing off! And stop standing there like a friggin' zombie and help me get these pills out of her!'

How To Save Someone From An Overdose

First, you will need to induce vomiting. A recipe to do this is as follows:

1. Four heaped tablespoons of table salt dissolved in a ½ cup of warm water.
2. Mustard powder may also be dissolved in water. It too is an emetic.
3. Fingers down the throat or stimulating the gag reflex with a toothbrush will also work, but may also scratch the back of throat and there is no certainty that the entire stomach has been cleared.
4. Afterwards, consume a litre of water.
5. Feed the patient caffeine for three hours and make sure they don't fall asleep.

I ran and got all the things that Meg shouted we'd need. When I came back into the toilet, Mum looked so vulnerable and limp and it shocked me because I'd always thought she was super-strong. But seeing her skinny chest heaving and gagging as Meg forced the salt water down her throat, and Mum vomiting all over the toilet bowl then gasping for air, I just couldn't bear it.

'There's a good girl, c'mon, get this down you,' Meg said to Mum as she supported her woozy body in her big arms. She mixed mustard powder to the salt water and made her drink it.

Dad's recorded voice echoed, '*… all food stocks are exhausted, all* *living animals slaughtered, crops are not planted for the following year, guaranteeing starvation. So begins the final...*' And this was all my fault, too, because if I'd never told Mum about Dad's recordings, she would never have gone looking for them.

'Quick! She's going to hurl again,' Meg said. 'Hold her hair out of the bowl, would ya, love?' Mum buckled over and puked violently.

'Good girl, good girl, nearly done,' Meg said, patting Mum's back. 'Haley! Go and fill up that jug, got to get more water down her. Oh, and make sure the coffee's on. And I won't tell you again – turn that fucking recording off!'

I did as she said and ran, guilt pursuing me. Why did I want to run from my own mum? I returned with the water, but was dreading going back inside. I felt sorry for Mum but something also repelled me. It wasn't the stink of vomiting that made me stay back. It was her weakness, frailty.

'Get it down you!' Meg barked at Mum. 'Now, next time you plan on doing yourself in, pick the right pills, love. You might as well puke these up. They won't kill you right away, but they'll bugger up your liver. Right, a little sip more of the lovely stuff!'

Meg forced Mum to drink and she retched so violently that her whole body rose off the ground.

When it was done, Mum was like a newborn baby, all wet and shivering in Meg's arms, and this made me feel even more abandoned. Mum was whimpering and it scared me, because that meant there was truly no one left to take care of me and Ben. She wasn't my bossy mum anymore, she was just a shuddering helpless body of a stranger who'd tried to abandon her children forever.

Mum's eyes tried to find me through her wet, pukey hair, like they were begging. I should have knelt down and hugged her, but I don't know, maybe it was the puke all over her, maybe not, but she made me want to run.

'So selfish,' I said, and I ran.

How To Deal With Weakness And Failure In A Parent

There is something seriously wrong with humans. For one, we secretly find failure and weakness in others repulsive and so we avoid them. Secondly, when we feel shit about avoiding them, we avoid them even more.

Trust me. I felt bad. I mean, I'd told Mum ages ago that I wished she was dead, but I didn't actually mean for her to actually try to do it, for Christ's sake! And here's me thinking we'd been making progress.

It wasn't like it was a real attempt – that was what I told myself. It was just a 'cry for help', which was actually kind of more appalling.

And Meg had said, 'Don't be daft. Your Mum's been popping those bloody Valiums like sweeties for weeks. She'd probably just taken one too many today and dozed off and dropped those pills all over the place.' Then her voice was stern: 'But don't tell anyone about it. Your mum made a silly mistake, that's all.'

Nonetheless, the thought of even being close to Mum gave me the shudders.

Meg said she couldn't be two places at once and that I couldn't go on like this – it wasn't fair me avoiding Mum like that. I had to go up to the bedroom and bring my mum her third coffee, and show her some pity. 'Come on, she's feeling guilty and she gave herself a hell of a shock. Go on, be nice to her, help her a bit.' Meg blamed herself, because she'd seen the signs but hadn't acted on it. 'Your poor mum.'

Meg gave me instructions not to let Mum fall asleep, to check if she was delirious or shaking, or had blue lips, to take her temperature and make sure she drank more coffee and water, more than she even wanted. Meg told me to fib to everyone else, that Mum just had a bit of a cold. But that freaked Ben out because he thought it meant Mum had the virus.

Mum lay in my bunk, ghost-white, and Ben was with her with his little surgeon's mask on, playing Doctors. There are times when his total obliviousness to everything is really useful.

'Can I go to No Man's Land and help Danny lay the pipes for Dad's water-system, Mum, can I?

'Go on then, scoot. Mum needs some rest,' I said.

Ben ran out and Mum and me were left alone. I was sort of beginning to understand that thing that men fear about women. My mum's silence and mine, in that room, as minute after minute went by, became like this whole other person, invisible and watching us, like a guilty ghost.

Mum closed her eyes and raised a hand to her chest and it sat there, perched like a bird on the grey sheets. I took her temperature and stared at her knuckles and they seemed old and wrinkled like chicken skin. Her eyes were shrunken cos they hadn't seen make-up in months. I wasn't going to be the one that spoke first. If we never spoke again that would have been horrible but less awful than me whimpering, 'But why, why, why? How the hell could you even think of doing it?'

Whether it was an accidental overdose or not, it came to the same. Mum had wanted out. Whether 'out-of-her-box' on drugs, or 'out of existence', it was the same difference. I felt betrayed.

Something in Mum's eyes said 'stay' and 'please'. Her hand hovered by my wrist, as if to restrain me if I ran. I stared at the window, sort of picturing her in that bathroom that night when Dad took those pills, back when I was a kid. I was struggling to try to understand and forgive – like, maybe she just took all those pills so she could understand him from the inside of her own body. Or maybe she knew more about what was happening in the outside world and it was too horrible to face.

It's the worst feeling in the world to know both your parents are weak and so scared of life. Like, what the hell is the hope for you?

She took my hand. 'I know you'll never forgive me, but try, please ... I'm sorry, I didn't believe him.'

And then she was deliriously going on about Dad.

'He told me,' Mum said, clinging to me, 'but I wouldn't listen ... I thought, if we could just be practical, get on with our lives, then all of this madness would go away.' Her hand was literally hold-ing me back from leaving. 'If I could give your father some new responsibility and keep him busy, I thought it would take his mind off all this, make him well. And he did seem better when I was pregnant again…'

'What, wait, you're saying you had Ben to keep Dad busy?'

A kid's life isn't like a puppy for Xmas, and now she was trying to say sorry, even for that, sorry for bringing my brother into the world. It broke my actual heart, but it explained so much, like Ben's eating disorder. Her fingernails were digging into me and I thought if there were any more horrible revelations, I would pass out.

'Seeing you with Danny,' Mum said, 'I realised we're never going to see anyone we ever knew again. Danny is the only young man you'll ever know from now on. I'm sorry, I wanted you to have a good life, better than mine.'

She was weeping, and she still smelled of puke. My poor mum, I just wanted her to stop, but she went on.

'I should have listened to your dad. He was right all along. Maybe it was me that drove him insane, like you said. Everything he said…' Her body jolted with tears. 'I didn't know. I didn't know. I was so wrong. I'm so sorry, Haley. I should have trusted him. I'm sorry, I'm so, so sorry.'

No one ever teaches you how to deal with a parent telling you their entire life has been a pathetic failure, and it's probably against the laws of nature to see your protector in need of protection.

She said, 'You and me and Ben. The virus is going to get us, isn't it, Haley? Or worse, the gangs. Forgive me, please, I'm sorry.'

It was actually like we'd swapped roles. I sort of blurted out some of her old words, like, 'Don't be silly, we need to be practical.'

I went to the bathroom and carefully pulled off two sheets of toilet paper, then I thought to hell with Meg's rations and ripped off a ton more and brought it all back to Mum. 'Here,' I said, 'blow your nose and stop crying or you'll have me blubbing too.'

Mum looked up at me and smiled weakly. She cried in my arms

and really clung and she said, 'Forgive me, forgive me,' and I said, 'OK, I do, now shh and stop making such a noise or Ben'll find out.' And I did forgive her.

She was just this poor woman who'd tried her very best but had been beaten by the world. I felt this surge as she clung to me and I told myself, I have to protect my mum now, it's my turn. I stroked her hair and kissed her brow and told her, 'There, shh now, we're going to be alright.' It was her old cliché, but it was true. I had to make it true or we were all seriously screwed.

What To Do When You Spot An Enemy

There's this whole procedure for checking the perimeter fence for any sightings of enemies. Danny taught me it and it goes like this:

1. Run to your hiding spot. Hide.
2. Check the safety catch on your crossbow, so that you don't shoot yourself by accident.
3. Get binocs ready.
4. Rise slowly to check for holes in the fence, or people beyond it.
5. Report 'all clear' and name the sector on your walkie-talkie.
6. Run again to next area and repeat procedure.

I was out on patrol in No Man's Land and it was raining and the sun was going down. I freaked. There was this distant dark figure coming towards me past the burned-out tractor. I got into the hiding position and raised my crossbow, then my binoculars.

This human was coming round the inside edge of the fence, not the outside, and it was definitely a man, and I couldn't see any holes in the fence.

He was short and squat like Ray, but how could it be Ray? Ray had taken to doing nearly all the night patrols, like he was living on a different schedule from the rest of us. I thought it was on account of how guilty he felt about Dad, and his drinking, like how he'd lost the plot completely over the last month and felt too ashamed to meet anyone's eyes.

But yes, it was Ray staggering towards me and I thought, thank God. But then I thought, shit. Because if he was looking for me it could mean:

A. He's pissed out of his head and he's coming to give me a row about dry humping Danny and to tell me never to go near him again. Or…

B. It's about the rice, or the rabbit stew, or any number of the other things I wasted that month.

But Ray just kind of lurched over the tussocks and there he was: standing silently and getting his breath, so close I could smell his B.O. His hands were trembling but maybe it was from booze withdrawal.

He nodded at me. Looked around. I guess I was nervous and just playing with my arrows.

'Getting good with the crossbow, I hear,' he finally said.

I shrugged, 'I guess.' Expecting him to segue into shouting.

'You see any smoke out there?' he said as he stared out at the fence.

I shook my head.

'Truck noise?'

I shook my head, thinking, wow, is this him like actually trying to initiate a conversation? And, is this a trick?

'Sounds of sirens? Police?'

I shook my head.

'Got to watch out for that, they're not on our side anymore.'

'Right,' I said, 'Chapter Ten.' And Ray sort of smiled. So I quoted it back to him: '"*Armed gangs with leaders who have defected from the police forces steal vehicles and go from town to town, village to village, hunting for medicine, food, commodities, water, petrol and safety. Sexual abuse and murder become commonplace and the gangs* spread further contagion. More dangerous still are the military patrols that could catch us in their net as they attempt to round up and eliminate the gangs.'"

'Good,' he said. And we were silent then, just staring at the razor wire fence. Then he sighed and turned.

Was that it I thought? Is this all there is to male bonding with men of few words?

He went to walk away then stopped. 'Wanted to say sorry,' he said, with his face down.

And I was like, what the hell?

'Wasn't good to you at the start. You're a good soul,' he said. 'Stronger than me when it was needed. Sorry.'

Wow. What could I say? Life was turning into a Sorry-Haley fest. So, I just stared at the heather.

'Don't know what I'd do without your father,' he said.

And he wiped his eye, but maybe it was because the rain was pouring on his bald head. I was cringing so much my actual teeth were grinding. It was kind of painful with the silence and this wind whistling between us, and kind of ache-y too. I dunno why but I sort of wanted to hug him.

'Kane,' he said.

That was random.

'Keep your eyes open for Kane,' Ray said. 'She was very angry with your dad before she left. If she's survived the plague, she might have joined the other side. Revenge thing. Understand? She could be a gang leader now.'

Now, that was terrifying.

'You see her on the other side of the fence, stay down, hidden. Call me or shoot to kill.'

'Oh … OK,' I stammered and sort of shuddered as I stared at the hills beyond the fence, like searching for her, right that second.

'Right. You and your mum do the fence by day,' he said. 'Danny and me, will take turns by night. Got to be ready for the mob when they come. Understood?'

I think I said, 'Aye aye,' or, 'Affirmative,' or I may have even frickin saluted cos I was nervous and a bit try-hard.

'Alright. Continue,' he said, then he turned and was gone.

Jeez, I was just so amazed, I had to have a seat there on a bunch of wet grass, and let it all sink in. Not the whole wet ass thing, but all that had transpired.

Now I had yet another secret to keep: Ray was actually kind of a sweet guy.

The world really was upside down.

I watched him turn into a dot then vanish into the fog near the house, and I let out this big breath, like I'd been holding it in and not even realised it.

Maybe there was hope for humans, after all.

How To Bury The Past Together

If you don't have a functioning freezer, then when a dead person (or limb) is stored in a shed this can cause great distress and spread bacteria. Do the following:

1. Bury the remains at a depth of more than four feet. This is to stop animals, like wild foxes, from digging up the remains.
2. Perform a unique and personal ritual to mark the event and to reaffirm the commitment of the group of survivors.
3. Use the opportunity to reflect upon the millions of dead and dying beyond.

It was a week later and, in some weird way, Mum and Dad's healing got stronger in direct proportion to how much Dad's amputated half-leg was stinking the place up, like a metaphor or something. It was also driving the scary security dog wild with meaty desires, so that lump of limb had to go.

We picked a spot out there in No Man's Land near the abandoned tractor and we all stood around in a circle and watched Danny finish digging the hole. He climbed back out and I took his hand, like a real couple at a funeral. I wanted us to be seen like that and no one made any objections. Not even Mum, but she was deep in a kind of trance and not really talking much.

Usually, like in the past, Mum would have yelled, 'Stop touching that boy, Haley!' and a huge fight would have broken out, no doubt with Meg and Mum going cat and dog at each other. But none of this happened and so we were kind of burying our past too, and accepting that there was no return.

A solemn ritual had to be enacted. Like it says in Dad's manual in the 'Deaths' chapter, if we were all going to accept each other, we had to bury who we were before, and realise we could never go back. We had to bury our 'lists of last things'. Dad had asked us to make this list of things that we might miss from the old world, but would never see again. To lay those desires to rest.

I laid my busted old phone in the hole and threw in my list, which was embarrassingly just like a shopping list, to be honest, because I'm so superficial. Dad couldn't bend so I took the bag of old technology from his hand and set it in beside his list and his stinky dead leg. Mum put her pair of heels in the hole, and the make-up from her purse and some pill packets, since she'd never need them again. Then Danny laid in his box of wooden aeroplanes and his stack of 'girls with guns' centrefolds. Meg put in the landline telephone and an old vinyl album from the Eighties. She had a list of things she'd miss, like, ten pages long. Ray laid in some empty bottles and one half-full of some random booze that he'd confessed he'd stashed 'just in case'. He made a secret sign to me, to say, remember, don't tell anyone about our little chat.

Then we stood, sombre in No Man's Land, all seven of us, the wind in our hair, staring into the grave, twitchy with every rustle or creak from the direction of the perimeter fence half a mile away. Plus, yeah, Dad's leg-stink added urgency to the ritual. 'Quick, Ben, it's your turn now,' I said.

Ben clung to Danny's old phone and his list of favourite sweeties and chocolates and his long-dead computer game console and he shook his head. 'Will it grow into a phone tree?'

I went down on one knee and whispered, 'Hey, I'm onto you, you just say things like that to be cute and get hugs and treats, don't you?'

Ben shrugged. Nodded.

'Come on then, Ben, we've all done it,' I said quietly. 'We all had to say goodbye to lots of things, so we can move on.'

He shook his head and stomped his foot. I was waiting for Mum or Dad to say, 'Ben, if you do it now, I'll give you some ice cream,' but that would have been majorly missing the point, since ice cream was on his list of last things.

Ben stared into the grave and the random things sitting inside it. It looked like some weird time capsule of mismatched junk. The name of the band on Meg's album was Kajagoogoo and they had big bleached haircuts. We should have been burying some Shakespeare or Plato but this was all our civilisation had amounted to.

'Go on, Ben.'

Ben looked up at Mum and then at Dad. They stood apart and Dad reached with his one good hand for Mum's hand, but because of the crutch, he couldn't reach. Ben stared at them strangely then he took the phone and kissed it and laid it into the ground and said, 'Bye bye, Granny.'

I heard a sob behind me and it was Ray, choking up, and that got to me. Meg hugged him and then she started. A domino effect took over and then Danny cried too.

Mum reached for Dad's hand and they clutched each other. Then I saw her circling his thumb with her own. She wasn't crying, she didn't look him in the eye; she just stared into the hole in the ground, gripping him so tight.

Ben turned and did a double take at almost everyone weeping, and he sighed and took the shovel and tried to fill in the hole. 'Jeezo,' he muttered, 'you grown-ups are so weird.'

As we filled the hole, Ray wiped his face and picked up his gun and checked over his shoulder and said, 'OK, let's be quick. We're not safe out here. Anyone could see us.'

Ben ran off ahead and Danny and Meg offered to help Dad hobble back to the farm at his one-legged pace, but he refused. He insisted that he take his crutches in one hand and Mum's hand in the other. I stayed behind, stunned and staring, not at the hole but at Mum and Dad, hand in hand, gripping each other for dear life. Then the most impossible thing of all: Mum rested her head against Dad's arm, and they stopped, and they must have thought no one was watching cos Dad kissed Mum's forehead and she snuggled her chin into his neck.

I was utterly crying and the rain kept pouring but I didn't care.

How To Plan Beyond Mere Survival

You have to have a plan for your life after the pandemic, otherwise everything just becomes rations and routines and fearful repetitions.

I lay in Danny's bed but not quite in his arms. I didn't want to make out. There were no stars through his attic window but the moon cast a glow over us. I thought about how this could actually work. Like, 'the future'. It blew my mind. I would live and die between these perimeter fences. I could get pregnant, like a redneck teenager, and have an actual squealing, smiling baby, with a name and everything, and feed it from my boobs. No, it was too gross. And what kind of irresponsible dick would bring a child into this cruel world? My sixteenth birthday was coming up and Danny and I had agreed that we would 'do the deed', with precautions of course. The date was set – two months and five days' time. I was pretty stoked but felt kind of guilty that I had a global catastrophe to thank for it.

'What are you thinking, Haley Crowe?' Danny asked as he stroked my face.

'Apart from how upside-down everything is?'

'Yeah.'

'I'm thinking, I'm going to stay right here in this bed with you tonight. For the whole night,' I told him. 'If that's OK? I mean you'll have to keep your underpants on and be a perfect gentleman and maybe even your jeans. But we can dry hump for a bit.'

'Jesus, Haley,' he said, 'do you have to speak like that?' Then we laughed and he said, 'But what about your parents?'

'I think we're kind of the most grown-up of all now,' I whispered.

We pashed and after some of the aforementioned dry humping, which made Danny very sore, he fell asleep. But I couldn't. I heard voices from downstairs. It was like an old half-forgotten human hum from when I was little. The Mum and Dad sound. I listened harder. It was them. And they weren't arguing, but taking turns, like low voice, higher voice, low voice, which meant they were actually listening and not talking over each other.

They went sort of silent and I'm sure I heard Mum having an emotional moment. Then a sound I'd never heard before, like a kind of distant barking, a hollow noise. It must have been Dad crying too.

Then there was a sound on the stairs. Dad couldn't get up with the crutches and Ray usually helped him get to his bed but Ray was out on patrol. It was a weird noise, like a heavy thump followed by whispers then a dragging sound, then another thump and a creak. Dad whispered, 'Wait, let me put my arm over.'

I lay there in the dark, focusing on their noises, trying to work out what pictures went with it.

'So heavy.'

'Sorry.'

'OK, now ... let me ... can you take my weight?'

'What if you fall backwards?'

'Here, let's try that. That OK?'

It was my still weak mum and crippled dad trying to drag each other up the stairs. There were groans and pain sounds and it went on for a whole ten minutes and at the end of it they were panting at the top.

I unpeeled myself from Danny's arm and had to have a sneaky peek from the attic hatch. And I saw the weirdest, most corny thing ever. It practically made me cry and barf at the same time. Mum and Dad supporting each other, all their slow way down the corridor. And Mum saying to Dad, 'Oh, Ed.'

I hid from view and waited to hear the sound of our bedroom door opening and to hear Mum's voice calling up for me when she realised I wasn't there, but their hobbled footsteps continued past. She was walking Dad to his bedroom and I heard every step on the creaking floorboards. I waited and there was the squeak of his door opening, then a bit of nothing, then the door closed but there were no footsteps walking away. So, Mum had gone into Dad's bedroom and totally stayed.

They were totally going to sleep in the same actual bed for the first time in, like, over five years. Mental! I had to stay awake to make sure Mum didn't go back to her room. An hour later and she was still with him. No doubt they were going through some *Swiss Family Robinson* negotiations, planning how they could make this work together. Then I heard them. At first I thought it was bonking but it was definitely just snoring. Mum and Dad, utterly sleeping in the same bed. I couldn't frickin believe it.

It was majorly impossible to sleep and every minute that passed this goofy grin stretched wider across my face.

I was finally falling asleep when I heard it. In the dark there were sounds coming over the mountains, like some vast choir of moaning and screaming from a hundred miles away and cold fear shot through my spine. By my dad's calculations the infected refugees would reach the highlands any day now. The noise sounded inhuman, like maybe it was what people became when they turned into animals. I could sense their force gathering beyond the wires.

I woke Danny and he said it was most likely just the wind through the fence. It did that sometimes.

How To Confront Your Enemy

How Not To React When Faced With A Wheezer (2)

Nothing can prepare you for your first sighting on patrol. You will panic. Your routine of having nothing to report over a whole month might actually increase your panic.

I dashed from a bush to the trench and scanned the perimeter fence through the binocs. 'Nothing to report.' The walkie-talkie hissed against my leg and I ran to the half-dug trench with the burned-out car next to it, got myself safe and concealed.

I was kind of enjoying being out of the safe house, too, cos one of the weirdnesses of having Mum and Dad get back together again was they really just couldn't stop doing embarrassing shit, like staring into each other's eyes, and laughing together, and saying, 'Remember the time we...' And actually necking – this has been confirmed by other witnesses. What in the actual fuck?

I'd come almost full circle and was near the end of patrol-time. The wind was remorseless and the caw-cawing crows were circling over some distant dead-thing and Dad had said that winter was a small mercy, as it would kill many of the infected and spare them further suffering. I had frozen ears and a clear, clean brain; there was something crisp about everything. I drank some water from my hipflask and got into position with the binocs.

I didn't see properly at first. The binocs were pre-focused on the fence and the movement happened on the other side. It was a human with some weird weapon in its hand, and it wasn't wearing any protective clothing at all – zilch. It didn't look like Kane but that was of little relief. It was a bloke with a bald head and he was standing by one of the telegraph poles and I started to panic-breathe. I threw myself down into the dirt and grabbed the walkie-talkie. 'One niner, one niner, come in.'

There was no reply, which was weird since Dad was always on the other end and it wasn't like he could walk away, so I tried again. Meg's voice came on, no wait, actually, it was Dad's: 'Seven eight, I copy. What's up, Haley?'

I told him there was a man on the other side near the gate and he didn't reply. I asked him, did he copy, and still no reply, just static.

'Copy that,' he finally said. 'Is it police? Is it one person, or many?'

I didn't know, because I'd been too shit scared to look again so I focused and could see the invader was wearing some kind of uniform: blue-grey with straps and an orange safety helmet. And the gun in his hand might have been some kind of nail-gun thing.

Dad said something like: 'Haley, listen. It might be an ambush. There could be a dozen others hiding. Remain concealed!'

But I told you about all this already, and about how I aimed the Ghost 350 arrow right at the guy's heart and fired it. So, I fully expected to see the guy spurting blood on the ground and for me to feel pretty guilty, but, when I finally opened my eyes, I saw there on the other side of the fence that the guy was bending over. Not doubled up in agony, just picking up this clipboard thingy. And my stupid arrow was nowhere to be seen.

Then the guy leaned on the fence and looked through it. A burst of static from my walkie-talkie. I hit the dirt and waited, counting breaths, then I rose again. The man tore a piece of paper from his clipboard, put it in a plastic sleeve and took the nail-gun thing and nailed the page to the nearest telegraph pole. He stepped away and was obscured by this clump of trees. I ran to the rusted stack of oil barrels, skidded down and looked again.

Dad's voice over the walkie-talkie: 'Haley, for God's sake! Don't risk being seen. You copy? Head back … immediately.'

Dad was making way too much noise so I turned him off.

None of it made sense. Like, shouldn't Dad be sending out Ray and Danny as back-up? That was our protocol. And why hadn't he asked me for my exact position, or whether I was within contamination distance of the wheezer?

The crossbow lay beside me, its chamber empty. To reload it, I'd have to stand and prime the wire with the foot-strap and the guy would see me, so it was out of the question. Ergo, I was without a weapon. I put the binocs on times four magnification and used the stump to steady my shaking hands. The guy's mask-less face looked fat and forty-something. He just walked away and stopped and pulled a car door open. I crept on my elbows and refocused and saw it was a Range Rover, grey-green colour. The man started the engine and drove away, just like that, so spookily nonchalant it could only be a trap. The vehicle had some sign on the back but I couldn't make it out.

I waited, watching it skid along the dirt track. I scanned 180 degrees for any other movement. No, the guy had maybe just been on a reconnaissance for a mob. I watched till I couldn't hear the engine.

Some random bird circled overhead and wind blew in the heather and all that 'time passes' crap happened before some instinct kicked in. I had to see what the hell he'd nailed to that pole. It might have been advance warning that our supplies were to be requisitioned by the army, or a warning about contamination or the war or something.

I took a risk and stood and reloaded the crossbow. I was a sitting duck and I seriously have no idea how I even did it because I was shaking so much. Fully armed, hyper-alert, I put on my sterile mask and my blue gloves, then I ran to the gate. I probably should've returned, like Dad had said, and the longer I was exposed the more danger I was in. I got the keys in sharpish and undid the perimeter gate and sprinted into the outer world, towards the pole with the sign. I was utterly out in full view and maybe even breathing in the guy's contaminated breath.

I snatched the paper in the plastic sleeve, and yelled, 'Keep the hell away from me, I know you're there!' just in case anyone else was hiding.

I backed off, tucked the paper under my arm, crossbow to eye, swinging side to side, retreating to the gate. I yelled, 'Don't make me shoot you!' I locked the gate as fast as hell, trying not to drop the damn keys or the paper, but I wasn't safe yet. I ran back to the trench and hid myself and counted and looked out and counted again. The coast seemed legit clear but my heart was pounding like Dad's when he nearly died, so I set down the crossbow really carefully before pulling the page out.

This is what it said:

Due to line vandalism, which has affected the distribution of electrical current in this area, this site has been disconnected until further notice. This property is currently not registered as an electricity consumer. To register, set up an account and book a reconnection, please call the help desk. Our hours are 8.30 a.m.–5.30 p.m. Monday to Friday, and 8.30 a.m.–2 p.m. Saturday.

There was a graphic at the top that said, *Northern Power*. Below, it said, *Energy For You*.

How Power Actually Works

There is power in wires, power in fear, power in your muscles, power in the lies you live by, and maybe even in the truth. I ran from the million voices sucking the air from me. I ran into what should have been danger, away from the farm, following the line of poles and pylons with their power and phone cables, through the heather, far from the track. I fell and stumbled on, unable to see for the stupid tears, telling myself it wasn't true, it was all a cunning government trick to make us turn against each other. I didn't run back to Dad because I had to know for sure, something real and not just the words, words, words that people twisted.

The power cables started to droop lower with each pole and that must have been what the vandalism meant. Then they were almost at head height. I clambered over the brow of a hill and stopped. There was a sound of something flapping in the air and then a colourful flash. I saw this long ribbon of yellow tape stretched over a large square: *Danger Keep Out.*

Within the cordoned square there were these two telegraph poles lying on the ground, cut clean through by a chainsaw. The black power cable lay in the mud, as thick as a snake, another chainsaw slash right through it, the copper and coloured cables decapitated inside. The heather all around was scorched black and the mud had this texture like oil and leather. Where the fallen pole had landed there was a spattered yellow sign with a stick-man being hit by a zigzag shape. I didn't know if it was safe to step in, if all that crap was still electrified. About a metre from the spot where the power cable lay, in the middle of the burned mess, I saw some green, melted rubber thing and it looked sort of familiar so I stepped in, not giving a damn anymore. The ground cracked under me like ice, and black mud oozed from the cracks. I kicked the molten thing and it rolled over to reveal the tread of a rubber boot, a man's size. It was the right foot.

Dad's boot.

I stared at it. Picked it up.

Bastard!

I ran back till I reached the perimeter gate, and it swung on its stupid hinge behind me as I shed my pointless crossbow and kept on running. Fragments flew together in my head as I raged back over No Man's Land and I was so frickin furious. I sprinted and fell and sprinted again, counting my breaths to control the anger. One, two, three. I ran on. One thing stuck in my mind. It was what Meg told me in the week after Dad's leg. How she'd believed in other apocalypses before. How Dad gave her faith and purpose.

I ran and my lungs burned and I felt so pathetic for not having put two and two together before.

My dad had met Meg and Ray in NA. They believed that he'd saved them, but it was them who'd given him his one big idea. Meg and Ray were like kids to him, stupid, gullible, believe-anything kids, the trial run for Ben and me. If he could brainwash them and save them, then he could do the same with us.

I slowed my pace as the farm appeared over the tussocks. I pictured it as Dad must have when he first came up with his idea. A lost place, barren and beautiful, forgotten even by the clouds. Not a place to escape to, but to hide from reality. I ran on, step by step by step. Past the dead car and the abandoned fridge and the screaming soldier target. I stumbled and fell. I got up and started again.

'Fucking Dad!' I wanted to kill him.

Meg and Ray couldn't believe in God but they could worship my dad and so he created this bastard child of an idea from both their needs. This mixture of Meg's apocalypses mixed with Ray's Twelve Steps. A new beginning after a cataclysm with numbered days and stages, starting from Day One.

I don't even want to tell you about the next bit.

I ran through the gates and past Ray and Danny, who were both working on the wind turbine. I pushed past Mum and Ben and they were carrying buckets of rainwater and calling after me. I guess I looked a state with wet eyes from the wind and maybe from rage and crying. Everything was fake. Every single thing the others were doing was just acting out the fantasy of a madman. I ran inside and down the corridor, to the cubbyhole at the end, where I knew my lying asshole dad would be hiding.

I found him with his bandaged leg-stump propped up on the desk among the scattered wires and circuit boards, and all of it was fake, fake, fake. He'd never planned to fix any communications at all. The internet was probably working, and TVs and electricity.

I stood trembling before him and warned myself that I wouldn't let him molly-coddle me or apologise – he would only nod at my accusations and if I began to yell this would give him time to concoct another lie. I had to make him speak, now, to hear it from his own mouth.

I handed him the piece of paper. His eyes scanned it, then rolled back into his head. I threw his melted rubber boot onto his desk.

'Fucking liar!'

'Haley,' he said, taking his time. 'I know what you're thinking but ... there's a reason for...'

I watched his scarred lips come to a stop, his eyes looked into me and I said something like, 'You could have died. What kind of asshole cuts through a power cable! What did you do, chainsaw them down then try to burn through them? And what happened to Kane, did you electrocute her, too?'

Dad started on his 'if you'll let me explain' strategy, his eyes spinning more webs of deceit. 'Yes, you're nearly right,' he whispered. 'Kane and I argued before I headed out past the fence. She'd been suspicious. Most likely, once she got to the towns searching for me, she'd have worked out I'd been lying, cursed us and never came back. As for the fire, I had a five-litre can of petrol, and when the cables came down, they sparked and the whole thing exploded under my feet.'

I was paralysed. There were no contaminated mobs, slashing and burning their way across the countryside. There was no military state of emergency.

A noise came from down the corridor. The door was open behind me. Dad took his crutch and bashed his cubbyhole door shut.

'How much longer did you think you'd keep fooling us?' I blurted out.

He tried to touch my hand but I pulled away.

'Don't bullshit me, Dad, just tell me, is everything really OK out there? Like, back to frickin normal? Is Granny OK? Are my friends going to school? Is there food in supermarkets? Is there no fucking virus at all? I swear, if you don't tell me, I'll go right out there and yell it all to Mum and Ben and everybody!'

'I really don't know all the details,' he said quietly. 'From what I can gather, the Asian flu epidemic that we fled from was contained after a month and didn't spread...'

'What about the video clips? The riots?' I yelled. 'Were they fake? Did you fake that up?'

'No, that was real,' he said. 'But old footage from five years back.'

'What the fuck? And everyone dying – did anyone fucking die? Tell me!'

'I'm sorry, Haley, I'll admit, I got my dates wrong. It was a foreign health scare, a few thousands deaths, not the pandemic I predicted. But I was convinced, still am, that we're safer here because it's only a matter of time until a real super-virus will...'

'Shut up, shut up!'

He was incredible, everything he said about Mum was true about himself: when he didn't like the truth, he just turned his back on it and forced everyone else to live his lie.

'Haley, listen, my timing was out,' my conniving, cheating, bastard father said, 'but there's no way this is going to last. You know it yourself, the number of recombinant pathogens out there, the multiplication of possible sources of lethal leakage ... It's coming, maybe next month, maybe later this year, maybe next, but it's an inevitability. The date is a mere technicality. It's better to be one year too early than one hour too late, right? We're safer here. Trust me.'

'"Trust me"? Fucking "trust me"?' That made me freak. How could anyone ever trust him again? How could me or Ben ever trust another living soul after this? That's why I hit him with my fists. I hit his chest, his chin. What kind of evil person would nearly kill himself to trick his family like this? What clinically insane monster would make Mum fall in love with him again? Mum was right all along. He had to be sectioned, forever. These were some of the things I yelled at him.

He tried to restrain my hands, begging me, 'Shhh,' but that just made it worse and I yelled at him to let me go. He said he was sorry. 'How else could I have got you to stay here? It was the only way to convince you – that's all.'

His grip was hard and his eyes were soft and breaking my heart. I yelled and yanked my hands back. 'I believed you! I love you! I trusted you and you tricked me! You total dick!'

What with me bashing him and yelling some why-why-whys and him trying to hug me, Dad fell from his seat, with a horrible one-legged thump, and I saw his stump was still bleeding and he was in massive pain. Everything changed. He looked so pathetic, his arms reaching up through his teeth-clenched pain.

'Help me up, Haley, please.'

And all that scar tissue across half his face and his big blue eyes made me think of him dead. I got full of pity and I helped him up and I gave him one last chance to explain. The shouting had burned out and I was crying a fair bit too. 'I just don't understand … Why Dad, why?'

He took his time. 'Look at families these days, Haley,' he said. 'Think of us six years back, me, you, your mum, sitting in the same room. Doing what? We never talked or sang. We were all on our phones and laptops, headphones in. Together in the same room, but we were all alone.'

It wasn't getting him off the hook. 'Try again, Dad,' I said. 'Last chance.'

'The other day I watched you, your mum and your brother pick strawberries together. Out there in the polytunnel. I planted them for you, three years back. You were all working together, picking and eating them, and your mum sang and you joined in. It was beautiful. You didn't even see me watching you. We've been happy here the last little while. All working together.'

I couldn't believe it, the fucked up logic of his. He kept going.

'We can live here and it doesn't matter what's going on out there,' he said, and it was so deluded and sentimental. Mum had been a hard-working, successful, corporate, single woman and he just wanted to turn her into some medieval strawberry-picking slave.

I told him Mum would hit the roof as soon as she found out the truth and he'd go to jail, for sure, and I'd have to give evidence against him in his trial, and I would.

'OK, you won't listen,' he said. He rummaged among his wires and gadgets, shaking his head. 'There's no point me … You should go and hear for yourself. Go listen to the real world and see what it has to say about itself. You've been away from it for a while, so it might seem very different to you now. Go. Maybe there'll be a news report; I haven't heard anything for weeks. Maybe the pandemic has started for real now. Maybe we're just a few months early. Here …' He handed me a tragic small wooden box with a dial and a winding arm on the back and some kind of speaker thing, all duct-taped together with a coat hanger. 'It won't work here. Go out to the perimeter and wire it to the fence.' He told me it was a self-charging, wind-up long-wave radio and he showed me how to use it, then he paused.

'Are you going to tell everyone today, Haley, or will you give me one last chance?'

I wouldn't speak and he was calm, tired, like maybe people on death row get before their final day. He looked me hard in the eye and said, 'OK, please don't do anything rash. Please, just think about it for a few days and then decide. If you want me to confess to your mum and the others, I'll do it, but if you're going to tell them yourself, I ask one thing of you – one thing only … That you give me some advance warning, a few hours, so I can make my own preparations.'

Preparations? What? Like a noose or a Kool-Aid or what? And that was just typical – now he'd turned the tables.

'You should think long and hard about the impact your decision will have upon others,' he said slowly. 'OK, and let me know first. I'll be right here.' Then he hit his leg. 'Not going anywhere, see. Deal?'

Yes, it was cunning of him to make it 'my choice'. Christ, you go to the end of the world and back and you can never escape your own stupid self. My old freedom-of-choice enemy had me by the throat yet again. Another fucking choice! Everyone's life was in *my* hands. Thanks a bunch, Dad, you lying psycho!

He held his hand out to me to shake. 'Deal?' he repeated.

I backed away clutching the radio, shaking my head.

How To Get A Signal From A Fence

Mum was carrying a bucket of milk with Danny. I pulled my jacket tight round the radio and ran past. I shouted that I'd forgotten my bow and was going back to get it.

I ran all the way and collapsed at the perimeter fence. The anger turned into breathless sobbing. I couldn't bear to sit there by the gate and hear the truth from some smiley asshole news presenter. And anyway, the radio needed winding up. I headed south. I stumbled over heather, over broken ground, away from the track, and something told me I needed a pure spot, somewhere with a sort of view. I walked into the wind, winding the radio-box as I went. The sun burned my eyes and one of those marsh birds that I didn't know the name of circled overhead, calling out in panic, swooping at me. 'I don't want your stupid eggs, leave me alone,' I shouted.

How do you find the perfect spot to hear the final truth? It's always going to disappoint. Like, where do you go to ask someone to marry you? So I just sat down at this random god-awful spot by the fence. I pulled out the clothes hanger aerial and fastened it to the fence with the pliers, so that the entire perimeter fence became a huge receiver, then I stared at the On switch.

One of my big procrastinations was coming on and I looked back to the farmhouse, then out to the gate. I closed my eyes and focused. I got this image in my head of people running and dust clouds in a city. Maybe this all started with the Twin Towers? Dad had done a story for the newspaper about families looking for survivors. Photos of mums and dads and kids tacked up on fences. He'd been in New York the week after and seen it with his own eyes. He'd been in a warzone too. I forget which one but maybe he had PTSD.

I couldn't flick the switch.

Then, like channel-hopping in my head, there was this picture of a family of four in the organic fruit aisle in Waitrose, smiling as they loaded their trolley with apples, bananas, pears, kiwi fruit, seedless mandarin oranges, all in plastic packets labelled with product names. There are one hundred and seventy brands of yoghurt in the world. There are three hundred and seventy-five brands of sunglasses.

I still couldn't do it. I heard a hawk in the distance, but I couldn't see it.

The view through the fence really wasn't awe-inspiring. I was staring out at a solitary hill and the sky was flat and grey. My truth-hill was deeply lame and not even worth a photo. It had a solitary, scrawny tree on it, bent over by the wind. I didn't know what kind of tree it was.

My fingers hovered over the ON button. Did I actually want Dad's apocalypse to be true?

I remember finding this weird news story online about these religious folk in America and they'd gone to the top of this moun-tain. They were, like, a mixture of Mormons and hippies. They lugged these canoes and rafts up to the top, because they were waiting for the second great flood. They believed the Mayan calendar predicted it, the last days, caused by a meteor strike that would melt the icecaps. It was supposed to happen in 2012, and ninety-nine per cent of the population of humans and animals would die, just like Noah's flood. They totally believed this and I was a mere tot at the time. These mountain-climbing apocalypse folk even had their pets euthanized to save them unnecessary suf-fering in the coming great flood. It was going to happen exactly at twelve seconds, past twelve minutes, past twelve o'clock on the twelfth day of the twelfth month of 2012.

I thought about how these folks were like Dad. About how they must have felt at the very moment when the meteor didn't strike and the flood didn't come. That awkward minute, when they double-checked their watches and the sky was pretty normal-looking and they said to each other, 'Hey, Darleen, maybe it's Eastern Standard Time, maybe we got another hour till the apocalypse starts.' And somebody else saying, 'Maybe the Mayan calendar's not totally spot on, Ron. Let's just stay here overnight with our boats in case the flood comes tomorrow.' And this other guy says, 'Well, I sold my house and cashed in my life savings to build this boat, so I'm not budging from up here till it happens.'

These folk had been willing the end to come for so long because it gave their life an incredible urgency and importance and a sense of togetherness and maybe even hope and love. Maybe they waited up there three nights on their mountain-top until one of them said, 'Shit, I bet we got the year wrong, Marge, what d'you think?' And then they started lugging their Noah rafts back down again, in deep embarrassment.

It was so sad, thinking of them making it back home and turning on the TV and everything was just totally normal. There's still home-shopping channels, and tits 'n' ass channels, and channels with fast cars and shoot-em-ups, and news people with fake teeth, grinning. Then they have this revelation that there was never going to be a meteor strike and they'd actually secretly desired it so they could escape from tits 'n' ass and fast cars and smiling news presenters. The humiliation of that. And they'd killed Fluffy the cat for nothing.

I remembered, the news story had said that this couple had come home from the mountain and, two days later, with one gun each, they blew their brains out, all over their kitchen. Oh, Dad!

The more I put it off, the more painful it would be.

I stared at this absurd little radio box held together by duct tape. I touched the dial. There was just a possibility that Dad was right. After all, he hadn't checked the news since his incident. A lot can happen in the world when you're not looking.

I turned it. The radio came on with a click. There was just static and I was relieved and thought maybe I could maybe put this off and come back for a tearjerker sunset some other day.

I turned the dial and there were fragments of talk, all mashed up, far away and dislocated. And that was a relief, since I didn't want to hear it all in one go. Then I re-adjusted the aerial against the fence and it was like a spark of noise, a sharp clear signal.

A woman was singing, '*Mister CashMan, give me some cash – boom boom boom boom. Mister-CashMan-dot-com, for an easy-payback, short-term loan.*'

I stared at the radio and the voice inside it changed. '*All this month at Glasses4U, we're giving away one set of contact lenses and a free pair of duplicate prescription glasses…*'

I stared at the little hill beyond the fence, and this mound of granite from millions of years ago, it didn't know or care about any of this. A voice said, '*Is male pattern baldness worrying you?*'

I changed channel and a woman said, '*After the recent Asian flu scare, tourists are now taking full advantage of cheap flights to exotic locations with a new boom in air travel.*'

'*… It's nah-nah-nah-Newsbeat with our hot tips for this year's Grammy awards.*' I turned the dial.

'*… If anything we're now seeing a vast growth in bio-lab-innovation.*'

'*… The anti-aging cream that will give you back your youth.*'

'*… You can too. We can all be winners, with the Big We.*'

'*Oh baby, baby, you make me feel so right. Oh baby, baby, all night.*' I turned it off.

The wind blew my stupid hair into my eyes. It whistled among the pointless razor wire and the wind didn't know the difference between the wire and me. It just did what wind does; it was stupid and meaningless and it would still be here a billion years after our dumb-assed species had died out.

Everything was normal, and normal was just fucking pointless too, and after all this we'd have to go back home.

I hated the wind and the planet and myself and I cried for the longest time.

How To Turn Rage Into Power

It's not like you can just tell the truth and everyone will be, 'OK, that's great.' No, there were human costs involved. I was so confused and angry and everything was going slo-mo. I was back at the safe house and walking past Ray. He and Danny had tools in their hands and they were teaching Ben about carburettors or something. In the last month, all trace of Ben's ADHD had gone. He'd lost weight, too.

I could tell them right now: it's all a lie.

Danny turned to me and saw I was upset. We'd sort of set a secret date to get naked on my birthday and we'd been holding hands a lot. But I walked away and left him standing there, confused-looking.

I walked on and was hit by these major visions of how things would be.

When I told Ray the truth, he'd slam that engine lid shut, drive out to the nearest pub and never come back. He'd drink himself to death.

Nice one, Haley.

But why should I care for Ray anyway? He'd threatened us at gunpoint.

I walked round the farm. My feet felt strange and light, as if I was walking through a memory. I couldn't bear to think about what would happen to Danny if I told him the truth.

I found Meg and Mum hanging washing out the back by the barns. Big, white sheets, they were still stained even after hand scrubbing and they were talking about this problem together. I kept hidden and watched Mum doing this dumb job she once would have called sexist slavery, and sharing it with a woman from a class she would never have mixed with before. They were comparing blisters on their hands and laughing together.

And if I told them, this fragile friendship would break in mere seconds. The linen would be dropped in the mud. Meg would be the last to leave here but when she did she'd go searching for her next apocalypse. The one that had probably been waiting for her all along. The needle.

But why the hell should I care? The truth has to come out in the end, everyone believes that, right?

Danny caught up with me and grabbed my arm. 'Haley, what's wrong? You look…'

'Just leave me alone.' I could have just exploded in tears into his big, stupid arms and blurted it all out. Why does the truth always have to hurt? When they knew, and Meg and Ray abandoned us, Danny and me would be left with the fear that the only reason we'd ever been together was that we'd thought there was no other choice. Like that stupid 'if only' song about being the only girl left in the world with the only boy.

He held me firm. 'Tell me, Haley, what's going on?'

If I told him, everything he had ever been told since he was small would collapse around him. He couldn't come to the city with me; how would he fit in? He'd been raised feral. He'd only done a year or two of school, he'd never had a friend, never been shopping. He'd see me talking to my old school chums and he'd attack them with a stone or some shit. He'd run away and steal to live. He wouldn't surrender his weapons. He'd end up in a juvenile detention centre, or in jail.

That look on his face. He loved me so much, but had I fallen in love with him, really? Or was that all just a fantasy I'd made myself believe in, like Dad's stupid apocalypse.

I hid my tears and broke away from him. 'Don't touch me,' I shouted. 'Just … fuck off! Go!'

I stumbled through the empty kitchen and imagined the knife, the cutting board, the cans, all covered in a veil of grey dust. I foresaw the apples shrivelled and brown, everything left lying where it was dropped on the day of truth.

The washing machine made out of the bicycle stood there, pathetic now, just a pointless invention by a desperate man. Somewhere out there in the hills Dad must have smashed through the water pipes and a vast pool of drinkable, wasted water had been forming into a pointless little lake. We could have had clean water and power all this frickin time!

And he'd said, 'One day, you'll thank me for this.'

I walked through the dark corridor to the quad and gazed at the solar panels, mirroring the sun back to itself. They were vain, stupid objects. There was power everywhere and millions of tons of food sailing happily in container ships, and pipelines were creaking with a whole planet full of oil. No virus and everyone out there, shopping, texting, tweeting, dating, jogging, flirting, buying, selling, trading.

I foresaw the polytunnel overgrown with weeds and saw the wind strip its plastic walls to a ghost shell. In truth, the whole apocalypse thing hadn't really mattered to Dad or Meg or Ray. They were just some folk who despaired at the lack of dignity in the world and decided to try to make some of their own. What a waste.

I stared at the goats, chewing their hay. Their ugly, boggly eyes ever suspicious. I'd never developed fondness for them and they shied away from me, stretching their necks against their metal chains. Who'd care for the goats, the rabbits, the guard dog and the chickens after the police came to take Dad away? Would the last person to leave here have the heart to shoot them, or just leave them to starve?

I pictured the crows tearing at the dead rabbits, white fur in black beaks.

Why did I have to be the one to ruin everything? Why couldn't I just keep on living in the lie? It wasn't fair.

'Haley!'

Mum was calling me but I had to be alone. I ran outside, passed her and Meg with their empty buckets.

'Help us fetch some water, would you, love?' Mum asked.

She called me 'love' and that too would end when we were back in the city. I ran on.

'What's got into her?' I heard Meg say.

'Raging hormones,' Mum said, and they laughed together.

I hid in the barn room with the battery rack and the electricity-generating bike. It had no windows and a lock on the door and that's what I needed.

How could I sit at dinner and say nothing? I leaned against the damp, dark wall and tried to weigh up the positives of telling them. There was just one that came to mind: after Dad went to jail, there'd be no way Mum wouldn't get me that X-Phone I'd wanted to help me get over the trauma.

So pathetic. Back to square one. Nothing learned.

I bundled myself up into a tiny ball in the dark corner against the battery rack, trying to vanish. No one knew where I was but I wanted to scream, stop picking on me!

How many days could I hold the toxic truth? And Danny's face pleading. 'What's wrong, Haley? I know something's hurting you.' He'd kiss me and I'd cry and blurt it out and then he'd be as good as dead. Oh, Danny.

I opened my eyes and there before me, in the cracks of the wooden door, was a spider web. It was freshly made and no bug corpses littered it. The light made it glow and it was mathematical and perfect. A home and a murderous trap, all in one. With a flick of my finger, I destroyed it.

Dad would be cowering somewhere, preparing more lies, but knowing he was finished. And after Mum exploded at him, and took his car and left with me and Ben, Dad would finally turn one of his many guns upon himself.

I worried about Mum even more. She'd have been away from work so long she'd have been fired. She'd have to make a big public song and dance about our abduction to get her job back. But worse than that, even when she was reinstalled in her lovely big house, with her Wi-Fi and her central heating, something would be dead inside her. She'd learned to love Dad again, and it was all a lie.

'Haley! Where are you?' I heard her calling out. 'Come and help me set the table.'

I stared at the electricity-generating bike. I was burning up and needed to do something with my rage. I disengaged the machine from the battery. There was no point in saving anything. I flicked the switch for the test bulb to turn it on. I climbed on and I pedalled. Hard.

I didn't cycle home in my imagination. I didn't think about roads and motorways. I stared at the wet, dark walls of the ancient barn and I pushed myself harder. I thought about muscles and lungs and breath. I watched calories turn into watts in the burn of the bulb.

I didn't picture all the people in the super gym in the city centre, all with their headphones on watching computerised landscapes synchronised to their cycling, all getting hot 'n' bothered, eyeing each other up like they were stars in pop videos, all alone on their treadmills.

I focused on the power in my legs, the tightening of hamstrings, my calf and ankles, and the hoarse heat in my throat. I thought about what it felt like to saw through your own father's bone. We are just meat and motion. The light bulb surged as I pedalled harder and then dimmed as I slowed for breath. This 60-watt bulb, with its tiny wire on fire, had become part of me. And no one would ever benefit from the power I created with my stupid body. So many people's lives are like that, just wasted energy.

I pedalled until my legs were muscle-locked and sweat poured from me, along with my stupid tears. I focused on that bulb with its glow that rose and fell in time with my anger. I ignored Danny's knocks on the door, saying, 'Haley, I know you're in there. Why's this door locked? Haley, you OK?'

I pedalled harder. The wet walls glowed brighter with my wasted energy. It was like Dad said, power is the tipping point. It's all about power. I had power over my dad. Over my mum. With just a few words, I could destroy them both. I had power over Danny and over our love. If I stopped pedalling for a second, the light would completely die.

How To Lie To Live

Big Lies Kill, Little Lies Save Lives

My favourite pop song at the moment is called *I'm On It*. It's your classic girls-just-wanna-have-fun, put-your-hands-in-the-air thing by this breathy bimbo called Shabba, but it's majorly lit.

I'm sorry, you probably think I'm back home in the real world now, but I'm still at the farm, at the perimeter fence, listening to the stupid wind-up radio.

And it's, like, another two months have gone by.

You can be disappointed in me. That's fine. I am, too.

Like I keep telling you, I'm shit at choices. Terrified of them. But I have an excuse, really. I had to make this horrible decision so I said to myself, I'd write it all down. Then I spent a few more weeks typing it all up on Dad's old laptop, and I had to power it with the damn bike.

I told myself to be ruthless and truthful and work out the evidence and all the outcomes, like Dad always said you should, then decide whether I tell Mum and Ben and Danny and Ray and Meg the truth.

Or not.

Now I've re-read everything I wrote and I've weighed all the pros and cons, I just can't put it off anymore. I have to make my final choice today and just accept that someone is going to get hurt.

I've been very worried about Dad. I mean, he's sleeping tons and maybe clinically depressed again, and one night I was sitting at the dinner table with everyone and Dad was twitchy, cos I've kept him living in constant fear for weeks and weeks with the 'when the hell will Haley give the game away?' routine. He wasn't touching his pheasant stew and he suddenly shouted, 'Haley, is there something you'd like to share with us all?'

And I could have said, 'Yeah, everybody, guess what I heard on Capital FM today? There's a three-for-two offer on T-shirts at Gap and the frickin pandemic didn't happen!'

But I said zilch. Maybe to torture him. I dunno.

I'm like Scheherazade, keeping our happy family alive by spinning out a fake story and they don't even realise it.

To be honest, I thought Dad might go so nuts that he'd just end up confessing and spare me the trouble, but that plan's been overshadowed by the fact that everyone else has lockdown fever. Last week another jet flew over and Ray shot an entire round of ammo into the sky, while Meg ran around trying to bleach every surface that the plane might have breathed on. Insanity.

And Mum's got pretty obsessive with the Armalite AR-10. She spends far too many hours shooting only-occasionally-edible birds. Plus, she's become a total tyrant in the kitchen. To be horribly honest, I even think she's happier being a rustic survivalist than she was a corporate zombie.

The one good thing about not spilling the beans about reality is that Mum and Dad will stay together. It's pretty clear that they're in love all over again. Imagine that, bonking a man with one leg! Gross. Seriously, this has been certified by independent witnesses and it's all so cringe.

The weirdest thing of all is, we're actually a better family than we ever were before. Maybe it's cos we've got no technology to hide inside, and no places to run away to. We're talking 'togetherness'. Like actually singing songs every night round the goddamn fire and making pots out of mud. So, in some mega ironic way, I got my childish wish. Maybe they could use this method in marriage guidance counselling.

Plus, Mum looks so much younger now. Maybe it's the diet of rabbit.

Talking of rabbits, Danny and me kept our appointment to

sleep together after my sixteenth birthday. Maybe that was the only reason I kept on pretending that the pandemic was real. I know, I know – I told you I'm shallow and selfish. You don't have to actually like me.

So we got naked together. But it utterly backfired. I couldn't bonk when the time came, because I just knew if we touched in that special way that the truth would just burst from me. Like, in post-coital chat, not during.

So that was the end of that. I mean Danny splooged and everything and it was gross and amazing and hilarious, but not anywhere near my lady bits. And then it all went sour between us, and now Danny feels he's done something wrong, like he's a crap lover or I don't find him attractive or something. Men are so insecure. So now he shouts at me, 'Why are you so secretive? What are you keeping from me?'

He thinks it's about his pecker, but it's about the pandemic. At least his pecker is real.

But it gets worse: I had to come up with excuse after excuse not to spend time with him, just in case I spilled the beans. So then things turned kind of shit, because now he's so convinced I don't love him anymore.

Every day I come out here to the fence to get away from his neediness and rejection-anger. 'Why are you avoiding me, Haley?' he says. 'God sake, what's wrong with you? Why are you so cold?' He's started banging his head off walls and majorly Heathcliffing it.

Withholding love is the cruellest thing of all. I'm sorry, Danny, but sometimes you have to protect people from the truth, like Mum and Dad said. Plus coming out here to write has given me some kind of space from our cabin fever, and sometimes us grown-ups need space from each other.

Every day now I pretend to go out on patrol with my crossbow and I come to this same spot by the lonely tree and I turn my walkie-talkie down low and stare out at the birds. They fly from one side to the other and don't even know what a razor wire fence is. They're breeding now and that's why they sing, I guess.

Some of them sit on the fence. Like me, metaphorically speaking.

Some days I really, really crave shopping in the mall again. And Snapchat. And Amazon deliveries, and having actual friends, though they mostly just talk shit about boys on social media. I miss Danish pastries and Brie cheese bagels. And freedom, I guess, whatever we thought that was.

And it's all still out there on the other side of the fence, a hundred miles away.

Some days the music on the radio fits the view – it's a dance tune and the clouds are racing by, or it's classical and they flow like a stream. Sunsets go well with hardcore but not disco. Distant rain is Mahler. Some days the radio says, '*Instantly makes you look ten years younger.*' Other days I hear them sing, '*Party party party,*' and I feel like a lying piece of shit. On other days men tell me about '*fluctuations in the Dow Jones Industrial Average*'. Most days, I feel like the fence is protecting me. On other days, it feels like a prison all over again.

Haley Haley, quite contrary.

If I tell them the truth now, then all of this will have been for nothing. Dad will be put in jail, and Mum will never trust anyone again. Worst of all, when she does find out, she's going to utterly despise me for hiding the truth for so long.

You know, it's actually perfectly doable to live a lie. Isn't that what most people do, anyway? I guess choosing not to decide was a choice in itself, after all.

I know what I have to do. In Dad's manual it says:

1. Trust to your intuition and take a leap of faith.
2. Take responsibility for your choice. Even if you choose incorrectly, you must brave up and 'own your choice'.
3. Even if you made a terrible choice and the results are

disastrous, you must live with it and not blame other people.

I just can't do it. I'm pathetic, such a waste of frickin space. I'll have to do it tomorrow. Tomorrow, I'll decide for sure. It's final!

Become A Guardian Of Last Things

To force myself to decide I went back to that special bit in Dad's manual, where he mentions the Guardians of Last Things:

Take a breath. Step to the edge of the ledge. Look down at the world you knew, far below. Jump or don't jump.

Good.

Your old self died in the fall. Leave it in the gutter and walk away. From now on, you are someone who has survived your own suicide. Every day from now on is a gift that cannot be wasted. This is your true Day One.

Now, leave the mourning of the many things and open up a new page in your head. Ask yourself: What I will need?

How much time do I have to build a safe house? How much money will I need? Should I gamble or should I work? Should I break the law?

Who matters to me? Who will I live for?

Most of us find our own lives empty. The thing to live for will be our children.

From now on, every single thing you do will only be for the sake of your kids' survival. Social conventions no longer matter. Ask yourself, what lies will I have to tell everyone, so that they will not interrupt my preparations or report me?

The general public will not survive anyway.

You will need to steal. Embezzle. Get weapons.

Suddenly, there is a reason to get fit. To get up early. To take night classes. To hoard. To plan. To build. Suddenly, every minute counts. Now that you have accepted the coming pandemic and your own death, you have a passionate, lucid reason to live. From this moment on, you will find beauty in the places that the world has overlooked.

You will feel the texture of time. Life will never have felt so precious, so urgent. Every second is now filled with purpose as the countdown begins. Love – that thing so derided in our culture, becomes your power source.

Know that you and your children will become the few who will survive. You will become the guardians of last things.

If You Find This, Please Download It, Then Run

If you are reading this, that's good. I found a tiny signal near the perimeter, so I'm going to try and send this all as an email attachment to Dad's old website. So maybe it'll be posted up there. Only, I don't know how much longer the internet will last.

Something big has happened. The biggest decision in my life has been made, and sort of not by me. Secretly, I must have wished for the darkest thing, and maybe out there in No Man's Land the forces of wind and rain heard my plea, because it started.

I heard it on the radio. It was breaking news on Bloomberg. It said: '… *a security breach at a virology lab in Dayton, Arizona, may involve highly infectious viruses.*'

I was in shock. This was three weeks ago and I double-checked it against Dad's manual, and everything was matching up, but Dad said never to trust the media and to learn to 'read between the lies'.

Then one day later, Russia Today said, 'Clusters of respiratory infections – on the Pacific Rim, in Japan and Taiwan – are not believed to be connected.'

And that was weird because why would they tell you this virus existed only to discount it? And I was getting major déjà vus.

Then the next day the German Chancellor said, 'These are wild speculations intended to destroy the amazing economic recovery after the last pandemic scare.'

I really wanted to tell Dad but I bottled it up, cos I needed to see if it was all just fake news and panic, like before. Plus, I'm no expert.

Then two days later, the BBC said, 'Four German bio-students have been arrested in Shanghai Airport attempting to smuggle twenty vials of lethal BSL4 pathogens out of the country. The airport has been shut down due to fear of contamination.'

And I was trembling and I had to make up lies to Danny so I could come out to the perimeter with the radio all day. 'Why?' he said. 'Can't you stand the sight of me anymore? Why do you hate me so much, Haley?' And I told him, 'Danny, I really, really, really don't. Believe me, you have no idea!'

That night, just like Dad predicted, the news said, 'Unexplained outbreaks are now affecting Japan, Taiwan, Australia, India and several EU Countries.'

Then the G20 went into emergency session, but they said it was about the economy and that these outbreaks were 'absolutely unconnected'. And then it ended with the usual talking heads from each country saying, 'Our government urges calm.'

Then this doctor said, 'The lungs are devoured by the virus, which causes aerosol contamination through coughing, breathing, blood, saliva and sweat.'

And CNN said, 'We can confirm that this is, in fact, the same virus that has appeared in over twenty-five countries after its initial appearance in India.' Then NDTV said, 'India furiously refutes American claims about the origins of the so-called Bengal Virus and has made counter-claims that the pathogen originates in the Dayton laboratory in the US.'

It was just like Dad said: there was no 'end' after the Covid pandemic. Just every country racing every other to control the trillion-dollar virus business, and all of them cutting corners and blaming each other for lab leaks and thefts. The last pandemic didn't make us 'more prepared' for a future outbreak. No, it supercharged every nation in a race to possess the most lethal pathogens and cutting-edge cures. It became like the Cold War. Pandora's box had opened. We were in the Pandemic Era now, with new mutations proliferating everywhere, as fast as the fake news that concealed them.

We'd learned nothing.

On that day Mum baked a carrot cake and made progress with Ben's home schooling, and so I had to hide all this info from her and everyone. I know it sounds utterly immoral, but I was wired, excited, terrified. Because, like, if the great pandemic did actually occur right now, but just a bunch of months late, that would've conveniently got Dad and me off the hook, and we'd be safe in hiding already, so I mean who's going to quibble over some dates, right?

Then the *Washington Post* said, 'The symptoms include flesh-eating infection and hemorrhagic fever. Leaked files claim the W.H.O. and C.D.C were warned about this lethal pathogen six years ago…'

That was it – I had to tell Dad. I got him alone in his cubbyhole and said, 'You total asshole, you were wrong about the dates but I think it's actually happening this time.' And I showed him the radio and told him where I got the signal and he said, 'Haley, I'm weary from all this. Wait and see. No doubt they'll manage to get it under control and it'll all just blow over again.'

I pled with him, 'But, Dad, how will I know? What's the final sign?'

He shook his head.

'Tell me!'

'Declaration of war,' he whispered. 'The President of the USA or Russia will say this is biological warfare, then there'll be a total news media blackout.'

Then his face went all regretful and he said, 'But, Haley, I was wrong. It won't happen. We should be glad I was so wrong. I'm sorry.'

I hugged him tight but not too tight to hurt him and I said, 'If it doesn't happen this time, Dad, I really am going to have to tell Mum. But please promise not to kill yourself, if I do. Please, I mean it.'

We shook on it. His burn-scarred hand in mine, like a metaphor or something.

The next day China dumped twenty trillion in US bonds and a CCP virologist claimed that the virus was an American bio-attack. The US government claimed that 'anyone who makes such accusations is playing into the hands of warmongers'.

 And that same day Danny cornered me by the cut-out soldier targets, all emotional, saying, 'You need to be alone, that's cool, I respect that. But you're keeping something from me. Just tell me what it is! I'm tearing myself to pieces here. Just tell me what I did wrong!' He was so brave and wrong and it was so hard not to just snog him and I whispered, 'Hey, handsome, I just need a few more days to be sure. That's all. Then I'll explain. Everything. I promise. OK?'

Then the weirdest thing was, I felt totally energised, like Dad must have the first time. And I even started to hope that the worst would happen just so all this unknowing would be over. I know that is totally sick and evil. How could I wish that billions would die? I'm sorry.

Then I heard this: 'The President of the United States claims that the theft of viruses from US laboratories, and their use in contaminating foreign cities, constitutes an act of biological warfare.'

He actually said, 'We are at war.'

I couldn't sleep all night. I had to creep out to the fence with my radio.

I feel sick to my soul and wired to the moon.

I'm still here now, waiting for news with Dad's old laptop, and the battery is dying and I'm keeping warm by typing. Is it fake news or is it really happening this time?

The sun is rising and the sky is pale. I'm hugging myself tight in the blanket I snuck out here. I need to pee and to wind up the radio again. I hope the world will pull itself back from the brink again, but one thing I've learned about humans is we keep making the same mistakes over and over, and the stakes just get higher and higher.

The news says nothing about the new pandemic. Nada. The news has died. I search the channels and there are only voices talking about movies and sport and fashion and who is hot and who is not, and adverts for insurance. I'm angry because how the hell can I know the truth if they won't tell me? But then I realise: this is it. The media blackout has begun. The military are preparing their hazmat suits. The weapons are being armed.

We never really realise we're alive, till it's too late.

The birds are singing the dawn chorus. No one will know what's hit them. None of you will.

It's final. This is it. I can feel it. It's starting. Now.

Of course I'm crying. Do six billion people really have to die?

I'm breathing in the coldest, cleanest air, ever.

I've made my decision: I'll tell Dad everything. I'll hug him and tell him.

He lied, but his lie has come true. I'll tell him, 'It's like you said, Dad: "Better to be one year too early than one day too late."'

As for Mum and Ben and the others, they know how to live off-the-grid now, so why spoil it? Best if they don't know, ever. We can just keep on living like this, and when the infected mobs attack the fence, we'll have had more time than anyone to practise our defence.

Yes, like Dad said: 'We're the luckiest people in the world. We're ready, we're prepped, we're in lockdown already.'

What do I want?

I want to live and to save Ben and my Mum and Dad, and Danny and his family, and maybe even have a kid one day and pass all this on. To be honest, my life was pretty pointless until all this happened. I think I know what life is for now. Kind of shit that I only worked it out now, though.

OK, I have to upload this.

I don't know if you or anyone else will ever see this. Or if me and my family will make it. I hope you're out there. Whoever you are. And that the ones you love are safe.

I have to send this now. The power's nearly done and I don't know how long my signal will last. If you can download this, I hope it will help.

Don't take the world for granted. Don't waste your life wishing it was better and blaming other people for your own shit. Face up to the worst thing that can happen and prepare for it. Learn how to survive practically everything. Love one another without fear. Learn how to hunt. Avoid eating rabbits if you can. Start packing your car immediately. Get the hell out of the city. Now.

That's all I've got.

Over and out.

Acknowledgements

It's impossible to thank everyone individually for each of the many generous things they've gifted to me on this project, from inspiration, to time, to labour, to pep talks and even (literal) therapy, so this will be a list in no particular order.

My thanks to Lionel Shriver, Gail Winston, Craig Hillsley, Sara Hunt, Jeanne Ryckmanns, Jane Cameron, Nicola Barr, Ross Murray, Creative Scotland, the Royal Literary Society, the Society of Authors, Patrick Jamieson, Irvine Welsh, Mark Buckland, Karyn Dougan Buckland, David Mackenzie, Nick Fox, Doug Johnstone, Lynda Obst, Tim Lott, Mark Cousins, Jenni Fagan, Collette Colfer, Melanie Stokes, Ian Rankin, Kathleen Kettles, Edna Morrison, Peter Cox, Iona Italia, Nick Hudson, Emily Ballou and the good people of Cove.

About the Author

Ewan Morrison is a multiaward-winning novelist, screenwriter, and essayist. His novel *Nina X* won the Saltire Society Scottish Fiction Book of the Year and is being developed as a feature film with an Academy Award–nominated director. He is the winner of the Scottish Book of the Year Fiction Prize, the Glenfiddich Scottish Writer of the Year, and has been nominated for three Scottish BAFTAs. He lives in Scotland.